THE OTHER ADONIS

Also by Frank Deford

FICTION
Love and Infamy: A Novel of Pearl Harbor
Casey on the Loose
The Spy in the Deuce Court
Everybody's All-American
The Owner
Cut 'n' Run

NONFICTION
The Best of Frank Deford
The World's Tallest Midget
Alex: The Life of a Child
Big Bill Tilden
There She Is
Five Strides on the Banked Track

THE OTHER ADONIS

A Novel of Reincarnation

FRANK DEFORD

SOURCEBOOKS LANDMARK™
AN IMPRINT OF SOURCEBOOKS, INC.®
NAPERVILLE, ILLINOIS

Published by Sourcebooks, Inc.
P.O. Box 4410, Naperville, Illinois 60567-4410
(630) 961-3900, FAX: (630) 961-2168
www.sourcebooks.com

ISBN 1-57071-745-1

Library of Congress Cataloging-in-Publication Data
Deford, Frank.
 The other Adonis: a novel of reincarnation/by Frank Deford.
  p. cm.
 ISBN 1-57071-745-1 (alk. paper)
  1. Reincarnation—Fiction. I. Title.

PS3554.E37 084 2001
813'.54—dc21

               2001031329

    Printed and bound in the United States of America
     BG 10 9 8 7 6 5 4 3 2 1

For Betsy and Tommy Kearns,
Double Ones

Acknowledgments

For their kindness and expertise in helping me research this book, my very special thanks go to Andre and Paulette Dierckx and Dirk Stoclet in Belgium. They were invaluable in helping steer me through Antwerp and through Flemish. For their generous advice and guidance with the manuscript, I am most grateful to Sharon O'Connell and Barry Rosenbush. For their determination and devotion in seeing the manuscript become a book, my sincerest gratitude goes to Sterling Lord and Hillel Black. For hanging *Venus and Adonis* upon its walls and letting me wander through its wonders, I am indebted to The Metropolitan Museum of Art and its most pleasant staff. And for inspiration, I bow to Peter Paul Rubens.

Frank Deford
Westport, Connecticut
June 6, 2001

THE OTHER ADONIS

◆BEFORE◆

In the dark, Peter Paul Rubens could hear nothing but the gentle breezes barely stirring the leaves near the top of the tallest trees at his magnificent villa. So still a summer's night it was. Besides, his famous showplace was adjacent to The Meir, which was the most fashionable square in Antwerp, away from the hurly-burly of the port's activity. So, rarely did any of the more raucous city sounds disturb the happy residents of Rubenshuis. Most mornings, Rubens himself would rise refreshed before dawn, then set off, walking a few blocks to attend four o'clock mass at his parish, Sint Jacobskerk—Saint James Church.

The great master had been widowed in middle age, and as perhaps the best known man in all of Europe—a diplomat of reknown, no less than the most honored artist—it had been assumed that one so wealthy (and yet so handsome, too) would remarry into the grandest of nobility. Instead, at the age of fifty-three, Rubens had found himself almost mystically drawn to Helena Fourment, the plump, sixteen-year-old daughter of a mere local silk merchant.

How joyous had been that union! Now, but four years later, by this sweet August night of 1635, Helena had already blessed Rubens with three children. The youngest was still nursing. Moreover, as her husband's favorite model, Helena had reinvigorated his work. Never before had the suave genius of Antwerp felt so fulfilled. In fact, Rubens's painting was now all the more ambitious because he had abandoned his political duties to concentrate solely on art—"la *mia dolcissima professione,"* he called his beloved work in Italian, the language he most favored of the six that he spoke.

Indeed, this, his fabulous mansion six years in the building, was itself like a Genovese villa that had somehow been transported north to Flanders. Well, really it was two separate houses joined by a portico. There, on one side, the Rubens family lived, while on the other, he and his assistants worked. Everywhere, though, he painted his Helena—in the main studio downstairs, in the other huge public rooms filled with statuary, or even outside in the bountiful gardens where peacocks roamed amid the fruit trees, from the portico to the honeysuckle arbor, between the jonquils and the tulips and the lilacs.

Sometimes, Rubens would paint Helena as the good Christian mother, attired modestly in her finest satin and lace, brocaded in gold. Other times, he would portray her as the most tempting pagan goddess, naked and sensual. Almost always, though, it was Helena who adorned his canvases, even as she embroidered his reputation and brought new joy to his soul.

Alas, after a magic—and temperate—life, one that had almost been free of any infirmity, Rubens had contracted gout. In time, the disease would go to his arm and inhibit his ability to paint, and soon enough after that, it would reach his heart and kill him. Now, in his fifty-eighth year, the gout would only come and go, from discomfort to remission. On his worst nights, however, Rubens could not sleep and he took to leaving his bed and walking about his estate, cursing *de gicht.*

He was again in discomfort this particular evening. It was the last minutes of August 15th—Assumption Day, that glorious holiday that celebrated the ascension of Mary, the Virgin Mother, into heaven. It was an especially important date in Antwerp, for Mary was the patroness saint of the city. The cathedral was named for her, and statues of her were erected, it seemed, on every street corner. An excess? Perhaps. But only of devotion. How better to show the cursed Protestants where the spiritual allegiance of Antwerp would always lie? All Christians might share—must share—Jesus, but Mary belonged to the loyal Catholic communicants of the precious capital of the Spanish Netherlands.

Rubens himself had, in fact, most cherished some of his early works that featured his first wife, Isabella, as Mary. Helena, for all her beauty, was yet too young and captivating to be a Mary. But, happily for Rubens, he had found at Saint James another woman who could serve as his ideal model for the Madonna until that future time when Helena could grow properly Marian of face and form.

Anyway, on such a soft and starry night as this—the Virgin's own!—Rubens decided not to go down to the garden. Rather, although struggling with his gout, he went up the stairs by his bedroom and then across the top of the living quarters into his own private studio. It was there that, alone, he sketched his favorite models. Always here, in private, is where he drew Helena in the nude. And likewise here, only a week ago, is where for the last time he had painted Elsa.

Poor, poor Elsa. Rubens threw open one of the windows and looked up to the Flanders sky, tearing up at her memory. For she was dead now, Elsa was—brutally murdered. Strangled.

He thought of her now. It was easy to remember her. Elsa had been so much fun to paint, always teasing him for his stuffy propriety, even holding up her big, pink bosom before him, promising Rubens a dandy time indeed if only he would sneak away from Helena one night to partake of her favors down at her room on the Burchtgracht. A lot of Rubens's models were whores. After all, what ladies of respectability would go naked—even for the master of Europe, even for posterity? But Elsa was so lively, so cheerful, that Rubens hoped that he might be able to hire her full time to take her away from the brothel.

But then, Monday night, they had discovered her body in the canal, down from what was called Bloed Berg—Blood Hill—the building where the butchers in town threw away the useless offal. When they spotted her, Elsa was floating out to the Schelde River among the blood and the guts.

Distraught when he learned of Elsa's terrible demise, Rubens himself had immediately gone down to the *scutters'* guild hall and told those private policemen that there would be a hundred-guilder reward for whomever apprehended the villain. The *schout,* the chief officer, was surprised. Why would such a man as the great Rubens care so for any whore, even if she did model for him? After all, there were these unfortunate endings for these disposable women all the time.

Rubens replied, "Did not Our Lord Himself extend the largest measure of his love to that other Mary, who was just such a woman as Elsa? Did not he promise the Magdalene eternal salvation?"

"Oh, yes, yes, yes, of course," cried the *schout*.

But never mind Rubens and his Mary Magdalene. Rubens and his hundred guilders! Suddenly, every *scutter* in Antwerp was on the case of the strangled whore.

And now, in his studio on Mary's night, Rubens thought of Elsa again and prayed for her. Surely, she was already with the Virgin in heaven. Then he walked across the tiled floor to the other window and threw it open, too, to peer across the Wapper Canal to the spires and gables of the city he loved. And he breathed deeply the cool Flanders air.

But hardly had Rubens begun to draw in the soothing night breezes than he heard the piercing cry. It seemed to come from his left, from somewhere around the next corner. Perhaps just down Hopland Street? Yes, it must be that close. Still, wherever it came from, the scream was so horrific that it assaulted his ears. In the silence, there had been nothing whatsoever to prepare him for that one long, blood-curdling wail that ended as abruptly as it had begun.

This is what Peter Paul Rubens heard that night of August the fifteen, 1635:

"...owwwlllleeeeeee..."

It was so dreadful a cry, so full of pain, that as soon as the silence returned, Rubens fell straightaway to his knees upon the tiles, crossing himself in the moonlight.

Immediately then, hearing nothing else, he retraced his steps, going back down to Helena's bedroom where she was up now herself, nursing the baby. "Such a sound, *myj wyfken*—my pretty wife," Rubens said, "as I have never heard before. First poor Elsa. Now this."

"Now what?"

"Be assured, Helena, some awful business has just happened in Antwerp."

"Well, sleep, *myj goeds man.* We will surely, soon enough, learn of the matter from the *scutters.*"

Which they would. Especially since, as with Elsa, it very much involved those whom everybody at Rubenshuis knew.

·1·

It was not spring fever that had troubled Nina this day. She had lived most of her life in New York, where spring, at its best, came only in fits and starts. This year, it didn't even seem that it would ever settle in—and here it was, well into May. You could not possibly contract any full-blown fever. At best: a twenty-four-hour spring flu. Rather, Nina was distracted by something real.

Somebody, she knew, was checking up on her. There had been too many odd calls, improper queries; too often, she had even felt that somebody was watching her, and—who knows?—maybe even following her. To this point, yes, Nina had been more curious than fearful. Still....

"Mother, I am not 'glossing over' your concerns. I am simply saying that it is a mistake to jump to conclusions." That was Nina's daughter, Lindsay, addressing her mother over the phone from her office in Washington. Lindsay went on, "You know how it is nowadays, with computers. There's no secrets out there. If you simply enter the Publishers Sweepstakes, that's enough to put your name on every list known to man—your social security number, pin number, mother's maiden name, date of birth, and expiration date." Lindsay paused. "Maybe, Mother, you didn't pay your bill."

"Don't call your mother a deadbeat."

"Well, are you in trouble with the IRS?"

"Lindsay, please. You know me. I pay my taxes *ahead* of time."

"Mother, all you have to do is stiff one credit card by mistake—maybe even *their* mistake—and the sirens go off to everything you're attached to. Really, I'll bet you've been naughty somehow, and don't even know it."

That made Nina sigh. She was sitting in her office, alone, her feet literally up on her desk. "Believe me, darling, I have not been naughty lately. *That*, I know."

Lindsay chuckled on the other end of the phone. "Still no boyfriend, huh?"

"Boyfriend? Not even any doddering, old-man friend."

"Sorry, Mom. But don't despair. It's spring, the time for *l'amour*...even for men."

"Oh, thanks. You're no help whatsoever."

"Really, Mother, it's the global village now, which means that there are no secrets and everybody is a gossip. Trust me; it's all some computer thing."

Nina Winston said yeah, probably, thanks, and good-bye, Lindsay. But, she kept thinking, the trouble with each and every younger generation nowadays is that all the members thereof tended to explain everything on account of computers and other mystical wonders of technology. But it stayed with Nina that maybe, just maybe, somebody—some actual human being—really was after her.

Oh well.

She swung her feet from off her desk and tried again to apply herself to the task at hand, which was the folder that lay where her feet had momentarily rested. It was even more difficult for Dr. Winston to concentrate because her next patient bored her so. Well, he bored her as a patient. As company, he was quite diverting—Mr. Floyd R. Buckingham. Call me Bucky. Everyone does.

Bucky. What a perfectly awful thing to be called by everyone. By anyone. Worse, every time that Nina had met with him—three fifty-minute hours' worth—she had learned nothing about him. As absolutely professional as Nina had tried to be, using every standard procedure, her sessions with Bucky were more cocktail conversation than psychiatric probing.

But, forcing herself once more, Nina opened Buckingham's file and reread it:

BUCKINGHAM, FLOYD ROBERT
age: 44
resides: Darien, Connecticut
education: graduate, University of Virginia
married: 16 years to Phyllis

Nina paused. Again. Every time she read the file, she came to Bucky's wife's name and thought: *Phyllis. I don't know anyone named Phyllis anymore.* Well, there was a particular reason this would occur to her. Nina was not Dr. Winston's real name. That was Thelma. She must be, Nina always thought, the last of the Thelmas. Besides, even when Thelmas ruled the Earth, little Thelma Winston hated her name. She took the name Nina for herself, just like that, one summer's afternoon after she saw Nina Foch playing second lead in a movie.

Now, the Phyllis diversion past, she returned to the Buckingham file:

children: Timothy, 13; Sarah, 10
occupation: publisher, *Snow Ski Vacations* and
  Summer Sailing magazines
referral: "Somebody gave me your name a few months
  ago, but I forgot who."
Comments:

FIRST SESSION—APRIL 23RD

"Mr. Buckingham speaks vaguely of doubts and fears, of midlife crisis, and other blurry concerns, which he does not articulate clearly. He is expansive—garrulous, really—in talking all *around* himself, but is unable (or unwilling) to explain quite what it is that he thinks is bothering him. Perhaps he needs time to get comfortable with me.

"Curiously, apropos of nothing, he did ask me once if I 'did' hypnosis. He was pleased to hear me respond in the affirmative, but displeased when I told him that I'd learned hypnotism from a dentist—rather than from some Svengali. I explained, then, how hypnotism was more about dealing with pain than power, which irritated him some. But, soon enough, B recovered his suburban *savoir faire* and was again more engaging than forthcoming. Drat."

SECOND SESSION—APRIL 30TH

"Ditto 4/23. Why did I get the feeling midway through our hour that B was doing a better job analyzing me? He certainly felt more trusting of me when I informed him that I, too, had been in counseling once. Men all like that physician-heal-thyself angle. (Of course, I didn't tell B that my counseling adventure turned *my* life upside down and destroyed *his* marriage, but where does it say that I must declare *caveat emptor*?) Anyway, what is B's worry? Yes, yes, I know that the male of the species always takes longer to reveal himself, but with B, something secret really does appear to be lurking there. Whatever, we'll not meet again for two weeks because he has some America's Cup boondoggle in San Diego, and is taking the wife along. B likes San Diego a great deal. Let me tell you about La Jolla, Nina! He did open up on that important subject."

THIRD SESSION—MAY 14TH

"More of the same, but he did bring up hypnosis again. Why does this intrigue B so? I explained once more, patiently, that on those rare occasions when I did employ it, it was more for diagnosis than for treatment. 'Well, yeah, it could be like that,' he mused. But when I tried to get him to expand on that, he deftly turned the conversation back to me—asking me to expand on my earlier revelation about why I had left my pulmonary specialty for psychiatry. B quite approved, endorsing my inner wisdom. Sometimes, I'd swear that B was flirting with me. But then, I'm a lonely old woman given to such delusion. Still, I am starting to feel more like a geisha. Shall I make some green tea next time? Please, B, fish or cut bait."

That was the sum of it—sparer even than Nina had remembered. It bugged her, too, for Nina was good at what she did; she didn't like giving up on a patient. She was professionally cagey, but so naturally empathetic that people—even men, even evasive men like Bucky—opened up to her despite themselves. Hypnosis? Nina was hypnotic simply as a good ear.

But then, there was a certain law of inversion that always worried Nina. Invariably, those patients who came to her all flap-gum, babbling from the start, had the least to reveal. Meanwhile, the reticent ones, like Bucky, might well be keeping the lid on the most painful anguish. Nina could not forget, either, his reaction whenever she felt as if she had zeroed in on something sensitive. Then, his eyes would go vacant, even as he maintained a smile and kept on talking. It was, she thought, as if he was lost in some sweet, private reverie—prouder still that he could enjoy this intimacy even as he kept on giving Nina a line. She had even coined a word for this response: "buckysmirking." All one word. "Buckysmirking." But it wasn't funny to Nina. It was maddening. Even a little eerie. And it was why she didn't quite yet want to give up on him.

So, she would see if she could call the smooth-tongued Mr. Buckingham's bluff. Nina buzzed her secretary. "All right, Roseanne, send him in." And Floyd Buckingham promptly entered, as jaunty as ever. He had a daisy in his lapel, which, although a new touch, was certainly in keeping. He bounded across the room in his long strides, reached across the desk, and gaily cried out "Nina!" as he handed her a copy of *Summer Sailing* that was fresh off the presses, freighted with shiny advertisements.

Nina thanked him. "I like the boutonniere, Mr. Buckingham," she added.

"Tut, tut, Nina, we agreed: first-name basis."

"First name at the couch, but Mister and Doctor at the desk. And, Mr. Buckingham, sit down here." Nina gestured to the chair across from her. Bucky, taken aback at this formality, even a bit chagrined, accepted the seat reluctantly. Nina, for her part, sat down too. "Look," she began, venturing firmness across the desk, "this just isn't working."

Predictably, Bucky tried to interrupt her, but Nina simply held up a hand and proceeded. "I do look forward to your appointments, Mr. Buckingham. I've always heard that the men from UVA were good company, and you have certainly held up that standard. But we're not just here for a tête-à-tête."

"I know," he said somewhat sheepishly.

"Oh? Sometimes I get the impression that I'm just another client of yours, that you're, uh—"

"Bullshitting?"

"Yes, thank you. I suppose that's the word I was searching for.

But it puzzles me, because you don't need me for that. You've got all those ski people and boat people"—she tapped the cover of *Summer Sailing*—"to converse with. And on expense account." Again, he started to interrupt; Nina even thought she saw the first signs of buckysmirking. So, quickly, she stood up.

Petite as she was, this hardly afforded her a commanding position, but it did at least imply emphasis. And, indeed, Bucky listened to her more intently as she began to address him anew in that doctorish tone that she had learned to employ—the one that expressed omniscience gently. "I think, Mr. Buckingham—I think—that you've decided that you should feel guilty. It's only an educated guess, because you've given me so little to go on. But you've obviously got a wonderful wife and two terrific kids. You adore your work, and you're very good at it. Obviously, too, you make oodles of money."

Bucky nodded, unabashed once more. "*Oodles.* Haven't heard that in years."

"I am a woman of a certain age. But you, you Mr. Buckingham, are in the very prime of your life. You have your health, you're slim and tall, and I can see you tan nicely, to boot. You're obviously not addicted to any substance—not even to golf. But you get along with everyone and have many friends, good and true." Nina paused. "Right so far?"

Buckingham sighed in the affirmative. "The worst was when I gave up smoking. Effortlessly. First time I tried."

"Exactly. But you look around and everybody else is getting divorced, or their kids are on drugs, or they've just been downsized—even though you're sure they're smarter than you—or they're losing their hair, or they're fat, or entirely too emotionally involved with the New York Knicks. So, naturally, all that makes you feel perfectly awful about your own success—your lucky self."

Buckingham was listening, which made Nina rather pleased with herself, so that she not only came round the desk toward him, but thrust a forefinger into the air. "And not only that, Mr. Buckingham, not only that—but you've heard of something called 'mid...life cri...sis,' and so you've decided, aha!, you must be in the midst of that. And so somebody gave you my number, and you've come here to chat me up in the hopes that I can make you feel even worse about how wonderful your wonderful life is. Right?"

He shrugged. "Basically."

She stepped over to a shelf and plucked off a large book. *The Diagnostic Manual of Psychiatry*," Nina said, hefting it. "It was about a hundred, hundred-fifty pages when I got into this twenty years ago. Now: four, five hundred. All kinds of new stuff. But look under *M*: still no Midlife Crisis."

"No, none in my book either," he said. And no buckysmirking.

So, Nina had smoked him out. Bucky really was just face value after all—no dark secrets or traumas. She was sort of disappointed; she was going to miss him.

Oh well.

"So, my professional advice to you, certified and approved"— Nina mockingly swept her arms around the room at her diplomas and citations—"is to stop using my time and your money, and instead, take that beautiful wife of yours out on the town. Then, just before you swoop her up in your arms, you tell her how lucky you are—and how grateful." Nina turned back then to bang the desktop. "Case closed, Sergeant Preston."

Buckingham applauded. "Well done, Doctor. You're very perceptive."

"Then leave, and Godspeed...Bucky."

But he shook his head then. "Sorry...Nina. I'm not quite finished." She slumped. He sat up and went on, "If I'd come to you a year ago, everything you just said to me would've been spot on. That's what they say in England when you get it just right. Spot on."

"Yes, I know."

"But things have changed." He drew a deep breath. "I'm sorry, but I haven't, uh, well, I haven't altogether leveled with you."

"All right, what haven't you told me? I mean, besides everything."

"Well, two things."

"And you're prepared now to let me in on these two things?" He nodded almost solemnly. "All right, and how would you characterize these two things?"

"Well, one is just very important. Huge." He paused then, pondering.

So Nina asked, "And number two?"

"Strange. Number two is the strangest thing you've ever heard."

"I've heard a lotta strange things in this job."

"Not this strange. I'll bet."

"All right," Nina said. "Then let's start with number one." She beckoned him to move to the corner, to the couch, which was familiar territory for them, but the ambiance now was suddenly new and different.

·2·

"The important thing," Buckingham said, "is that I am in love with another woman."

Nina gritted her teeth. Oh great, she thought. All this time, all this build-up, only to hear the most hackneyed, predictable revelation from a man in an *alleged* midlife crisis. She sat back in her chair. She knew what Buckingham expected of her: a psychiatric certification of his angst that would justify his infidelity. Midlifers thought she could be like the school nurse. Bucky has a little temperature, so please excuse him from his marriage for the rest of the day so he can go get laid.

Hoping that her professional face didn't betray her personal irritation, though, Nina proceeded with the approved script. "And how long has this affair been going on?"

"Oh, it's not an affair."

"So, you love her from afar?" Oops...Watch out, Doctor, Nina told herself, your facetiousness is showing. But Bucky didn't notice.

"Always, I'm afraid," he replied, without irony. And suddenly, then, his voice was almost tremulous. "Nina, from the moment I laid eyes on her, I knew—I knew—we'd been intended for each other...forever."

"When was that?"

"Twenty years ago."

"And you loved her all this time?" He nodded. "Bucky, will you tell me her name?"

"Constance."

"Well, uh, what brought this twenty-year romance with Constance to, uh, a boil?"

"I met her again."

"When?"

"February eleventh."

"Where? Come on, Bucky, help me out. You're not being cross-examined."

"Okay, okay, I'm sorry. Lemme stand up." He rose from the couch and began to pace. "It was on a plane, American 362—the three o'clock from O'Hare. I just made it. And I really had to get back. It was my son's thirteenth birthday. Jesus. But the instant I entered that plane, I swear, Nina, I could feel something. My head was swimming."

"Forgive me, Bucky. It can be a long run, O'Hare." Maybe that wasn't sympathetic, but damn it, Nina had to get a little substance back into all this poetry.

"No, no, no," Bucky replied emphatically, holding his arms up. "This was different. It was like the atmosphere on Earth had changed. Finally, I had to get up. I was in first class. You know, I fly first cabin."

"Of course."

He paused at her tone, and, for just a moment, the old Bucky returned. "I'm sorry. That really sounded horseshit of me, didn't it?" he asked. Nina shrugged. "Anyway"—and the grave new Bucky was speaking again—"I got up and headed to the back of the plane. You know, turning back the little curtain. I had to. I knew Constance was there. I swear. I hadn't laid eyes on her in twenty years, but there was no doubt. *No* doubt. I even whispered it out loud: 'God Almighty, Constance is here.'"

"And she was?"

"Twenty-six C, aisle. By the time I actually saw her, I was hyperventilating."

"And Constance?"

"She just said: 'I knew it was you, Bucky.' Just like that. So I sat down next to her. And my heart..." He touched it. "I'm sorry, I know this sounds so phony."

In fact, Nina was mesmerized. She couldn't help but believe what Bucky said. Every detail. He had invested such intensity and such sincerity—such purity—into what was usually so God-awful tawdry and ordinary, that Nina had forgotten to take any notes or even to turn on her tape recorder. She pushed the button now. "And how was *she?* How was Constance?" she asked, much too anxiously.

"She put her hands like this," Bucky said, thrusting his own hands under the opposite sides of his jacket, up under his armpits. "She had to. Otherwise, she told me she knew she would've grabbed me."

"And to that moment, it had been twenty years since you saw her last?"

"Uh huh."

"Okay, how long had that lasted?"

Bucky turned back, to stand before Nina in some form of supplication, holding his hands out to her. "I'm telling you, there never was any *that*. Never. I swear, I've never touched Constance, never kissed her, never even been alone with her." And he stared, helplessly, right through Nina.

"But you are in love with this woman?" He nodded. "And she with you?"

He nodded again. "I'm telling you, we are meant for each other. I mean, we were always meant for each other."

Nina rose and pointed to the couch. "Okay, Bucky, you sit back down. I stand up and pace. That's the way it works. Get comfortable. Start from the beginning." He followed her orders, taking off his jacket as he fell back onto the sofa. "You wanna glass of water?"

"If you mix it with scotch."

"I'm a psychiatrist, not a bartender." That gave them both a chance to smile, and she poured him the ice water. "Now...."

Bucky took a swallow. "We'll start with Philadelphia," he said, and with that announcement, he leaned back and began talking, all but oblivious to Dr. Winston. "It was that fall after I graduated from UVA. I really didn't know what I wanted to do. In fact, that whole summer, I'd just farted around down the Jersey shore. But I met an old buddy there, and he worked for an ad agency in Philly—

I'm from Philly myself—and he thought maybe that was something for me. So, they gave me a shot and started moving me around, trying to figure out where the hell I fit in.

"And one day, they had some project in marketing, so I went over there. And there was Constance. And it was just like on the goddamn plane in February. I mean, Nina, I could feel it the minute I walked into her little office. I swear to you, I was in love with her right away. I can see her now—the skirt, the blouse had these little purple flowers on it, her hair up...I'm sorry, I won't bother you with all that."

"No, no—do," Nina said. "Whatever you remember."

"Well, right away, Constance ducked her head. And I was sure I knew why, because she had the same feeling I was feeling—only for her it was even more complicated because she was already married. She was just out of college, but she was married. Girls still did that then."

"I remember."

"Constance had met this guy like the first week in college. She went to Smith and he went to Amherst, and they met at some goddamn mixer. He was a big-deal sophomore, cherry-picking the new Smithies. She never went out with anyone else in college. Constance is a one-man woman, you see. She just had the wrong one man and didn't know it. They're still married, too. Still. And he doesn't know, the poor sonuvabitch, all this time, she's been meant for me."

He paused for another drink of water. Nina wrote the word *meant* on her pad. It struck her the way Bucky kept referring to the romance as some sort of *fait accompli*. Then he barreled on. "Of course, neither does Phyllis know that all this time I've been meant for Constance. It's not fair, really, is it? Anyway, suffice it to say—I like that: 'suffice it to say'—suffice it to say, I went, basically, out of my mind the next two weeks working around Connie every day."

"On the marketing project?"

"Yeah. And I know what you're thinking, Nina. Did I ever express my feelings? And the answer is a thousand times...almost. Actually, though: never. I mean, the lady is not only married, she is a friggin' newlywed. Just that June, after she graduated. That's why she's in Philly. He's there in med. school. His name is Carl. Amherst Carl. Constance is taking courses at night for her masters and working in the ad agency to help support Amherst Carl. And she's a whiz, Nina. Numbers, statistics, all that crap. A genius. She does the same stuff for Merrill Lynch in Chicago now. Went to Wharton—the whole nine yards. She wouldn't have anything to do with a jerk like me if it wasn't that it was, you know, meant to be that way."

Nina underlined *meant*. She didn't have to prod him. The words were pouring out of Buckingham now, devoid of any self-consciousness.

"One night it was my birthday. September twenty-seventh. I was, uh, twenty-three that year, so four or five of 'em took me out for a birthday drink after work. Bookbinders. That's a big deal in Philadelphia, Bookbinders. And guess what?"

"Constance comes along."

"You got it. And this is the first time I'd ever been, uh, off the premises, you might say, with her. And, one by one, the others left. Truth is, they probably felt uncomfortable being around us. I know there were whispers."

Without so much as a please, Bucky held out his empty water glass, stiff-armed, in the general direction of Nina. She took it and refilled it as he rattled on.

"Constance doesn't drink, but she said she'd stay for one more Coke. And we were laughin', and then we were getting serious, and she's telling me all about herself. And then, just like that, I guess she started to feel guilty because she starts talking all about Carl. Carl and Constance. Constance and Carl.

"But I'm just looking at her and thinking: no, it's Constance and Bucky. Come on, Constance, say it. Say it. Tell me you love me. But she didn't say it. And I couldn't. You know how it is sometimes, Nina. You're absolutely 100 percent sure, but you can't be positive. You know? I mean, *suppose,* just suppose I'm wrong? I didn't know then—"

"Know what?"

"Know...well, I'll get to that. That's number two. That's the strange part. Okay?" Nina didn't push it; she only nodded. Bucky's shoulders sagged. "So, she left. She had to go to class. And there I am, sitting all by myself at big-deal Bookbinders. But I knew, then. I knew. I had to get my ass outta there. I don't mean Bookbinders. I mean Philly—away from her. So, the next morning, I walk into the boss's office, and I say, thanks and all that, but I've really decided that I wanna go to New York. Fact is, I'd never ever in my life wanted to go to New York, but I figured it's where you go when you wanna escape. Right?"

Nina sat back down in the chair next to him and agreed.

"Yeah. So I dropped by and said good-bye to Constance. I was still hoping that she'd fling herself at me, but she didn't."

"Suffice it to say," Nina said, but sweetly.

"Yeah. Suffice it to say. We just stared at each other for a while, and then I went back to this little cubicle I had, and well...I cried. Have you ever cried for love, Doctor?"

"Yes, I have, Bucky."

"I know I'm not supposed to ask you stuff, but—"

"It's okay."

"Yeah, boys aren't supposed to cry. But I cried my eyes out. And then I left. And I didn't see Constance till that American flight number 362, last February the eleventh."

He took a considerable swallow. "That *is* quite a story," Nina said.

"Yeah, I'm sorry, but I gotta walk around." In fact, he walked in a circle, eventually coming to stare at the wall.

Nina finally said, "You never talked to Constance again—no contact at all?"

Bucky turned back, leaning up against the wall, arms akimbo. "No, never. I just tried to forget her. And a few years later, I meet Phyllis. I was starting to do pretty good then. I can sell magazine pages, Nina. It's a silly little thing, but it's my thing. I was making some good bucks—not oodles yet, but good bucks—and so, I proposed. I'd almost forgotten Constance by then. Almost." Suddenly, he pushed off the wall, holding his arms up, palms out. "Wait a minute. I don't want that to sound wrong. I love my wife, Nina."

"I understand."

"I really love Phyllis. I do. It's just that always and forever, I have to love Constance. It's crazy, isn't it?"

"Sorry, we're not supposed you use that word with patients," Nina said, trying to make things a little lighter. "And you haven't seen Constance since—"

"Haven't talked to her. We got off the plane. We're both shaking. I thought I was going to pee in my pants. Excuse me. Then we found an empty gate, and we just sat there and stared at each other for a long time. Finally, I touched her. I took her hands. I just had to touch the woman I love." Nina nodded. "And then we just stared some more. You know that expression, about how a guy undressed somebody with his eyes?"

"I do indeed."

"Well, it was like that with both of us—only it was like we were both undressing ourselves of all our things, all our everyday stuff, all our...lives. We were naked to the heart. To the soul. You know?"

Nina was hushed at the vision Bucky's words conveyed. Nor did she really understand, at first, that his question was not rhetorical, that he really wanted her to respond. But when she saw his eyes pleading for certification, Nina not only heard herself saying, "Yes, I do," but adding, "I had that happen to me once, too."

She could not believe she had volunteered that to a patient. Hell, Nina thought, why shouldn't she just lie down on the couch and tell the good Dr. Buckingham everything? What was it about this guy that made her so susceptible?

"Really?" Bucky asked. "When was that?"

Nina got back on track, waving him off. "Some other time, Bucky. I really think we have our hands full enough now just trying to deal with you."

"Yeah," he concurred.

So, Nina faced him again, clasping her hands before her in her most pronounced no-nonsense pose. "You were telling me about undressing souls," she declared. "At LaGuardia."

"Yeah, so I finally said to Constance: 'Look, I love you. I have to love you. I can't explain it, but I felt that way the minute I walked into your office twenty years ago.' And you know what she said? 'Me too, Bucky.' Just: me too!"

Nina had to smile. Bucky went on, "So Constance said then: 'All right, now what do we do?'

"And I said: 'Look, we gotta be sure. We gotta give this some time.' You see, Nina, even then, I'm trying to tell myself this is crazy, that it'll all go away."

"But it won't?"

Bucky shook his head. "You sound like Constance. That's what she said, flat out: 'A month, a year, whatever, it won't ever change, darling. Ever.' But I told her I had to have some time to sort it out. 'Gimme to the summer. I'll call you in six months—August the eleventh.'"

"And that's it?"

"That's it. We squeezed each other...hands—just hands. And both of us said 'I love you' again, and then she just stood up and walked away, down to the baggage claim. I waited a while, and then I went home to my kid's birthday party."

Nina let his words trail off into silence. She glanced down to her watch. "If you don't mind, Bucky, I think that's a good place to stop for now."

"Yeah."

"Okay, and since you've told me about the important thing, next week you can tell me about the strange thing."

"Aw, I can't *tell* you, Nina."

"Come on, whatever it is, I'm sure you can tell me. If you've told me all about this, then—"

"No, no, no. I mean I gotta take you out and show you this."

Nina tapped her foot, making a little joke. "Bucky, I'm sorry, but the class rule is: no field trips."

But suddenly, then, he stepped before her—so direct, so firm, that Dr. Winston might even have been frightened if she didn't think she knew the man so well. "No, no, Nina," he snapped. "You *must* come see this."

She fell back, startled. "Well, I—"

"It's not far. Only three, four blocks."

Nervously, but curious now, "Where?"

"The museum."

"The Metropolitan?" He nodded. Nina considered. She shouldn't even have considered considering. But she did. Despite herself. Despite her professional demeanor and her personal instincts. Despite. So—despite—she stepped behind her desk and checked out her appointment book. "All right, if it's that important—"

"It is. It *really* is."

"Okay, day after tomorrow, I'm through with my last patient at four."

"I'll meet you at the museum. Out front. A few minutes after four."

Nina waggled a finger, trying to lighten things up a bit. "But I'm telling you right now: I don't do this for all the boys. This better be good *and* strange."

"Oh, it's very strange, Nina. Very, very strange." He reached up, took the flower from his lapel, and grandly, presented it to her. "Forget me not, Doctor."

Nina laughed. "Don't worry, Mr. Buckingham. You're a hard man to forget."

·3·

Two mornings later, when Nina arrived at her office, she was
greeted by a police officer who was there with Roseann. Poor
Roseann—she was beside herself. "Oh, Doctor," she cried out,
"someone broke in last night."

The cop nodded gravely. Someone had indeed gotten in—man-
aging, it seemed, to force open a casement window. Nina loved
those old windows; she would crack them and let in good old-
fashioned New York City air. "You might want to look around, Doctor," the officer said, "but it appears he had to beat it outta here
pretty quick when he tripped the motion alarm."

"We don't think he even got into your room," Roseann said.
"Just here." Her arm swept around the waiting room.

The cop pulled at the casement, making sure it was shut
tight. He was not, however, approving. "I'd have bars put over
this, Doctor."

"I guess," Nina replied. But she'd always resisted that idea. A few
doors off Fifth Avenue, a doctor's office—bars on the windows. The
thought was just abhorrent to her.

"They have nice designer-style bars," the officer informed her,
helpfully. "Curlicues and what-not." Nina thanked him for that
security fashion tip, then took a coffee and went into her own
office, closing the door behind her.

She needed time to pull herself together. There was, after all, no
denying it any longer: somebody was, for some reason, trailing her.
"Let Lindsay try and attribute a break-in to computers," Nina said

out loud to no one, smirking. Then, to herself, "Jesus, I'm talking to myself again."

That was all so ironic. It had just never occurred to Nina Gaither Winston that she would ever be left alone. Sad sometimes—probably. Sick—it happens to everybody. Unsuccessful—maybe. Confused—well, yes and no. But alone? That had simply never crossed her mind as a viable possibility. Yes, of course, the husbands do die first, but no, they don't die in their fifties. That wasn't in the plan. Anyway, Nina had always just assumed that if Kingsley did (as the insurance men always put it) "pre-decease" her, she would surely be that one American widow—in what was it officially now: in a million? in a blue moon?—who would find another guy.

After all, Nina liked men. Most women her age were really tired of men—all the boorishness, all the golf, all the games on television, all the, well...all the men bullshit. What most women Nina's age wanted was *company*. Nina didn't want to settle for company. She wanted men. She had always liked them, always been their friend— she had been as faithful to Kingsley as the day is long. Well, of course, until Hugh. And there's the rub. There's the goddamn rub. Now Kingsley was gone, and Hugh wouldn't have her.

And Nina was damned if she was going to go on a cruise.

She sipped her coffee and tried not to think about the break-in, tried not to think about how someone was after her. Yes, of course, she could call Lindsay and say I-told-you-so, or call some girlfriends for some pointless commiseration. But why bother? Instead, she picked up her first patient's file, determined to *lose herself in her work*. Isn't that what you're supposed to do? Only she couldn't manage that now, because her thoughts kept flying ahead from the day's first patient to the last.

Yes, today was the day that she was going to rendezvous with Bucky at the museum. And the prospect charmed Nina. It wasn't just the strangeness of what he promised. There was even a tint of danger, sort of. No, she wasn't afraid of Bucky. But yes, she was afraid of where Bucky—Bucky's story—was taking her. Ultimately, Nina was afraid of herself. Call it off. Cancel.

She would have, too, but the truth was, that as much as Nina hated to admit it to herself, there was a certain personal anticipation here. A date. It was like a date. Well, almost. Close enough. We'll meet at the museum. We'll have some innocent fun, a few laughs. Why call that off?

Of course, Nina knew very well that reputable doctors shouldn't go meet patients after work simply because they had something strange to show you. But Bucky was good company...and, okay, he was cute, too. He looked like one of those movie stars, like whatshisface. No, not the real star stars from the disaster pictures, or the guys playing opposite Julia Roberts—no, not your Mel Gibson or your Tom Cruise, but one of those almost kinda stars who play the exasperated father in the family movie, or the white guy with Eddie Murphy. That was Bucky, and she was going to meet him at the museum. So there.

Nina even had to admit: she had dressed for Bucky today. A trim maroon suit that kept her looking properly "professional," but that still showed her femininity to its best advantage. Nina had a fine little figure. *Pert* is the word you would use if, in fact, anybody actually used the word *pert* anymore. And, more importantly, Nina looked younger than she was, which was officially, certifiably, fifty-three years old.

Her mind remained distracted. The patients came and went, but Nina Winston was not a particularly good doctor today. With Mr. Armistead—poor, tedious, well-meaning Mr. Armistead—Nina even began to wonder if she could seduce Bucky. Just thinking theoretically, of course—and never mind all the ethical canons of her profession. Just blue-skying, kicking it around...but, if she did *theoretically* try to seduce Bucky, could she? After all, when it was the other way round, when she went to Hugh for counseling, didn't he seduce her? (It was *he* who seduced *her*, wasn't it?) Anyway, turnabout is fair play, and it certainly made sense, seducing Bucky. His marriage seemed to be falling apart, but he wasn't scheduled to contact his assigned dreamboat again for another few months. There was a window of opportunity here.

And then, to herself, Nina thought, "You are perfectly asinine."

In the mirror, two hours later, after her last patient, Nina checked herself out. She turned around, looked back over her shoulder, and thought: I have one great little ass. That's the advantage of starting out with a little ass. You can maintain it as a great little ass, while all the big asses that men rave about get to be too-big asses.

Next, Nina examined her face in the mirror. She'd had a little laser work a couple of years ago. Doug Frazier had done it for her. They'd been in medical school together, and he was gay, and Nina could always talk to him. In fact, Doug was the only person she ever told about Hugh. Even then, though, she only confessed to Doug about Hugh after she found out that Kingsley had cancer. That had put Nina over the top, guiltwise: her husband's dying, while she's screwing another guy.

Oh well.

Doug had helped more with her face than with her guilt. She looked deep into the mirror. There were no lines to speak of. She stood back. The whole package was, in fact, pert.

So, out the door and up Fifth Avenue she walked. And there he was. Even before she had crossed the street up by the Stanhope Hotel, she spotted Bucky. He was high up on the steps of the museum. He had on a double-breasted gray suit with a pink shirt—she could pick that out, even from a distance—and a handkerchief of another shade of pink protruding from his breast pocket. "Hey, good looking," he hollered, gaily, as soon as he saw her.

Nina waved back, marveling how wonderful it must be for anyone to be so assured. "You know what you are?" she asked, as she came up the steps toward him. "You're what we used to call a *bon vivant.*"

He laughed, but only for an instant, because then there was a bit of uncomfortableness for them both, inasmuch as the convention of this time called for one of them to peck the other on the cheek. But this was still a doctor-patient meeting, even if it wasn't in the office. Typically, though, Bucky went right to the heart of things. "I don't think you're supposed to kiss your doctor."

"No," Nina replied.

"Well," he went on, "if I were going to start kissing doctors, I want you to know, I'd start with you, Dr. Winston."

Despite herself, Nina blushed. So, quickly, then, "Now, you're going to show me the...strange?"

"Right this way." He handed her a little admission button. Today it was an ugly sea green. Why, Nina wondered, did The Metropolitan Museum of *Art* feature such awful colors? Bucky ushered her up the last of the great front steps to door of the museum. "Really, it's very strange," he assured her.

That made her pause. There was no give in Bucky's voice now, no playfulness. In fact, he spoke *sotto voce,* lacking any expression whatsoever. Buckysmirk had become buckyblank. Nina was almost frozen, the one foot still poised to move into the building. It would have been easy—a little embarrassing, perhaps, but easy nonetheless—to conclude this little adventure right here, to voice second thoughts, to confine their appointments to professional territory, to her office. But instead, Nina held her tongue, and side by side with Bucky, she strode into the Metropolitan.

◆4◆

In Chicago, in the Merrill Lynch office where Constance Rawlings worked as a stock analyst, Terry Schulbach, her boss, was despised by virtually all the women; he was known as "Schulbeast" or "Mr. Slimebach." In fact, almost alone among those women who tolerated him was Constance. It was certainly not that she had been spared his crude come-ons—especially considering her superior anatomy—but simply that Constance was so amazingly controlled, detached to the point of frostiness. She was perfect for her job—analyzing economics, studying companies, creating market profiles, which would then be forwarded up the line, leading to recommendations to buy or sell.

Probably, in fact, Constance had grown even more insular, distant from the everyday world around her, ever since she had renewed her acquaintance with Bucky. So it was that in Chicago at the same time that Bucky and Nina were entering the Metropolitan, Constance appeared at Schulbach's office, and, closing the door behind her, took up the seat across from his desk.

Ignoring his usual transparent ogle, she spoke coolly to him, "This is confidential, Terry."

"Hey, Connie," he said, leaning forward, "better from your lips to my lips, but, from your lips to my ears—it's safe with me."

"Good," she said. "I want you to arrange a transfer to New York for me."

"Oh, Connie, noooo." But then, in the next moment, Schulbach came together professionally. "You're the best person in this office."

"Then, I would expect you to relay that assessment to New York so there won't be any problems."

"Don't worry. They know how valuable you are." He pulled out a pad. "All right, when?"

"I'll be leaving in August. Around the eleventh."

"Carl moving to a new hospital?" Schulbach asked idly, pulling out some forms.

"I'm not at liberty to reveal the reason," Constance answered, rising. "And I will expect you to honor this information that I've entrusted to you."

"You can take it to the bank, Connie."

"I'd also like the rest of the afternoon off," she went on, leaning over, without guile, even while Schulbach gazed directly down her cleavage. She placed a folder before him. "I've finished the e-Micro-Graphics file."

Schulbach tapped the cover of the report, then stood up, and, as formal as he could be, he declared, "It's been a privilege working with you, Connie. I know I kid around a lot, but I'm serious: you're the best analyst I've ever had. Thanks."

"My pleasure," she said, and turning, left his office and went to the parking garage. There, in her forest green Nissan, she headed onto the Edens Expressway toward Lake Forest. No radio, no CD. No, now that e-MicroGraphics was out of the way, she could devote all her thoughts to her beloved Bucky. She imagined the two of them alone, soon enough, watching the sunset together. She imagined them drinking champagne. Yes: for this, she would have a glass. She would have two! Constance cooed to herself. She imagined Bucky kissing her. She imagined Bucky undressing her. She imagined them making love.

No. They weren't in bed. Instead, they were in a shower together, soaping each other. But now that that was the image, Constance dwelt on it. She didn't really know why—why they were in the shower. Sunsets, champagne, kisses—sure. But she had never once stood in a shower with Carl, let alone with any other man, let alone even thought about it. But having met Bucky again had revitalized her imagination. Suddenly, Constance daydreamed. She visualized things in the brightest colors. Her memory was more vivid, too. So much came back to her. It was as if Bucky had, by his reflected light of love, put a shine on old things gone dark.

Why, when Constance had been a little girl, she had possessed such clear, odd memories. She had grown up in a city, in Rochester, New York, but she told her parents of cows, sheep, and tall sailing ships at anchor, then moving across a sea—curious visions that her mother and father found amazing...but benign. *What sights these children see on television now!*

But little Connie knew that these sights had not come to her from a screen in the family living room. She had *seen* these very things herself, alive, with her own eyes. That is why she certainly never tried to tell anybody about Bess. If Mom and Dad wouldn't believe about the cows and the ships, what would they make of Bess?

Poor Bess. Poor, dead Bess, in her pretty, long, blue gown with her cold, blank eyes, staring up at Constance from the shallow creek where she lay, drowned. How did Bess get there? Why was Constance looking down at her? How did Constance even know that her name was Bess? Constance couldn't remember that. But she knew it was Bess. Of that she had no doubt. Bess.

It also helped, too, that there was a way that sometimes Bess could be driven from her mind. That vision would suddenly be replaced with a pattern of diamonds. It was always the same pattern, and it was always in red and black. In fact, the first time that Constance saw a checkerboard, she thought: so that's what I've seen in my mind every now and then. It's just a gameboard. But then she looked more closely, and Constance realized that in her red-and-black vision, the pattern was diamonds, not squares. And it was a much more complicated pattern than the checkerboard.

First of all, the diamonds in Constance's mind were not aligned horizontally as they are on a checkerboard. Rather: more diagonally. Furthermore, the pattern was fixed in an odd fashion. Between vertical rows of pairs of red diamonds, there was a cluster of four red diamonds, then a solid line of black, then a cluster of six red diamonds, then another solid black line, then another four red-diamond cluster, another solid black line, another cluster of six red diamonds, and so on, over and over. In Constance's mind, no matter how many times she envisioned the pattern, this is always exactly what she saw:

But then, over time, as little Constance grew up, as her miniature world expanded, as she did indeed remember things from television or from family trips, all these exciting new sensations overwhelmed the bizarre old ones that had been squirreled away in her mind. Soon, what she thought of was cars and trucks and Captain Kangaroo and Mister Greenjeans and teachers and the sights of Rochester—not sheep and sailing ships. Not Bess. In fact, when Constance first remembered Bess again the other day—suddenly, as she rode up alone in the elevator at Merrill Lynch—she couldn't even recall her name. It had been so many years since last she had seen Bess. But the vision was just as clear as ever it had been back in Constance's childhood: the pretty, young woman in the long, blue gown, empty eyes staring through the clear, shallow water where she lay on the pebbly bottom.

But Constance did not dwell long on Bess. The vision always came and went because her mind always fled back to Bucky. Six months, he had said. August the eleventh. Only eighty-two days to go.

At the stables near her house where Constance rode, she changed into her riding clothes—a floppy sweatshirt, boots, and jodhpurs. She tied her hair in a polka-dot ribbon, then pressed on her helmet and mounted her bay gelding, New York Minute. She adored riding. It had so quickly become Constance's favorite activity—she, who had never otherwise held any interest in sports.

Proctor Lee watched her now, as Constance guided her mount about the ring, taking each jump smoothly, clear all around. Proctor Lee had taught Mrs. Rawlings how to ride twelve years ago. He had taught hundreds of her North Shore neighbors the same—how to ride, how to jump a horse, how to perform in a show ring. He marveled at Constance. In almost forty years of teaching, he'd never encountered a student who'd been more adept so quickly. At first, in fact, it had depressed Proctor that Mrs. Rawlings had come so late to the sport, for otherwise he imagined that she could have been the very best, a champion.

Immediately, Constance could do everything he taught her. Straight back, perfect seat, balancing her buttocks there on the horse's back, then working her legs independently, the one or the other—just the right amount of pressure—guiding the reins with exactly the touch he had instructed her. But as perfect as Constance was at following his directions, Proctor Lee also saw soon enough that Constance lacked that mutuality, that canny ability to blend with the animal, to become one—that talent that every outstanding horseman or horsewoman instinctively possesses. It was always a perfect technical ride that Constance gave; it was also, however, never a fluid one, never quite pretty.

Oh, she would win some ribbons—even an occasional blue or red in a small show if the judge was a man. Even now, as Constance paused after another loop over the jumps, Proctor Lee couldn't help but stare at her, shaking his head at the beautiful tableau that she and New York Minute formed—the absolutely gorgeous woman, sitting tall and still, astride the magnificent steed. But she was just too mechanical; Constance Rawlings in repose, even lost in a baggy sweatshirt that masked her voluptuousness, was far more beautiful than she was in action, in animation.

That was why there was no more that Proctor Lee could teach her.

Back in the stable, Constance didn't bother to change out of her riding clothes because she wanted to wash them when she got home. She came into the house, and there was Carl, in an easy chair, splayed out, exhausted, watching the five o'clock news, sports, and weather on WLS. "Hard day, honey?" Constance asked him.

"Yeah," he mumbled. "Long."

Constance said, "I'll make it better for you." Without fanfare, then, she pulled off her sweatshirt and tossed it aside, undid her bra, and stood in front of her husband, reaching up behind her head, untying the polka-dot ribbon that held her hair. Dumbfounded, but altogether pleased, Carl raised his hands to caress his wife, just as the ribbon came untied and her hair tumbled down around her bosom, hiding his hands in the swirl. Constance sighed at his touch, but only for a moment, for then she leaned down, undid his fly and threw her mouth upon him, swiftly bringing him to his joy.

Thereupon, without further ado, Constance scooped up her clothes, went upstairs, and stepped into the shower. She let the water splash all over her, tilting her head back, imagining that it was a waterfall on some desert island, and that now it was Bucky's hands (not her own), that drew over her body, pausing to touch all the precious parts.

"Oh, Bucky darling," Constance said, opening her mouth, letting the shower water rain on her tongue, over her shoulders, pelting all her body. "Oh, Bucky, only eighty-two more days."

·5·

Bucky and Nina strolled across the museum lobby, around the information desk, toward the grand staircase directly before them. "Up we go," he announced. Nina touched his sleeve, then pointed over to the left, to an escalator. "Gee," Bucky sighed, "I didn't know that was there."

"I didn't think so. Can I ask you, Bucky, exactly how many times were you here before, you, uh, discovered whatever it is I'm about to see?"

"Well, Phyllis and I brought Sarah here a few years ago after we took her and a couple friends to the Central Park Zoo, but then it started raining."

"Any port in a storm."

"Yeah, I guess I'm really not much of a museum person."

"Suffice it to say," said Nina, as the escalator deposited them on the second floor, and Bucky started to steer her over to the large section of European paintings. They were fortunate in that this general area wasn't crowded, because, adjacent, the Metropolitan was featuring a special exhibit of the works of Mary Cassatt, and this was drawing the bulk of the crowds. Idly, Nina asked, "Have you seen the Cassatts?"

Bucky puzzled. "I don't think I know them."

Nina shook her head, grinning. They took some seats in the middle of an empty gallery . Nina said, "Mary Cassatt was an American painter, but she spent most of her life in France. With the Impressionists." She paused. "You *have* heard of the Impressionists?"

"What do you think, they don't learn us anything at UVA?"

Musing, Nina said, "I've never understood why there are so few female painters. All the women writers, and almost no women artists."

"I think it has to do with the boobs," Bucky replied. Straight-faced.

"I'm sorry?"

"The boobs." He pointed to a couple barebreasted paintings. "Most art is boobs, so I think men throw themselves more into it." Only after a few moments did he let a little grin spread, and she realized he was putting her on. Maybe. Nina punched him, lightly, on the arm.

"I do like some of it," Bucky added, then, his voice taking on more seriousness. "Sometimes, you know, I only play the Philistine. It's what I'm supposed to be, a bozo selling ad space for magazines. The work doesn't lead much to salons and ballets."

"Yes," Nina said, keeping a straight face herself, "you do a good job of masking your intellect."

An older couple strolled by, and Nina and Bucky fell silent; a gallery is not conducive to private conversation. Only when the people moved on did Nina ask, "So, what brought you back here? Another rainy day at the zoo?"

"In a manner of speaking, yeah. It was back in March—the twelfth to be exact. I was going for a kill with a client. I mean, this was a whole new product category we'd been trying to crack, and I was sure they were coming into both my books. They were from outta-town and took a suite across the street, at the Stanhope. They were seeing a lot of magazines. I was so confident. I mean, Nina, this is my business. You get so you can tell if somebody's gonna come into your tent, and with these guys, I was so sure, I'd gotten room service to bring up two champagne bottles. And on one of them, there's a little ski cap, the other a sea captain's hat. Those are kinda our symbols—*Snow Ski Vacation* and *Summer Sailing*—"

"Yeah."

"But then the guy says, sorry, thanks but no thanks—and I am crushed. Devastated. I was gonna drown my sorrows at some bar, but I came outta the Stanhope and I saw the museum across the street, so I decided to retreat into culture instead."

"Serendipity?"

"Is that another one of the Impressionists?" Nina tapped his arm again. "So, I came in and started walking around. Helter-skelter. Checked out the Egyptian stuff first, all the yucky mummies, that old Temple of Dunbar, Dendur—whatever. Then I dragged up those goddamn stairs and ended up in here."

"This room?"

"Yeah, I sat right here, feeling sorry for myself, staring at that picture." Bucky pointed to a large painting on the long wall facing them. "It's called *Apollo and Aurora*, and, you know, I thought it was kinda neat. Better than those damn mummies."

Nina studied the work. It was very florid, Apollo standing up in a chariot, Aurora next to him in a starry blue gown, scattering flowers to the winds. "It's terribly romantic," she said, "but then, you do possess a romantic view of the world."

"Doctor, you don't know the half of it," Bucky said, and he reached for her hand, just long enough to help pull her up. "So then, I moved into the next room, just ambling, like this." He imitated himself ambling through the door, not stopping till he approached a bunch of Rembrandts.

There, he caught his breath. "Okay, now this is it. Imagine me that day—March twelfth. I'm all alone, walking from this room into that one"—he pointed to the gallery ahead, number twenty-seven—"and I just stopped dead. I could feel it...exactly like I feel the same thing now." Bucky gulped and bit his lip.

"What? What do you feel?"

"I feel Constance. And weirdness. All mixed together."

Nina reached out, and took hold of his sleeve before he could advance into gallery twenty-seven. "Now wait, Bucky. Explain to me: what do you mean you can feel Constance here?"

"Nina, I can't *explain* it. If I could explain it, I wouldn't've come to you. It's just like back on the airplane or in Philadelphia. It's just...Constance. And love."

Nina tried to gain some control. "Okay, I know you're trying," she said, "so let's do this. Can we, like, reenact? Can we walk into that room now exactly the way you did the first time?"

"Okay. But you stay with me." And this time, when he reached out and took Nina's hand, he held it firmly. They stepped into gallery twenty-seven that way, together. But as soon as he came through the door, Bucky's step faltered. It was almost as if a stiff wind had blown into his face. He nodded to her, caught his breath, and plunged ahead again, turning to the right. Then he stopped a second time. "Right away, I looked around. I mean, I knew Constance had to be here."

"But she wasn't?"

He didn't answer, only shrugged. Then he turned to face the first painting. "That's when my eyes fixed on her," he said. Nina saw: it was the Madonna. Still holding Nina's hand tightly, Bucky stepped up the painting. She saw that it was entitled *Holy Family with Saint Francis*, and it was by Peter Paul Rubens.

"Rubens," she said.

"Yeah. 'Course, I'd heard of him, but then I didn't know who painted this. I was just mesmerized by the Madonna. Like now. I just wanted to keep on staring at her—and I'm not very religious, Nina. That's not it. I'm not even Catholic, like you. But then suddenly I felt myself being pulled along this wall. Just like now. I wanna keep in touch with the Madonna, but I gotta move along. I *have* to."

Nina was pulled along with him, but she didn't hear everything Bucky was saying. Her mind was short-circuited. *I'm not Catholic, like you.* How did he know what religion she was? She would never volunteer that information to a patient. In fact, Nina purposely tried to keep her office neutral of gender, of background, of religion—certainly religion. And plants, not flowers. Flowers can seem too feminine. No personal photographs. No memorabilia. Paintings of the hotel school. And, above all, *nothing* religious. So how did Bucky know she was Catholic? And wait a minute: hadn't he once made a passing reference to "your daughter?"

But these thoughts were literally yanked out of her mind because Bucky had pulled Nina past a small painting in the middle of the wall to arrive before the huge canvas next to it. They stood before it, and she could actually feel some kind of sensation that emanated from him. And, my God: if she could feel this *from* him, what must he be feeling himself? Bucky was even trembling a little, taking deep breaths, his eyes fixed on the painting in some mixture of awe and adoration. She was, frankly, disturbed. Even a little frightened. "Come on, Bucky," she said, "let's sit down."

Of course, a lot of it was what was happening to Nina, too. She had to sit down herself. No patient of hers had ever affected her this way.

Bucky did momentarily regain some of his equilibrium when she turned him away from the painting, and when he slumped to the bench in the middle of the room, he could speak again. "That's exactly what I did the first time," he said. "And all the other times."

"What is it?"

"You look at the picture." As he kept his own eyes away, Nina examined the painting. It was dominated by two large forms, a man and a woman. He was strong and powerful, with some type of orange toga draped over him in such a way that his muscular back and arms and his magnificent, flared calves were altogether visible—and so simply perfect, so beautiful, so defined. Nina was even assured, staring at the man, that once upon a time, God had made better men's bodies Himself than men did today, tricked up with steroids.

By contrast, the woman holding onto the man was fat and chunky, nearly formless, save for a lovely pair of breasts. Her legs were even downright ugly. Nina would have known at a glance, anywhere, that this was also a Rubens. *"Venus and Adonis,"* Bucky said. And then, a long, worrisome pause, as he found the nerve to say the words, "That's us up there." He held out his hand, and Nina saw that it was shaking. "That's us up there—me and Constance."

"Bucky, come on, you know Venus and Adonis are mythological."

He turned to her, and crossly, "I know *that*, Nina. Don't patronize me, for Chrissake. I mean, Constance and I were the *models* Rubens used. I can feel Constance up there. I swear to God, I can smell her. I know now: we were together in Holland in 1635." And now Bucky spoke softly, tears—of love? of fear?—forming in his eyes.

"I know it, Nina. That's what's strange. I know I'm looking at me and the lady I love when we were together three hundred and fifty years ago."

Nina just said, "Oh, I see." After all, Bucky was so matter-of-fact; he made it all sound so plausible.

•6•

"Think carefully now, Bucky. Did you ever see this painting before?"
He shook his head vehemently. "Are you sure? A lot of times we find
that somebody saw something way back—even early in childhood—
and it made a deep impression in the subconscious, so that it came
out years later in some unusual fashion—like this."

"Look, did I see it in some old schoolbook? It's possible. But,
hey, it's not the friggin' Mona Lisa."

"Ever hear about Venus and Adonis?"

"Well, like everybody, I know she's the goddess of love, and he's
the ultimate hunk. But, no, I never knew Venus and Adonis were
gettin' it on."

Nina had to smile; she'd never quite thought of the gang from
Mount Olympus *gettin' it on.* "Well, how 'bout Rubens?"

"Painted fat ladies, all I knew." He snuck a peek back at the
painting. "I guess Constance was a little chubbier in that life."

"It was the style," Nina said. "But hey, more for a guy to love."

He laughed, momentarily his old self. "Now me, of course, Nina.
Get a load of me. I was a real piece of work then."

"Yeah, a real studmuffin." Nina turned back then, to look again
at the painting. "I don't remember the story. Did you ever know it?"

"Hey, Nina, I'm telling you. I didn't know Rubens, I didn't know
the painting, I didn't know the story. I swear, all I know is what I
made myself read in that little notice posted on the wall."

"Tell me."

"Well, you gotta start with the little kid up there, tuggin' at

Adonis's leg. That's Cupid."

"I could guess that," Nina said. Cupid was blond and rosy-cheeked and also tubby like Venus. He had wings and—the dead giveaway—his bow and arrows lay at his feet. He was looking up at Adonis, pleading with his eyes, his fat little arms wrapped around one of Adonis's massive thighs.

"Yeah, everybody knows Cupid from Valentines. And anyway, the deal is that he's been dickin' around, like little kids do, and one of his love-potion arrows accidentally grazed Venus. Now, she's a goddess, but Adonis is only mortal. The sonuvabitch might have been built like a god, but he was still just another guy."

"Early Schwartzenegger."

"Yeah. Only here's where the plot thickens. Venus just happened to be staring at that great bod when she got nicked by Cupid's arrow. So she absolutely loses it over the guy. But still, she's a goddess, so she could tell the future, and she knows that lover-boy is gonna get killed if he goes out on a boar hunt."

"So, that's the moment that Rubens painted," Nina said, pointing at the picture.

Bucky said, "Exactly," but he still kept his eyes turned away. "See, Adonis has got this pretty, *naked* lady pleading with him to stay with her, but he won't listen."

"Just like a man."

"And, sure enough, he was killed by a boar."

"The original tragic love story," Nina said. She stared hard at the painting, searching for clues, trying to comprehend it all.

Suddenly, though, Bucky grabbed her hand again. "Look, I'm sorry," he gasped, "but I gotta get outta here. I've never even been able to stay this long."

"I understand," Nina said, and keeping hold of his hand, she guided him the other way out of the gallery, into the eighteenth-century paintings, then through a maze of other rooms. They moved so rapidly, with such focus just on getting away, that neither of them noticed the tall, gray-haired woman in a most fashionable flowered spring *chapeau,* who had been sneaking peeks at them from the next gallery . In fact, so quickly did Nina and Bucky move that it was all the woman could do to turn away and hide her face, pretending to study a Dürer.

Past the woman, they rushed through the elegant British portraits, out to the top of the great stairs. "Hey, where ya takin' me?" Bucky cried out.

"Just hang on for the ride," Nina replied, and they flew down the steps, made a U-turn at the bottom, back through the European Sculpture Court to an elevator. They piled on, and when the doors opened, Bucky was surprised to be outside on the Roof Garden that overlooked the museum's Egyptian obelisk and then all of Central Park beyond, green and thick with trees.

"Hey, this is really gorgeous," Bucky said.

Nina was pleased. Bucky seemed to be returning to his more normal effervescent state. She let go of his hand and let him just drift around, wandering through the statues, gazing over the park, looking out to the city. Still, he didn't say anything. Eventually, they found their way to the south end of the garden, past a bulky black statue called *Standing Woman,* to where, on the Fifth Avenue side, a little peninsula extended out from the rest of the garden. They plunked themselves down on one of the benches. But it was a long time before Bucky finally looked at Nina and said, "You think I'm loony-tunes, don't you?"

"No, but I can tell that something in that gallery affected you in a very...uh, unusual way."

"But you don't believe me, do you?"

"Bucky, please understand: what you're telling me is not exactly easy to believe. It's not just that it's a fantastic story. To me, it's even more complicated. I'm devoted to a religion that doesn't espouse the concept of reincarnation. If I accept your, uh, your adventure in time, I have to question the most basic beliefs of my own faith."

"Yeah, that's one reason I wanted you."

Nina looked up sharply, curiously. Once again, Bucky had said something about her which at least seemed to indicate a personal knowledge that he shouldn't own. But it was innocent enough, and for the moment, she let the matter pass again. Instead: "Have you told Constance about this?"

"No, I swore to you. We haven't talked since that one day—February eleventh. Besides, I wanted to talk to someone like you first."

"All right, Mr. Buckingham, this is hardly the place to offer any diagnosis, but given your state of mind, it wouldn't be fair if I didn't at least venture some thoughts. Just understand this is instinctive, shoot-from-the-hip. Okay?"

"I won't hold you to it."

"Good. All right," Nina began, "you have had, in your life, a huge emotional upheaval with Constance. I'm not about to advise you on that subject. I'm not a preacher, I'm not Dear Abby, and I'm not a horoscope. But, whatever, this attraction is obviously tearing at you. Now, you and Constance—you're what I call a retro-romance. It's not that unusual. Typically, it involves a man and a woman—usually just about your age—who were high school or college sweethearts, and they meet again, and—"

"But Connie and I were never sweethearts."

"All right, all right—it's not a *classic* retro-romance. But you're back with somebody you were in love with once, and it evokes what you remember as the good old days—when all of life was summer at the Jersey shore. But now it's mortgages and an advertiser who doesn't buy your pages and a marriage that isn't all hearts and flowers. But, ah, the old girlfriend. She was perfect then. It's easy to convince yourself that everything will be glorious again if you just take up with the angel from the past."

"That's what you think?"

"I told you this was a quick read. But this situation is not uncommon. Adonis and Venus *is* uncommon. Bucky and Constance isn't. And to be sure, your situation is even more pure, more idealistic, because Constance was never more than a sweet dream to you." Bucky nodded. Nina went on. "And I'll acknowledge that if we forget for the moment the rather essential complication that you both happen to be married to other people, then you and Constance make a very compelling love story. I know you believe that, Bucky."

"I really do."

"I know. And when you add to that this deep—very real—sense you possess that you two are somehow, as we say, 'meant for each other,' then I can see how you could, in your mind, make this leap into other lives. And what better lever for your dreams than Venus and Adonis, as painted by that romantic master, Mr. Rubens? You walk in, you see—"

"Nina, damn it, I told you: I didn't even know the story. I had the feelings even before I got near the painting."

"Okay, okay. A point taken. But, Bucky, you were upset by the business deal gone wrong, you are carrying this retro-romance around, it *is* a very romantic scene, you *did* recognize Cupid, and taken together it was somehow enough to convince you of this journey through the centuries."

"You do think I'm loony-tunes."

Nina shook her head vigorously. "No, you're missing the point. I think you're one of the sanest people I've ever met in my life—which is precisely what makes everything you tell me sound so damn persuasive."

Quickly then, he snapped at her, "Okay, hypnotize me, Nina."

"Why?"

"You know. Maybe you can take me back to the seventeenth century, to Amsterdam, to Rubens."

Ah. So that was where the fascination with hypnosis came from. Nina nodded, and replied, "Really now, Bucky, you make it sound so simple. *Take me back!* As easy as take me back to the mall. Take me back to that good Italian restaurant. Come on. If it was that easy, and if we really do live again and again, then that's all we'd do: go back. It'd replace television."

"All right. I know. But how many sane people—You said I was sane."

"In a moment of weakness."

"How many sane people ever get these feelings I have? You know, besides Shirley MacLaine." He chuckled at that. So did she. And of course, that sort of humor was what made Bucky so damn much more convincing. Those patients of Nina's who were acting, or just laying it on thick, always gave themselves away by being too intense by half.

"Look, Bucky—okay, I have hypnotized some people. But I told you: mostly to try and help deal with some physical pain. Or I've tried to stop someone from eating compulsively. Or smoking."

"And you've had some success," he interjected—a statement, more than a question.

"Well, yes, I have. And yes, I have helped people go back into their past to try and find out why certain things upset them. But never—*never*—has anybody I've hypnotized starting talking about a past life."

He leaned forward, with that mischievous old look in his eye. "All the more reason to believe it, if I do make it." Nina shrugged at that. "Hey, come on, what's to lose?" he fairly cried out.

"All right, Bucky, I will think about it."

"Thank you, Nina," he said, and he reached over and took one of her hands and held it in both of his. There was nothing improper in the gesture, for Nina could sense the genuine gratitude that flowed with his touch.

Still, she knew she shouldn't have accepted even such a benign clasp so easily. Damn, Bucky, damn you. He had taken her over the line again, to where she no longer quite knew whether she was his doctor or his friend...or God knows what she wanted to be. The trouble—and Nina recognized it—was that it was not a matter of her hands briefly touching his. Rather, it was a matter of her whole self being so entangled with this man and his bizarre story.

And Nina was the one who was the psychiatrist.

Bucky dropped her hand then, but went on, so sincerely, "Just to reveal myself to anyone—that's why I had to be certain that I could trust you. I guess, in a way, I was examining you more than you were me. If I was going to tell you all this crazy stuff about me, I had to be so sure about you. I had to—"

Suddenly, something seemed to register with Nina. Something was wrong, something out of whack. "Bucky? Did you check up on me?" But even before he could answer, she recoiled—she *knew*—and then she raised her voice—more shrill, more accusatory. "Did you have someone spy on me?"

"Well, sure, you know, just the usual kinda background check—

computers, records. Hey, Nina, I hadda be sure. I couldn't talk to just any Tom, Dick, or Harry about this stuff. I never before—"

"You common...you, you," Nina hissed, rising from beside him—and caring not at all that everybody there turned to look at her. "That creep of yours broke into my office the other night."

"No, no, Nina. He's not that sorta snoop."

Nina had her hands on her hips now, glaring down at Bucky. She had to glare. She had to keep her anger in a grimace, or otherwise she knew she'd start to cry. "No. No, it's not done that way, Mr. Buckingham. No—you're *way* out of line, buster. And you can find somebody else to give you the green light so you can tiptoe through the ages with a little pussy on the side."

Jesus, Nina thought: *pussy*. Did I actually say *pussy*? Did I actually say it out loud on the Roof Garden of The Metropolitan Museum of Art?

Oh well.

At least that made it easier for her to turn her back on Buckingham and bolt away, past the grotesque statue of *Standing Woman*, under the arbor, through the glass door, to the elevator. She could feel everyone staring at her. And snickering. It must have looked like the poor older woman had...oh, to hell with how it looked. Nina never even glanced back at Bucky. She never relaxed her formidable pose. She strode onto the elevator.

Even when she got off on the first floor her face was still frozen in fury. She tore down the corridor—so fast, in fact, that her appearance caught by surprise that tall, gray-haired woman in the most fashionable spring *chapeau*. As a consequence, when the stranger turned quickly away from Nina as she rushed by, that action called attention to itself. And to the woman. Nina looked over at her. But she didn't know her, so she didn't slow her gait.

Still, even as she hurried along, through the Italian piazza, towards the Great Hall, to escape out to Fifth Avenue, even as she gritted her teeth, even as her eyes misted up, even as she cursed Bucky under her breath, even then, there was a part of Nina that longed to detour, that yearned to go back up to gallery twenty-seven, back there to visit with Venus and Adonis again, to study them and to try—try!—to understand. Nina had to force herself to stay the course, to hurry down the steps, out into that world that was, for sure, the here and now.

·7·

The huge bouquet was waiting for Nina the next morning. Hardly breaking stride, she plucked the note from the flowers and pitched it into the trash basket. "I want these out of here immediately," she told Roseann. "Itsky-outsky."

"Yes, Doctor."

"And when Mr. Buckingham calls, and he will, you are to advise him that I will not speak with him, now or ever, nor will I respond to any letters, faxes, email...or carrier pigeons. And Roseann...."

"Yes, Doctor?"

"Don't worry about being courteous to him, either."

Stepping then into her own office and closing the door behind her, Nina lunged for the telephone. She knew that if she hesitated, even for a moment, she would lose her nerve. Bang-bang, she punched the seven digits.

Two rings. No, he's probably not there. Three. He is not going to answer. If it's four, it's surely going to be a phone machine. What then? Hang up and call back later? Leave a message and hope that *he'll* call back? The fourth ring. That awful, demanding fourth ring. A click. His voice. "Hello, you've reached Hugh Venable. I'm sorry—"

Nina fell to her seat, squirming. Amazing. It was the first time she'd heard that voice in five years. Surely, she'd always assumed she would bump into him. Excuse me: *bunk* into him—it's New York. God knows she bunked into everybody she didn't want to bunk into. But no. "...I'm away from my desk right now, but if..."

Just the way the words tumbled out. The timbre. Hugh Venable could recite the alphabet and send chills down Nina Winston's back. Hugh Venable could say, "...you'll leave a message, I'll get right back to you," and she would swoon. "At the beep."

It beeped. She panicked. Go on, go on, her little voice told Nina, you're not a goddamn teenager. Okay. So, she heard her big grown-up voice say out loud, "Hugh. Surprise. It's Nina (quickly, add) Winston. I hope this isn't out of order of me, but I just..." (Go on, Nina, go on. You've identified yourself.) "...and I just, uh, have had something come up—professional, Hugh—nothing personal at all..." (No, you didn't have to add that. That was too defensive. Go on, go on—and be casual.)

"And I'd just love to touch base, see if you're alive and well. Okay? Thanks. And the drinks are on me." (No, no, you weren't supposed to add that. Too social. Not until he says, let's meet somewhere. You giddy little girl. Quick—don't end on that. So...) "Bye for now." (God, that could only have been worse if you'd ended up saying "*Ciao.*")

Of course, if only Nina had known:

Hugh Venable walked into his office just as his own message ended. He started to reach for the phone. But then he heard Nina's voice. And he froze, until out loud, this is what he whispered to her voice: "Still, the sound of all the nightingales in heaven." And when her message was ended, he only listened to her words again. "Damn you, Nina," Hugh said at last, "you weren't supposed to do that." But even then, he knew he'd call her back—and, in fact, it only took him four more hours and a Bloody Mary at lunch for him to work up the nerve.

In the meantime, Roseann informed Nina that (of course) Bucky had telephoned her.

Nina replied, "I don't even want to know, and if he calls again, you tell him it is pointless because you have been instructed, on pain of death, not even to tell me that he has called."

Roseann nodded. By now, she was convinced that the young Mr. Buckingham and the Widow Winston had been conducting a torrid affair right under her nose.

When Nina came back from lunch, where she had treated her-self, indulgently, to a hot dog with sauerkraut, potato chips, and a carbonated orange drink, which she had purchased from a vendor working the museum trade, another policeman was in her office. Roseann was beaming. Officer Gomez introduced himself and announced, "Good news, Doctor. We caught the perpetrator who broke in here."

"Really?" Nina asked, totally surprised.

"Yeah, some druggie. We nabbed him early this morning, just 'round the corner, trying to break into another doctor's office. Looking for drugs."

"But I'm a psychiatrist, Officer. Why would anyone come in here? There's probably more drugs in the average East Side medicine cabinet than I keep here."

"Look, these guys don't pause to get your resume," Officer Gomez said. "We still catch these characters breakin' into dentist offices, lookin' for gold. Idiots. Dentists mostly stopped using gold for inlays years ago."

"Well, thank you, Officer," Nina said. "I'm delighted to know that all this has been resolved in such an ordinary fashion. Just a run-of-the-mill perp, right?"

Gomez smiled. "Yes ma'am. The NYPD always gets its perp."

They laughed together, and Nina was so pleased to know that the intruder hadn't been Buckingham's spy, that she might even have considered being marginally more forgiving of Bucky. How-ever, just then the phone rang, and momentarily, Roseann held it out to her, saying, "A Mr. Venerable? Returning your call."

"Venable?" Nina mumbled, as convincingly as she could feign some confusion.

"Oh yes, yes, of course. I better take this in my office." She also made sure to close the door behind her and kick off her shoes before easing into her chair and chirping, "Oh, hi, Hugh. Thanks for getting back to me."

"Well, it did catch me off guard."

She pushed the mute button so he wouldn't hear her catch her breath. But they had spoken! They had exchanged words. Dr.

Winston was an adult SWF having a phone conversation with an old...uh, friend. It was going to be okay. "Everything all right?" Nina ventured then, unmuting.

"Oh, fine. Like the job. Miss the flock. But the students are bright, and they keep me on my toes. And you?"

"Well, you know, it's the same fruitstand here. And that's why I called, Hugh. One of my patients brought up a subject I thought you could help me with. If we could just, uh, get together for a few minutes sometime."

"Might it be better to do it on the phone? You know what we agreed, Nina."

There it was. Nina paused. No damn it, she'd gone this far to try to see Hugh Venable again, so there was only so much more of a fool she could make of herself. Onward: "Well, Hugh, I thought perhaps the statute of limitations had run out on that prohibition. Yes, we certainly could do it on the phone, but couldn't we also at least show each other how we've held body and soul together?"

Hugh held his hands over the phone. "Temptress," he sighed in a stage whisper. And then to her, "Well, all right Nina, although I'm sure your body has held together far better than mine."

Nina grinned. Already, it was easy talking to Hugh the way they used to—so natural, by turns funny and profound and endearing. How had she actually spent five years of her life not hearing that voice? "And your soul?" she asked.

"Ah, I like that Nina. I think we're putting together a mighty fine country and western song here. 'You held my body together, but took my soul apart.'" And then he sang that. Worst singing voice in the world. God, it was sweet for Nina to hear that man sing again.

So, he agreed to meet her after work. After work! Split the difference. She'd go over to the West Side, and he come down from Union Theological Seminary to meet at a place in the Seventies he'd heard about. Yes, tonight. In just a few hours. If only she'd thought about wearing a more glamorous—sexier?—outfit today.

Oh well.

Hugh hadn't seen her since she gotten the laser treatment. That should be enough, the first time back.

Suppressing her ecstasy, Nina came out of her office. Roseann looked very concerned. She pointed to a package that had just arrived by special messenger. "I think it's from Mr. Buckingham," she volunteered fearfully.

"Well, let's open it up," Nina said. "However distasteful the gentleman, I don't think he's the bomber type."

And, indeed, it didn't explode. Instead, when Nina unraveled the bubble packing, she exposed a doll—a mournful man wearing a fedora. There was a button and Nina pushed it. Immediately, the man began to speak in a sniveling voice, pouring out apologies, "Oh, please forgive me...I'm so sorry...I swear, I'll never do it again...A thousand pardons... Can I ever obtain your forgiveness...? Oh, woe—"

Nina flipped off the switch, pretending not to be the slightest bit amused.

But then, how long could she stay mad at the irrepressible Mr. Buckingham? Sure, he had snooped on her, but he hadn't been responsible for the break-in, had he? Besides, if it hadn't been for Bucky, why, Nina wouldn't have found the excuse to get to see Hugh Venable again—at last, this very night, somewhere, at a quiet little table in the corner.

·8·

Hugh was already there when Nina arrived, waving to her from the back. It was obviously a very trendy place. For a man of the cloth, the Reverend Venable was always up on these kinds of things, ahead of most curves.

Happily for Nina, there was a crowd at the bar that she had to negotiate her way through, so she could keep her eyes off of Hugh as she approached him. Nevertheless, by the time she reached him, her knees buckled a little anyhow. He looked magnificent. If he had aged a day in five years worth of days, it was not apparent. He looked yet so manly, so powerful, so...so Adonis-like...had Adonis just not gone on that silly wild boar hunt, but had lived on up into his fifties.

"Well," he said to her, "you haven't lost it, Dr. Winston."

Nina pecked him on the cheek. Having gone through this sort of thing with Bucky, Nina had decided that *not* to peck him on the cheek would be more awkward. "Don't you get any older?" she asked, sliding into the booth across from him.

"My secret plan is to retire as some eighty-year-old parishioner's boy toy."

Laughing, she noticed a drink before her. It looked very much like a martini. Certainly, it came in a martini glass. "What is this?"

"A martini, of course. They're back in fashion."

"God, I haven't had a martini since I was a virgin."

"See? Some things you can get back."

Nina took a sip. The gin burned—nicely—but when she looked back up, planning to go right on bantering, Hugh's expression had changed, the twinkle gone. He had to watch himself. He had given her the martini, and with it, he had doled out some repartee. But just so, just that much. "It is nice to see you, Nina. But I won't pretend I think it's a good idea."

She caught her breath. What made her think it could all be as if nothing had happened? "Well, then, maybe I shouldn't have pushed this on you. But I did think you could help me." She took another sip. How bitter the gin was this time.

"So, what's up?"

"Well, if you'll give me just one peremptory challenge, your Honor."

"I didn't mean to sound brusque, Nina. But we agreed this was over."

She thought: *you* agreed. But she only said, "I do want to thank you for that lovely note when Kingsley died."

"It must have been so fast, the cancer."

"A wildfire, they told me." A sigh. "Maybe that's best."

Hugh kind of gestured to himself. "Did he ever know?"

"About us?" Hugh nodded. "No, I'm sure he didn't. Thank God." Suddenly, it was terribly uncomfortable, and they heard all the noises of the world all around them. Nina managed to change the subject, sort of. "Your children?"

"You mean, did they know about us?" Reluctantly, she nodded. "Not you in the specific. I think they both suspected there was another woman, but I just told them the same half-truth, which was that I'd simply fallen out of love with their mother. And Lenore has been very sweet, pleading with the kids not to hate me. She always figured there was someone else, but she's been a gem, undeserving of—"

"All right, all right—make me feel even more guilty."

Sheepishly, Hugh reached over, patting her forearm. "I'm sorry, Nina. That wasn't very thoughtful of me." Quickly, though, he withdrew his hand and threw it up in the air. "But you see, that's precisely why this can't ever be any good. Too much guilt, both ways. So, let's get professional. How can I help you?"

Nina smiled wanly and put on her therapist face, the one that heard but did not engage, that saw but did not involve. "Well, there's this patient. Fascinating guy, really, because he's so incredibly normal. Except—" She stopped.

"Come on, I'm all ears."

"He thinks he's lived in the past."

"Ah, so the subject here is—"

"Reincarnation. Yes."

"Rubbish," Hugh declared, all disdain, before going back to his martini.

"Rubbish? Just...rubbish?"

"Well, I'm assuming you're asking me as a theologian. Certainly, there's enough nonsense written on the subject—exceeded only, I suppose, by the stuff on the Kennedys and how to lose weight."

"So then, as a theologian?"

"As a Christian theologian, there's simply nothing in the entire Christian canon—or for that matter, the whole damn Judeo-Christian heritage—that gives a nod to reincarnation."

"Nothing?"

"Look Nina, I'm well aware that tens of millions of Hindus and Buddhists and all sorts of other people believe in reincarnation. I make no mockery of that. And it's not just in the East. The Dalai Lama is practically an American pop figure nowadays, and he's the very essence of reincarnation. Obviously, no one *knows*. But from the perspective of a traditional westerner, Christian or Jew—" He paused. "I suppose your patient fits in there."

"Yes."

"Well, there's simply nothing in our common heritage that supports that belief."

Hugh took another sip of his martini, and Nina noticed it was almost finished. She gulped at hers to catch up, to be prepared if the waiter came over and Hugh was inclined to order another. "Of course," he went on, "those who want to believe in reincarnation put, shall we say, a new spin on scripture. A favorite, for example, is from John, when Jesus tells the apostles: 'In my father's house, there are many mansions.' Well now, somehow, people who want to believe in reincarnation have decided that many *mansions* is really code for many *lives*. Beats me how they've arrived at that, but hey, if it rows your boat." Suddenly, he stopped and looked quizzically at Nina. "Wait a minute. *You* don't believe in reincarnation, do you now?"

"No, Hugh. It's just that this patient has had a very compelling experience."

"Well, hell, be my guest. But Jesus really wasn't all that complicated in what he said. I'm pretty sure that if he was trying to tell us that we were going to keep on coming back till we got it right, then he would've come right out and said so: 'In my father's house, we recycle souls.'"

Nina laughed. She always enjoyed Hugh most for his irreverence. She had never dared sneak into his church to hear him preach. It wasn't because she was a Catholic and he was a heathen Lutheran; no, irrespective of religion, it was because she was a woman sleeping (in sin) with the guy in the pulpit. Nevertheless, she'd heard that Hugh brought the same kind of conversational wry wit to his sermons. "Oh, come on," Nina said, "haven't there been all sorts of dissident Christians and Jews who believed in reincarnation?"

Hugh leaned back, arms akimbo. "Sure. Matter of fact, I went out with one after the divorce."

"You did?"

"I'm afraid that was my anti-Nina period. If it couldn't be us, the last thing I wanted was a pale, cut-rate version of you." Pointedly, Hugh neglected to mention that he was still in that period. Every woman he went out with, including his current *enamorata,* bore no resemblance—of appearance or personality—to Nina. "She used to argue reincarnation with me. It was basically her contention that the early church had covered up all the pro-reincarnation writings. Great conspiracy theory stuff! You see, she argued, if people knew they were going to get a lot more rides on the merry-go-round of life, they'd be much harder for the church to control. Pretty good argument, too. But she was cuckoo—a lotta fun, but off-the-wall."

"Well, did she bring up all the stories about people under hypnosis who remember details about past lives—all sorts of things that can't be explained? You know, they speak strange dialects, know secret hiding places from centuries past, all that sort of thing."

"Ah, yes, Edgar Cayce and that crowd," Hugh replied. "Well, I jes can't 'splain eet, Lucee. And I am impressed—I'll admit it—that the *kinds* of reincarnation memories do make sense, in a way."

"How's that?"

"Well, it's documented that an inordinate number of people who claim to recall past life remember dying violently. Somebody eighty-sixes you with a poleaxe, yes, that would tend to stay with you, I suppose. And children who are presumably innocent of practicing any humbug—they often display the most vivid, inexplicable memories of some time past. But then these recollections fade as they grow older and get overwhelmed by their quote, new life."

Nina nodded. Hugh went on. "But look, there are lots of things we can't explain, and my suspicions about reincarnation are considerably heightened by the fact that most people who claim these lives from the past invariably say they were Columbus or Cleopatra or George Washington. Funny, isn't it? Nobody ever turns out to have been a peasant from Bolivia, even though there have been a helluva lot more Bolivian peasants than there have been George Washingtons. Now, if you go out to the nuthouse—"

"Heavens, my good Reverend Venable, that's terribly politically incorrect."

"Yeah. If you go out to the nuthouse, and a guy's walkin' around like this"—Hugh thrust his hand into his jacket front—"and screaming, 'On to Waterloo, Josephine,' we stick him in a rubber room. *But:* same guy comes into your office, lies down"—hand in his jacket again—"and says that under hypnosis, you take him at face value."

Nina had to smile, even if she did say, "I see your doubts about the efficacy of the noble psychiatric profession have not been modulated in my absence."

"Nina, I am no less dubious about those dear folks who have near-death experiences. They all walk down the same bright tunnel, and they all see the same great white light, and then the Jesus figure in white, beckoning—the whole nine yards. I am dubious of that, even though I want desperately to believe that, to believe everything those people say."

"You're more of a skeptic than I realized, Hugh."

"No, Nina." He held up his glass, staring at it, before he drained the last bit. "I'm a man of great faith—otherwise my life has meant nothing. So, I must have faith that my faith is the right faith." He shrugged. "Now, having made that pronouncement, I'll give you two good reasons why I'm full of it."

Smiling, Nina held out her hands: a go-ahead gesture.

"First, if we were in Bombay right now, or in all sorts of other places in this world, reincarnation would be the holy order of the day. So you're welcome to remind your patient of that. He's got a huge peer group out there, and I'm sure they're all smarter than yours truly."

"Noted. And the second reason?"

"Look, Nina, I got dealt some pretty good cards. Just being born in America. But more: reasonably well-off, reasonably intelligent, good family, good friends, good health...." (Plus, Nina thought, handsome to a fault and incredibly charming.) "In the whole scheme of things, I'm what? One out of a thousand? One out of ten thousand? Blessed. That's the word for me. I've been put on this earth, blessed by God. And you too, Nina. Of course, I've screwed things up a little."

"With my help."

"We're not flagellating ourselves here. I'm simply toting up the score, and having done that, I'd rather take my chances on making heaven than on coming back here. Next time, if there is a next time, sure as shootin', to even things out, I'm gonna be that Bolivian peasant. So maybe none of what the theologian has told you has anything to do with anything rational. Maybe I'm just scared of reincarnation."

The waiter appeared. "Shall we do this again, sir?"

For just an instant, Hugh seemed ready to order another round, but he caught himself, and instead, "No. We're finished here." *Finished.*

He dug into his pocket, but Nina piped up, "Please—it was my invitation. I'll put it down as a business expense. 'Two martinis— interviewed potential Bolivian peasant.'"

With that, Hugh stood up. Nina wanted to stop him. She wanted to tell him more about Bucky so that he would advise her to stop dealing with him. She knew it was best to give up Buckingham as a client. She knew how professionally out-of-order she had behaved. She knew the whole business was too bizarre to be healthy. And she also knew that Hugh could tell her to do what she couldn't tell herself: call it off. Pronto. But there was no more chance. It was only, "Sorry, Nina, gotta run."

His eyes were everywhere now but upon her. So easy had it been for Hugh to look Nina square in the face when he was talking about some subject, something inanimate or theoretical. Now, though, he could barely glance at her when he said, "Nice to see ya again, Nina. You still look like a million bucks—and I hope you find some terrific guy."

"Thanks," was all she bothered to say—although when Hugh turned away and began to weave out, never looking back, she did mouth to herself, "Thanks, but I already found one."

Well, maybe it would have made Nina feel better to know that after Hugh left her so abruptly, he went directly to his girlfriend's apartment. Her name was Marilyn, and she looked not at all like Nina, nor acted at all like Nina. But still, he thought he might be in love with Marilyn.

The reason Nina might have felt better about this is that Hugh had not originally planned to see Marilyn this evening. He had some term papers he absolutely *had* to grade. But after he had been with Nina, if only for that little while, just one martini's worth, he felt that he had to be with Marilyn. He had to reaffirm his feelings for her. He had to make love to her.

He did, too. Only, all he thought about was Nina.

This is what maybe, had she known, Nina would have felt better about. Or, maybe not.

·9·

There were balloons and flowers from Bucky the next day, and the day following, a singing telegram. It was performed by a guy dressed in sackcloth, carrying a large bag that had written on it: Ashes. He sang a medley of apology songs, including "I'm Sorry" by Brenda Lee in falsetto, "I Apologize" by Billy Eckstein in a deep baritone, and "Sorry, I Ran All The Way Home" by The Impalas in great animation. Then he left a note from Bucky, which pleaded for Nina to call him.

She resisted as best she could. Who's sorry now? Still, Nina could not put Floyd Buckingham out of her mind. Whatever had occasioned that intense reaction from him in gallery twenty-seven was as weird as it had also seemed real. So finally, after a couple of weeks, Nina simply could resist temptation no longer.

She needed to buy a small birthday present for a friend, and so she rationalized that the best place to purchase something would be at the Metropolitan gift shop. So, with her membership card, she obtained the day's admission pin—a too-pale lavender it was this particular afternoon—and steered herself directly to the shop on the main floor.

There, browsing in the jewelry section, her eyes suddenly lit on some earrings. They seemed so familiar. She drew closer. In silver, gold or pearl: a single teardrop hanging down. And closer still, the name: Venus Earring. Nina couldn't believe it. But yes, it was indeed the very earring visible on Venus in *Venus and Adonis*. Is the whole damn world suddenly Venus and Adonis? The clerk came over.

"Beautiful, aren't they?" he said. "They're from a Rubens painting we have up—"

"Yes, yes, I know it."

"These were poor Princess Diana's favorite earrings. You see them in so many of her pictures. The silver. But they're all always popular."

"The pearl," Nina said. "I'll take a pair of the pearls."

"Of course. The *real* Venus."

With the earrings, then, Nina pretended to herself that she was just moseying about, ending up strictly by random in the *R*s of the book section. (Ah, feigning unconscious behavior; you need a good psychiatrist, lady.) And sure enough, there as if she could have expected it, was not only a book about Rubens's work, but one that featured *Venus and Adonis* on the jacket. Venus: her Venus earrings shining, her pale pink cheeks, and the most adoring gaze, staring beseechingly into Adonis's absolutely perfectly handsome face. Never was there better evidence of what Sir Joshua Reynolds had observed once, that all of Rubens's subjects appear to have "fed on roses."

Rushing to the cash register and totally forgetting to buy that birthday present, Nina hurried through the Great Hall. Outside, slinking about halfway down the twenty-eight steps, way over to the side, she started to read the book by covering the page with her arm as if it was dirty pictures. First she read Rubens's biography, which was much more interesting than Nina ever imagined. He was the quintessential Renaissance Man who was not only an artist but a diplomat, a friend at most every court that mattered in Europe. Devout Catholic. Civic leader. Rich. Sensitive. Adoring father. Beloved husband. *Twice,* beloved husband: Isabella, then Helena after Isabella died. Damn, they don't make men like this anymore.

Then she turned to read about the painting *Venus and Adonis* itself. Painted, 1635. Rubens would have been fifty-eight then, just starting to be hampered by the gout that would kill him only five years hence so that he might, one eulogist proclaimed, "go see the originals of all the great pictures he had left us." *Venus and Adonis,* Nina read on, was itself something of a copy of a similar work by

Titian, which Rubens had seen in Madrid in 1628. Hmmm, even the masters cribbed a little. Shakespeare, Nina remembered, never once wrote an original plot. (Of course, the Bard had never met Floyd Buckingham, either.)

By the time she had finished reading, there was no sense in Nina even trying to kid herself anymore. She had to return to gallery twenty-seven; she had to visit Venus and Adonis again. Had to. This time Nina sort of snuck up on her prey, entering the gallery from the door on the other side. She paused there for a moment to study the large family portrait directly across the room from her quarry—and, of course, now she knew exactly who those people were. Rubens, himself. Helena. One of their children.

But as soon as she turned around to face *Venus and Adonis*, she was in that painting's thrall. And she knew it. Bucky had won. Nina could not look at the work without somehow seeing Mister Floyd Buckingham of Darien, Connecticut, metamorphosizing into Adonis. Why, Adonis might just as well have had on a double-breasted Joseph Abboud and a Turnbull and Asser shirt, as he did the reddish cloak that Rubens had draped around that powerful young body.

Closer, closer. So transfixed was Nina that she attracted the wary eye of the vigilant blue-grey garbed sentinel of gallery twenty-seven. He edged closer, ready to pounce if this odd woman might try to perform some random act of desecration. But then, to take it all in, Nina backed up, sitting on the bench in the middle of the room, and the guard relaxed. By now, Rubens's glorious figures all but moved before her eyes. There—there was precious little Cupid, tugging at Adonis—stay with my mistress, *stay!* And there was the lead dog, looking off to the thrill of the hunt. Come, our master, lead us! And Venus—Venus, above all! Venus, reaching for her hero with both arms, pleading with him, her sweet lips imploring him in what could only be the prelude to a kiss!

But still. Adonis pulls away. How, Nina thought? How could this foolish man go off on some idiotic hunt, leaving this lovely woman behind? For Chrissake, Adonis is actually going to leave the goddess of love and go off with his stupid dogs, and—

Suddenly, to her complete surprise, Nina felt a strange hand on her shoulder—and then the smug announcement, "I knew you'd come back, Nina."

She only sighed. In a curious way, Nina was relieved she'd found Bucky—even if she knew she'd have to admit that he had won, he had lured her back into his lair. Whatever. "Sit down, Mr. Buckingham," she said, trying her best to sound irritated.

"Thank you," he said, but placing himself at right angles, so that he was facing away from *Venus and Adonis*.

Nina sighed. Who was she kidding? Angry? She was absolutely enthralled by this adventure, even as it frightened her. So: to hell with it. To hell with arm's-length, decorous, professional behavior. Everybody gets one freebie in life, what the gamblers call a bisque. So: "Come on," she heard herself saying, "I'll buy you a martini."

"Really?"

"Where have you been, Buckingham? Martinis are back."

So, they left gallery twenty-seven, Bucky raising his cupped hand, as if offering up a martini toast to the Madonna there in the company of St. Francis, and then, gaily, he escorted Nina across Fifth Avenue to Nica's, the sidewalk bar at the Stanhope. "Martoonis,—goodness, gracious," he exclaimed, holding out Nina's chair—a green and cream rattan. Then he sat down beside her, their table for two right by the wildflower boxes that lined the sidewalk.

"Aw, come on, big old Adonis can't handle a modern martini?"

"Two Boodles martinis, straight up, very dry, don't bruise the gin," Bucky proclaimed to the waiter, shooting his cuffs. But then, straightaway, he turned back to Nina, his face serious, his tone somber. "I am very sorry, Doctor, for uh, investigating you. It was wrong of me, and I have no excuse." Nina nodded. "But this I swear to you, too: my guy did not break into your office. On my honor."

"I know that's true now, Bucky. I jumped to conclusions."

The martinis came. "They are not bruised," said the waiter. "No hemorrhaging at all."

"Wiseass," said Bucky, as soon as he turned away.

"Takes one to know one," Nina cracked. "So, what did your private *dick* find out about me—assuming, that is, they still call 'em private dicks."

He sighed. It wasn't easy to embarrass Floyd Buckingham, but he didn't feel comfortable about what he'd brought on himself. He even looked away, following the cabs that sped down Fifth Avenue. When he turned back, he tried to speak as blithely as possible. "Well, all right, Doctor, no flies on you."

"Come on. That's what the dossier said? Just: 'No flies on Dr. Winston. Pay on receipt.'"

"No, that's just my succinct summation. You want more detail?"

Nina held up her glass. "Bruise me."

"Pretty boring. You have an impeccable credit rating. You even pay your taxes *ahead* of time." Nina grinned sheepishly. "And professionally, you are not only admired, but held in some heavy awe. I picked the right doctor—that's for sure." He raised a glass to her. "So, that completes my report, Madame Chairman."

"Oh, come on, Bucky, fill me in on the juicy personal gossip."

He shrugged. "I'm sorry: you're whiter than white. Live alone, East Side. Like the theater. Some concerts. Would sell your body—although, apparently, you haven't done so yet—to see Placido Domingo sing anything at Lincoln Center." Nina nodded and sipped. "You vacation every summer in Rehoboth Beach, Delaware, where you spend a week with your only child—sorry, I forget her name."

"Lindsay."

"Yeah. With Lindsay and her husband. You also usually travel abroad once a year. Turkey and Greece last October." Nina nodded. "Go with friends. You were, uh, widowed. I'm sorry, Nina."

"Thank you, Bucky."

"You're five years older—at least—than I thought you were. Of course, there was the little"—Bucky smugly tapped his eye—"laser work you got a couple years ago." She grimaced. "Hey, you asked for it, lady. And anyway, for reasons which elude both me and the private dick, you presently have no steady beau. God, what's the matter with the older guys?"

Nina rolled her eyes. "The matter with the older guys, Mr. Buckingham, is that they are simply younger guys grown up."

"Oh, I get it. The problem is with guys, generically?"

"You catch on." She looked into her drink. So, Nina thought proudly, she and Hugh had managed to keep their affair utterly secret from the world. "And that's it?" she asked, just to be sure. "That's all the dirt your man could dig up on me?"

"Yeah. Pretty thin soup, I'm afraid," Bucky said, but then he turned in his rattan chair, even twisting it a little, so that he could look directly at Nina there beside him. "Like I said, I picked the right doctor—and the right person. And now I want you to help me, Nina. Please."

"In which particular area—the current passion, or the past life?"

"Both. Because I know they're connected. Listen, what I have to do right now—well, me and Constance—that's our problem. I don't need a shrink to tell me who I've fallen in love with or how that complicates my life. But I do need a shr—"

"Wait. Here's the deal, Bucky. You don't call me a shrink. I don't call you a two-timer."

He smiled sheepishly, little-boy-like. "I stand corrected. But what I do need from you, Dr. Winston, is for you to try and help me understand how it is that I know—*I know*—from that painting, that I have lived a life before. In the seventeenth century, in Holland. And that the woman I love now lived with me then, too."

He was altogether animated, throwing his arms around, pausing long enough only to toss down the rest of his martini as if it was Mountain Dew. He waved to the waiter, instinctively holding up two fingers—even if Nina's drink wasn't half gone. She didn't notice, though, for she was reaching down to pull her Rubens book out of her Metropolitan shopping bag. She held it before her chest then, covering it with her crossed arms. And then she drew a breath and began.

"Bucky, Peter Paul Rubens wasn't some unknown hack. In fact, he'd be a solid A-list celebrity today. His life is very well documented." With that, she uncrossed her arms and laid the book on the table so that Venus and Adonis, in close-up, were suddenly staring at Bucky. He gasped. Nina jabbed her forefinger at Venus's chubby face. "That, Bucky," she said, "that was Rubens's wife."

Bucky was rattled. "Whatdya mean?"

"I *mean*, the model for Venus was Rubens's second wife, Helena." Nina turned to another page, showing Helena in a portrait with two of her children. The hair color was more auburn than Venus's blonde, but the facial resemblance was undeniable. "Or look," Nina went on, showing Bucky *The Judgment of Paris*, where the pudgy Venus appeared again. "Did you ever notice the painting across the room from *Venus and Adonis*?" He shook his head, obviously baffled by all this.

"Well, check it out next time. There's a family portrait that Rubens painted of himself and Helena and one of their sons." She leaned closer, mimicking swiveling her head. "You can stand sideways in the middle of gallery twenty-seven, and see for certain that Venus *is* Helena—look one way, and then the other."

Gingerly then, Bucky began to flip through the book, as Nina kept talking. "Rubens's first wife was Isabella. She was sloe-eyed, with a long, pointed nose, fairly thin. He seems to have loved her dearly, but she really wasn't his type. So, after Isabella died, Rubens married Helena, even though she was only sixteen, and he was fifty-three. But she absolutely fit his mold. It was almost as if he'd been fated to marry her."

Bucky's head jerked up from the book. "A man after my own heart," he said.

"In any event, Rubens and Helena were as happy as man and wife as they were artist and model. They had four children, and—"

Bucky looked up. "So, what are you telling me?"

"I'm not *telling* you anything. But what I'm *saying* is that the Rubenses were, from all accounts, the perfect couple. Yet you tell me that you have the feeling that you were Adonis and your true-life ladylove was Venus. But we know that Venus was Mrs. Rubens. Now, you couldn't have been having an affair with the painter's beloved own wife right under his nose...could you?"

Bucky ran his fingers through his hair, pondering this introduction of conflicting new evidence. Luckily, the waiter brought the next round, so he could dive into another martini. "Don't be snide, Nina. And tell me this," he growled, leveling an impolite finger at her, "if old man Rubens loved his child bride so much, how come he went around painting her naked all the time? For the whole world to see. I mean, the mother of his children."

"Why, land sakes, Mr. Buckingham, I didn't realize you were so puritanical. Certainly, that didn't seem to bother Helena—especially since the guy doing the painting was not only her husband, but indisputably the most passionate painter of the flesh we've ever had." She sipped her drink. "Of course, it's also true that Rubens ran a full-scale studio. Rarely did he paint a whole picture all by himself. He'd design the painting and sketch the main figures, but usually he'd get his assistants to do most of the painstaking work. It's certainly possible that he only used Helena's face for Venus, sketched her body up in his private studio, then got an assistant who specialized in painting the human figure to fill in the rest. Or sometimes Rubens would use what we'd call a body-double today. Rubens employed a lot of the ladies of the night for his models."

Bucky approved of that idea. "Yeah. That makes sense, Nina, because every time I look at the painting, I always feel more, uh, association with Adonis than Venus. And now I understand. It's probably only Constance's *body* I'm seeing up there."

Nina shook her head, smiling. "I guess I'm just never gonna dissuade you, am I? I suggest Constance was a whore, and you buy it." Bucky smirked a buckysmirk. "All right, lemme try something else," Nina said.

"Shoot."

"Facts. Your facts are all off. You keep talking about being back in Holland—you and your Venus living in bliss in Amsterdam."

"Yeah." He said that confidently, but he eyed her warily.

"The trouble is, Rubens wasn't Dutch. He was Flemish. Big difference. *Huge* difference. The Dutch and the Flemish hated each other. Holy war. Protestants and Catholics. Rubens never lived in Amsterdam. His whole life—when he wasn't traveling—he lived and painted in the city of Antwerp. That's in Belgium now. You're just making up stuff, Bucky." His shoulders slumped; Nina rushed to go on. "Look, I don't mean you're trying to deceive me. But whatever has happened to you—with Constance—has obviously been very traumatic. You've had a good marriage, wonderful family, and bang, out of the blue—or anyway from out of twenty years ago—comes this woman who turns you upside down."

Bucky started to interrupt. Nina reached over, holding her two fingers before his lips. "Hush. You're getting a full-service therapist for the low introductory price of a couple of unbruised martinis, so let me finish. Now, I don't know what it is about that painting that moves you so. I have no idea why you actually identify with the man and the woman in it. Maybe Constance simply reminds you of Venus, maybe—"

"No, no—no way. Constance doesn't look anything like Venus. And anyway, you tell me it can't be her face, but she's not at all fat, and I've never even seen her boobs, and—"

"Okay, okay. Let's not be quite so, uh, literal. There are all sorts of things that we can connect in the mind in subconscious ways. You were upset. You've fallen in love with another woman. You've just lost a big magazine deal. You stumble into the museum, you see this painting—bingo. Who knows what clicked? And now you've convinced yourself."

Bucky had been listening courteously, but now, suddenly, catching Nina completely by surprise, he banged the heel of his hand on the table. "No!" he shouted—and loud enough, too, that some other patrons turned to look. So he leaned closer, lowering his voice without diminishing the urgency of his tone. "No, Nina—you listen to me now. You're so rational. You're saying, well, you said Rubens was in Amsterdam, but he's really in Antwerp. You said Venus was your girlfriend, but she's really Rubens's wife. So, Bucky, you gotta be all wet.

"But listen to me, Nina. Doesn't that prove I'm not settin' you up? I didn't go study this stuff. Hell, at first I didn't even know Rubens did that painting. I was just mesmerized by it. I just saw me. I saw just Constance. Somehow. I could feel us up there. But Rubens? All I ever knew about him is he's the guy who liked to paint fat broads. And I just assumed he was Dutch. Flemish, Schlemish. I'm no art critic, Nina, but just put me under hypnosis, and I swear to you I'll be *in* that studio, wherever it was."

Satisfied, he reached again for his second martini. She finally finished her first. The people rushed by on the street. The cabs were jamming up, the start of theater traffic. As much as New York might be celebrated as a city for the night, that was really only so in midtown. Uptown, here, Nina always knew that the city is best now, at twilight. She slumped in her chair. "Okay, Bucky, I can't beat you. So, just let me be very practical. Let's suppose I did hypnotize you."

"Now you're cookin' with gas."

"I said *suppose*. And let's suppose we followed the hypnotism-chic reincarnation manual and we took you back to your child-hood. Then I said, all right, now go back, back, etc., etc., and all of a sudden you told me: yeah, I'm back here in the artist's studio in 1635, and today I'm all dressed up in an orange sarong because I'm the Adonis the world-famous Peter Paul Rubens is going to paint. Also, look here, here comes my girlfriend, and she has all her clothes off, etc., etc.—"

"Etc."

"Well, it wouldn't mean diddly, Bucky."

"Why?"

"What we try to do in hypnosis is to reveal thoughts that don't lie on the surface—*repressed* in the vulgar vernacular. We try to bring things out. But here you are, already telling me and the world that you're Adonis from Antwerp. So, hypnotizing you wouldn't mean anything. You see? You'd only be playing the record back to me in hypnosis that you've already sung, live. You've crammed for the test, Bucky. You've even put an apple on the teacher's desk. I'm part of all this by now, and so just my voice, my inflection, is capable of tricking your mind into releasing all that you've subconsciously rehearsed with me." For gentle emphasis, Nina laid her hand on the book cover, on Venus's face. "It's pointless."

But then, suddenly, his hand was covering hers. It was nothing like that soft, understanding touch that he had offered to her back on the rooftop garden the other day. This was different—and if it was not a menacing grasp, it certainly was a firm one. Nina raised her head, uneasily, to look into his eyes. "You're scared," he told her.

"Yes," she whispered.

"I know. I'm sorry."

"It's all right. I know you didn't mean to scare me."

"No."

"But it's just all so real, Bucky. No matter how I try, I can't shake that."

"Because it is real."

She sighed. "Suppose, suppose—" Her voice trailed off, and when their eyes caught on one another again, Nina and Bucky knew what they must do.

·10·

Uneasy, still somewhat rattled, Nina opened the door to her office, switched off the alarm, and turned on the light. Bucky went into the bathroom, and that gave her a chance to compose herself...some. When he came out, Nina said, "Among the things which no self-respecting psychiatrist would do, one is to meet a patient away from the office. And—"

"And?"

"Go out to a bar with a patient. And—"

"And?"

"Drink dry martinis with a patient. And—"

"And?"

"Get involved with a patient."

"Involved?"

"Let me be honest, Bucky. I know I'm not doing this as a doctor. I'm doing this because you've fascinated me. Because I'm curious. Because I like you. Those are all the wrong becauses."

He waited for her to ask him to leave. Instead, Nina simply said, "Are you ready?"

"Are you sure?"

"Of course not. Are you ready?"

"Well," Bucky said. "The two drinks I had. They won't—"

"Look, there're night-club hypnotists all over America putting on a good show, hypnotizing drunks in the audience. I'm sure you'll be fine."

He nodded. "Okay, so what do I do?"

"There's no hocus-pocus. It's really not unlike any of our other sessions. We'll get comfortable."

"Lie down?"

"No, sitting up is fine. I'll make it dark, with a candle you can focus on. But don't worry, I'm not doing any Vincent Price stuff with a sparkling pendant."

"You just talk to me, right?"

"Exactly. And if a subject wants to get hypnotized—and, surely, no one ever wanted that more than you—and if you have the right disposition—and you certainly seem to—then you'll go under, nice and easy. All hypnosis is really self-hypnosis, you know. I'll just be holding your coat, so to speak." Nina paused. "And, for that matter, I'll take mine off. I need to be relaxed, too."

Bucky helped her with her jacket, slipped off his own, and unloosened his tie. Nina also kicked off her heels. She was just turning to lead Bucky to the couch, when all of a sudden, there was a knock on the door. "Jesus," Nina said.

"Who the hell?"

"Who is it?" Nina cried out.

"Police, ma'am."

Nina peered through the little peephole. Sure enough, she recognized the same officer who'd been by a few days before. She opened the door to him. "Remember, I'm Officer Gomez, Doctor." He nodded toward the other cop, a woman. "Officer Sabatini."

Nina greeted them both. "Is there anything the matter?"

"Well, Doctor, you know there's been the trouble with break-ins in the offices 'round here, and we saw the light on, and so—"

"I appreciate your vigilance, Officer, but I, uh, sometimes have evening hours, and my patient, uh—"

Both Nina and Bucky saw the cops sneak a quick glance to one another. They knew exactly what they were thinking. Attractive, older female doctor: shoeless, jacketless, gin on her breath, flushed. Handsome younger "patient": jacket and tie off, gin on his breath, flustered. "Of course," said Officer Gomez, suppressing a knowing leer. "Can't be too careful."

"Oh no, thank you," said Nina, closing the door behind the two cops. Although just then, as she started to shut it, she idly glanced up. Across the street in the dusk under a street light was a woman looking in her direction. Hadn't Nina seen her before? Tall, gray-haired; she had some kind of a hat on. Where? But the woman turned away then, stepping back into the shadows, and—

Oh well.

It went out of her mind. Nina closed the door and bolted it, and when she turned around, Bucky stepped up to her and gently took her by the shoulders. "You still okay?" he asked.

"Fine, really. Just a little put out. After all, there goes my well-cultivated good-girl reputation in the neighborhood."

He dropped his hands. "You sure you wanna go ahead with this?"

Nina shrugged. "What the hell, why not? The whole thing has sort of vague sexual connotations anyway, doesn't it? I mean, Bucky, no reflection on your honor, but right now, I do feel sort of like those times when I went to bed with somebody, even though I knew I shouldn't have."

"Dr. Winston—heavens to Betsy!" Bucky cried, in mock horror, hand before his mouth.

"Oh, don't worry—not that often," Nina replied, laughing. "Not often *enough*." He laughed. "Come on now, just sit down and relax. I'll be right in." Then what she said hit her, and in chagrin, she banged her hand on her own forehead. "Good God," Nina yelped, "now I sound like a hooker."

But, following Bucky into the room, she placed a candle on the table between them, lit it, and turned out the lights. Then, facing him directly, looking into his eyes, speaking softly, Nina told him to relax, to be comfortable. No need. Barely had she uttered a word before she knew he was in a trance, fading back within himself, at peace somewhere. It was too easy. And so, chatting now, talking about coziness and serenity, about trust and sweetness, she flipped on the tape recorder and encouraged him to think of the past. "Do you remember your childhood, Bucky?"

He beamed. "Of course. Terrific childhood. Wonderful."

"Well, can we go back there, Bucky? Can we?"

"You bet," he said—but in an enthusiastic voice higher from the mature man's she'd just been listening to.

"Where are we?"

"Down the shore."

"Oh, where 'bouts down the shore?"

"Cape May," Bucky's little voice said, irritated. "You know we always go to Cape May."

"Oh, of course. Sorry." Then, quickly: "How old are you, Bucky?"

"Six and three-quarters."

Nina remembered he had a birthday in September, and if this were summer at the shore, then that would be soon, so she asked him what presents he wanted. She asked what grade he'd be going into; she asked about his friends and his favorite things. There was no stress, no anguish. Little Floyd Buckingham appeared as happy and easygoing a child as was big Floyd Buckingham guileless and content an adult. So, Nina idly whiled away more childhood time with him, using the extra minutes primarily to relax herself. She was gaining her rhythm now, slipping more securely into her professional role. And so, she took another sip of water and decided to move on—which was, to move back.

"Bucky, can we remember the earlier days? Can we go back before school, back when you were even younger?" And promptly, he was changed again, smiling and nodding, altogether accommodating, acting like a baby. Not goo-gooing, not like some foolish adult playing a role at Charades, pretending to be a baby. Had Bucky carried on like that, Nina would've been sure that it was just a pliant patient trying to please the doctor. But no, with Bucky, there was just enough of a child, just a baby's agreeable manner.

It was going so well, so smoothly. "All right now, Bucky, let's see if we can go even further back." Bucky smiled his assent. He didn't talk, though, because, of course, babies don't talk. "Further back in time," Nina went on, "further, further—"

Bucky nodded at her. But suddenly, then, Nina was surprised to see his face begin to change. It was no longer that vacant, happy, baby face. It was growing different, showing surprise—even, it seemed, some pain.

"Are we further back, further—"

And now, even more to her shock, came the new voice, one that was different altogether, both shriller and more guttural, so unusual that Nina found it hard to believe that it was emanating from Bucky's mouth. But it was. The voice said only: *"Yah, yah."*

Nina was astonished. My God, she thought, what *is* this? "Tell me," she started to say. "Where—"

But at that moment, without warning—without any warning whatsoever—Bucky's eyes widened in horror and he fell from his chair, upon his knees, onto the carpet. His hands flew to his chest, and then, in even greater despair, they reflexively flew up high, and his screeching voice pierced the night. What Nina heard Bucky scream was: *"...owwwllllleeeeeee..."*

·11·

Bucky looked around, astonished to find himself down on his knees. After his scream, Nina had felt that she had to rush to bring him out of his trance. He'd been too agitated. And God, but the chills still reverberated through her own body, the echo of that horrible howling still in her ears. She put on her most reassuring face, but she could not stop thinking: if the mere sound could affect her so, then what must have happened to Bucky...somewhere...some-*time*...to make him actually emit such a noise?

"It's okay," Nina said, "you've just been very restless. Very animated."

He stood up brushing off his knees. "Well, did I—?"

Nina shook her head. "Not what you wanted, no. Sorry. You were terrific at going back into your past—back to a very charming little baby Bucky. But then...something stopped you."

"What?"

"I don't know. You got"—Nina searched for the best euphemism—"uh, upset about something." Nervously, Nina rose and rubbed her hands. "Bucky, please, let's not forget that maybe that's it—baby Bucky." He frowned, so she sought to offer him more consolation. She had to. Whatever Floyd Buckingham had encountered in his mind was terrible, and Nina knew that if there was any chance whatsoever of finding out what may have happened to him—in whatever existence, real or imagined—then she could not press fear upon him now. Besides: *first, do no harm;* the patient's well-being was a damn sight more important than the doctor's curiosity. So, feigning nonchalance, Nina threw up her hands. "Look, we just couldn't break through something. And that's not unusual."

"Damn. Does that mean it's a no-go?"

Nina casually flipped off the tape recorder and turned back on more of the lights. "No, not necessarily. It just means we'll have to give this more thought." She glanced over at him again, surprised to see him tucking his shirt back in. He'd exerted himself so when he screamed that he'd pulled his shirt clear out of his pants. So, composing herself anew, putting on her most professional face, Nina strolled into the waiting room where she picked up the appointment book on Roseann's desk. "Okay, let's talk again. Just here—no hanky-panky, no martinis." She glanced down. "Tuesday at four?" He shrugged in the affirmative.

Then Nina picked up her purse and took out a little package. "Here, a present for you."

Bucky opened it in delight—then shock when he saw what it was. "Earrings? You're giving me earrings?"

"Look closer at 'em."

He held them up. "Oh my God, they're Venus's. Where did you—?"

"They're very popular. Right in the Metropolitan."

But it didn't seem as if Bucky was listening anymore. Instead, he was holding the earrings high, gazing at them, lost in his own new trance. Suddenly, he dropped his eyes to Nina. "I got it!" he cried out.

"Got what?"

"Constance doesn't know any of this stuff. She never heard of you, doesn't know Adonis from Adam, doesn't know Rubens." He waggled an earring before Nina. "Hypnotize Constance."

Instinctively, Nina backed up, folding her arms across her chest. Why, if there were a psychiatrist studying Nina Winston, she would say that hers was a classic defensive body language. But the scream—Bucky's awful scream—Nina could still hear that. She was still scared. But even more fascinated. Constance. Of course. Nina wasn't even surprised when she heard herself telling Bucky, "Okay, Constance." He pecked Nina in delight on her cheek.

As soon as Bucky was gone, Dr. Winston threw some water on her face. Then, despite herself—who hypnotized whom?—she picked up the tape recorder and played with the REWIND until she had it right there. PLAY. The scream. And no matter that now she heard it, alone, prepared for it, in the bright light of her own office. Still, her whole body shook.

Nina turned off the tape. So abruptly had Bucky stopped. The howl. Then: nothing. Just kneeling on the floor, his face full of anguish, his eyes staring. At the candle? At...what? Why? Nina rewound the tape and pushed PLAY for another instant. Again: the howl. No. Enough. STOP. Make some notes while it's fresh in your mind, and then fly home, ladybug.

She took the tape out—don't be tempted anymore—laid it on her desk, then began to scribble down all her recollections. Finished, she left the notes there by the Rubens book, stood up, and reached for her jacket. That was when the phone rang. No one knew she was at the office except..."Bucky?"

But, no answer. "Bucky, don't play games." She heard the phone click off.

Oh well.

At least: no heavy breathing. She put on her jacket. And her shoes. She picked up her pocketbook.

Outside, the evening air was as fresh as anything you could order from an L.L. Bean catalogue, so Nina decided to hoof it home. Working a random diagonal, then—a block across, then down one or two, just drifting with the lights, she headed east for her apartment in the Sixties.

It was funny how quickly she felt it, though. Hardly had she reached Madison when Nina sensed that she was being followed. That was all the more weird, because she had never been followed before—not ever, not once in her life. But it was like the first time she'd known a strange man was staring at her with lust in his heart: sixteen years old, in a mini-skirt, her little rear and boobs barely enough to qualify as jib and ballast...but instinctively she had turned around, and sure enough, there he was, lounging in the doorway, smoking a cheroot, giving her a once-over. So.

Casually now, in the security of the intersection of Madison at 78th, Nina glanced back. But she couldn't spot anyone. So, she crossed 78th, and like she'd learned in the spy movies, she pretended to study a shop window, using that ruse to glance back idly to see if anyone else had stopped. And: well, there was another woman, across Madison, up at the next corner. Nina's eyes were drawn to her. Unfortunately, her eyes didn't draw very well right now because she'd taken her contacts out back at the office. Still, she could see this: that as soon as she spotted the woman, the woman stopped in her tracks, pretending to obey the DON'T WALK sign, even though in New York, nobody paid any attention to DON'T WALK signs.

No, Nina wasn't really scared yet. No real danger. Lots of people around. And, after all, it was only a *woman* who seemed to be following her. Still, when she whirled south again, moving briskly toward 77th, past her all-time favorite East Side Nineties block— two bakeries, a bank, and two jewelry stores—when she paused there and snuck a peek back, the first genuine fear struck her. From the light of a well-lit store, Nina could make out the identity of the person following her. And:

It was that tall, gray-haired woman in a hat.

Now—now Nina remembered her. That day at the museum. And earlier tonight, across from her office. How long had she been tracking her? Days? Weeks? So now, curiosity blurred into fright, and Nina quickened her pace, crossing 76th, stepping as fast as she could. At 75th, to be absolutely certain that this strange woman was after her, Nina took an abrupt right, doubling back toward Fifth. And sure enough, the last she could see before the building on the northwest corner blocked her view, was that the woman had reached the Carlyle Hotel in the midblock between 77th and 76th, and was now rushing out of the sidewalk shadows, cutting across Madison, nimbly negotiating the traffic.

That was enough. No more cat-and-mouse. Nina hailed the first cab and jumped in. "Make the light at Fifth—quick!" she cried, and he fired the taxi ahead, cutting under the last of the yellow light, swinging downtown onto Fifth. Nina looked back just in time to see the tall lady bend herself into another cab. There was no doubt now. "Go through the park!" Nina cried out.

"I can't do that till 66th, lady."

"All right, all right. Just step on it." (*Step on it,* Nina thought. Nobody says *step on it* in real life, and I just have.)

"You being followed, lady?"

"No, no, it's just a prank." Nina glanced back again, but of course, all the cabs were yellow, so that was pointless. Anyway, the turn to the West Side came, and the driver began to traverse the park.

"Okay, lady, now where to?"

Nina gave him directions to circle back, to take her to her apartment on the East Side. He stopped asking questions. And he made good time. Even then, though, Nina made sure to have the right fare and tip ready for him, so she wouldn't have to wait for any change. She dashed into her building.

"Jaime," Nina said to the doorman, "I'm having some difficulty with a, uh, former patient. Tall woman. Gray hair. Probably wearing a hat. She may be coming here. I am *not* at home."

"Of course, Doctor." Jaime liked this little intrigue. The Soviet Union had had its consulate just down the block, and there'd always been rumors that the CIA had monitored the Commies out of this very building. Why, Jaime hadn't enjoyed this sort of mystery since the Cold War ended.

Nina rushed into the elevator, and she could hear her house phone ringing in her apartment even before she could unlock the door. She grabbed for the receiver. "Jaime downstairs, Doctor. Your patient was here."

"She asked for me?"

"No, she just got out of a taxi, looked in—you know, saw me. So, I started to walk right at her, and when she saw that, she turned and hurried away, down toward Lex."

"Thank you, Jaime," Nina said, but it was cold comfort. This was getting serious. The woman knows where I live. Nina wanted a drink. But she had already had two drinks. Two *martinis,* for God's sake. Instead, she decided to compose herself by going into her bedroom and lighting a votive candle. She would hypnotize herself. She'd learned how to do that years before, when she was training to hypnotize patients.

Nina stared at the candle, breathing deeply, talking to herself—softly now, in cadence. But, right away, she knew it wasn't flying. She couldn't block the tall woman out of her mind. And the scream. Bucky's scream. The woman. The scream. No use. She couldn't remember the last time she'd been unable to hypnotize herself. Well yes, then, she could remember: it was after that evening when she'd first cheated on her husband, when she'd made love to Hugh.

But on that occasion, there'd been an alternative. That time, anyway, she could go to church and pray for the forgiveness of her sins. Which she did. But what could Nina do now? She turned on the light and blew out the candle.

That was when the phone rang. She stared at it, the ringing. The tall lady, of course. She'd obviously been the hang-up at the office. But Nina was mad now. She wanted to talk to her, to confront her. Another ring, and Nina pounced on the phone. "Hello," she said—the word more interrogation than salutation. But there was only silence on the other end. "Come on," Nina snapped. "Come on."

The woman's voice responded to that. "Put Bucky on...please" —the last word more command than courtesy.

Nina snapped back. "You followed me. You know Bucky's not here."

The caller pondered this. Then, after a few moments, she said, "Yeah, my foot." And then the click, gone.

Nina couldn't help but stare at the phone. *My foot.* It was almost a little-girl thing to say. She couldn't even remember the last time she'd heard anybody say "my foot." It made everything weird even weirder. *My foot.* Shaking—literally shaking—Nina reached for the telephone again.

·12·

"I'm really sorry," she said, when Hugh answered. "I'll never do this again."

He was cross. "Damn it, Nina. We agreed."

"I know, Hugh. But I just had to talk to someone. I'm scared."

That restored his sympathy—and then he could also hear her voice cracking, hear the muffled sound that tears on the verge make, as Nina told him about being followed, about the woman in the hat, her calling her up. She had to talk to him, had to listen to him.

Of course, isn't this the way it had started the first time—six, seven years ago? Then, Nina wasn't frightened. She was simply upset and unsure. Lindsay had left home, and she and Kingsley were alone, and that was different—not necessarily bad or good, you understand...just different. But for some reason, Nina had lost some professional confidence. She had started taking every patient's trauma and travails home with her, questioning everything she had said, everything she had suggested, all day long.

She knew she had to see somebody. Psychoanalysts have to themselves be psychoanalyzed before they can even begin to psychoanalyze other people. Why shouldn't Nina see another psychiatrist? But that seemed so insular to Nina; she decided she'd rather talk to her priest. Besides, there was a certain attractive perversity to that, too, inasmuch as psychiatrists were supposed to be so godless. Only, Nina couldn't stand her old parish priest, because he represented to her all the hidebound, anti-female stuff that she despised in the Catholic Church.

That was when one of her best friends, Diane, suggested that Nina talk to her minister, who was, Diane proclaimed, absolutely the most sensitive—and charming—man in the world. Diane was a Lutheran, ergo her minister, Hugh Venable, was a Lutheran, and that all seemed too much of a reach for Nina—and for Hugh. But Diane was persuasive. So, strictly as a courtesy to their mutual friend, the two of them—the Catholic communicant and the Lutheran minister—agreed to meet. Both, in their own minds, figured they'd go through the motions for about fifteen minutes. Only Nina and Hugh fell in love with each other in the first five. So, he became her counselor.

After their fourth counseling session, as a way (she said) of thanking him for all his guidance, Nina asked Hugh out to dinner. It was totally transparent. He made sure to wear his clerical collar, so that if anybody saw him dining with this attractive woman, they would assume that it was church business. She picked a restaurant with bright lights. After dinner, on a pretense, she had their cab drop her back at her office, and on a further pretense, he came inside for a moment. Both of them, by the way, perfectly understood these pretenses.

Feigning to look for something, Nina opened the top drawer of her very reliable desk in her very reliable office, which was neutral and non-threatening to all who might enter. But there, staring up at her—and him—was the detail from the Sistine Chapel, God touching man. Hugh was quite astounded. "Why?" he asked.

"Before I meet with every patient, I always open this drawer and look into it. It reminds me that no matter how dead-end somebody's problem might seem to me, there's still another answer for that person."

"You're quite amazing, Nina. You don't need my help."

"Yes, I do," she said.

Fifteen minutes later they were making love. He still had on his clerical collar, and it was upon her psychiatrist's couch where they consummated their passion. Neither of them had to dwell on the symbolism. Besides, it was all so glorious. *Bliss* was the word that occurred to Nina—a word that she had thought was previously only to be found in silly romance novels for silly woman.

Soon enough, too, Nina regained control of her confidence in her work. But, of course, she and Hugh had created quite another, larger problem for themselves, which Hugh would finally solve (well, after a fashion) simply by running away. He stopped seeing Nina, and ashamed of himself, of his sin, he divorced his wife and resigned as a pastor to take up being a teacher at Union Theological Seminary.

Now, all these years later, here was Nina again, seeking his help and his love. But then, as she talked to him over the phone, Nina heard the buzzer in the background at Hugh's apartment and heard him say, "Just a second, Nina, it's someone at the door."

Nina looked down at her watch. It was nine o'clock. Only very special people came to the door at nine o'clock—and invariably, when very special people come to the door at nine o'clock, they tend to stay once the door behind them closes. Nina especially arrived at this conclusion after she heard a woman's voice coo, "Hi!" and she heard Hugh say, "Wow, you're stunning."

Stunning—that had been the word he had always used for her. Why had Nina ever thought it was just her word? Now, she understood: every dime-a-dozen bitch was stunning.

In any event, Nina didn't hear anymore because Hugh had then cupped his hand over the phone as he told his girlfriend, Marilyn, "Oh, it's just one of my old parishioners." And then he uncupped the phone and said to Nina, "Sorry."

"No, I'm sorry, Hugh. I didn't know you had company."

He let that go. "Look," he said instead, "your door is locked and bolted, and the doorman won't let anyone up under any circumstances?"

"Yes."

"So you're safe."

"Well, yeah, I guess." So he reassured her that she was fine, but to please call him tomorrow if she were really still worried. *Take two aspirin, my dear, and call my office if the fever doesn't go down.* The cursory sonuvabitch. Nina thanked him and hung up.

God, but she still loved that man.

God, but she was still scared.

Nina took some Excedrin PM and fell asleep. Hardly two hours later, however, and she came wide awake, the martinis and the confusion roiling her system. And then the phone rang. She waited in the dark. It had to be the lady of the hats. And this time, she wouldn't bite. She let it ring. And then her message came on. And then a response. "Hello, Dr. Winston..." But it wasn't the woman. It wasn't any woman. The man's voice said, "I'm sorry to be calling so late, but this is Officer Raftery, nineteenth precinct, NYPD, and—"

Nina grabbed for the phone. "Yes, yes. This is Dr. Winston."

"Doctor, I'm sorry to bother you, but someone has broken into your office again." Nina sighed. "We came as soon as the alarm went off, but whoever it was managed to get away. Very professional."

Nina asked, "Can you tell if anything—"

"He broke in that same casement window, but nothing else appears to be disturbed. And he played the alarm like a violin."

Suddenly, even in the dark of her bedroom, Nina could see her office before her. And she knew. She knew absolutely. So, very calmly, she said, "Officer, what phone are you on now—where in the office?"

"I am, you know—your secretary's desk."

"Okay, here's what I'd like you to do. I'd like you to go into my office—to my desk. You can see it from where you are, right?"

"Yes, ma'am."

"Good. Right on top there, there should be a coffee table art book with Venus on the cover."

"Venus? Will I know Venus?"

"Officer, it's a fat, naked Venus, but, you know: Venus."

"Okay, gotcha."

"And right next to the book, there should be some handwritten notes and a tape."

"Video tape?"

"No, just a regular old tape—audio tape. Would you go in there now and see if they're still there?"

It was all for effect, she knew. They were gone—stolen. But, anyway, she sat up in the dark waiting for Officer Raftery to return.

Well, she was going to have to get bars on the windows. Much as she hated the idea, that was settled. She heard steps coming back, the phone being picked up. Officer Raftery said, "I found the Venus book right where you said."

"But no tape."

"No, ma'am."

"And no notes."

"Well, there's the one—to you."

"*To* me?"

"Yes, ma'am. It's addressed to you. Very neat-written, almost artistic, you could say."

"And what does it say?"

"It says: 'Dr. Winston—Sorry I have to borrow this, but it may be our Rosetta Stone.'"

Nina had him repeat the message, but it remained hopelessly meaningless. "Well, is it signed?" she asked.

"Yeah, I guess so, maybe."

"So, what's the signature?"

"That's what I mean, Doctor. I can't tell you that. You know that lettering that's almost like ours, but not quite? Like Russian, I think."

"You mean Cyrillic?"

"Yeah, I think that's it. You know, like some of the letters are exactly like ours, like *O* and *B* and *C*. But, then, some look all crazy."

"And that's the signature—in Cyrillic?"

"Doctor, I guess it's a signature. You know, it's at the bottom."

"Do you have any idea what it says?"

"Not really." This is what Officer Raftery was puzzling over:

ДВОУМОУ ОДИНС

Raftery did make a couple of stabs at explaining what the various letters were, but, of course, he couldn't even venture a guess about how to describe the Дs and the Иs. Anyway, it wouldn't have made a bit of difference. Nina didn't know Cyrillic any better than she did earned runs averages or how to find Orion's Belt.

"Thank you, Officer," she said. "I think I'm just supposed to say: dust the note for prints and test the handwriting. That's the person who broke in."

"Don't worry, Doctor. We'll get an expert to find out what those Russky letters mean, and we'll let you know."

So, she thanked him, hung up, and tried to think of something else, something nice. Invariably, that something else, something nice she thought of was Hugh. And it was now, too.

Of course, certainly Nina would not have thought about Hugh if she had known, that right now, at his apartment, he was lying next to Marilyn. She was nestled in the crook of his arm. But Hugh was only staring up, worrying about Nina and thinking how he could never again, in good faith, make love to Marilyn. Or to any woman but Nina Winston. Just one martini with her, a couple of phone calls, and he was completely, madly back in love with her. That is what he was thinking about, in the specific, as Nina was thinking about him in general.

Only, Hugh thought: how? It was Nina who had scarred his faith, ended his marriage. How could he ever allow himself to go back to her? Oh, why did Nina Winston have to be so damned *stunning*?

·13·

Monday, as soon as Nina was finished with her last patient before lunch, Roseann came into her office. She had two things to relate to the doctor. First, somebody from the 19th Precinct had just called. There were no fingerprints on the note, but they had shown it to a Russian expert. The words in Cyrillic read: DOUBLE ONES.

"Double one?" Nina asked. "You mean like eleven?"

"No, the officer specifically told me that the Russian lady said 'Double Ones'—plural. And it's pronounced, uh"—Roseann ventured the phonetic spelling—"*Odin Dvoynoy.*"

Nina shook her head. "What could that possibly mean? Double Ones?"

Roseann said it beat her.

"Okay, what else is up?"

"There's someone here who'd like to see you."

"A referral? Appointment?"

Roseann frowned. "No. She just now walked in and says she wants to see you about...Mr. Buckingham."

Nina brightened. She'd always had some feeling that, even as the woman of the hats trailed her and broke into her office, she would also, soon enough, reveal herself. Somehow, Nina had a sense that the mystery woman was her companion of sorts in the saga of Bucky. "Of course I'll see her," she told Roseann.

Immediately, though, as soon as the stranger came through the door, it was obvious to Nina that this woman wasn't that woman. But just as quickly, and even before she introduced herself, Nina was sure she knew who this was—standing there before her, tall and lithe and stylish, in her Donna Karan black pants suit and a gray Isaac Mazrahi sweater. The woman fidgeted, brutally unsmiling.

Of course, Nina was not put off; rarely did anyone first come to a psychiatrist confidently. But the woman in the Donna Karan seemed almost surly. She was, in fact, loaded for bear. As much as she had avoided confrontation throughout her life, as uncomfortable as this was going to be for her, the woman had decided exactly what she would say. She had rehearsed that, and now before she even introduced herself, Phyllis Buckingham ungritted her teeth, narrowed her eyes, and snapped, "Have you been screwing my husband, Doctor?"

Nina was so unprepared for such a blunt accusation that she was able to answer reflexively, without any guile or artifice. "The truth of the matter is," she replied, "that right now, I don't happen to be screwing anyone at all."

That, of course, was the last response that Phyllis had expected—not only the content, but the tone: blasé, mixed even with a little whimsy. So, with no rebuttal at her command, all she could do was slump down into the chair, so deflated that Nina even rushed around the desk to console her.

"I'm sorry, Doctor," she finally managed to say, "but I'm just so confused."

Nina handed her a Kleenex box. "Excuse me: you *are* Phyllis Buckingham?" Phyllis nodded, sniffling. "Well, Mrs. Buckingham, maybe I can appreciate your suspicions, but I can absolutely assure you that my relationship with your husband is strictly doctor-patient."

"How long has Bucky been coming to see you—appointments?"

Nina leaned back on her desk. "Technically, I shouldn't answer anything about my dealings with a patient, but you're obviously aware that he has been seeing me, so I won't stand on ceremony. About two months now."

That helped Phyllis clear her head, sufficient to move back on the offensive. "If you'll excuse my layman's ignorance, Dr. Winston, but do dates at the Metropolitan, then cocktails, and a little private

evening *therapy*"—ooh, how that word dripped with insinuation—
"back here at the office...." Purposely, she paused to glance over to
the couch. "Does that now constitute a professional relationship?"

This time, Nina was the one caught off guard. So Phyllis barreled on. "Even when I called, the first word out of your mouth was
my husband's name. *Buckkky.*"

"That was you?"

Phyllis sat up confidently now. "I don't follow my husband,
Doctor. But I had confided my suspicions that he was...running
around, and by chance, one of my friends that I'd told had been at
the museum. She saw you there with Bucky, and then later, she
walked by your little tête-à-tête at the Stanhope bar, and—"

"So then she followed us to my office and called you?" Phyllis
nodded. Nina fought to suppress a smile. After all, even in her dis-
combobulation, she had to laugh to herself that, since the woman
of the hats had also been spying on her, it must have created quite
a pedestrian jam there on the Fifth Avenue sidewalk that evening, as
all these snoops reconnoitered her activity.

"Well," Nina went on, "I acknowledge—and apologize—for that
professional indiscretion. But, I assure you that it was not premed-
itated. It was a chance meeting at the museum."

"My foot," Phyllis snapped. "The last time Bucky was in *any*
museum was when he was also singing in the Mormon Tabernacle
Choir."

"Let's just say for now that he's struck up a particular new interest at the Metropolitan." Phyllis scowled. "And we came across each
other there, and then after a cocktail"—well, Nina fibbed, with the
singular—"which was strictly my suggestion...after that, I can promise you that nothing of impropriety happened between us in this
office. Nothing."

"But isn't that rather unusual, taking a patient to—"

"Yes, absolutely."

"Then can you explain to me why—"

"I'm sorry, Mrs. Buckingham, but you'll have to ask Bucky about
that. He's not bound by any confidence with me, as I am with him."

Phyllis was not altogether satisfied with that response, but she was at least beginning to grow somewhat comfortable. "You can understand, can't you, that I just assumed that this was all about another woman?"

"Yes."

"Well, if it really isn't you, then—?"

"Now, please don't read anything into this, Mrs. Buckingham, but I'm sorry, I must honor the strictures of my—"

"Okay, okay," Phyllis growled—not really accepting what Nina said, but only going along in the manner of a prosecutor who had been silenced by a judge, procedurally. "Okay. But the fact is that, suddenly, a few months ago, Bucky began to change. Never happened before. Of course I imagined it was another woman. What else? Then I find out he's traipsing into a psychiatrist's office after a couple of drinks with a woman. Bucky—going to a psychiatrist? You know, Doctor, the only thing wrong with my husband is he's too normal. And then I start thinking about it, and it dawns on me: of course, the other woman *is* a psychiatrist."

Nina said, "Didn't your friend mention that I was a bit too long in the tooth for such an attractive younger man?"

Phyllis tossed her head in condescension. "Hey, Bucky's always had a thing for older women."

"Really?"

"You mean he hasn't told you that? He hasn't told you about Jocelyn?"

"Jocelyn? I'm sorry."

"Then he's B.S.ing you, Doctor. Jocelyn Ridenhour was the love of his life—the one before me. And she had to be fifteen years older than Bucky. Funny thing about him, Doctor. As boyish as Bucky can be, he's always gravitated to the company of older people. I don't mean just women. So many older men you'd never imagine would have anything in common with him, have taken to Bucky in business. He's just sometimes this old soul. I know he woulda married Jocelyn if she hadn't been sooo much older. So you see, Doctor, forgive me, but you fit the profile." Nina chuckled, but then Phyllis hit her with this: "Of course, you are a little short for his taste. Bucky likes us tall and leggy."

As quickly as she could process that, Nina asked, "And this Joce-lyn—she was tall, huh?"

"Oh yeah, just like me. And eccentric—not like me. That's about all I know about the lady."

Well, well, well, Nina thought. What have we here? How many loves of a lifetime does Mr. Floyd Buckingham have? Constance? Jocelyn? And not to mention such a chic and adoring wife? Still, Nina rather liked Phyllis, admired her gumption for confronting her—especially since it was so obviously out of character. "You know, Mrs. Buckingham," Nina said, "if you had the courage to come see me, why don't you just ask Bucky yourself about—"

"Because I'm scared. Because, all of a sudden, I don't know if I know him anymore. But at your next session with him..."

"Tomorrow."

"I would like you to tell him I came here."

"All right."

"Maybe then he'll explain to me why he's acting so differently, why he could possibly feel the need for psychiatric help."

"Of course," Nina said, rising, escorting her to the door.

Phyllis waited there, though, before she held out her hand. Eventually, instead, she said, "I'll bet you like Bucky, don't you, Doctor?"

"Yes, I don't think it's inappropriate for the psychiatrist to admit that."

"I know. Everybody does. Everybody likes Bucky. We all are crazy about him. The children and me, the dog and the cat. My mother likes Bucky so much more than she likes my father. All of us, we love Bucky. And so, if you're really not sleeping with him—"

"Phyllis, I'm not. I promise."

"Well then, if you could just help bring him back to us from wherever he's gone to, I'll be very grateful." And quickly, then, before Nina could see the tears cloud up in her eyes, Phyllis pivoted and walked straightaway out that door, through the waiting room and the front door, out to Fifth Avenue, where it had begun to drizzle.

Nina watched her go, then held up a hand to Roseann—five fingers spread out. Five minutes. She rushed back to her desk and

wrote the name down. JOCELYN. No question about that. But: RIDEN-
HOUR? Or maybe it didn't have an *h* in it. RIDENHOUR? Or maybe an
ei: RIDENHOUR? That is what Phyllis had said, hadn't she?
R(E)IDEN(H)OUR. Yes, yes. One of those ways.

Nina grabbed for the Manhattan phone book. Try that, first.
Try it without the *e*, but with the *h*. Richey, Riddle, Ridello...Riden-
hour. There weren't that many of them. But there was the one, plain
as day: RIDENHOUR *Jocelyn*. No pussy-footin' around. No mere initial,
no: RIDENHOUR *J*. Nina was the same way. What crazed pervert is
going to be fooled by an initial? WINSTON *Nina* is what it said for
her. Who's kidding whom? You put down WINSTON *N.*, everybody
knows it's a woman. So what's the point? Good for her. Good for
RIDENHOUR *Jocelyn*—even if she did follow Nina and break into her
office and steal from her.

The address was downtown, The Village or SoHo, or that new one
that makes all the columns, wherever it is. TriBeCa. Or *TRI BC* if it's a
woman district. Anyway, for now, Nina preferred just to call. Not to
talk. Not now. Just to call. Leave a message. Jocelyn Ridenhour should
be at work now. Just leave a message on her phone machine.

Nina dialed the number. And here came the fourth ring. But, no
click. No phone machine? Fifth ring. Sixth. Seventh. There is no
phone machine. Doesn't this lady of the hats named Jocelyn Ridenhour know this is the twenty-first century? After the eighth ring,
Nina hung up.

So, she picked up the pad—the same pad that Jocelyn had written the note to her on—and printed this on it:

> *If you are* ДВОУМОУ ОДИНС,
> *Please return my tape & my notes.*
> *Contact me & I promise: no police.*

Then, just to be mischievous, Nina added:

> *Have a nice day* ☺

Two can play this game.

She found a blank envelope, addressed the letter, sealed it, and
put it in her pocketbook to mail.

·14·

Over and over, Jocelyn Ridenhour listened to the tape, trying to fathom it. She would even get down on her knees in her apartment and pantomime the scream, trying to better imagine what Bucky was saying. And why.

Read through Dr. Winston's notes again. "On knees...Absolute agony on his face...Sees what? (It must be *awful*.)" Read them over. Listen to all Bucky said when he was in the trance. Even listen to Bucky and Nina talking briefly afterwards, before she flicked off the recorder. Do it all again. But, still: what was he screaming? Why was he screaming?

Anyway, as pragmatic as Jocelyn could be, going about her task, the sheer horror of the wail affected her no less than it had Nina. It was a cry and a shriek and a moan all together.

She had called Bucky, of course—called him regularly since that time in March when he had come to her, confused and disturbed, and she had told him to go to a therapist. Get hypnotized—maybe you can get the answer that way. That was when Jocelyn had given him Nina's name. Jocelyn had heard about her. Dr. Nina Winston: as respected and reliable a shrink as a man could find.

But, by now, Bucky's reluctance to talk anymore to Jocelyn had too much frustrated her and annoyed him. The last time she'd called him, he'd all but hung up on her. "Damn it, Joc, how many times do I have to tell you? I know how interested you are. I know you gave me the shrink's name. But this is my business. And I'm not going to tell you anymore. Now, don't call me again. Good-bye."

That was when Jocelyn started assuming the initiative herself. This could be too important. Besides, she'd already written Sergei and Ludmilla. Yes, perhaps she'd contacted them too quickly, promised them too much. Certainly, that did put more pressure on her. And certainly, Jocelyn appreciated now she shouldn't have broken into Dr. Winston's office. That was foolhardy. That was two counts, breaking and entering. Theft. And there also must be an official, legal term for following someone. Stalking? It was all so foolish going after the doctor, anyway. The doctor's not going to reveal anything to her. She can't. She's a doctor. Yes, Jocelyn admitted to herself, she'd been wrong to rush it, to take all these chances.

Just give Bucky time, and he'll tell her everything. He always did.

So, Jocelyn played the tape again, down on her knees, mouthing the scream.

She grew positive that it must be a name that Bucky had yelled. Ollie? Or maybe it was Al, with a trailing shriek. She thought back, then, all their time together. Bucky loved to talk to her as much as he loved to make love to her. But all that time, all that she ever heard him say—Jocelyn could not recall Bucky even once mentioning an Al or an Ollie. (Well, not counting the times he'd twiddle his tie, doing a very bad imitation of Stan Laurel talking to Oliver Hardy.)

So then Jocelyn thought: well, maybe it wasn't a name. Maybe it was a word from a foreign language, like *alli*. Could there be such a word? So, she searched foreign-language dictionaries—Spanish, French, German, Italian—for all the possible spellings. But: nothing like it. *Allez* in French, *ole* in Spanish. No, no—that wasn't the sound. Not quite. And, anyway, you didn't get down on your knees in pain to scream those kind of words. No.

One day at lunch, Jocelyn went into a large bookstore, and in the travel section, she asked for a Flemish-English dictionary. Hadn't Bucky told her about gallery twenty-seven, about Rubens? Wasn't that the start of it all? Maybe Bucky was crying out in Flemish. Unfortunately, Jocelyn learned, there is no such animal. There is no Flemish language. Instead, she discovered, Flemish is simply a

dialect of Dutch. Well then, she asked for a Dutch-English dictionary. But: no word in Dutch even remotely approximated that distinct sound that Bucky had uttered: "...*owwwlllleeeeeee*..."

Jocelyn's frustrations were growing. Her interests in other
things wavered. She turned off the phone machine and stopped
painting. Her mind would wander at work. And every day, as soon
as she got back to her apartment, she would rush to the phone
and contemplate calling Bucky. But she was getting a hold of herself now. She knew she must not irritate him any more. Be
patient, Joc. Be patient. We are dealing with centuries here. Maybe
eons. So what's a few more days? Still, she knew she was so close.
And to think that Bucky could be the one. After all this time,
everywhere in the world—and Bucky had the answer for them.
Bucky. Right here.

Of course, this also: now why couldn't it be me? That was the
greatest irony.

All that Jocelyn knew about reincarnation, about life past,
about lives past—yet never could she get an inkling of who she
might have been before. The shoemaker's children had no shoes.
Ah, yes, and Jocelyn Ridenhour had no past lives.

Finally, she had to write Sergei and Ludmilla to tell them that
things must wait a bit. But don't worry: soon enough she'd be coming to visit them. By the end of the summer, no matter what. And
then they'd start to work things out. Jocelyn had contacts. Soon, the
whole world would know what they knew. Soon, the whole world
would believe.

Jocelyn did send them some money to help them continue their
studies.

But, Jocelyn was stymied. So, with nothing else to do, she went
out and bought another hat. It was a large straw bonnet with a flowing pink ribbon—just the perfect sort of hat for a lovely English garden party in Dorset during Wimbledon fortnight. Or, if no one
invited you to an English garden party in Dorset during the fortnight, then it was the perfect sort of hat to wear in your New York
apartment, as you played the tape, again and again.

And again and again heard: "...*owwwlllleeeeeee*..."

And though the chills went up and down her spine, as they always did, there was no more. No more to learn from it. Nothing new, nothing else. Once again, Jocelyn got up off her own knees and adjusted her new straw bonnet with the flowing pink ribbon.

•15•

The knock upon Nina's office door came only five minutes after she had begun her first hour of the day with the garrulous Mrs. Harrison of Rye. All the more amazing, because Roseann was under stringent orders never to bother Nina when she was with a patient, except under the most extraordinary circumstances.

Nina opened the door. "I'm sorry, Doctor, but it's Mr. Buckingham."

"Where?" Nina whispered, glancing about the waiting room.

"I mean, it's *about* him. I think he's under arrest."

Barely apologizing to Mrs. Harrison, Nina grabbed the phone. The voice on the other end declared, "Dr. Winston, Robert Fernandez. I'm head of security at the Metropolitan Museum, and—"

Nina tore up Fifth Avenue, dodging traffic, and was there at the security office in five minutes, tops. Fernandez, a slim man in a business suit—plainclothes—escorted her into his office. She was surprised; she had expected Bucky to be there—like waiting in the principal's office until Mommy came.

Fernandez anticipated her question. "We're holding him," he informed her, beckoning Nina to take the chair across from his desk. "This whole thing is very unusual, Doctor," he went on, shaking his head in evident puzzlement. "Normally, something like this happens—" He stopped. "Well, nothing like this has ever happened. But, you know, somebody gets in trouble, we call a lawyer, maybe the family. He specifically asked that I call you."

"No, Mr. Fernandez, I appreciate your consideration. Mr.

Buckingham is my patient. Now, can you tell me what he did?"
Fernandez shook his head. "Well, to be truthful, we're really not
sure *what* he did do. All we know is, the museum opens at nine-
thirty. Nine twenty-five, a guard finds Mr. Buckingham sitting
upstairs in a gallery."

"Gallery twenty-seven?" Fernandez's eyes flew wide open, and
Nina smiled wanly. "Mr. Buckingham has something of a, uh, fancy
for a particular painting in that gallery."

"Okay, that helps."

"So how did he get there?"

"Well," Fernandez replied, "he wouldn't go into any detail till
you arrived, but he did tell us he spent the night inside the
museum."

That stunned Nina—no less, evidently, than it had baffled
everybody else. "But don't you have cameras and sensors and all
that?"

"Doctor, this place is guarded like Fort Knox—has been ever
since Murph the Surf stole the diamonds. So how Mr. Buckingham
secreted himself is very important to us."

"Nobody has done this since Murph the Surf?"

Fernandez shook his head ruefully, and it dawned on Nina then
that inasmuch as nothing seemed damaged or missing, the author-
ities were more interested in *how* Bucky had gotten away with his
nocturnal sojourn than they were in extracting a pound of flesh. So,
Nina said, "Mr. Fernandez, I can assure you that my patient is no
threat to anyone, nor to anything in this museum, and if I can speak
with him, I'm sure that I can gain his promise that this will never
happen again."

Fernandez pondered this. "I gotta know how he did this," he
said.

"So, let's find out," Nina replied—and with that, Fernandez
picked up his phone and asked that "the intruder" be brought into
his office.

Bucky entered—if not manacled, still closely accompanied by
two uniformed guards; nobody was taking the modern-day Murph
the Surf lightly. He barely looked up at Nina, mumbling a "thank-

you." His suit was rumpled; he was unshaven, bowed of posture, sheepish of aspect.

"Bucky," Nina said, "I have assured Mr. Fernandez here that you are not out to steal anything. Nor to harm anything. However, you have obviously trespassed—"

"But I didn't damage anything!" Bucky cried out, coming into his own again.

Respectfully, Fernandez replied, "Sir, if I snuck into your house and spent the night, I would not be welcome there, even if I didn't do any damage—would I?"

Bucky nodded. Nina took up the interrogation. "Did you actually spend the whole night in the museum?" He nodded again. "Did you break in?"

Bucky protested vigorously. "No, look." Incongruously, he still wore a little admission button in his lapel. It was an especially hideous puce. "I came in late yesterday." And then, quite proudly, "I'm a member of the museum, now."

Nina buttonholed Fernandez, gesturing to the door. "Can I talk to you?" He nodded, following her out.

"What's up?" he asked, when they were alone in the corridor.

"Look, I know how serious this is, Mr. Fernandez. But Floyd Buckingham just has one little problem, and that problem, incidentally, has something to do with the museum. But he's a model citizen."

"He hasn't got any record," Fernandez volunteered.

Nina was delighted to learn that Fernandez had discovered that; it put another arrow in her quiver. "Right! And he's a great husband and father; respectable—he's a prominent magazine publisher—the whole nine yards. If Mr. Buckingham tells you what he did and how he did it, and then you let him off, and he promises never to do it again..." Nina shrugged, throwing herself on the mercy of the museum.

"Can you guarantee me he'll never do it again?"

"Mr. Fernandez, I can't *guarantee* anything, but I can ninety-five percent guarantee it, and if he does do it again—yes, I can absolutely guarantee that he won't hurt anything."

Fernandez pondered that. "He's gotta tell me everything."

"Of course."

"And no compromises. If I let him walk, I don't ever want to see his butt back in here again. Ever."

Nina nodded—although she was put off by Fernandez saying "butt." God, Nina hated that word. "Ass," she thought, was so much better. But nowadays everybody had concluded that "butt" was more respectable. So, she nodded solemnly and declared, "If his ass is ever back in here, he deserves whatever you hand him."

"Okay," Fernandez said, and they went back into the office.

"Bucky," Nina said, steel in her voice, "tell Mr. Fernandez everything he wants to know."

Bucky got the picture. "Okay," he began, "I came into the museum late yesterday afternoon and went up to twenty-seven. See, I have, uh—"

Nina interrupted. "Mr. Fernandez understands the gist of that situation."

Bucky nodded. "But there's always people passing through, and I decided I had to be alone there. Somehow. So I started lookin' around."

"To hide?" Fernandez asked.

"*Just* to hide, sir. I mean, I know what terrific security you got, all that. I knew I couldn't sneak up to twenty-seven during the night. I knew that. I just wanted to be positioned for some private time the next morning."

Fernandez shook his head. He was beginning to have his doubts that he should let someone as bananas as this back on the street.

"Well, lemme tell you," Bucky explained, "it's not easy to find a place to hide here. I did see some nice big vases down in the European Sculpture Court, but they're way up on pedestals. No good. Finally, I worked my way up to the north end. All the Egyptian stuff. You know that?"

Fernandez frowned. "Mr. Buckingham, it's my job to know every inch of this museum."

"Oh yeah, of course. So, anyway, I end up in that huge hall where the temple is."

"The Temple of Dendar?"

"Yeah."

"Don't tell me you hid in the Temple of Dendar?"

"Oh no—no way, José," Bucky said—but then he remembered that Fernandez was Hispanic, and he worried that maybe "no way, José" was anti-Hispanic. So, quickly: "I mean, that place has gotta be wired, lasered. Nobody could hide *in* the temple. But outside. Outside, where the temple's been eroded, they've constructed these big blocks—concrete, I guess. They're just like steps. And I could see this little ledge up in the back, and so if I climbed up the blocks and lay down, there was no way you could see me."

"But the guards?"

"The guards are *great,* sir! They are all doing their job. But they are all around the front of the temple, where they should be, like stopping people from taking flash pictures and videos. Which they should. Which is their job. But nobody's looking around near the back of the temple, because who cares? Right?"

"Right," said Fernandez, shaking his head.

"All I really had to worry about was some visitor seeing me. But it was late; there weren't many left. Still, just to be sure, I took off my little entrance button"—Bucky pointed to his puce lapel pin again. "I'd noticed all you officials wear little ID tags around your necks." Fernandez fingered his. "So, what I did was, I took off a shoelace, and I had a little acetate folder in my wallet, and I put one of my frequent flyer cards in there. The United looked best—a nice, rich blue." Bucky reached into his pocket and brought out his makeshift tag. Fernandez held his head; Murph the Surf had come to this. "Then see," Bucky went on, "I punched holes in the acetate, ran my shoelace through that, and hung it around my neck. From any distance, you know, it looked like I was a big muckety-muck."

"Holy Mother, I don't believe it," Fernandez moaned.

"All right, now it's five o'clock. It's only a few more minutes till closing. I walk up to the temple, around the side, where the big blocks go up, and act like I'm kinda checking it out. I pretend to make some notes. I can see nobody's paying any attention to me. So—bingo—quickly, then, I scramble up the blocks and lay down on the ledge." And that's where Bucky stopped.

Everybody waited.

Finally, Fernandez said, "And that's it?"

"That's it. I never left, all night. I was a little scared about dozing off and rolling off. But, you know, I still caught forty winks here and there."

Fernandez covered his eyes.

Bucky made sure to console him. "Sir, your security is terrific." Fernandez shook his head. "No, no—think about it. Your system is based, logically, on the premise that you have to protect yourself from somebody who's up to no good. Why the hell should you care about somebody all harmless who just wants to spend the night?"

Fernandez did sort of mumble in support of that logic. Nina had to duck her head and pretend to search for a Kleenex in her pocketbook. Ah, yes, Bucky was back on his usual roll. "I mean, sir, I knew if I moved so much as a foot off that ledge, some laser is going to start ringing whistles all over the place. I am dead meat. So, I just lie there. All night. Finally, around quarter to nine this morning, I start hearing a lot of activity. I've still got my little United Airlines ID on"—he fingered it; Fernandez grimaced—"so I see the coast is clear, and I walk down those steps like I'm in charge. I make a bee-line to the men's room—whew—wash up, then go up to twenty-seven. I got there about ten after nine, and, yes, just what I wanted; I was all by myself. Mission accomplished. Couple more minutes, I'm gonna leave, but then the guard sees me. You have really got some terrific security people working for you, sir." Bucky shrugged. "And that's it. That's all she wrote."

"Unbelievable," Fernandez said. He started to pace about. "But, I believe you. And I believe your doctor." He waved a finger in Bucky's face. "So, okay, I'm gonna let you go. *But!* But, I'm tellin' you, sir: your butt is *persona non grata* in The Metropolitan Museum of Art from this moment on. Hereafter. Anybody sees you back here—ever—you're arrested. Now, you can live with that?"

"Yes sir, I can. But I promise you: it'll never happen again. Thank you." He stuck his hand out then, and if somewhat reluctantly, Fernandez accepted it. Nina also thanked him, and then she left, Bucky behind her.

Outside, coolly, she only said, "Let's take a walk."

"I'm sorry, Nina. Uh, don't you have any patients?"

"Patients? Excuse me, Bucky, but *you* are a patient—and right now, in fact, you're more of a patient than I ever imagined."

"I guess," was all he said, softly—and they walked on, then, without speaking anymore, down Fifth Avenue. At the south end of the museum, across from 80th Street, Nina steered him around back.

The Metropolitan is incredibly jerrybuilt. The classical front, along Fifth, was actually constructed long after the museum was originally designed; other sections came along later, juxtaposing architecture of stark contrast. For example, the path that Nina and Bucky walked on now, at the south end, went by a sloping modern glass wall that abutted the beaux-arts front. That huge glass precipice gleamed in the morning light so that the day's sunbathers were already assembled beneath, catching the rays from what amounted to a giant reflector.

Nina steered Bucky further along, toward the tunnel that headed out to the obelisk and the Great Lawn. The grass had just been cut, and already lovers had taken to lolling about and artists to working at their easels. Bikers rode by. Joggers loped, lost in their Walkmans. Nina pointed to an empty bench by the tunnel, and they slumped down together there. She waited without a word, until at last Bucky realized that it was up to him. He lifted his head. "I masturbated," he said, softly.

"You what? Where?"

"Sitting there, looking at Venus and Adonis."

"Did you plan that, Bucky? Was that why you wanted to be alone in twenty-seven?"

He shook his head, dispiritedly. "Oh no, Nina. Nothing like that. It just happened. I was there, alone, looking at the painting. And I could feel Constance. I was overwhelmed, and, all of a sudden, I—" He shrugged.

"Ever do that before?"

Gaily, Bucky held out his hands, up right before her face. "Hey, Doctor, no hair on my palms."

Nina reacted instinctively. She took her own right hand, and slapped it down hard on his. "Goddamn it, this isn't funny," she snapped. "And stop smirking. Don't you get it, Bucky? You risked your whole reputation, your whole career, your whole life back in there. Just imagine the headlines." She held up her own hands now, as if they were a newspaper. "Met Masturbater!"

He ducked his head, shamefaced. "That close, Mr. Bucking-ham," Nina went on—only this time she held up her thumb and forefinger, barely apart. "You were that close to losing that whole glorious existence you've created. And there's no explaining your-self. 'Oh please, your Honor, it's very understandable. See, Venus is my current, would-be mistress, just like she was back in the seven-teenth century in Antwerp. Soon, too, I'll be shacking up with the same lady, who also lives in the twentieth century, and though I barely know her, I'm going to leave my wife and children and run off with her. But in the meantime, I'm sure you'll understand that I have to rendezvous with her painting in the museum and make the best of it.'

"And, of course, the judge is just going to say: 'Oh well, Mr. Buckingham, that explains it all. Case dismissed.'" And Nina brought down an imaginary gavel.

It was Bucky who held up his thumb and forefinger now. All the usual bravado was gone, all the cheek, all the charm that invariably passed him through the narrow portals of convention that blocked most other people. "Yeah, that close," he sighed. "I know. I'm losing it. Aren't I, Nina?"

"I guess," she replied truthfully. "I guess maybe you are."

"Yeah," Bucky whispered. "But I can't help it, Nina. I can't stop any of this."

And then, in the next moment, he began to sniffle, and then he began to cry—great tears, great wracking sobs. The good Dr. Win-ston could only reach over to her patient, to the disconsolate Buck-ingham, take him in her arms there on the park bench in Central Park, hold him, rock him softly, and assure him that it was going to be all right. But...

But, it didn't seem to Nina anymore that it necessarily was going to be all right.

·16·

That afternoon (after he had called Phyllis with some ridiculous alibi which she did not for a moment believe), Bucky arrived at Nina's for their appointment that had already been scheduled. Moving immediately to the couch, he plopped himself down and began to deliver a torrent of gratitude and apology—all of which was sincere, but overdone, nonetheless. Bucky also explained that he had already sent a personal note of appreciation to Robert Fernandez and had made out a nice check to the Metropolitan.

When he had concluded this recitation, Nina said, "Okay, for now, we'll skip over these remarkable events of the past twenty-four hours. I have something else to ask you."

"Shoot," he called out. Already, some of the jauntiness was returning.

Nina, still standing, templing her hands before her face, withdrew them, and then leaning down, inquired, gently but firmly, "Bucky, tell me, Constance...her last name?"

"Rawlings."

"Is Constance Rawlings real?"

His eyes darted about, confused. "You mean Constance—now?"

"Yes, let's just confine this discussion to the present century."

"Jesus, Nina, you don't think I made up Constance?" She drew closer yet—if not for intimidation, then certainly for emphasis. "Well then, Constance Rawlings of Chicago is not to be confused with Jocelyn Ridenhour of New York, is she?"

This time, all the air went out of Bucky. "How did—?"

"If there is a difference, tell me about Jocelyn."

"Well, of course there is. There's Constance, and there's Jocelyn. But how the—?"

"Never mind *how*. I'm the one with the questions."

Bucky mumbled an "okay," sipped some water, and then he began: "I met Jocelyn about a year after I left Philadelphia and came up to New York—advertising agency. She was in the art department, divorced then—and even though she was a lot older, we hit it off."

"What does 'hit it off' mean, exactly?

"Exactly what you would think 'hit it off' means."

"How long did the affair last?"

"Oh, a couple years. Really, right up till I started getting serious with Phyllis. By then, I'd left the agency, gotten into magazines, and when I broke up with Jocelyn, that was the last I saw of her until—"

"Until when?"

"Well, a couple years ago. Jocelyn's won some kind of art director's prize, and there was this award dinner I had to go to, and you know, we chatted—the usual: you're looking great, terrific to see you—and we said, hey, let's have lunch. And we did. Went to Gabriel's. But that's it. I haven't seen Jocelyn for months."

This wasn't a lie. On the other hand, it wasn't exactly the truth. It was Clintonish. *Seen* was the operative word. But Nina wasn't informed of the subtlety, and so she took off in another direction.

"You ever tell Jocelyn about Constance?"

"All of it—walking into that office with her, getting all tingly. Jocelyn was fascinated. She's always been into whatcha-callit—the spirit world, stuff you can't explain."

"But you never told Phyllis about Constance?" Bucky shook his head. "So, you told things to Jocelyn you wouldn't tell your wife?"

"Hey, come on, you're twisting that, Nina. When I was going out with Jocelyn, we knew it was just a, uh, thing. Look, she's a good fifteen years older than me. We were making it, sure, but it was never really any typical boyfriend/girlfriend stuff. I could talk to Jocelyn about everything. In fact, she was the only person—I mean, before you—that I ever told about Constance. Now, do you really think I could tell Phyllis that no matter what happened in my life, there is this one woman who is meant for me—and it's not her? Come on."

Nina allowed him that. "Fair enough," she said.

So now he shot back at her, "Okay, who told you about Jocelyn?"

Nina pretended to study her nails. "Oh, just somebody named Phyllis Buckingham." Bucky's head snapped back. "Some friend of hers told her about our little tête-à-tête at the Stanhope, and so she came in yesterday and asked me about us."

Bucky flew off the couch. "Damn it, that's not fair of Phyllis."

Nina smiled foolishly at him. "Oh, poor Bucky—not fair to Bucky-wucky. But it's fair that you're planning to take off and leave her, no warning, come this August 11th. That's fair."

He bowed his head. "As usual, I'm all screwed up."

"Sit back down," Nina ordered him—and he obeyed. "Now, not surprisingly, your wife told me to tell you that she's noticed a change in your behavior toward her. She's suspected another woman and decided it might be me. I denied that, but I didn't reveal anything else. She's very much in love with you, Bucky." He nodded, guiltily. "And she's very confused. You've gotta tell her something."

"I guess," he mumbled.

"All right, then tell me something else." Bucky perked up for that more pleasing alternative. "Take me back to gallery twenty-seven this morning. You are there, alone at last with your Venus. I know this is difficult to put into words, but try and help me to understand. Tell me exactly what you felt, how you were thinking."

"Can I lie down?"

"Of course."

Bucky lay back, let his suede loafers slip, loosened his tie, and closed his eyes. Nina flipped on her tape recorder, and at last, he began. "There is, first of all, just this warmest, sweetest wave that sweeps over me. I remember when you hypnotized me, and I just felt so at peace. But in the museum, it's like peace-plus. It's like being in love, and making love—but all beyond that. That moment, that... Nina, it's like a spiritual climax." He paused, but he didn't open his eyes. "I'm sorry, I shouldn't be so graphic with you."

"That's okay, Bucky. I have had some passing familiarity with climaxes."

He permitted himself to open one eye and look at her, smiling wickedly for an instant, then he closed it back and resumed. "I just felt so at home this morning. And it wasn't only looking up there at Constance and me—you know, Venus and Adonis. But now that you've told me it's Rubens and Helena on the wall behind me, I can feel their warmth, too." He sighed, and Nina, intrigued, understood that Bucky had, in some sense, put himself into his own trance. "It's like we're all together back at the studio. All of us. The little boy—Cupid—and the other artists, and Ollie, and I could swear, I could feel the Madonna looking right at me. I could almost hear her, like she's talking directly to me and saying: *it's okay, Bucky, go ahead, it's okay*. And that's the last thing I remember, before, you know. It's just so warm. I feel like there's a color over top of me, over top of us all."

Nina's head picked up. "A color?"

"Yeah, yeah."

"What kind of color?"

"I'm not sure now. But I knew it then. I had the same feeling, a color all over me, back when I met Constance in Philadelphia."

"But you can't remember exactly what color? Is it a colored sheet that's over you? A colored tent?"

"No, no, Nina. It's not a colored *anything*. Just a color."

"And you can't remember what color?"

Bucky put the heel of his hand to his forehead and thought hard. "I think it's just rapture, Nina. And rapture is a color, but right now, I'm just not sure which color."

Nina listened spellbound, something nagging at her, until carefully, she ventured: "Would it maybe be…silver?"

"Yes, God yes!" His eyes came wide open. "How did you know, Nina?"

She looked away, shaking her head. "I don't know, Bucky. Maybe I just always thought rapture had to be silver."

"Yeah, and maybe I'd remember better if it wasn't just the paintings. If I really was with Constance herself again."

Nina got up out of her chair and walked back and forth. He cocked an open eye toward her. She stopped. "Okay, I agree," Nina said. "You're right. It's time to bring Constance into this."

"Hallelujah!" Bucky cried out, swinging his legs around, clapping his hands.

"All right, calm down. Just tell me how to contact her."

Bucky dove into his billfold. "Here's her number at work."

Nina took the slip of paper and dubiously said, "You promise, she doesn't know I exist?" He shook his head. "She knows nothing about Venus? About Adonis?"

"No, I swear it."

Nina jotted the number down. "Okay, I'll call her."

"Oh, thank you, Nina. God, thank you." Beside himself, he pecked her on the cheek, then boyishly, he skipped away, snapping his fingers.

Nina waited till he was almost at the door before calling after him. "Wait a sec. I wanna ask you one other thing." He stopped. "You know anyone named Ollie?"

"Ollie?" She nodded. "What is this: Double Jeopardy for two hundred?" But Bucky did search his mind then, until, at the last, he put a silly expression on his face and started fiddling with his tie.

Nina said, "You can spare me a bad impression of Oliver Hardy."

He shrugged. "Sorry, only Ollie I know."

"Okay, forget about it. We shrinks work in mysterious ways."

Bucky grinned, waved, and was gone through the door—never happier.

Nina, though, immediately went back to the tape recorder and rewound it, bouncing the buttons until—there it was: "...we're all together back in the studio. All of us. The little boy—Cupid—and the other artists, and Ollie, and I could swear, I could feel the Madonna looking..."

Unmistakably: *Ollie.*

And he didn't even know he'd said it.

Nina clicked off the tape and walked over to her desk, thinking, wondering, until at last, she opened the drawer there and stared in at God reaching out to Adam. Even when she closed the drawer back up, though, it was several more minutes before Nina could bring herself to call the 312-number that Bucky had given her. It rang only once.

"This is Constance Rawlings," said the no-nonsense, no-frills voice on the other end of the phone.

·17·

As much as Nina always loved art, it had certainly never occurred to her how perfect museums might be for assignations. But, that is where, so often, she and Hugh used to rendezvous—the Metropolitan, the Whitney, the Museum of Modern Art. There, in public, they would, by chance, accidentally, bunk into each other. *Why, how nice to see you again, Ms...? Oh yes, of course: Mr. Venable. And are you here for the Magritte exhibit?*

Often afterwards they would go to her office and make love on the couch that was meant for therapy. Looking back, it all seemed so tawdry.

Well, because it was tawdry.

Today, it was funny, though. In the past, Nina had met Hugh so often at the Metropolitan, so now when she looked up from where she was sitting by herself in the Tiffany Court and saw him coming toward her, there was some disjunction of time in her mind. She merely thought: *Oh, here comes Hugh now.* It took a few seconds for it to register. *Oh, my God, it really is Hugh! Now!!*

Of all the places in all the museums that had been their favorite foreplay, this was the one location they loved the most: the sun streaming in through the skylights, falling upon the lush greenery, and all the wonderfully eclectic statuary. There was everything from August Belmont frowning down from his massive chair, to a glorious angel on high blaring her trumpet, to Indians and bears and panthers, to Pan playing his pipes in the middle of the fountain pool. And it was from that direction now that Nina saw Hugh ambling toward her, holding his sports jacket over his shoulder with a crooked finger. It had been five years since last they'd met each other here, but he sidled up to her bench as if it had been yesterday.

"You know, Nina," he began, "all those other times I was in museums, I only had eyes for you, but today, as I was searching for you, I noticed how many good-looking women there are on these premises. A veritable garden of female pulchritude. Just my luck, I only figure this out as I approach three score years."

"You really must be more observant in your dotage."

"I mean, Nina, if the man in the street only knew. The museum: *the* place to pick up chicks! Not only that, but just by being here, you're *ipso facto* that rare and sensitive male of the species—not just another one of those pigs who frequent bars and hockey games."

Nina laughed. And: isn't it amazing how you can always hear a fountain better when you're in love? She heard the water, absolutely distinctly, splashing upon Pan. "So, what brings you to me?" he asked.

"You called, remember? You were upset."

Suddenly, Nina didn't hear the fountain. Sweetly, she snapped, "Yes, I remember. But it seems to me that was several days ago, and the dragon must have long since gobbled up the damsel in distress."

Hugh simply chose not to respond. Instead, "So, I dropped by your office, thinking we might have lunch, and was finally able to pry your general whereabouts from out of your Gorgon of a secretary. Then I made a beeline here." He swept his arms about the courtyard. "I remembered: this was always your favorite place."

"Funny," said Nina, "I always thought this was *our* favorite place."

"Yes," was all he said, softly, so then Nina could again hear every drop of water falling in the Pan fountain. And even clearer, hear Hugh say, "God, doesn't that fountain sound great?"

Nina nodded, beaming. "Yes, I needed this. I needed to come back to a place where I knew I'd be comfortable...and safe. There's something really weird going on, Hugh."

"This is the same reincarnation stuff?"

"Uh huh. And not only that, but this is where it all traces to—a painting upstairs by Rubens."

"The guy who does all the—" Hugh held up his hands, cupped, before his chest.

"Oh, thank you for that, sir," Nina cracked. "But please, don't limit yourself." She made the same cupped gesture. "Couldn't we also say 'vah-vah-va voom?'"

"My, a little testy, aren't we?"

"Actually, Mister Art Expert, Rubens painted many beautiful things. But who would know? Mention Rubens, everybody just thinks big, fat boobs. All the painters in history, this would be the one I get involved with." But she was laughing now, and gaily, taking Hugh's hand, she tugged him with her into the middle of the courtyard. "Maybe that's why I like this place so. It's the one place in the whole damn museum where I don't have to put up with big tits. Everywhere else, every artist: big tits. But here in the Tiffany Court: a refuge for my small-breasted sisters."

"Hear, hear," Hugh said in a stage whisper, "down with big tits!"

"Yes, indeed," Nina cried out. "Look—my heroine." She pulled Hugh over, to stand before a statue entitled *Memory*. It was of white marble, a woman, sitting on a rock, looking into a mirror. Her toga fell down to expose one breast, but it was a most unmuseum-like breast: just a fine and dainty charm.

"Or up there!" Nina said, pointing above to Saint-Gaudens's *Diana*—a glorious sylph, the very antithesis of Rubens's voluptuousness, poised upon one nimble foot, pulling on a bow. "You know," Nina mused, "I like to believe that at least once upon a time, I looked very much like that—sans bow, of course."

Hugh looked down upon her, eyes of sensuality, but cut by the sweetest smile. "Yes, if once upon a time was just five years ago—yes." Nina squeezed his hand, and the fountain all but roared in her ears.

They walked on in silence until they arrived before another secluded bench. Hugh gestured to it. "Well, do you wanna talk to me?" he asked. "As your clergyman."

Nina collapsed onto the bench. "Oh sure—my clergyman. Officially, to my crowd, you're just another heathen."

"Well, all right. As *a* clergyman?"

She pondered that for a moment as he sat down next to her. But

Nina was, after all, desperate to talk to someone, and yes, Hugh was a clergyman, so maybe she could walk a fine line in the realm of patient-doctor privilege. She drew a breath. "Okay," she said, "he—my patient—thinks he's lived in the past. Buc— ...he's convinced that he lived back then with this woman he loves now—this woman who is not his wife."

"And no doubt you mean: this woman *other* than his wife."

"Precisely. And what really makes it unusual is that he's sure he can see the two of them in that Rubens painting. As the models. That's the truly eerie part."

"Can you tell me which Rubens?"

Nina only paused for a moment. "Why not? In for a penny, in for a pound. It's in gallery twenty-seven: *Venus and Adonis*."

"Venus?"

"Oh yes. Venus—the real deal. But, actually, Adonis is the looker. Yum, yum. Absolute hunk. Darling button eyes. But anyway, Venus—the one who might've been the model for Venus in 1635, who's the modern-day girlfriend—she comes in to see me tomorrow."

"You've never met her?"

"No. I'm nervous as hell. Oh, Hugh, it's all so spooky—all so damn real. I really have this sense that if things develop in a certain way with her, why, it's almost as if that painting proves it. Proves reincarnation."

"Really now, Nina, let's not be—"

"No," she snapped, "you don't know. You can't imagine. And here I am in the middle, Hugh—as scared as I am fascinated."

"This then—it has something to do with the woman who followed you the other evening?"

Nina sighed. "Yeah, somehow. But I think I know who she is now."

"Then call the police."

"No, I'm trying to reach her myself."

Hugh stood up, unbelieving. He planted his foot on the bench and stared down at her. "Are you crazy, Nina? Are you plumb outta your mind?"

"No, not really. I'm pretty sure she's an old girlfriend of, uh, Adonis. And I have her number. I called her, but no answer."

"You really shouldn't have."

"Yeah. So, I wrote her a letter."

"Oh, that's great thinking, Nina. She gets the letter and goes after you with an AK-97 she brought mail-order from Alabama."

"Well, actually, I haven't gotten up the gumption to mail the letter yet." She patted her pocketbook. "But today—I'm determined to mail it before I go back to the office."

"Then, for God's sake, at least tell me her name. Just in case."

"All right, all right. Just because it's nice that you're worried about me."

"Of course I am. I—"

Impulsively, Nina reached up and draped her hands across the knee that rested there. Then, upon her hands she laid her chin, her eyes peering up at him. It was all so cute, these two old grown-ups acting like teenagers, that people were sneaking vicarious peeks at them—that fine line between nosiness and disgust. But Hugh and Nina didn't take notice, because the fountain all but sounded like Niagara now. To both of them. "The ironic thing is, Hugh, that all this talk I'm hearing about love through the ages—a man and a woman meant only for each other, forever—it only makes me understand how I know we're meant for each other, too."

That embarrassed him (much as he enjoyed hearing it). Besides, now he saw people ogling him. Gently then, Hugh removed her head from his knee, put his leg down, snatched up his jacket and retreated to the other side of the fountain, toward the Tiffany panels. Nina followed after him, playfully grabbing his forearm. "Oh come on, Hugh, don't be a silly goose. You know you love me, too."

"Of course," was all he replied.

"Then for God's sake, darling."

"Nina, for God's sake—and for ours—we went all through this years ago."

"Yes, we did. We went all through how cheap we both felt, because you had a wife and I had a husband—neither of which is the case now."

"Well, I'm sorry, Nina, but cheap is as cheap was."

Nina folded her arms. "You're right, Hugh. You don't need reincarnation in your life. You're still a seventeenth-century Puritan."

"Don't be a wiseass, Nina. It doesn't become you." He sighed, smiling wanly. "When I was in the seminary, I remember a lecture on the Ten Commandments. The old teacher told a rare joke. He said that after Moses came down the mountain and read out the tablets to the Israelites, he got a call to go back up the mountain. When he returned, Moses gathered all the people together again, and he said: 'Well now, I have some good news and some bad news. The good news is, God changed his mind and cut it down to The Seven Commandments.' And there were great cheers from all the Israelites. Then Moses went on: 'But the bad news is, God says adultery still counts.'" Hugh shrugged. "I'm sorry, Nina. Adultery still counts."

She frowned at him. But she didn't give an inch. "Okay, Jehovah," she said. "I have some good news and some bad news. The good news is that I love you. And the bad news is that I'm always going to love you, and so I'm not going to just fade away and let you wallow in your guilt with those stunning bitches you try to forget me with. So there."

Aghast, Hugh simply stared at Nina. So, she intently closed the last bit between them and kissed him full upon his lips, only pulling back in her own sweet time. Then, she took out the letter to Jocelyn, wrote out her name and address on another piece of paper, and slipped it into Hugh's jacket pocket, speaking as matter-of-factly to him, as if she was giving him a grocery list. "There," she said. "In case I'm found in the East River. Or disappear into another century. And don't forget now, go see *Venus and Adonis* in gallery twenty-seven before you leave the museum."

She started to walk away then, but stopped and turned back. "And Hugh, one more thing," Nina said. "Whenever you come to your senses, give me a call and tell me when you can drop over to my place, so we can have some drinks and a candlelight dinner and then make love all night."

He would have heard her open the glass door and go into the medieval section, except that the fountain was so incredibly loud.

·18·

Well, Nina had to admit to herself: Constance Rawlings truly was stunning.

But, as we know, nobody has it all. Nina immediately noticed that Constance was stylistically challenged—everything just a bit out of kilter. "How do you do, Mrs. Rawlings?"

"My pleasure, Doctor." There it was, to the naked ear. Nothing intrinsically wrong with saying "my pleasure." But somehow, just as Proctor Lee saw Constance ride a horse: not...quite...right.

And those clothes. A perfectly attractive light blue summer suit. Right for the season—but altogether too resort-y for New York. Besides, Constance wore it with a large black patent leather belt and matching black pumps. Once again: a smidgen off. But still: enough. If Nina's daughter, Lindsay, had shown up so attired, Nina would have thought: somehow...somehow I have failed as a mother.

Nina also found out, quickly enough, that Constance was reluctant to provide any cooperation. "Please be informed that I do not wish to offer myself up to your prying," is the stark way she phrased it.

Nina was caught short. Patients might have second thoughts when first they encountered her, but they were never hostile. "Then I'm sorry you bothered to come so far," Nina replied, coolly, closing the folder (for effect) on her desk, "for I'm unable to be of any help if you resist my...prying."

"It's nothing personal," Constance said, at her most impersonal.

"No, not to me." Nina paused. "But I'm sure Bucky will take it personally. As I explained on the phone, this was at his request."

That did seem to register with Constance, so to dramatize the point, Nina rose. "You need not take up any more of your time, Mrs. Rawlings. I respect your wishes."

Constance did not budge. Instead, she spoke deliberately. "Please sit back down, Doctor. Do not conclude that a failure to be enthusiastic must indicate a failure to be cooperative." If Nina did not sit back down, neither did she show any more displeasure. As much as she hated to admit it to herself, she didn't want to lose Constance. Instead, she only clasped her hands before her and said, "I understand you're a stock analyst." Constance nodded. "I appreciate that a dispassionate approach is crucial in that field, but here we must deal more with emotions."

"I can turn it on, Doctor. That's not the issue. It all just seems so unnecessary to me."

"How's that?"

"Oh really, it's perfectly obvious that Bucky and I are intended for each other." Constance even shook her head in some exasperation. Whereas Bucky accepted whatever fate had driven the two of them together, he took that with a certain amount of natural wonder and some healthy confusion. Constance, though, simply concluded it was the way things are. Life was *a), b), c),* or *d) none of the above.*

Nonetheless, as they began the session more formally, Constance promptly started to recite the story of that first meeting with Bucky with vivid recall. Then, moving on, her tale of their chance encounter of February 11th featured a recitation of detail that so perfectly jibed with Bucky's version that, for Nina, it might as well have been a part of the Baltimore Catechism. Constance only diverged in expressing pique that Bucky had required them to go through a "grace period" before taking up with each other. "But of course," she allowed, "what with Bucky's children in school and my own daughter preparing to go off to college, I would agree that it will play less havoc with their lives if Bucky and I strike out together during the summer school vacation."

That tied Nina's tongue. For all the emotion Constance displayed, she might as well have been discussing a dentist appointment or the twenty-thousand-mile check-up for the family car.

Finally, Nina found herself. "Now, that does beg the question—just a devil's-advocate-type-thing, you understand—that to make such a momentous decision, it might be best to get to know each other a little better before, uh—"

"Doctor, I appreciate that it may sound too unequivocal to someone in your profession, but you must understand that there is no gray area here. Bucky and I are simply intended to be together." She shifted in her seat, ever so slightly—a rare movement, that. "I've long been agnostic. I am, therefore, under no spiritual delusion that a god has sent Bucky to me. I'm sure it's just a matter of the laws of chance."

"Oh?"

"It's logical to conclude that every one of the billions of us on this planet has someone who is best suited for him or her. The ideal mate."

Nina strove to put some poetry into this formularization. "As the old love song goes: 'For every man, there is a woman, for every woman there...'"

"Absolutely. At least by some infinitesimal measure. It's just that what are the odds that, on all the earth, you would meet that one best love?" Then she folded her hands, alerting Nina to something new on the conversational horizon. "May I ask, Doctor, are you married?"

"No, not presently."

"Well, imagine. It is within the realm of possibility that the one man best suited for you is, in fact, only blocks away. Or, it is statistically just as likely that he is residing on the island of Negros, in the Philippines."

"So," said Nina, getting into the mathematical spirit of love eternal, "we all probably end up settling for second best."

"More likely: eighty-seven thousand, four hundred and sixty-third best," Constance declared. That passed as a joke for her, and she chuckled. "But, you see, Bucky and I are that rarest statistical anomaly—the one man meant for the one woman, who actually did meet each other. Alas, we just happened to come together after I was married to another man."

"A day late and a dollar short," Nina offered, but Constance was not interested in that sort of folk arithmetic. Nina went on. "So, obviously you have no fears about moving ahead to a life together with Bucky."

"None whatsoever. And, you know, Doctor, you may have noticed that Bucky and I are marked by somewhat different personalities."

"Yes, I think it's fair to say that no one would ever call you two peas in a pod."

"Precisely. Laymen might say: opposites attract. More obvious to me: we bond on deeper levels. Bucky and I are simply meant for one another. I expect it will be absolute perfection when we do have sexual intercourse—a flawless physical expression of an ideal union."

Well, that summed that up.

But at least Nina was given an opportunity to consider what tack to take next, because Constance inquired about the bathroom. Nina had concluded long ago that it was revealing of a patient how one addressed that subject. There were, she had decided, distinct differences between those who asked "to use the john" and those who inquired if they might "go to the bathroom." Likewise, there were differences between those females who called it "the little girl's room," "the ladies' room," or "the women's room"—the latter invariably being among the more ideological of feminists. Moreover, those of either gender who preferred the more euphemistic "restroom" were usually her most difficult subjects, those least likely to volunteer anything. (Nina had originally thought the recalcitrant Bucky must be a restroom type, until he abruptly asked if he could "pop into the can.") As for Constance, Nina decided right away that she would be the sort to use the word "lavatory." Because: that's exactly what it was.

And now, as Nina looked at her notes, she heard Constance say, "May I visit your lavatory?"

Nina could not resist replying, "Yes, the powder room is right there." That made her irritated at herself; Nina was afraid she was allowing her own personal considerations to block out her professional objectivity. It wasn't that she disliked Constance (although she probably, in fact, did), but it was just so damned disconcerting, trying to put her together with Bucky. A lavatory person with a can person. Moreover, Nina knew who Constance was replacing. Phyllis Buckingham was so attractive, so sympathetic and...well, so much like Bucky.

Constance returned then, sat back on the couch, taking the exact same proper position, crossing her long legs at the ankles. Nina began again, tentatively. "I imagine it's been difficult for you at home, since you made this decision about Bucky." Constance looked at her, a bit unsure, so Nina amplified. "I mean, has your husband noticed any change in your behavior?" (Nina caught herself before she added: "...the way Bucky's wife has.")

Constance only answered, "No," amplifying that response only when she realized that Nina expected a bit more. "As you can probably tell, Doctor, I'm not the sort of person who wears her heart on her sleeve. Carl is not particularly demonstrative either, and if he is suspicious, he certainly hasn't given me any reason to think so."

"I see," Nina said.

Then, out of the blue: "I've given him a lot of fellatio." Nina was taken aback by such a bald announcement, but Constance assumed her failure to respond promptly indicated some lack of understanding. "You know, in the vernacular: blow jobs."

"Yes, of course. Blow jobs."

"You're aware how much men like them—though I don't speak with any broad firsthand experience. I was a virgin when I met Carl, and he remains the only man I've ever had sexual intercourse with. But, that is what I understand."

"Yes," Nina said, retaining a strict noncommittal stance on the subject.

"I never particularly enjoyed providing fellatio for Carl. Didn't actively dislike it, you understand. But, just not my cup of tea. After I saw Bucky in February, though, I began to think often of him in that context. So I began giving Carl fellatio while fantasizing about Bucky. As you might imagine, Doctor, my husband has been very pleased with this arrangement."

"I see. And how is your daughter?"

"Elise."

"Yes, are you concerned that Elise'll be terribly affected when you leave her father?"

"Fortunately, it works out quite well."

"It *does*?"

"Yes, for this will happen exactly as Elise departs for college, to a new phase in her life. Happily, she's chosen to attend Oberlin, which is in Ohio, so that will place her almost midway between her father in Chicago, and me here in New York with Bucky."

Nina nodded. Well, that took care of the marriage and the family. Carl gets a year's worth of blow jobs, Elise a nice, centrally located college, so everybody should be happy and move on. Nina swallowed and took another approach. "Mrs. Rawlings, what's your family heritage?"

"You mean, ethnically, that sort of thing?" Nina nodded; she was wondering if there could be any Flemish connection, any Belgian past. "Not very exciting, I'm afraid. Quite mixed. No tribal customs handed down." She shifted her position, trading the right ankle on top of the left for the left on the right. "My maiden name was Bauer."

"German."

"Yes. Some people, in noting my reserve, have suggested that there is a Teutonic streak in me, but honestly, whatever German was originally in the family has long since been blurred. My mother was a McDonald. She used to joke: no relation to either the farm or the hamburger." Constance chuckled at this family humor, and Nina joined in.

"Mrs. Rawlings—"

"Oh, I wish you'd call me Constance. After all, it's our secret, but I won't be Mrs. Rawlings much longer, will I?"

Nina shook her head, sort of. "Well...Constance, do you have any particular outside interests—hobbies, clubs, anything like that?"

Immediately, she brightened. That alerted Nina. Heretofore, the most incredible thing about Constance had been her utterly even nature. Nina had thought: I have met the human level playing field. But now, Constance perked up with genuine delight. "Show jumping. It's my passion. After Bucky, of course."

Nina threw herself forward in her chair, so happy was she to see a spark fly off Constance. "Why...why do you love it so?"

"Oh, Doctor, there is, at once, such a great peace to it, but such a great thrill. Everything we do in the show ring is so even, so fair— the same route, same fences, same challenge, same judge. And yet, there is this wonderful sense of being in command that comes from handling your animal." She paused, smiling in reverie. "But I must completely depend on my horse. So you see, my power is only part of the equation. There is such a glorious balance to it all."

Nina nodded, posed a few more perfunctory questions that went nowhere, and then stood up, asking Constance if she would agree to return tomorrow.

"If you wish."

"You understand: I'm giving you another opportunity to duck out."

Constance's bosom heaved impatiently. "I would have thought by now that you would have learned that I finish what I start."

Nina indicated that she understood, but: "I wanna try something new—hypnosis."

"Oh, I see where you're going, Doctor. Plumb the subconscious to find why the woman is so desperately in love with Bucky."

"Something like that."

"Well, be my guest."

"Have you ever been hypnotized before?"

"Yes, once. My husband and I were in Miami Beach at a medical convention. There was a hypnotist in the hotel nightclub, and much to Carl's surprise, I volunteered. As it turned out, I was an absolutely perfect subject."

"Really?"

"Oh yes. But then, I understand hypnosis. I know it's not hocus-pocus, but basically quite straightforward. The hypnotist had a field day with me." Constance laughed heartily at the memory. "Yes, he even had me going around to the others on the stage, taking their belly buttons." She held out her hands. "I was carrying them all over. Not actually, of course."

"Yes, I understand," Nina said. "You'll obviously be a terrific subject for hypnosis. And one other question. The Metropolitan is just a few blocks up from here, and—"

"I'm sorry. The Metropolitan what?"

"The Metropolitan Museum of Art."

"Oh, I see. I'm afraid I've never been there. Art can be decorative enough, but it's just altogether too subtle for me."

"Well, that's all right," Nina assured her—which was true enough, inasmuch as she was pretty much making this up as she went along. "You see, I like to take some subjects up to the museum, use certain paintings as a sort of Rorschach test. Perhaps we could take a stroll up there during one of our sessions."

"Fascinating," Constance said. "That sounds like such an original approach."

Nina had saved a couple of hours in the middle of the next day for Constance, but when it came out that she was an early riser, Nina suggested they meet first thing, and they agreed on seven-thirty. Constance paused at the door. "Will you be talking to Bucky?" she asked.

"Before tomorrow?" Constance nodded. "No. Why?"

"Oh, I know I have no reason to hope for it, but I had let myself dream that you might tell him to come see me. I'm just down at the Sherry-Netherland." Suddenly, she showed Nina a little-girl smile. "Between you and me and the lamp-post, I hoped he might spend the night with me."

"I'm sorry, but I really think it really would be better to finish up our work here before—"

"Of course, Doctor, that's most unlike me—getting ahead of myself."

"I understand," said Nina. "And I do thank you for coming."

"My pleasure," said Constance.

·19·

Nina prepared meticulously for the next morning. She was going to go to bed early and rise early, ready herself for Constance, to be at her very best in trying to take this woman of the millennium back into time, back to Antwerp in the year 1635.

The day's meeting had made Nina even more anxious, too, because she had learned that if ever there was a perfect subject, it surely must be Constance Rawlings. It was not only that she was so enthusiastic about undergoing hypnosis and professed to be so malleable a candidate. More than that, Constance was a veritable *tabula rasa* when it came to the pertinent matters at hand. While Nina had made sure not to influence her by mentioning reincarnation, Constance had herself volunteered that she was not only without religion, but held no belief in the spirit world. For Constance, there was no soul, no future life, no past life. Our existence was only and all a circumscribed show ring.

Moreover, she possessed only the most limited knowledge of art or history, and she had no hidden family memories that could account for any possible lingering heritage. Instead, Constance was, by her own definition, an altogether literal person, lacking any vivid imagination. She could not recall the last novel she had read. She rarely went to the movies, never to the theater, and watched little "fanciful" (her word) television. It was impossible to believe that Constance Rawlings could make anything up out of whole cloth, nor that anything but facts and reality lurked in her mind. She was simply ideal.

At the same time Nina was contemplating her meeting the next morning with Constance downtown, at Jocelyn Ridenhour's third-floor walk-up, the buzzer rang. Expecting no one, she went to the intercom and asked who was there. "Well, my heavens," she said, "a blast from the past."

Jocelyn buzzed him in, waiting at the open door, accepting a fond kiss on the cheek as he moved inside. "To what do I owe this unexpected honor?" she asked.

But Hugh Venable only responded gruffly, hands on his hips. "I'm not here to play games, Joc," he said. "What in God's name are you doing to Nina Winston?"

Jocelyn sashayed past him. "Ah, I should have known," she said. "The love of your life." Frowning, he followed her into the kitchen, where, automatically she poured two cups of coffee. Jocelyn Ridenhour always had on a pot of coffee; she had been a personal Starbucks long before coffee was invented in Seattle, Washington. "Tanzanian," she explained, "from the highlands of Kilimanjaro."

"The subject isn't coffee, Joc," he said, sitting on the counter. "Go on, tell me what the hell you're up to, following Nina all over Manhattan."

"No, first you tell me. How do you know about me?"

"Dumb luck. You're going to get a letter from Nina. God knows why, but she wants to meet you—and I made her give me the name of the nutty woman. And lo and behold..." He waved to her.

Jocelyn blew on her Tanzanian. "I'm afraid you don't know the half of it, Hugh. I also broke into her office—twice."

"Broke in? Are you out of your mind?"

Jocelyn shrugged. "So, how did she know it was me?"

"I don't know."

"Honestly?"

"Honestly. And Nina doesn't know I know you, either. So, okay, now can we start at the beginning?"

Jocelyn mulled that request, then hoisted herself up on the bend of the counter, so that she sat catty-cornered from him. "All right, I believe in reincarnation."

"I certainly know that. God knows, we discussed the matter enough."

"Yeah, but how long's that been since we were going out? Three, four years? I was a novice then, Hugh. Absolute naïf. But I've really studied reincarnation since then, and I've come across the most incredible teachers. Their name is Mironov—Sergei and Ludmilla. He's an Orthodox priest in Russia, she's his wife. They live in a little town somewhere up near St. Petersburg."

"How'd you find them?"

Jocelyn shrugged. "The Internet, of course."

"Ahh: www-dot-reincarnation-dot-org."

"Don't be a wiseass, Hugh. That's especially unbecoming of someone whose life's work is faith." He dropped his head in apology. "Of course, I know: reincarnation in the West is more philosophy than religion—exactly the opposite of the way it is in the East." She sighed. "But when Sergei was denied the right to preach during the Communist years, he and Ludmilla spent much of their time studying. They came to believe, Hugh, that the soul is reincarnated in other bodies. And is this really so much to accept? Think of how complicated the process is to build a baby. Well, if a baby can be born with a brain and eyes—and all the rest—why can't a soul be put in there, too? Sergei and Ludmilla believe all this, you understand, as devout Christians. They're not kooks. They follow Jesus' teachings no less than you do."

"And you, Joc?"

"Well, you'll be pleased to learn, Hugh, that the Mironovs have really brought me back into the fold. And my beliefs may not be all that unconventional. Sergei has found a lot of research indicating that some of the early Christian prophets espoused reincarnation, but that any references to that were simply expunged from what became the one true Bible. And the big Jewish honchos were delighted to second the motion."

Hugh started to interrupt, but Jocelyn plowed on. "I know. I know. That's old hat. But trust me: Sergei and Ludmilla have taken things much further. Wait here."

She jumped off the counter, returning with pictures of the

Mironovs that showed a rather ordinary looking Russian couple—he bearded, she babushka-ed. Jocelyn also held up a ream of papers, which, at a glance, all seemed to have been written in Russian. "This is the heart of their work."

"You can read Cyrillic now?"

She shook her head. "But I've had it read to me. And now I'm ready to arrange for a full translation—and publication!" Her face beamed. But then, Jocelyn had always been such a grand romantic that sometimes it could even leave her vulnerable. "This is so important, Hugh—so beautiful!" And now, brimming with ardor, she stood even closer, looking down on him, where he sat on the Formica. In her enthusiasm, Jocelyn could be quite intimidating. Rather formally, then, she asked, "What is the most we humans can aspire to, Hugh?"

Confused, unprepared, he wondered at first if it wasn't some kind of trick question. But that wasn't Jocelyn's style, so finally, he ventured the obvious. "Love," he declared.

"Of course," said Jocelyn. But Hugh wasn't off the hook yet. "So, what is the greatest love?" As he paused to respond, Jocelyn barged ahead. "Love your neighbor, of course, is wonderful," she told him. "And love God. No argument. But also, both your neighbor and God can be awfully abstract, can't they?"

"Well..."

"You know they can. You know that, as a human being, the greatest expression, the fullness of spirit, can only be achieved by loving one other person. And likewise attaining the love of that one other. That's the hardest, Hugh."

She slammed the Mironov papers with the back of her hand, indicating where this judgment came from. Hugh didn't dispute her, only said, "Go on. I'm listening. I always listen to you, Joc."

"Even when you think I'm full of shit."

"Even when I think you're full of shit."

"Do you now?"

"Go on."

"We simply cannot achieve completeness as a human being without participating in the totality of a living relationship. A woman"—she touched her chest—"with a man." She touched his. "One male with one female. No abstraction. No: I love God. Or: I love my neighbor. Why, I even love my bad neighbors in Serbia who rape and murder at will. No, no, to fulfill your life as a person on Earth, you must find that one other person. Sergei and Ludmilla, for example, know they've achieved the ultimate, but it looks like I'll have to come back, because I've never found that one man that I can form a whole loving life with."

"This information is not going to go down easy with the Pope," Hugh observed.

"Hey, didn't I tell you about not being a wiseass?" But this time Jocelyn laughed easily as she poured the rest of the coffee into his cup. "I'll make another pot," she assured him. "I have some wonderful Jamaica Blue Mountain."

"No, this'll be enough," Hugh answered. "But, you know, I would love to sit in an actual chair."

"Well, why didn't you say so?" Jocelyn exclaimed, and she led him into the living room—parlor? Jocelyn had decorated each room in her apartment in a different fashion. This one was Victorian, filled with bric-a-brac and doilies; her studio was art deco; her bedroom Scandinavian modern; her bathroom done up like a ladies room at a 1940s-style supper club (you had to see it). Now, as soon as they had plunked themselves down together on the old-fashioned divan, Jocelyn went on again. "One of the first things that Sergei discovered is that there are certain couples who find each other in one life, who are absolutely made for one another, but who are then pulled apart."

"Why?"

"Oh come on, Hugh, is there no poetry left in your soul? For all the same reasons that troubadours have always had jobs. Death. Ironic circumstance. The wrong class in a class society. The wrong religion. One or the other already married to someone else. Whatever. So, Sergei—no, actually this was Ludmilla—came up with a name for these lovers." She flipped through the papers till she found the right Cyrillic words. "Double Ones."

"Double Ones?"

"Yeah, I like that." She grinned smugly. "In fact, the last time I broke into Nina's office, I left her a note, and I signed it like that—but in Cyrillic: Double Ones."

Hugh only shook his head, more in amazement than disapproval. "Jocelyn, you do know that the police put people in jail for that sort of thing?"

"Of course I know, sweet-pea," she said matter of factly, "but then, I've never been obsessed before."

In her apartment, Nina went over the final elements of her strategy for trying to take Constance back in time. She wrote down a few key words that she might employ to trigger her regressive memory. Nina hoped that Constance could resurface in the past without any prodding, because she recognized that the more "hints" she gave her, the more that critics might argue that Nina had simply led Constance on.

So, she decided, that if she had to suggest something, first it would be a fairly neutral item. She settled on the Schelde River, by which Antwerp lay. "Does the Schelde River mean anything?" Then Antwerp itself. Then peacocks and greyhounds—because Rubens kept many of both on his estate. If Constance's memory still was not jogged, then would Nina get more specific. She decided, at that point, that she would mention the name of Helena, Rubens's wife. Then, if necessary: 1635, the year.

Nina wrote all this down, in descending order. If none of these various clues bore fruit, only then would she play her last card. Only then, finally, would she utter to Constance this one last word: Ollie.

Hugh patted Jocelyn's leg with understanding, almost avuncularly. "Okay, I get the picture, Joc, but help me some more with these Double Ones."

"Well, Sergei suspects that if Double Ones somehow manage to encounter each other, their souls can connect. The way he expresses it is that a soul is like a wireless message or maybe now—to bring the technology up-to-date—a byte in cyberspace. They're searching for bodies to inhabit, so—who knows?—maybe that special love from one of the Double Ones signals the soul of the other. Sergei doesn't pretend to know the spirit world, Hugh. He's not some kind of mystic. He's just...wise."

"Okay, so what's this got to do with Nina?"

"Bucky," was all Jocelyn said.

"I'm sorry. Bucky?"

"You really don't know anything, do you?"

Hugh shook his head. "That's what I told you."

"Well, Bucky appears to be the quintessential Double One, who, by chance, dropped into my lap." Jocelyn chuckled. "Bad imagery. The first time he dropped into my lap. The second time into my faith." Jocelyn pulled her long legs up onto the divan, gripped them with both arms, and lay her chin on her knees. She began to talk. She started by explaining who Bucky was, how they met. "It was really quite wonderful, Hugh. I made him feel mature. He made me feel immature." She paused, grinning at the memory. "Once he did tell me about his total fixation with another woman. That hurt me, but it was spooky enough that I understood how he *had* to tell someone." And thereupon, Jocelyn related all that Bucky had told her about Constance, when they had chanced upon each other in Philadelphia.

"Double Ones," Hugh piped up—but this time without any flippancy.

"Clearly. Only, of course, I didn't know anything about Double Ones then. And anyway, Bucky and I were winding down. He'd met a younger woman, and he'd marry her, so we lost track of each other."

"How long are we talking about?"

"Oh, a long time, Hugh. Maybe fifteen years. Then one night we ran into each other again, so we had a couple of lunches—strictly innocent. But, at some point in there I mentioned my interest in reincarnation. I promise you, I wasn't proselytizing." Jocelyn pursed her lips. "No reference to Double Ones, to how deeply I believed. Just mentioned it in passing. It was like I'd told him I'd joined a bowling league." Hugh nodded, taking it all in—quite fascinated, really. "But it obviously all registered with Bucky, and one evening a few months ago—I can tell you exactly: March the twelfth—he called me in an absolute panic and said he had to see me." That, as Jocelyn explained, was the day that Bucky had first happened upon *Venus and Adonis*.

"I went back up to the Metropolitan with him the next day, and it was positively frightening. He was breathing hard, shaking—literally. I mean, he held onto me for dear life. And, Hugh, I knew this guy. He'd been like a lover *and* a son to me—if that doesn't sound too inappropriate—and I'd never seen anything like this from him. Scratch that: I'd never seen anything like this from anybody."

"So, you mentioned Double Ones to him."

"Oh no. Never. I realized right away that Bucky could be the key to unearthing secrets. I wanted to keep him pure and untainted. Like, that's why, when he asked if I knew a psychiatrist who could hypnotize him, I didn't recommend somebody I knew who believed in reincarnation."

"Ah, so that's where Nina enters the picture."

Jocelyn leaned over and patted Hugh's arm. "You have no idea how regularly her name would just *happen* to come up." Hugh ducked his head, embarrassed. Jocelyn went on. "Enough about my broken heart. Back to Topic A. And here's a coincidence." She leaned forward again, picking the Russian papers off the table. "Sergei and Ludmilla have compiled a list of well-known people in history who are almost surely Double Ones."

"Like who?"

"Like don't be nosy. Like I'm saving that for the book. Who the hell ever heard of Sergei and Ludmilla, up there in darkest Russia? Or some guy named Bucky? But a bunch of big names will get people into the tent. And nowhere in history are there more obvious Double Ones than Peter Paul Rubens himself and his second wife, Helena. Classic Double Ones. Rubens was, essentially, painting pictures of her years before she actually entered his life. She was only sixteen when he married her, and he was almost your age."

"This is love? Some rich old goat and a baby-fat blondie?"

"Your sarcasm is getting the better of you again. And, Hugh, I can't speak for Peter Paul Rubens, but I'll tell you this. When I stood in that Rubens gallery with Bucky and he said he was looking at himself in a painting and he can feel Constance up there too—sense her, sense them both as Venus and Adonis—well, I mean, I knew, Hugh. I *knew*. It was eerie."

Eerie. That was the same word Nina had used. Hugh couldn't escape it. Whatever it was, whatever had happened. He knew these two grown-up, intelligent women well, and he knew what different sorts they were, but they both had been profoundly affected in the same manner by this one man, this Bucky, and his bizarre experience.

But Jocelyn wasn't finished. "There's more, Hugh. I couldn't wait to get home to contact Sergei and Ludmilla,"

"More?"

"Sergei's convinced that it's almost surely a couple hundred years before a soul returns to earth. It's no shuttle flight, back-and-forth kinda thing. And now: photographs." She said that portentously, pointing to her old family portraits on the table.

"Photographs, what?"

"Well, very soon now—okay, maybe a century or so from now—the people who return to earth are going to start seeing their former selves in photographs. Obviously, it isn't going to happen to everybody, but never before have we had our images captured so perfectly—and so widely. And seeing something as intimate as your own face—or that of a person you knew well—that's bound to register. And bound to confuse. You pick up a book, and there in some innocuous crowd scene, is a person who strikes you, who fazes you. Or you're watching some historical documentary on television, or—"

"—you walk into a museum, and—"

"Exactly! You're catching on, Hugh. Bucky and his ladylove have, in effect, prefigured the photographic recognition of past existence. Compared to the number of people who've been photographed, there's only been a handful of portrait models through the pre-photography centuries. And Bucky was one."

Jocelyn was really excited now. She was flailing her arms. It reminded him of one other occasion when she got so carried away about something that he jammed one of her hats on her head—in order, he told her, to tamp down her brains, as you would a fire. But

Hugh sat tight now; he just watched her jump and stomp about. The enthusiasm—the faith!—was extraordinary to observe in action.

"Oh, it's hugely important, Hugh. Bucky seeing himself! And Bucky seeing his old love, too. They're Double Ones, Hugh!" For happy emphasis, she slapped his foot, which lay across his knee, jiggling there. "Don't you see? These two could independently verify each other's memories from the past. We've never had anything like that before. And they can actually see themselves. Exactly as they were. Rubens was not only a genius. His work was the most exact, the most lifelike."

"Better than Kodak," Hugh said.

"Yes! And get this: Bucky just saw her again. Constance—his Double One from Philadelphia! Absolutely, by chance, after twenty years, they run into each other on a plane." Jocelyn leaned down and took Hugh by the shoulders. "Don't you see? We've got to get hold of her, bring her here, hypnotize her, too—then show her *Venus and Adonis*." Jocelyn let go of his shoulders, but raised her hands to the heavens, beaming. "Suppose, just suppose, she recalls everything Bucky does? Suppose she reacts the same way when she sees the painting? It's proof, Hugh, proof."

"Well..." He was only being politely dubious, but Jocelyn sneered at him anyhow, the way all true believers treat the recalcitrant. Anyway, Hugh was content merely to be evasive. He remembered now how Nina had told him that Constance was coming to New York, and he didn't want to reveal any of that intelligence.

No matter. Suddenly, Jocelyn dashed across the room, calling for him to follow. He did. Into her studio, past an easel that sat there empty, to a CD console. A tape was sticking part way out. "Listen," Jocelyn ordered.

"What is this?"

"It's the tape I stole from Nina's office."

Hugh reached down, grabbing for it. "Jocelyn, you can't!"

But too late. Just then, the voice keened: "...*owwwllllleeeeeee...*"

He recoiled, the same shocking reaction as Nina, and as Jocelyn, when first they heard it. "My God!" he cried out, the sound scraping his heart. "Who?"

"That's Bucky." Jocelyn flipped off the tape. "Or anyway, that's the voice Bucky had in 1635. I'm sure."

Reflexively, Hugh still covered his ears, as if he were protecting himself from the possibility that that horrific sound could sneak back and assault again. Finally, lowering his hands, he asked, "What's he saying?"

"I don't know. Just a wail. Maybe it's a name. I'm not sure. And Bucky doesn't even know he did that. And Dr. Winston won't help."

"Hey, come on, Joc—what do you expect? You stalk her, you break into her office."

"She's written me that letter, hasn't she?" Jocelyn had trumped him, and he frowned. "You don't have to protect her, Hugh."

He reached down then, and took Jocelyn's hand, wending his way out, through the parlor, only stopping at the door. "Please," he said, "just promise me you'll call me before you try anything else with Nina."

Jocelyn patted the hand that held her left hand with her right. "Oh, I'm jealous, Hugh. Here I am, telling you about stuff that can change the world—about life itself—and all you're worried about is...her."

Well, he couldn't disagree. "You pegged me from the first, Joc. I loved Nina the second I laid eyes on her." But quickly then, he let go of her and dashed away, turning back only to wag a finger. "And don't you say it."

But Jocelyn merely grinned, and she certainly did say it. "Double Ones," she cooed devilishly, but without a doubt in her mind.

·20·

How fresh Nina was! How invigorated merely by anticipation. Why, she had come wide awake at five-thirty, but relaxed, rarin' to go. She was waiting in her office, prepared for Constance, even though she arrived a few minutes early herself. "I told you, Doctor, I'm an early riser," she exclaimed.

Nina tried not to dwell on Constance's outfit—plain gray slacks, with open-toed, white shoes, a bright appliquéd beaded blouse and large turquoise earrings. Rather, they exchanged compliments on how stylish they both looked. Nina was herself in a simple tan suit, with a buttoned blue blouse. With air conditioning, she was usually quite comfortable in that, but the excitement heated her up, so she slipped off her jacket, taking the seat opposite Constance—the lights off, the one candle burning between them.

And Constance was absolutely right about herself. If Bucky had been an easy subject for hypnosis, Constance was the model. "Relax," cooed Nina, "relax all your muscles. Feel that relaxation moving down your body. Your neck is sooo relaxed, and now your shoulders, your arms..." It seemed to Nina that Constance was already gone, but she played out the litany: "...your wrist, your hands, your fingers, all so relaxed. You feel so pleasant, so relaxed—you're going into a sleep. Oh, what a fine, natural sleep. Deeper and deeper..."

Constance's breathing was slower, almost regulated—the classic give-away that she had fallen into a trance. To be certain, Nina asked her to raise her right arm. It drifted up, and Nina took it. A floppy nothing. Then, she sought to induce what is called limb catalepsy—wherein the hypnotist suggests that the arm is rigid and will not move without permission. "Your arm is growing stiff, hard—completely firm," Nina said, and instantly, she could feel Constance's arm tighten. "Why, your arm is locked so tight you can't even move it, can you?"

Constance shook her head, but her empty eyes gazed straight ahead. "Fine, fine," whispered Nina softly. "Now, I'm going to count down, and when I reach 'one,' then you'll be able to relax your arm, and you'll drop it into your lap, and there it will join the rest of your body in this deep, wonderful sleep.... Three... two... one." The arm promptly came down, even as the rest of Constance collapsed into Nina's authority. "You are so light. You are drifting back... back..."

Immediately, Nina returned Constance to when she first met Carl Rawlings, and immediately Constance came with her. It was all so easy. Yes, there they were at the Smith-Amherst mixer, and he approaches her, and she finds him cute, and they dance and talk. She even likes him enough to permit him a serious goodnight kiss. Carl is an ambitious young man, already intent on becoming a doctor. She admires that. She allows him to deflower her the Saturday night after the big Amherst-Williams football game. "Deflower" is the actual word Constance uses.

On rolls Constance's tale of romance. By the end of her sophomore year, she and Carl have decided to get married. It's all so pat, especially inasmuch as Constance talks about it clinically. Nina, in fact, is getting bored. She decides to jump ahead to Bucky. "So, now you've married Carl, you're working at the advertising agency in Philadelphia, and one day in September—"

Nina doesn't even get a chance to go on. Constance breaks into a smile. She starts to glow. She comes utterly alive. Constance barely changed her tone when Carl deflowered her. Now, Bucky merely steps into her office and she tingles. Constance is atwitter.

"I hear this voice. I don't recognize it, but it is so perfect. The voice. I'm sitting at my desk, listening." Constance perks up; she is almost like some animal, cocking its ears. "I have on a white summer dress, with little violets all over it, and now I'm shaking. I don't know why. It's just this new voice. But there is something in it—the way the words come, the tone. I don't know why. But I'm enthralled. And I'm nervous. I'm thinking: I better go to the lavatory. I start to get up, but here he comes to the door."

Nina leans forward. Hypnotic subjects can respond in one of two distinct ways. Either they observe themselves in action, out of their own skin, so to speak, or they more or less perform as actors. Constance would do both. She would start to act out a scene. When she met Carl at the dance, for example, she actually held out her hand to Nina, shook it, and said, "Hi Carl, I'm Constance Bauer."

Now though, she has shifted to the other posture, watching herself from a distance—almost as if it's a home movie in her mind's eye. She sees another man introduce her to Bucky. She sees herself catch her breath. But suddenly, then, she places a hand across her breast and speaks to Nina—well, parenthetically. "You're not going to believe this, but my nipples have gone hard. Just from meeting this strange man. I'm so embarrassed. Thank God nobody can tell. But I'm so confused. I'm actually thinking about making love to him—right here, right now, right in my office. I don't know what's happening to me." But even as she puzzles, she is beaming. And then, before Nina can ask anything else, Constance announces, in a very distinct voice, "It's all silver."

Nina is excited. "Silver? What is silver?"

"*Every*thing is silver. Somehow, the whole world is silver."

But Nina has no chance to ask more, for Constance rolls on, talking about the absolute thrall she finds herself in every time Bucky is in her presence. And she can tell he feels the same. She *knows*. Somehow, she even knows that Bucky is seeing silver, too.

And now they're at Bookbinders, and she is on the verge of confessing her love. But she can't. She is waiting for him to speak first. After all, just suppose she had it wrong. Maybe she is so overpowered by Bucky that she only imagines that he must love her too. She is a married woman. She can't blurt out this incredible secret. Anyway, he will. Surely, he will.

But he doesn't.

And so the next day, he comes to her office and tells her that he's going to New York. And as soon as he leaves, she cries. And, before Nina now, Constance cries. It is fascinating. But, of course, it only confirms what Nina has already come to know, that Bucky and Constance have some powerful attraction for one another. Okay. But is there anything more?

So, Nina thinks, go girl. Let's see if we can hit the jackpot right here, now. She has rehearsed what she would say if they ever got to this point, so here goes: "Maybe you've loved someone like Bucky before." Constance shakes her head vigorously. "Maybe, Constance, maybe. We do forget things. Sit back again, Constance. Try to go back now. You are so light. You can go back further than you've ever imagined. I'm going to count backwards, and when I finish, maybe you will be somewhere else. Maybe you can find someone else you loved. Back then."

Constance obeys. She closes her eyes. She is so peaceful; numb even, in a way. "Five," says Nina. "Four, three, two, one—"

Nina barely gets the "one" out before Constance rears up in her seat, elbows out, knuckles pressed upon her waist, a sneer upon her face. She snaps, "So, what would it be, love?"

And in no more than that instant, just like that, Nina knows that Constance is no longer Constance. Furthermore, Nina is fairly certain that she is a man—her pose, her tone, her manner—and Nina also thinks she has heard an accent. It sounds British. Constance is apparently into some form of what the reincarnationists call xenoglossy—speaking a strange dialect. *So, what would it be, love?* Six words, and Nina is sure of this. And Nina is thrilled. And Nina is scared. She ventures, "We were talking about love."

Constance cocks her head. No, stop: Nina can't even think of her as Constance anymore. This is a man before her. The Man cocks his head. "Eh?" he says. "'Tis funny how you talk. Where be you from?"

Nina says, "America."

The Man appears altogether puzzled by that. "Pray, where would that be?"

The way he says that. It is not, Nina thinks, just British English. That is the accent, yes, but it is...where has she heard someone talk like this? Wait. Yes. Shakespeare. The Man sounds as if he is in some Shakespeare play. Is The Man Shakespearean? Maybe "America" wasn't yet commonly used then. Nina's mind is racing. Virginia! Surely, all the British were familiar with Virginia. She tells him, "Virginia. I'm from Virginia."

"Ah," says The Man. "I was myself thinking of making sail to Virginia."

"You were?" Nina has clicked. The Man leans closer, for they are both straining to pick up the nuances in their respective strange dialects.

"Aye. 'Twas only weeks ago, towards the last o' thirty-four."

"Sixteen thirty-four?"

The Man snorts. "Are you daft, love? Would you think: 1434? Eleven thirty-four? Would you have me Methuselah? What, but 1634, in the reign of our Charles?" The Man leans back in disgust, momentarily scratching his crotch before folding his arms akimbo. "Marry, I wouldn't be talking to such a fool were she not so pleasant a thing to gaze upon."

Hmm, Nina thinks, and she flirts back. "Surely, I'm too old to waste such flattery."

The Man sits forward again, a leer in his eye. Nina doesn't even see Constance anymore, doesn't even see her turquoise earrings framing that lecherous grin. He chuckles, "'Tis the best fucks, I've found, are often enough you older ones."

"Watch your tongue."

"Oh, you'd be a lady, too?"

"More a lady than you're accustomed to, I'll warrant." (*I'll warrant*, Nina thinks. Did I actually say, "I'll warrant?" Never in my life have I said "I'll warrant." But if trying to sound like Shakespeare helps...)

Suddenly, though, The Man sticks out his hand. "'Tis the ones pose as ladies are often the best fucks, too," he declares, and with that, The Man's hand is upon Nina's breast.

She is too shocked to respond right away. She just looks down at it—the hand, there. It is, after all, still Constance Rawlings's hand, even if it is The Man operating it. Nina remains frozen, staring. But the hand is not functioning like every other man's hand that she has allowed to intrude upon her breasts. No, this one is darting about, fingering her bra. It is, Nina decides, a very confused hand, altogether lacking the bravado its owner has otherwise evidenced so far. Anyway, enough; she grabs the hand and throws it back to its owner. "I'm not one of your strumpets," Nina snaps.

The Man is not discouraged, it seems. Only puzzled. He merely points now to Nina's chest. "Zounds, what have you within?"

Nina tries to fathom his meaning. Then, quite decorously now, The Man sticks his finger closer to her breasts—but this time, it is clear, in curiosity rather than lust. And now Nina understands. The (rattled) Man has never encountered a bra before. Men may act with women the same in 1635 as they do now, but in 1635 bras are still almost three centuries yet to come. So Nina offers a bit of a smile, even, helpfully, pulls her blouse over just a smidgen to reveal the edge of the undergarment. "It's called a brassiere," she says. "French."

The Man shakes his head, with a what-will-they-think-of-next expression. "The bloody frogs. Soon, I warrant, they'll wrap chains round your cunt."

Before she knows what she has done, Nina has reached out and slapped The Man square across his face. The turquoise earrings shake. Immediately, Nina is horrified. Would this bring Constance out of her trance? But there is no need to fret. The Man only holds his cheek and laughs. "A wild bitch you are for one calls herself a lady."

Nina, relieved, gets a little coquettish. "A lady accepts no familiarities if she doesn't even know the gentleman's name."

The Man howls at that. "A gentleman you would have me? Ah, 'tis Cecil Wainwright, my duchess, for ere I be a gentleman, you only be short a queen."

And, so saying, he bows to her from his seat.

"So, Cecil, is it?" (Nina pronounces it, as he did: Sess-ull.) "You were telling me how you almost set sail to Virginia."

"Yes, duchess, 'twas a bit of trouble suggested that." He stops abruptly.

"What manner of trouble?"

"'Tis my affair."

"Don't worry, Cecil. I'll tell no one."

"Aye, and were you to, 'twould be the last." Nina recoils a bit at that ominous charge. "For I would do no less to you as I did to her."

"Her?"

"The one brought on the trouble."

"Where?"

He pauses, but only for an instant. Cecil will talk to Nina. And he does: "In Norfolk, whence I hail from."

"What was her name?"

"Bess." And then a sigh. "'Twas a shame what came to pass betwixt us."

"Which was?"

"The lust we shared."

"Ah," said Nina. "Was Bess pretty?"

"Prettier'n you, duchess, and you're fairer'n most, e'en despite your years." Nina nods; well, it is, after all, a compliment. "There wasn't a man in all Norfolk wouldn't say Bess wasn't the loveliest in the county. But she wasn't to have anything to do with a mere farmer's son such as I."

"But Bess did?"

"God's wounds, she threw herself upon me."

"Women do that to you, don't they, Cecil?"

Oh, how he loves hearing that. "'Tis a bloody curse to be as fair as God fashioned me," he declares, unabashed.

"Your vanity is a match for your visage," Nina cracks back.

"I only mouth what the lasses lavish upon my ears." He holds out his hands in some form of supplication. "Pray be as honest as is your wont to be tart: in all of your Virginia, have you ever seen another man so advantaged by beauty?"

Nina smiles her agreement, sure that with Cecil, flattery can take her far. "So, 'twas that charm that Bess could not resist?" He nods, smugly. "Vowed she had to save herself for some noble husband, but she could not help but give herself unto me." He shrugs. "In truth, 'twas as easy as this hard." Cecil points to his crotch. What an insufferable, boorish ass, Nina thinks. But she must restrain herself and keep playing to his conceit. Besides she is almost sure what follows next, and yes: "Too soon then, Bess tells me she is with child."

"And you wouldn't marry such a pretty thing?"

Cecil shakes his head in disbelief. "Are you mad? I would take such a prize in a nonce and spend the rest of my life at leisure—for Bess's father is as grand a landowner as graces Norfolk. But he would have run me through had he but known I had run through his daughter, in my fashion."

"And so?"

"We met, where oft we did, in a quiet meadow by a little creek there that runs to the River Wensun. And there Bess told me of her plans to wed a certain gentleman's son of a neighboring estate—he now at home on leave as an officer in one of His Majesty's regiments."

"Did the officer know Bess was pregnant by you—by another?"

Cecil shakes his head. "No. 'Twas her scheme to accept the marriage, allow him to have his way with her, and then advise him 'twas he had put the bun in her oven."

"Such a scheme would allow you to escape the father's punishment," Nina said.

"Aye, but it enraged me, for I loved her."

"You loved Bess, truly?"

"Though I may have poked her, 'twas not without affection."

"And so?"

"And so we argued, and when she bid me farewell, I sought to claim my prize one more time, but she wouldn't allow me that liberty—for now she was savin' her precious self for His Majesty's lieutenant. And I became a fury, I did." Cecil lowered his head—although whether expressing remorse or affecting it, Nina could not be sure. "My rage o'ercame me. And before I knew what ere possessed me, I had killed the lass I loved."

The revelation comes, at last, so quickly. Nina holds her breath, in shock. Cecil raises his head, to stare at her. "I have told ye, now. God forgive me, I had to confess my awful sin to one other, but should ye breathe a word...." He shakes a menacing finger at Nina.

"I have pledged my confidence," Nina replies, solemnly—fearfully, too.

"I meant not to harm so much as a golden hair upon her head. I swear to you," Cecil says, looking at his hands.

"You strangled her?"

"Before I knew what I had done, she was lifeless in my grasp."

"What did you do then?"

"Gently—gently as we had embraced so many times upon that same greensward, I allowed her body to fall upon the ground, and I but stared at it—with as much love as regret."

"And then?"

"I carried poor Bess to the stream there, hit her noggin with a rock—for she could feel nothing now, angel that I had made her—and laid her down, so that when she was discovered, it would appear that she had tripped and fallen, hit her crown and drowned there. But oh..." All of a sudden, Cecil drops his head into his hands, holding it in despair. "But, ohhh my. The Lord knows how to punish the unjust, does he not?"

"What did the Lord do to you?"

"He made it, He did, so that in the clear water, Bess appeared to be looking straight up, into my cursed eyes. Oh, so content she looked—not unlike those very times when like that, she lay, after I had given her ecstasy. And my bane is that I can ne'er forget that sight o' her. God's wounds, I see Bess now in that stream better than I see you afore me. 'Twas my intent to turn her over, upon her face, as a body would, had it stumbled and fallen. But not so much as a moment longer could I stay. Not with Bess's face so lovely in my vision." He buries his head again.

"So, what did you do then?"

"Promptly, I took away for Londontown, and 'twas in a tavern there I heard tell of a ship bound for Virginia. So I came down here to Gravesend, thinking that if I could but sign on, I could find me a new life o'er the sea. Poor sinner though I may be, I know someone of your discernment recognizes a man full of Christian quality."

Uh oh, Nina thinks. The leopard is getting his spots back. Bess is dead; long live the new Bess—whatever wench hoves into Cecil's sight. Or, right now: me, Nina. But, she presses on. "So why didn't you go to Virginia?"

"The sailing was delayed. But I stayed here in Gravesend, and sure enough, t'other day, I learned of a passage to Amsterdam, thence to Genoa, and their need for able-bodied seaman. So I signed on, and we sail on the morrow." He leans forward now, all the remorse vanished, and most of the alleged Christian quality, too. "So, duchess, on what will be my last night upon English soil, for lo, how long, I could not chance upon more agreeable company than you, to drink some now, then to enjoy our flesh abed together."

Cecil even starts to reach out again to Nina, totally unrepentant, his predator eyes gazing upon her. She pushes his hand away. "But I've hardly met you, Cecil, and you've told me of such a horrible thing you've done."

Cecil grins. He has an answer for everything—at least with women. "No fear o' that. This very day, I became a new man. Cecil Wainwright, the farmer of Norfolk, is no more—and his past mischief is gone with him. In his stead, signed onto the ship, is a sailor from Sussex—I with a new name, as sure as Wainwright may be with the devil." He is so blithe, so used to his way, that he obviously expects Nina to forget that he's killed a woman simply because he's taken on an alias.

But now the blood is rising in Nina, her curiosity racing. Yes, yes, she thinks, I see what is coming. Quickly, then. "So, sir, pray, what be your new name?"

"Oliver Goode," he declares, sitting tall in his chair, grinning proudly—especially, Nina knows, at that perverse choice of last name.

But, of course, it is not the last name she cares about. It is the first. Oh, she is not at all surprised, not any more, and if she shivers some when she hears it, it is only mostly from her anticipation. It is amazing, really, how easy the words tumble off her lips, as Nina says, "I see, and may I call you Ollie?"

·21·

"Such familiarity suits me well," says the man Cecil, who is now Ollie, "although I would soon hope that intimacy not be ours in name only." He rolls his tongue round his teeth to enhance that salacious vision.

Nina shifts uneasily, sneaking a glance at her watch. It is only eight-twenty, with plenty of time left before her first regular appointment. She doesn't want to pull Constance out of her trance, but neither does she want to stay here in Gravesend, where Ollie seems intent only on seducing her. He is so much the—oh my, Nina almost thought "lady killer"—he is so much the ladies man, that Ollie is certain that any woman's demurral is only a coquettish delay. Has no girl ever turned him down? Nina must gain control here. Sweetly, she asks, "Will you grant me a favor?"

"What boon is that?" he replies, so graphically stroking his crotch, that Nina all but sees a bulge beneath Constance's slacks. Constantly, in fact, Nina finds that she must concentrate in order to keep seeing the appliquéd blouse and the breasts filling it to remember that this is a woman before her. This is Constance Rawlings of Chicago and the here and now—and not a randy man named Cecil Wainwright, a.k.a. Oliver Goode, from 1635.

"A game to play," she tells him.

"Would it be for only two?" he leers, fondling himself even more overtly. Nina nods. She even winks. "Sure, and I would play with you, duchess."

"Good. But you must do my bidding."

"I like a woman takes a hold of the pole herself."

"All right then, gaze upon this candle," Nina says, holding it up before Ollie's eyes. "And follow the light. We are moving together, Ollie. You and me. We are taking a trip."

"Together?" he murmurs, but vaguely now, his hands finally falling limp in his lap, his eyes shifting after the candle.

"Of course, together, just you and me. And when I finish counting, we'll be there: three... two... one." She lays the candle down. He sits up, looking around. "Do you see where we are, Ollie?"

Suddenly, he is agitated, fearful, his head twisting about. "God's wounds, I must take leave of here."

"Why?"

"You must know. That cur's son Burleigh has set all of Amsterdam after me."

"Why, Ollie?"

"'Twas not intended. If Burleigh's woman had just kept her tongue."

"Who is Burleigh?'

"The second mate. From the moment we board in Gravesend, he's on my arse." But now a twinkle, the Ollie that Nina first met. "Yet wouldn't you know, we but dock here, and I chance to meet this woman—the very one Burleigh pokes when ere he comes here— and she takes a likin' to me, and soon enough, we're under the sheets."

"And she—what's her name?'

"Caterina."

"Caterina was going to tell Burleigh?"

"Aye, she was. Informs me herself, never such a fuck she's had in all her life, but it wasn't her pleasure."

"To fuck you?" Nina asks.

"Aye."

"So, you had your way with her?"

"Let's not be babes, duchess. Sometimes the lasses will say they're not so inclined, even as you can all but see the smoke risin' from their cunt." He leans forward. "Marry, I've been thinkin,' you might be that breed o' cow yourself."

Nina is not for discussing the point. She only asks, "So what happened...with Caterina?"

"What could I do but silence the wench?" Ollie stares at his hands. Nina gets the picture. Cecil Wainwright, alias Oliver Goode, emanating from Constance Rawlings, is a murderous, brutal creature, all too quick to react with savage fury. Nina shivers. Ollie looks around, then cries to her, "I cannot keep here! Burleigh will have 'em searching everywhere for me."

"Where can you go?" Nina asks. "I'll join you there."

"Will you now?"

"'Course I will, Ollie."

He thinks. "Well, I'm told the Spanish Netherlands isn't far distant."

Nina has never heard of that—let alone knows where it might be. The Spanish Netherlands? Isn't Amsterdam in the one-and-only Netherlands? So, "Where would that be?"

"South o' here, only two-days ride. They called it Flanders 'fore the bloody Spanish papist bastards took it over."

"So, I'll meet you there," Nina sighs, adding that certain come-hither tone that he appreciates. Expects.

"Pray, look for me at the docks. I'll be after a ship to sign onto. Maybe Virginia this time." A wink. "Maybe us together."

"Maybe," Nina coos, holding the candle up again, asking him to focus, even as Ollie keeps turning his head this way and that—still wary that Burleigh must be closing in on him.

Finally now, he stares straight into the candle. "Where, Ollie?" Nina murmurs. "Where in the Spanish Netherlands will you find a ship?"

"Antwerp, duchess. Antwerp, I'm told, is the city I want."

Of course, but somehow Nina already knew that, didn't she? Wherever these Spanish Netherlands, she was positive that there would be Rubens's city, there would be Antwerp. At last, Ollie will be in Antwerp, and she—Nina—will be with him, because by now she is almost as hypnotized as he...well, as Constance is.

Yes, yes. But whoever Constance may be now, wherever, Ollie was the name Bucky screeched. And this Ollie is a cold-blooded killer. Two women murdered by his bare hands. Minimum. And, of course, now Nina can visualize it: Bucky down on his knees, screaming Ollie's name. Pleading. It must be. Yes, Bucky is pleading with Ollie. As his hands are poised about his neck. *Please don't strangle me. No please...*

And she could suddenly remember what Hugh had said, "It's documented that an inordinate number of people who claim to recall past life remember dying violently."

But the pleading does no good, and the fingers splay out, tighten. Just as with Bess, as with Caterina. Then: "...*owwll-llleeeeeee...*" And silence.

Dead silence.

But wait, Nina thinks. If Constance somehow was Ollie, a man, then of course, Bucky must have been... The vision is so clear that Nina throws one hand up over her eyes, and—

"What kept you, wench?" The voice. Ollie's.

That snaps her back. She puts her hands on her hips and glowers at him. "Oh, I'm a wench now, am I?"

Ollie roars. It is amazing. He is beside himself, smiling. Smiling? No, beaming. "Ah, whether you be a whore or a queen, I care not," he booms. "And you can keep those fine tits o' yours wrapped in that fancy French armor, for I've found me a far better pair, I have."

"Really?" Nina has never seen Ollie like this before.

He ducks his head, all but blushing. "I have met the woman I truly love."

"Was not Bess that?"

Ollie holds up a hand to shush her. "Pray, you are sworn to silence." Nina nods. "Besides, Bess was barely a woman. Margareta is all a woman. With your ken, duchess, but without your years."

Margareta. So—could she have been Bucky? Of course. If Constance had been this man, then Bucky must have... "How did you meet Margareta?" Nina asks.

Ollie smiles broadly again. "'Tis quite amazing. Upon my arrival here that other forenoon, e'en at this very spot where now we discourse, 'twas only my purpose to find a vessel and sail off. A carvel would be to my liking, but I would settle for a fair boyer—whatever, only to be gone. Then, what do I discover, but the bloody Dutch have blockaded the river up by the North Sea. Once, I am advised, this is a port would put Amsterdam in its shadow, but now there's only small barges can ply the river. A friend I have met asks that I journey with him down the coast to a place they call Dunkirk, where a fellow of my strength and disposition may well be taken onto one of the privateering ships there. This strikes me as a pretty game, but just then, unawares, someone approaches me."

"Margareta?"

Ollie scowls at Nina. "If it is my tale you seek, duchess, you hold your tongue. Pray no, 'tis a gentleman, most well attired, and though weak in the king's English, he identifies himself as an assistant in the studio of one Peter Paul Rubens."

Nina only nods. It is as if she knows what will transpire before Ollie reports it.

She inquires, "Did you know of this Rubens?"

Ollie shakes his head. "Upon my oath, I had no acquaintance with his acclaim. Indeed, at first, I hold some suspicion, for the gentleman who has approached me—Cornelis, by name—treads with light feet, and I have been bothered by those bugger boys before." Ollie slams his fist into his palm to indicate how he has handled that situation. "But I listened to him best I could, whereon he informed me that Rubens is at work upon a painting that includes a personage who might be a match for my own fine figure." Ollie flexes to underscore the point. "He then quotes me a most handsome sum, and I agree to consider his proposition."

"So you went with Cornelis to Rubens's house?"

Ollie snorts. "House? Such a house as his makes cottages of castles I have seen in England. It is upon The Meir, the grandest square in all of Antwerp, but among so many tall trees that when you find yourself within, you might as well be in the midst of any countryside. Why, peacocks wander the gardens no less than chickens or ducks of the better manor I have known. And I am advised that this house of his is of a style that would make a Genovese sailor feel as if he had ne'er e'en left home. Withal, once within, I am straightaway ushered to meet this Rubens. And instantly, I am put more at my ease, for it is obvious *he* is no honey boy, but a full man, no less than I. Why, e'en at so many years—and he must be fifty if he's a day—he has fathered three babes with a new wife. Moreover, he speaks as good an English as that which I have heard in any part o' Norfolk."

"What language do they speak here?" Nina asks.

"Zounds, you're in Antwerp, and you don't know?"

"But I've just arrived."

"Why it is *Vlaamach* they speak," Ollie says, pronouncing "Flemish" as the natives do, because he has never heard the word in English.

"Do you speak any *Vlaamach*?" Nina asks, trying her best to duplicate his pronunciation.

"A word here and there. 'Tis the same tongue as Amsterdam. Then he grins, delighted. And, almost boyishly, savoring the words, *"Mijn schoun Margareta."* Nina shrugs. Ollie sighs. "My beautiful Margareta."

"And does she love you too?"

"Ja, ja, ja!"

"And where did you meet your beautiful Margareta?"

"At Rubenshuis. Upon the top floor, in the master's private studio."

"Is Margareta in the same painting as you?"

Ollie chuckles. "No, no. Margareta is in another painting. You'll be hard put to guess who Mr. Rubens makes of her."

"Try my imagination."

Instead, Ollie teases her some. "More funny yet, I am in the painting with Rubens's wife. Her name is Helena." Ollie leans closer, in conspiracy. "The master is an old fart, and struggling mighty with the gout, but his Helena is younger e'en than I. And God's wounds, she poses naked as a babe. I've seen whores with more shame."

"Really? You've seen Mrs. Rubens naked?"

He leans back. "Well, not herself now. Mr. Rubens takes her up to that private studio of his upon the highest floor, and alone there, bids her unrobe, and then, what he calls, 'sketches' her. But then he takes the sketches and paints o'er top them—and 'tis there I've seen Helena as bare as the nose upon your face."

"So, you've never truly seen the lady herself without her clothes or decency?"

Ollie guffaws. "You would not say that were you, as I, to see a painting of her. Marry, Mr. Rubens can paint tits—and other divers parts of the body—to a finer aspect than God in his heaven ever made them. I would wager that I can see Helena better upon that canvas than Rubens does himself when he pokes her abed."

"So, Ollie, is he painting you naked, too?"

He laughs. "No. The master's put me in some manner of sheet. Bright orange it is, and wraps round me."

"Do you know the name of the painting?"

"To be sure. Helena and I are portraying Venus and Adonis—"

"Adonis?"

"Aye, I'd never heard tell of him, but the moment Mr. Rubens lays eyes upon me, he screams out to Cornelis in *Vlaamach*. When I ask the great gentleman to speak in my own tongue, he says, 'Why, Englishman, I have just exclaimed to Cornelis that he has found me my Adonis. Not only are you, in visage, the match for any man, but truly, I have not chanced upon such a figure as yours since I used a bald-headed brute named Adriaen in *The Ascent to the Cross*."

"Have you seen that painting?"

"No, 'tis in the cathedral with much of the master's work. But Margareta promises to take me there."

"But she has not yet?"

Ollie suddenly looks away. "I best reveal no more to the likes o' you."

"But you know I can keep a secret. Whatever you tell me will ne'er escape my lips." (*Ne'er*, thinks Nina; now I have actually said "ne'er.")

Anyway, he does accept her word, if grudgingly. "True enough, you do hold a confidence as well as—more's the pity—your modesty."

"Why, Ollie, how could I be immodest before you if you have given your heart to Margareta?"

He roars at that. "Hold still, duchess. Not yet am I married, and no man unwed—and precious few wed—must restrict himself to a

single piece. If it's yet your pleasure to taste a little of this treat"—
Ollie merely points to his crotch this time—"you need but follow me
toward Rubenshuis, thence round the corner, to Hopland to a
house there that the master also owns—where I reside alone in the
grandest circumstance."

"You have your own house?"

"Just so. For when I comprehended how taken Mr. Rubens was
by my aspect, I drove a hard bargain. I feigned but little interest in
his enterprise, maintaining that I would instead prefer to strike out
for Dunkirk, there to seek a ship of prey to sign onto. Whereupon,
he not only raised the original offer, but he volunteered to provide
me with lodging in this other house he owned—and to stock the
larder there, as well—for as long as my services were required to be
his Adonis."

"So you have privacy when Margareta joins you?"

"And 'tis a privacy sorely required, too, for my sweet must leave
a husband by her own hearth."

Nina is hardly scandalized by this revelation, but neither has she
had any reason to anticipate it. "Ah, so your Margareta is a married
woman?"

"She would hardly be the first of her fair sex to stray from her
nuptial vows," Ollie replies, smugly. "But make ye no mistake,
duchess, Margareta loves me so—as I her—that we would well share
our rapture on a bed o' nails were that our only trysting place." He
laughs heartily. "Nonetheless, such sumptuous accommodations I
do enjoy, that 'twas a whore named Elsa—she, a great favorite of the
master who also poses for him in his private studio—who granted
me her services free, only that she might lie betwixt such fine
sheets." He pauses. "But God as my witness, I have been done with
that cow since Margareta granted me her charms."

"And Margareta was posing when you met her?"

"She was. And when Mr. Rubens noticed how taken I was with
that sweet countenance, he bid her remain there in his private studio to divert me."

"In what fashion, pray?"

"Well, 'tis hard work posing."

"Oh come now, a big strong man such as you?"

Ollie shows some irritation at that. "I wager you'd not say such a thing if you knew how the master has me twisted about like a pennant round a maypole, holding some big staff with my left hand, while peering down."

"Why are you staring down?"

"Because, duchess, in the painting, Adonis is looking upon Venus, upon her very tits—but I have not that pleasure, for the master is sketching me alone. Me? I have nought to gaze upon, save the floor. Moreon, all the while, Mr. Rubens has one of his assistants read Latin to entertain *him*. 'Twas a chore that was showing on my brow."

"So Rubens had Margareta remain in the studio?"

"He did. He placed her at my feet, where my eyes would cast down upon her—and not upon the harsh red patterns of the floor, those that all but crossed my eyes."

"Well, that certainly made posing more agreeable."

"True. Yet it remains a most wearing position."

"Oh, it doesn't sound that uncomfortable," Nina says, egging him on. "Show me."

"Pshaw. A fie upon you, duchess. Enough that I must set myself so long in the studio, that now you ask me to do the same—only for your merriment."

Nina flirts a bit. "Oh, just for a moment, Ollie—so if ne'er we meet again, I can always remember you as Adonis."

Flattered, Ollie rises, and for the first time in several minutes, Nina is once more wrenched back to reality. Now again, it is a woman she sees standing before her, the earrings and lipstick, the female face and form. Once more it is Constance Rawlings.

But just as quickly, Nina sees Adonis return. Yes, there he is. It is Ollie who spreads his legs apart, feet slightly out, right foot forward. He is set. *Adonis* is set. Now he twists, holding his left arm high, uncomfortable, all the more so that he has no prop to grasp as his spear. Then, finally, he contorts himself more, setting his gaze down upon a Venus who would be there. He even cants his head exactly to stare at his love.

Nina gasps. As much as she was prepared for this pose, she must catch her breath. It is perfect. It is uncanny. It is exactly that impossible, twisted pose of Adonis in the painting—and such an unnatural, discomfited position, that no one could possibly make it up. No one. *Zounds, God's wounds,* Nina says to herself.

"Enough for your pleasure?" Ollie sneers after a few seconds—although really, he is enjoying his act. Ollie likes being Adonis. As what vain man wouldn't?

"All right, but tell me one thing?"

"Aye," he says, relaxing.

"If Margareta isn't Venus, then what painting is she in?"

"Mr. Rubens has almost finished it," Ollie replies. "He only brought her back to touch up some things."

"And that's when you met her?"

Ollie grins. "It's called *Holy Family with Saint Francis.* And my Margareta is"—he snickers a bit—"she is the Madonna. But methinks she is herself no virgin." That pleases him, both his humor and his memory of their love. So, to punctuate his joy, Ollie suddenly twists back into his pose again—although this time he changes the tilt of his head just enough to look smugly upon Nina.

Well, she thinks, staring back at him, what a wonderful irony that the other Adonis is really a woman, and the Madonna is a man.

·22·

After Constance left, Nina was essentially useless for the rest of the day. Oh, the patients came and went, and she responded to them, but almost unconsciously. Roseann said that Lindsay had called, but Nina forgot to call her back. All she could think about was Constance. Ollie.

Ollie was going to kill Margareta.

No, Nina. Nina, please. Ollie *has* killed Margareta. In 1635.

And there must be a rational explanation to all this.

She opened her desk drawer and stared at God touching Man, giving him life. For the first time, Nina thought: if He can give a new life, why can't He give life again and again? Isn't that, really, just a technicality of faith?

The phone rang. It was Bucky. "Have you seen Constance yet?" he whined, sounding like a little boy.

"I've been in touch with her," Nina replied, which was the truth, if not the whole truth and nothing but the truth, so help me God. "When I'm finished with my examination, I'll call you."

But how did she handle things with Constance from here? After she'd brought her out of hypnosis, Nina had only told her that, yes, she'd been a most revealing subject. And yes, she'd assured Constance, she had indeed confirmed her undying affection for Bucky. But Nina volunteered nothing of her regression, nothing of Cecil and Ollie, nothing of Rubens and 1635. She still was taking pains to make sure that she did not in any way influence their visit tomorrow to gallery twenty-seven. They would enter Rubens's room together,

Constance unaware, and then Constance would, like Bucky, see Ollie and Margareta. Maybe. Or maybe, like everyone else, she would only see the Madonna and Adonis. Anyway, Nina would watch her.

After their session, Constance herself had stepped out of Nina's office into the swelter of Fifth Avenue. Early as it was in the day, the heavy July air shimmered before her. She glanced down and there was Bess, lying in the stream where a sidewalk should be. This time, too, Constance remembered her name. She had always known it was Bess when she was a little girl, and now, suddenly, she knew it again. Perhaps she should mention this oddity to Dr. Winston tomorrow; probably everybody had inexplicable memories like this.

Downtown at Merrill Lynch, Constance spoke to the department chief about her transfer to the New York office. Delighted; *pro forma*. So, Constance went up to the top of the World Trade Center. The sky was blue but the air was dirty, and so looking northeast toward where Bucky resided with his (first) wife and children, Constance was unable to make out Connecticut.

So Constance went to Central Park and rented a horse. Only a half hour in this heat, said the stableman. Constance rode out, thinking of Bucky. It was excruciating to know that he was right here, now, in this very same city, and when she trotted, posting up on her horse, she began to imagine that she was making love, sitting astride Bucky. Up and down. It was very clear to her. Also, unbearable. She had to break her mount into a canter so that she would not post, would not think about making love to Bucky.

Nina was leaving the office just then. Never mind that it was the hottest part of the hottest day of the year. She needed to walk, to move. By the time she got to her apartment, she was sticky with perspiration. All over. Oh, but that felt good and primeval.

Hardly before she closed the door to her apartment behind her, she started stripping off her damp clothes. She only paused when she unhooked her bra. Nina held it up, visualizing Constance/Cecil/Ollie reaching out a hand, fingering it in curiosity. And she thought: if, say, you were a scam artist and if this were all some sort of incredible fraud, and Bucky and Constance—and Jocelyn Ridenhour, too—if all of them were in league, and they had made all this Venus-and-Adonis stuff up out of whole cloth, and somehow they could fake being hypnotized and somehow they could contrive this whole complicated scheme, still...still, nobody would ever think of touching a bra and then asking what it is. Nobody.

Only finally did she let the bra slip from her hands and step out from her panties and into the shower. She simply stood there letting the water run all over her, not even bothering about soap or shampoo, only standing under the spray, replacing a sticky wet with a wet wet, until—was that the phone?

She grabbed a towel, if only to stand on when she picked up the receiver. "Nina," said the voice—and now, suddenly, every drop of water that clung to her suddenly glistened and tingled.

"Oh Hugh," she chirped, "what a wonderful time to hear from you."

He didn't respond in kind. Instead, rather formally, he asked, "You free tonight?"

"Yes."

"Good. Could you come to my office at the Seminary at eight? Brown Tower—Broadway and 120th."

"Oh terrific. I need so much to talk—"

He cut her off. "There'll be someone else here, too."

"Someone else?"

"Jocelyn Ridenhour."

Only then did Nina realize that she was standing, dripping wet, the air conditioner blowing on her, as the erstwhile tingly glistening drops were now just so much drab cold water that made her shiver.

Jocelyn was already there when Nina arrived at Hugh's, an office as cluttered and idiosyncratic as hers was neat and specific. Maybe that made it slightly easier for Nina, that Jocelyn—seated in an old wing chair over to the side amongst a freestanding stack of books and some squash rackets—almost blended in, just another eccentric artifact midst the hodgepodge. But then Nina saw Jocelyn's face more clearly, and she recognized her familiar form as she rose tall to greet her—and that made Nina cringe a little.

Jocelyn, without ado, announced, "Dr. Winston, I'm here to apologize for my behavior." Nina neither said anything in response, nor did she deign to offer her hand. So, Jocelyn spoke again. "What I did was inexcusable."

"Yes," Nina said then, ice cold.

Hugh, who had remained standing, more or less as a buffer between the two women, now spoke, "I must tell you, Nina, that Jocelyn and I have known each other."

"Oh?"

"Several years ago," Hugh went on, emphasis on the *several*, "we had a brief, uh, thing." Emphasis on the *brief*.

The qualifications of time notwithstanding, that revelation infuriated Nina. Hugh had actually been screwing this crazy woman, who had chased her all over, broken into her office, and generally scared her out of her wits. Her anger was tinted with jealousy, embroidered by betrayal. She turned from Hugh to face Jocelyn. "I also understand you had a *thing* with Mr. Buckingham." Jocelyn nodded. "My, have you slept with every man I know?"

"Nina!" Hugh cried out.

But Jocelyn deflected the cheap shot into a glancing blow. She gently touched Hugh's arm. "It's all right, Hugh. And really, Doctor, I don't think two men makes a quorum in Manhattan." Then she sighed, with a wistful little smile. "Besides, despite all my wiles, I could never make Hugh forget you."

"Jocelyn!" Hugh gasped.

At least Hugh's embarrassment did make Nina feel a bit more kindly. Quickly, though, she put back on her unforgiving face, turning again to Jocelyn. "I believe you have some notes and a tape of mine, too."

Reaching into her purse, Jocelyn pulled out a manila envelope and handed it over. Nina glanced inside. "Did you make copies?"

"Of the tape yes, but I destroyed it." When Nina looked skeptical, Jocelyn added, "I swear to you."

"She did," Hugh added. "Jocelyn and I have talked a great deal about what she did. And why."

"Well?" Nina asked.

So Jocelyn began trying to explain herself. She started with her interest in reincarnation, moved onto her association with Bucky, their visit to gallery twenty-seven, and, most recently, to Jocelyn's frustration that Bucky would no longer respond to her. Nina sat down as she listened, crossing her legs in that fashion that only women can, that perfectly indicates impatience. Indeed, when Jocelyn finally concluded her whole long explanation *cum* apology, Nina only shook her head and sighed, "But to break into my office, to—"

Hugh stopped her abruptly. "Damn it, Nina, this isn't easy for Jocelyn. Haven't you ever in your life done something you knew was wrong, even as you did it because you cared so much?"

Nina turned sharply to Hugh. *You sonuvabitch,* she thought. *That isn't fair. You know goddamn good and well that making love to you isn't the same thing as breaking and entering.* But, softly and defensively—hurt—Nina only uttered "Yes," and let it pass.

Maybe Jocelyn understood. Anyway, she changed the subject. "I got your letter," she said. "Would you like to know about Double Ones?"

Nina shrugged. "Yeah, what is all that?"

So, Jocelyn explained. She even showed Nina photographs of Sergei and Ludmilla. And when she was finished, Nina had grown more curious than angry. "So," she said, "you think Bucky and Constance are these Double Ones?"

"Oh I'm convinced of it. Especially after I saw the way he acted in the Metropolitan." She paused. "Dr. Winston, do you believe in reincarnation?"

Nina glanced quickly over to Hugh. "I never have, no."

"But could you now?"

Nina considered her answer, and purposely, when she finally did respond, she looked more toward Hugh. "I don't know. Frankly, I don't know what to believe anymore." Hugh frowned. Nina went on. "You know, it's funny. We all agree it's likely that somewhere in the universe there's another planet with life on it, and we accept the possibility that some space ship can travel for light years—centuries—and appear here. But when I think about it, isn't that more fantastic than that God can send a soul back to the *same* place?"

It was a small concession, but Jocelyn appreciated it—especially when she saw Hugh grimace—so she took it as the right moment to leave. This time, too, when she held out her hand, Nina accepted it. Jocelyn said, "Doctor, I happen to believe that we've come upon something that is exciting and important, and if I can help you in any way, please let me. Otherwise, I swear to you that I will stay out of your life."

Nina said, "Thank you."

Jocelyn stopped at the door. "However, I should tell you this. A couple of weeks from now, the beginning of August, I'm going to St. Petersburg to visit Sergei and Ludmilla. And I've changed my itinerary to return by way of Belgium."

"Antwerp?" Nina asked.

"Of course. I just want to see it there, see where Rubens lived with Helena. I'm pretty sure they were Double Ones, too. And I want to see Rubens's house. It's perfectly restored, you know. And I want to see his studio, where I'm sure Bucky and Constance posed. I want to feel as much of it—as much of them—as possible, especially for whenever Bucky talks to me about it again."

Jocelyn turned to open the door. "Have a safe journey, Joc," Hugh said, and she stepped in to the hall.

Suddenly, though Nina called after her. Jocelyn turned back, surprised, unsure. "Will you do something for me, Jocelyn?"

"I owe you."

Nina snatched a pad off Hugh's desk and wrote on it. "When you're at Rubens's house, do you know: do they still have records?"

"What kind of records?"

"Well, like who worked for him, who he paid?"

"To be his models?"

"Exactly."

"I was already thinking about that," Jocelyn said.

"All right, look for these three names," Nina said, handing her the sheet. She had written down: Oliver Goode, Cecil Wainwright, and Margareta. Jocelyn's hands shook a little as she read them—

especially when she saw the "Oliver." Ollie, for sure.

However, Jocelyn only said, "Just Margareta?"

"For now. If I come up with the last name, I'll let you know."

"Okay."

"And if there's any police records."

"Police forces really hadn't been created back in the seventeenth century," Hugh said, interrupting—but helpfully.

"Okay. Whatever. Any death records." Nina took a breath. "All right, was a woman named Margareta murdered in 1635? Was she strangled?"

Jocelyn gasped with excitement. "I'll see what I can find," she said, and she put on her hat—one of those sort of upside-down bowl-type hats that British Air stewardesses are required to wear. Then she turned away, disappearing jauntily down the hall.

Hugh arched his eyebrows and said, "Murder?"

"You have no idea," Nina answered, "what I am in the midst of."

"Are you all right?"

She evaded that. Instead, "I'm gonna see it through."

He took her by the shoulders, gently. "Oh, Nina, I wish I could do something."

"You can."

"I can?"

"You can love me." And with that, he said nothing, simply took Nina into his arms and kissed her as she had kissed him in the Tiffany Court—only now, of course, they were alone. She responded, wrapping her arms around his back and drawing him as much into her embrace as he had taken her into his. At last. Again. It was so sweet and passionate, alike, that Nina knew this was the prelude to a whole night of love, whole. At last. Again. Mischievously, she even thought: you took me on my couch—you defiled my very office!—and now, turnabout is fair play, and I'm going to screw you right here on your desk at the Union Theological Seminary.

But then for no good reason, Hugh pushed her away. Incredibly, he said, "You must go now."

"Go?"

"I'm sorry, there's someone I'm supposed to see."

"Now? It's nine o'clock."

"Well, it's an appointment."

"It's a woman, isn't it?"

"Of course not, Nina. It's a student. A male student." That was such a bald-faced lie it wasn't even necessary to label it as such.

"I am so tired of this, Hugh."

"I am too. And I'll call you. Soon. I swear."

Nina looked at him in disgust. At the door, she said, "Quite a day for me, Hugh. I started out with a guy who murders women. I end it with a guy I wanna murder."

Hugh didn't—couldn't—say anything. He only watched Nina go. Then he rearranged himself and composed himself so that he could go over to Marilyn's. There, she greeted him in a dressing gown the color of peaches. Straightaway, Hugh said to her, "I'm sorry, Marilyn, but I've always loved another woman."

She replied, "You know, Hugh, I thought maybe that's what it was."

In her hotel room that night, Constance woke with a start. She was seeing Bess again, lying there. Bess—whom she always saw when she was a little girl back in Rochester. Bess, in her long, blue gown, lying in the creek, staring up with her vacant eyes. Yes, there she was again—there was Bess. But, no...wait. It couldn't be Bess. This was a dark-haired woman, and she was not nearly so pretty as Bess. She was not reposing amid the pebbles of a stream, but was instead, sprawled undressed upon a bed, naked except for some sort of yellow scarf that was tied in a death-knot around her neck. What Constance found the most odd of all, though, was that although she had certainly never met the dead woman, she knew her name, which was Caterina.

Perhaps she should mention this curiosity to Dr. Winston, too.

·23·

Constance recalled going to a museum on a school field trip, but otherwise had no memories of art, so that when Nina escorted her up to the European paintings the next afternoon, it was as if she was guiding her into some foreign land. Oh, Constance did recognize some names—Rembrandt as they passed through gallery thirteen, then Goya, and for some reason, Filippo Lippi—but her recognition was in the manner of people who had learned the names of the presidents in grade school but really couldn't tell the difference between Madison, Buchanan, or Coolidge.

Constance did say she liked some of the paintings, but more as you might express a preference for a certain wallpaper or bathing suit. Actually, she was most fascinated by the distribution of the paintings upon the walls—appalled at how much space was "underutilized," as she described it. And then:

The instant she walked into gallery twenty-five, adjacent to the Rubens's room, Constance changed. She began to grow alert and curious; she fidgeted, looked all around. "Is there something...?" Nina asked, leaving the question open-ended.

"I don't know," Constance replied, befuddled now, and even more disturbed—exactly as Bucky had reacted when first he chanced upon this territory. "There's something eerie I feel," Constance added, more agitated. And then, as she approached the entrance to gallery twenty-seven, her head swiveled about and she cried out, "Bucky! Bucky is here!"

The few other people in the gallery scurried away, giving her a wide berth. The guard, standing between the two rooms, went on alert. *Oh my God,* Nina thought, *it can't be.*

But, of course, Nina knew this is exactly the way she supposed it would be.

As if following a scent, Constance advanced into twenty-seven through the door to the right—the other side from where Bucky had first come in. This put Constance right next to *Venus and Adonis.* She stared at the painting in awe and wonder. Then she gasped, "I'm home. I'm home."

The guard looked around through the other door, eyeing her dubiously. Obviously, everything he had been taught about deranged people suggested that, momentarily, this strange, beautiful woman was going to pull out a knife, a nail file—something—and slash the masterpiece before her. He edged closer.

Constance was trembling some now, so Nina took her hand. "I'm there, Doctor," she said. "I'm there."

"Where?"

"I'm home, in that painting. How can that possibly be?" Shaking more, she moved a step up, searching for some clue that would explain this irrational reaction to herself—she, the most rational of human beings.

Nina kept playing the straight man. "Whatdya mean you're in the painting?"

Constance tore herself away from staring at *Venus and Adonis* long enough to look beseechingly at Nina. "I feel it, that's all. Am I the fat lady?"

"I don't know, Constance."

"Who painted this?"

"Rubens."

"Who's he?"

"Peter Paul Rubens. A very famous Flemish painter of the seventeenth century."

Constance didn't even seem to hear. Instead, suddenly, as if summoned, she let go of Nina's hand and dashed the few steps to her right, past the small Van Dyke in the center of the wall, to the painting of *The Holy Family with Saint Francis.* The guard was there, taken aback by Constance's move, but ready now to pounce. And now he tensed, for Constance's chest was heaving, her eyes wild. She simply let loose her pocketbook, letting it fall to the floor. Then: "Bucky!" she cried out. "Bucky is here!"

Nina saw her reach out. Too late to stop her. Constance stretched up on her tiptoes, trying to touch the painting. The figures were just a bit too high, beyond her reach. The guard lurched toward her, crying out, "Don't touch that, lady!"

There was no evidence that Constance heard. Instead, with her whole body straining, she reached up again, uncaring that her short tan dress hiked up high on her thighs. Nina couldn't help but notice, too, that Constance's dress was ripe with perspiration. Still, Constance couldn't quite reach the Madonna, so she bent her knees, preparing to jump.

The guard couldn't wait any longer. He grabbed Constance—although decorously, he avoided her torso, only seeking to pull down her right arm. When he did that, though, Constance extended the left. So without a choice, the guard stopped being polite and grabbed her firmly around the waist. But Constance immediately reacted, angrily gritting her teeth, slamming an elbow back into his chest, catching him off-balance, so that he staggered back with an "oof," nearly falling down.

Just then, another guard, this one a tiny woman, hearing the commotion, rushed in from the El Greco gallery to support her comrade.

Nina, frozen in shock, regained her senses. "I'll get her, I'll get her!" she screamed, lunging at Constance, grabbing her around her chest, yanking her away. And somehow, that violent thrust seemed to bring Constance back to her senses. All of a sudden, she stopped her thrashing and looked around, horrified. Then, she tore out of Nina's grasp, and eluding the poor guard who was just regaining his footing, she tore off, willy-nilly, through the nearest door toward the Dürer gallery.

Nina scooped up Constance's pocketbook and rushed after her, scrambling ahead of the guard. "Don't worry, I'll get her outta here," she called to him. Unconvinced, he followed, but at a distance.

Nina caught up with Constance. She'd stopped running, and was simply standing there, stock still, in the corner of the next gallery, appalled at herself, her face in her hands. Tenderly, Nina embraced her, whispering, "It's okay, Constance, it's okay." And then, holding her hand, Nina led Constance down the huge staircase into the Great Hall, around the information booth, out the front door.

It was sweltering outside, but never mind—they simply collapsed there, on the steps. Nina kept an arm around her shoulder. Constance gasped for air, shaking her head. Finally, she looked at Nina, but "What?" was all she could manage to say.

Nina knew she had to level with her. "What happened in there to you—that's exactly what happened to Bucky three months ago."

"But...why?"

"I don't know why. It only seems—I mean, anyway, Bucky thinks that you two both had an earlier life, together. He thinks you were both models for Rubens."

"Who?"

Constance had been so entranced, Nina's original reference to Rubens hadn't registered. She explained again who the artist was. "He painted in Antwerp. The two paintings that affected you were probably done in 1635."

"My God, could it be?"

"Constance, I don't know. I don't have the foggiest."

"Well, what next?"

Nina had already decided what that must be. "I think it's best that I go over what I know with both of you."

"Together?"

Nina nodded. "I'll call you after I speak to Bucky."

Constance broke into the most glorious smile. "Let's meet at my hotel room," she said. "I'd prefer the privacy."

Nina agreed. What the hell? She knew as soon as she left Bucky and Constance alone they were going to pounce on each other, so she might as well expedite the inevitable and start them off in a bedroom.

Constance rose, dusted off her bottom. "I need to ride," she announced, and without another word, she strode away from Nina, down the steps, walking briskly in the heat along Fifth Avenue. Nina watched as all the men turned to look at her in that way men always looked at Constance, with as much wonder as lust. It was odd, too, that even as she witnessed this welter of admiration for Constance, Nina felt a certain sadness for her...although she wasn't quite sure why.

As soon as Nina hung up, after telling Bucky—a thrilled Bucky, an amazed Bucky, a beside-himself Bucky—that they would be meeting with Constance tomorrow afternoon, she began to make some notes. Nina decided that she would *not* tell them that Ollie was a murderer. That was too much for now—especially since she didn't want to prejudice Bucky in the event that she hypnotized him again and was able to get past the scream.

But even as she outlined what she would tell them, her heart began to race. Merely the anticipation of meeting with the two of them together, of talking to them about past life. She struggled. Her mind zigged and zagged. And her next patient would be here in five minutes. Oh, if only she could talk to someone about this. If only...Hugh. And now she was thinking about Hugh. Why had he acted the way he had last night? Somehow, she knew she should give him the benefit of the doubt. On the other hand, she also wanted to give him a piece of her mind. So, she dialed Hugh, even if Nina hoped he wasn't there. She wanted to talk to his phone machine.

Nina liked phone machines. People were always bitching about having to talk to machines, but Nina quite enjoyed that. Yes, she preferred talking to real people, one-on-one, face-to-face. That, after all, was what she did for a living, and she did it very well. But Nina found telephone conversations so lacking in definition, in dimension. She wanted to see how people looked when they spoke to her, how they acted. Nina was probably too visceral a person. Visceral persons are not, as a general rule, good telephone persons.

But phone machines. Nina liked them right from the get-go, as soon as they were invented. Because, with phone machines, you didn't talk *with* people, you spoke *to* them. You could deliver soliloquies. Now that we had phone machines, soliloquies were back.

This, in particular, was the soliloquy that Nina delivered at this moment:

"Hugh, I've waited impatiently to hear from you today because I have never thought you were common. But you cannot kiss someone as you did last night, and then send that someone off and not call and explain to that someone the next day. You can't do that unless you are common.

"I especially wanted you to call, Hugh, because I am discombobulated today. I am meeting with the, uh, Double Ones tomorrow afternoon in her room at the Sherry-Netherland, and I am scared as hell, and I need to be with someone, and the only person I want to be with under these circumstances—or, indeed, under many circumstances—is you. So, I would appreciate it if you would get back to me so that I can be with you tomorrow after I leave the Double Ones. I guess that'll be five-thirty, six, something like that.

"So please call me, or I will have to conclude that you really are common, which would surprise me, because as you know, I love you, and I have always prided myself on my good taste, and it seems impossible to believe that I could actually fall in love with someone common."

Hugh did not call back. Nina did not sleep at all well that night.

Bucky was more distracted than Phyllis had ever seen him. He told her that he would have to stay in New York the next night, because he had a client to take to a women's basketball game at the Garden. "A what?"

"It's a new women's summer basketball league, and this client—well, it's a she—and this is the one thing in all the world she wants to see. I think I'm gonna get a lotta pages outta this."

As weird as Bucky was behaving, Phyllis believed him. It was all too outlandish an excuse, a women's basketball game in the summertime.

Bucky did not sleep at all well that night.

After she rode in Central Park, Constance asked the hotel concierge to get her a ticket for a musical. She wanted to be distracted. The

concierge suggested *Miss Saigon*. It did not hold Constance's attention at all. Not even when the damn helicopter landed right on
stage. She was not only too keyed up about seeing Bucky, but she
could not put out of her mind the inexplicable behavior she had
exhibited in gallery twenty-seven.

Constance did not sleep at all well that night.

She kept seeing a dead woman in water. But no, it wasn't Bess.
Constance knew that right away. Bess was so beautiful and clean,
lying there on the bed of pebbles. This woman was altogether different—herself and the water, too.

The woman was heavy and red-haired. And the water. The water
was so dark. But it was red, too. A blood red. And the woman was
drifting along in some sort of a channel. Moving with her, too, were
all sorts of debris. And then Constance watched as the redheaded
woman drifted out of her sight, under some building.

But even then, even as the body disappeared, Constance remembered the woman's name. It was Elsa. So clearly she recalled it: Elsa.
And now she could see her before she was in the water. When she
was still alive. A hefty woman. Busty. Big, flouncy bosom. And vulgar. But not rotten vulgar. Rather: naughty vulgar. Bawdy. Yes, Constance could see Elsa perfectly. She could even hear her laughing.

Constance shuddered at that recollection, and tried to think of
Bucky instead.

Slowly, too, Elsa did fade away, but it was not Bucky that she
visualized then. Rather, Constance saw the red and black diamonds,
lined up as always in their unique pattern. But that calmed her and
finally she could slip into a sleep, the one that would carry her into
the morning of that day in her life, when at last, she would have all
to herself the love of the only man she had ever wanted.

·24·

Nina escorted Bucky up to Constance's room. "I'll give you two minutes," she barked at him like a schoolmarm. Normally, he would have had some wiseass comeback, but now he was ashen and nervous and without repartee. Certainly, without smirking.

Constance opened the door, and Nina stared at the two of them staring at each other. Constance was lovely, far more simply dressed than ever—probably because she had dressed to undress. A plain dress of brown and white, buttoned all the way down the front. She was without jewelry, and barefoot—and altogether, Nina thought, presented some rare combination of sensuality and innocence. Anyway, without a word, Nina closed the door in her own face, leaving them inside the room together.

Immediately, Bucky took Constance in his arms. It was, really, the first time they had ever touched, and they kissed with such power that they seemed to all but suck the breath from one another. But they needed to affirm their love, too, and so at once they exchanged vows, for forever and always. Then Constance fell upon his chest and pleaded with him to hold her, tighter. He did, too, only after a while, Bucky knew he must say, "We have to let Nina in."

And so she entered, as coldly professional as she could be, with a blank expression purposely plastered upon her face. Nina put two chairs next to each other (separating them just enough to keep Constance and Bucky out of actual physical contact), bade them take their seats, and then sat down on the side of the bed herself, facing them. Then straightaway, without ado, Nina began:

"I do not understand what is going on—only that something incredible has happened between you two, and that somehow, *somehow*, it relates to pictures painted by Peter Paul Rubens in the year 1635 in his studio in Antwerp. For now, I'll leave it to you to decide whether we're dealing with reincarnation or some other phenomenon or"—Nina threw up her hands—"God knows what. But let's not speculate on that for now. Let me only tell you what I know. Okay?"

Bucky and Constance looked over at each other with excitement, then nodded enthusiastically. So, Nina took out her notes, even though most of what she'd learned was emblazoned on her mind. Quickly, she recapped the past of their lives—their current lives—acknowledging to them that under hypnosis, they'd both vividly recalled the same incidents from Philadelphia, almost verbatim. "You also both expressed—in talking to me and under hypnosis—the same sort of instant physical—or metaphysical—attraction for one another."

Bucky smiled shyly, Constance more triumphantly.

Then Nina moved onto a discussion of their similar extreme reactions to the Rubens's paintings in gallery twenty-seven. Bucky gasped. Constance ducked her head, losing her usual bold assurance. "Yes," Nina started to explain to Bucky. "I took Constance up there yesterday."

"I completely lost it," Constance admitted. "I'm afraid I kinda hit a guard, didn't I?"

Bucky's mouth flew open. Nina threw back her elbow in imitation of Constance's action. "Well, I'd say you just kind of jolted him. But you should know, Constance..." She stopped then, turning back directly to Bucky. "I assume you'll allow me to tell everything."

He knew what was coming, and chagrined, he nodded. So Nina faced Constance. "A few weeks ago, Bucky somehow managed to hide himself overnight in the Metropolitan so that he might be alone in gallery twenty-seven, and he, uh—"

"I jerked off," Bucky said.

Far from being appalled, Constance merely reached toward him, waving with understanding.

Nina went on. "Luckily, no one caught him in the act, but he's been barred from the museum. And given your own behavior yesterday, Constance, you might—at least for now—want to steer clear of the place."

Constance kept her counsel. Nina continued. "Okay, we start getting really spooky here, but bear with me. I'll try to speak as directly as I can, without editorial comment. Now, I've sought, as Bucky requested, to take you both back beyond this life, into—"

Constance's hands flew up. "So, that's—"

"Yeah," Bucky said.

"I apologize for not leveling with you, Constance, but it's more productive to try that without a subject's being a party to the effort."

"I understand."

"With Bucky, as I told him at the time, I had no real success. There was only one thing you said—"

"I did?"

"Yeah. You, uh, uttered the name Ollie."

"Hey, you asked me about that once."

"Right. That time you referred to Ollie while we were talking, without even realizing it."

Now Constance said, "Ollie?" in that way as if the name rang a bell.

"You know it?" Nina asked.

"Well, yeah, it seems to ring some kinda bell."

"Well, there's a good reason why. Whereas that one name was all I could get out of Bucky, when I regressed you, you moved back very easily into 1635."

"Wow!" Bucky cried out, and even the unflappable Constance looked up in delight. Almost unconsciously, too, they reached across the great abyss that Nina had created between their two chairs and managed to touch fingers. She let it pass. Bucky said, "Tell us about Constance and—"

"In a moment," Nina said. "First, let's go back to the museum. There are, of course, two Rubens that grab your attention. But listen," Nina leaned forward on the bed, "you two react quite differently to the two paintings. Bucky, you've always been much more affected by *Venus and Adonis,* but Constance, you totally lost your composure when you came to the other—to *Saint Francis Meets the Holy Family.*"

Tentatively, Bucky and Constance turned to look at each other, both nodding, affirming Nina's analysis. She went on."You see, Bucky, from the first, you were convinced that you were somehow in *Venus and Adonis.* And you were just as sure that Constance was in it, too. Okay, leaving aside for the moment the question of how this might be, we naturally assumed that you, Bucky, the man, must be Adonis, and—"

"Of course!" he cried out, actually jumping to his feet, pumping his two fists into the air.

"Of course what?" Constance asked.

Bucky looked to Nina and she held out her hands, indicating that he had the floor. So Bucky declared, "Connie, you were Adonis." Then to Nina, "Right?"

Nina said, "Go on."

"And I was the Madonna." When Constance looked confused, he kneeled before her, taking her hands. "Don't you see, Connie? It's so obvious now."

Nina said, "Just try to remember, Constance. You were stunned by *Venus and Adonis.*"

"I remember. I said: 'I'm home.'"

"Exactly. She did, Bucky. Because somehow you knew you were home, Constance. Because Adonis, up there—that *was* you." Nina paused, catching herself. It was amazing how easily she was speaking now without any qualification or reservation. *That was you* —you, a twentieth-century woman *had been* a seventeenth-century man. That's what Dr. Winston had said. Without admitting it, she had at some level in her own mind leapt over the line. Oh well, onward. To Constance: "But it was only when you saw the Madonna that you lost control."

"Because Bucky is the Madonna," she ventured—tentatively.

Nina nodded. "And because you love him. As you loved that woman he once was." Constance and Bucky looked over to one another, rather like a couple of kids who shared a neat secret. Nina spoke to him: "But you, Bucky, you always reacted to the Madonna in a more casual way—like she was a good buddy, a confidant."

"Which she certainly was, since she was me."

"I guess." Nina shrugged. "Anyway, you acted completely differently in front of *Venus and Adonis*. Of course, at first this was complicated somewhat because, naturally, you thought Constance must be Venus."

"Only Helena is Venus."

"Wait a cotton-pickin' minute," Constance snapped. "Who the hell is Helena?"

Both Nina and Bucky smiled and filled her in on Helena's place in the Rubens's family. Bucky also said, "What's amazing is, that time I was jacking off—I knew, deep inside, that a part of me was doing it because of Adonis. And that just embarrassed me more, because I thought, now, on top of everything else, I'm turning gay."

"Have no fear," Nina said, "your rampant heterosexuality is safe for yet another century."

It was the closest they'd come to a joke all afternoon. Constance, though, barely broke a smile. She only got up, said, "Pardon me," and went into the bathroom. Bucky looked up, almost shyly, at Nina. "How ya doin'?" she asked him. She meant: right now, all this.

But he answered, "Oh fine. I'm planning a sailing trip."

"The whole family?"

"Yeah. Up the Sound, into the Atlantic. I was thinking: better do it now before the kids get too old."

Nina went along. "Gee, that sounds great." But, she thought, this is just like it used to be, back in the beginning, when Bucky was afraid to talk about anything real, so we just chatted about everyday stuff. So, here he was, prattling on about a family vacation, as if the love of his life—of all his lives—wasn't right there with him, and that soon enough, they would start talking again about how they lived together in the year 1635. So, Nina continued in the same blithe vein. "I'm going to San Francisco myself next week."

"Great."

"It's a convention, but I'm using it as an excuse just to get away." She didn't add: away from you. Away from all this madness. And away from the man I love who loves me, but won't even call me back.

"Wine country?" Bucky asked.

"No, I don't think so. You see, Bucky, I like wine just fine. I mean, I like to drink it. But really, I don't like to analyze it and talk it to death."

Bucky laughed, relaxed. "Yeah, Nina. That's what I like about you: you always get it just right." He reached out then, and for just a second, he touched her hand. Nina winked at him, and then they sat back until momentarily, Constance returned.

Nina treated everyone to Tic-Tacs, and then she resumed. "All right, now we come to Constance under hypnosis. You spoke to me in a voice that belonged to an English sailor who had just signed onto a ship bound for Amsterdam." Nina paused. "He went by the name of Oliver Goode."

Bucky caught it right away. "Ollie!" he called out.

"Ollie," Constance said. "I was Ollie."

"Oh yes," Nina said—although for just a moment, her mind wandered, because she looked at Constance and knew she'd been Ollie, and she looked at Bucky and she knew he'd been Margareta. And surely Ollie had killed Margareta—killed the woman he had loved. And there they were, before her. But then she caught herself. *Hello, Nina, that was 1635—back with the Pilgrims.* And she regained her perspective and resumed the narrative. "Now from Amsterdam, Ollie went overland down to Antwerp to pick up a new ship, but in 1635, Antwerp was blockaded by the Dutch—the Protestants. Ollie told me all this, and when I went back and read up on the period, it checked out perfectly." Nina glanced at Bucky. "Spot on," she said, with a British accent. He smiled.

Constance was only impatient. "What happened next?"

"Well, a man named Cornelis sees Ollie and tells him that Rubens is looking for a strong, handsome man to be the model for Adonis. So, he tags along to Rubens's house, which is by a canal called The Wapper."

"You mean like Burger King?" Bucky asked.

Constance frowned at such frivolity, but Nina said, "Yes, spelled a bit different, but the same pronunciation. More important, Rubens's house is still there today, only now the canal is filled in as a street: Wapperstraat."

"The house is actually still standing?" Constance asked.

"Perfectly restored—exactly as it was in 1635."

Constance crossed her arms before her and shook her head, charmed at this revelation.

Nina continued. "So, as soon as Ollie arrives at Rubenshuis, the master takes one look and considers him the perfect Adonis. He even compares Ollie favorably to another muscular model he'd used years before in another famous painting entitled *Ascent to the Cross*. I found a picture of that, and, yup, big strong guy right in the middle. Constance, it's amazing what you—what Ollie—told me. The detail." She took a sip of water and went on. "As it turned out, Rubens was so taken by Ollie that he gave him a very nice salary, plus he let him stay in an extra house he owned, right around the corner. On Hopland Street."

"Is that house still there, too?" Constance asked.

"Well, Hopland Street—it's still there. But the house, I assume it's gone. It wasn't anything special. Except..." Nina paused, "...except it was in that house where Ollie carried on an affair with the woman who posed as the Madonna."

Reflexively, Constance looked at Bucky, and he directed a thumb at his chest. "Me," he said.

"Well," Nina said, "anyway, her name was Margareta."

"Last name?"

"Don't know."

"Did they marry?" Constance asked.

Nina passed for the moment on revealing the fact that, inconveniently, Margareta was already married to someone else. She just said, "It was at this point that I had to end the session with you, Constance."

Her disappointment—and Bucky's—were palpable. "When do I get to do it again?" Constance asked.

"After we get a chance to digest all this. Maybe it's a blessing that Bucky and I both happen to have vacations coming up."

"My husband and I are going away, too. Jackson Hole." She looked at Bucky. "That's where I plan to tell him that when I get back, I'm leaving him for you, darling."

"Well, it's up to you two," Nina said, "but I would suggest that you both hold off on those plans till we've finished this business."

Constance got her back up. "What's this gotta do with the price of eggs? We know we love each other. Now we know we always have."

She turned to Bucky for affirmation. He looked a little unsure. Nina jumped in. "Look, this is powerful, mysterious stuff. In a way, you've waited for each other for almost four hundred years. Another couple weeks…"

Bucky took Constance's hand. "It's a good point, darling. If we get distracted with our own lives, it could be that much harder when we concentrate on trying to find out what happened back in Antwerp."

Nina spoke up again, "And, Bucky, I've come up with a better idea how I might get you to regress next time. It's your call, but I'd ask you both to put off any dramatic changes in this century until we've done our best to resolve what happened in that other time and place."

Bucky glanced at Constance, but without waiting for her response, he declared, "I think you're right, Nina." Constance nodded then, herself, if not with great enthusiasm.

"Fine," Nina said, grabbing up her papers, "so we'll regroup in another couple weeks." Just then, though, her eyes fell upon a word underlined boldly in her notes. She hesitated. After all, she could all but feel the electrical field that Constance and Bucky were sparking; never had Nina Winston wanted more desperately to depart a premises. But, she said, "I'm sorry, hold your horses. There is one other thing." And then she spoke just the one word: "Jocelyn"—which provoked such a startling reaction from Bucky that Constance's head jerked up, too.

"For Chrissake, Nina," Bucky whined, "why bring her up?"

"Because she's contacted me personally, and because she has

something interesting to say that at least deserves to be heard. By you both."

"All right, who's Jocelyn?" Constance asked.

"An old girlfriend," Bucky told her, although averting her eyes.

"Oh, that's nice."

Nina stayed out of it.

"An *old* girlfriend, Connie. We're talking fifteen years ago. Jesus, you were already married. What was I supposed to do, take up celibacy?" That mollified Constance sufficiently for him to continue. "When I first saw *Venus and Adonis,* I had to talk to someone, and I spoke to Jocelyn because I knew she had an interest in reincarnation. In fact, she was the person who suggested I go see Nina."

"Strictly second-party referral," Nina said, picking up the thread. "I'd never met the lady—never did until Bucky refused to talk to her anymore. She was very curious about our sessions."

"Damn Jocelyn," said Bucky.

"And what did you reveal, Doctor?" Constance asked, harshly.

"Nothing. But she already knew about you."

Constance whirled to Bucky. "You told her?"

"Years ago, I *had* told her about us back in Philadelphia. That's all."

Constance mulled over that revelation, then declared, "No more." Nina wasn't altogether sure whether that referred to Jocelyn or this meeting, or both. Anyway, she moved quickly ahead to end things, all but announcing "In conclusion," the way boring speakers do.

"All right, let me wrap this up," Nina did say. "The issue is not so much that Jocelyn knows about you, as what you might like to know about what she told me." Whereupon, Nina went over Jocelyn's devotion to Sergei and Ludmilla, to their belief in reincarnation, and particularly, to their understanding of the concept of Double Ones. "Jocelyn is naturally most fascinated with you two, because she believes that together you can virtually prove that Double Ones exist."

"I guess," Bucky said.

Constance was not so pleased. "Meddler," she groused. "And

you stay away from her, Bucky. I don't want any old flame of yours—or anybody—snooping around like I'm some specimen, studying me the way I study companies. We'll end up as freaks on the front page of *The National Enquirer*."

Nina stood up. "Fine. You owe Jocelyn nothing. I just wanted you to know that this woman sincerely believes that you two can absolutely prove the existence of reincarnation." She paused before adding, "And may God help you if she's right about Double Ones, because if she is and if you two are, then *The National Enquirer* will be small potatoes. So, you wanna stop all this now, I understand."

Constance announced, "No, we will just never speak to her—and you tell her that, Doctor."

Nina said, "I will," and then rather formally, shook both their hands. As she stepped into the corridor, the door closing behind her, she heard Bucky call after her, "Thank you, Nina."

Nina said, "My pleasure."

·25·

Bucky stepped toward Constance. At last, alone. But just before he took her in his arms, she held up a hand to halt his advance. "Wait," she announced. "You are never to see her again."

"Nina?"

Constance shrugged. "Well, in time perhaps we should abandon her, too. But I mean Jocelyn. That woman is wicked, and her nosiness can only mean trouble for us. Our love is only ours." Bucky nodded, intimidated by her intensity. "Swear to me you'll never speak to her again."

"I swear," he said formally, although at this moment, brimming with ardor, Bucky surely would have sworn to anything that Constance requested of him.

"Good," she said, and, instantly putting all that aside, she tossed her head back, running her hands through her hair. Bucky stood transfixed, then, as Constance brought her hands down further, to her dress, and began unbuttoning it, one by one by one. She tossed it aside, then tapped at the hook to her bra between her breasts. "You undo it," she said.

Bucky did. "Now, pull them down," she said, nodding to her panties. He followed that sweet order, too, then stood back and gazed upon her, unadorned. "I wanted you to see me first. I'm real. We're real."

"You're magnificently beautiful," he said, and he tried to kiss her, but instead, Constance pushed him back and began undressing him, until they stood there, real, before each other.

Constance fondled his erection. "Do you remember," she asked, "when this was me?"

"I'm not sure, Connie. Do you?"

"I think so, yes." He placed his hands on her breasts. "And yes, I remember me doing that to you."

But Bucky did not say any more, only lowered her upon the bed, where they were furious in their passion, and as perfect in love as Constance had told Nina that they must be. Moreover, for them both, there was this, too: the most amazing bright silver filled their vision—alike, whether their eyes were open or shut. "Do you see the silver?" she whispered.

"Yes."

"Double Ones," she sighed. "We are Double Ones." And for the first time in all her life, Constance Rawlings cried tears of joy.

In the lobby, Nina started toward the revolving door onto Fifth Avenue that would take her back into that cauldron of...no, she thought: not cauldron. Cauldrons were 1635. Who knew cauldrons any longer? So, let's see now. Wok. Yes, wok. She was about to walk out into the wok of a city. But, so what? Nina's whole body was a slop of perspiration from what she'd gone through upstairs; besides, she was steaming even more because that rotten preacher hadn't called her back. But then she heard: "Dr. Winston..."

She looked back. It was the concierge. Nina nodded. "Your cab is waiting."

"My cab?"

He gestured that she precede him out into the ghastly heat onto 60th. "Your cab, madam." And it was. Only it was not a regular yellow cab, but a hansom cab, the perspiring driver dozing aloft, as the poor horse sipped at a water bucket. "Juanito," the concierge shouted, "this is Dr. Winston."

Juanito stirred, picked up his top hat, then clambered down, bowing with a flourish. Nina took her seat under the little roof that blocked out some of the sun. But it didn't matter. The heat didn't matter. All the fear and wonder of Bucky and Constance were instantly gone, because—obviously, indisputably—this chariot had been ordered by Hugh Venable, erstwhile common creep, now puta-tive sweetest man in the world.

"Lead on, Juanito, driver of the gods and goddesses," Nina cried out gaily, luxuriating in her own lovely sweat as the horse clopped along. All the years she'd lived in New York, a lifetime, all the horse cabs she'd seen, all the tourists going in them to the Tavern On The Green, never had Nina even considered taking one. Never. Ah, but now it was different, for somewhere—momentarily—Hugh would emerge from off a blistering sidewalk to sit by her side.

Onward. Then just before the cab turned onto Central Park South, suddenly, a young man emerged from by the hot-dog stand, running toward Nina. From behind his back, he pulled out a large bouquet of white roses, presenting it to her with a grand flourish. "From a devoted admirer," he proclaimed.

Clutching the roses, Nina replied, "Tell my devoted admirer that *I* admire both his flowers and his exquisite taste."

Nina did not even notice any longer that it was blazing hot and that she had wilted, her hair a perfect mess. She did not even think of Bucky and Constance, their bodies locked in time and space, making air-conditioned love for the ages. Nina only smelled roses, and Nina only thought of Hugh.

At Seventh Avenue, where Juanito turned the cab into the park, another young man materialized. In a waiter's apron and bow tie, he carried a silver tray—upon it a lovely glass shaker and a single mar-tini glass. As soon as the carriage halted, he stepped up, stirred the drink before Nina, then handed it to her. "From someone who wishes you to be as refreshed as a sylvan glade," he announced.

Nina held the glass high. "Inform that someone," she replied, "that even as I am cooled by his gracious concern, my lips remain hot for his." She sipped, then, tingling from the gin and the knowl-edge that somewhere ahead, at one of these romantic stations of the cross, Hugh himself surely awaited.

Perhaps now? Perhaps right here, where the road bent? No, it was only a young woman who arose from a bench there. She carried a beautiful old silver mirror, and when she climbed aboard the car-riage, she brushed Nina's hair, and then held the mirror up, so that she could apply her own lipstick and blush. Then, from the pocket of her maid's Provençal apron, the lady-in-waiting removed a perfume bottle, placing a drop at Nina's wrist, behind her ears, and most decorously, in the cleft of her breasts. "Envy, from Gucci," she announced. "Your admirer finds your beauty can only be enhanced by a scent as light and floral as this summer's evening."

"Tell the admirer that my beauty is evanescent, for it appears only to his eyes, and is revealed to no other but he."

The great chariot proceeded along, around another bend. And there—yes, there sat Hugh. He was wearing cream trousers and a short-sleeved white shirt trimmed in green and blue. He looked handsome and young and debonair—very much the sex object. As Juanito slowed the carriage, Hugh rose languidly and lifting his own martini glass, he inquired, "May I join you?"

"You may, sir."

"You look absolutely gorgeous," he said, climbing in beside her.

"Oh, it's just something I threw together for the global warming."

More seriously. "Everything go okay?"

Nina shrugged. "About what I expected. I'm fine, but I'd also just as soon not talk about it."

"All right with me. So, can I just tell you that I love you?"

"Of course you can. You can kiss me, too." He did, tenderly. He might have kissed her more fervently, but there were the martinis to worry about.

"I love you, too, Hugh." Appropriately then the carriage slowed, and a young man with a mandolin—yes, a mandolin—fetched up aside Juanito, where he began playing soft and lovely mandolin favorites. Nina grabbed Hugh's arm and pulled him closer. "I didn't know you could be so romantic."

"I guess I never had the chance before. Back then, circumstances lent themselves more just to lust."

Nina drew away. "Goodness gracious, I hope that hasn't been eliminated from the new model."

"Oh, no, no. The new model is romance and lust. Package deal."

Nina drew her forefinger across her forehead, then flicked away real sweat. "Whew," she sighed, as a new song began. It sounded very much like "Greensleeves." But then, many of the songs sounded like "Greensleeves." In truth, Nina decided the fellow probably wasn't a very good mandolin player—even though she had very little experience in rating mandolin players. So, she just said, "I am impressed, Hugh."

"Well, even seminary students are crass enough to suck up to their professor. But I must say, even I hadn't counted on a mandolin player surfacing."

Nina just cooed, kissed him on the cheek, and patted his thigh a little. The cab slowed then, Juanito steering it to the side of the road. Hugh stepped down, offered his arm to Nina, and together they strolled to a little grove of trees. They were still in the midst of New York City in the midst of a heat wave, but suddenly now, Nina felt cool and altogether at peace. It was an ideal way to be, for when Hugh turned to face her, he said this without any warning whatsoever: "Nina, will you marry me?"

And she did not miss a beat, replying straightaway, "Why yes, Hugh, it would be my happiness and my honor." With that, she raised up her pretty face to his and gently kissed him upon his lips, falling into his arms. Then Nina began to cry for joy, which she had done often in the past, but not for quite a while.

The mandolin began to play again, a sweet song. Yet another young woman appeared, she holding high a fancy cushion that was velvety and tasseled. Nina saw right away that there was a ring upon it. As Hugh snatched it up and placed it upon her finger, she could see that it had one magnificent diamond in the middle, set off by other smaller ones, with a ruby placed at both ends of the arrangement.

"It was my mother's," Hugh said. "My sister always imagined that she'd get it, but I traded her a necklace and the sideboard and some china for it."

"You knew you would marry again?"

"No, Nina. I knew I would marry you."

The ring bearer threw paper flower petals at them as they laughed and returned to the carriage. They went to Nina's apartment house. As she alighted there, she held up her left hand one more time, watching the sun play off the diamonds. "So," she said, "you will make an honest woman of me."

"No," said Hugh, stepping down beside her. "I am making an honest man of me."

·26·

Nina had assumed they would make love right away. Instead, they danced. They waltzed. All over the apartment. Nina and Hugh waltzed to Strauss and they waltzed to "The Tennessee Waltz," and they waltzed to every waltz between the Danube and the Mississippi. It was what Hugh had planned; he'd brought a CD of waltzes with him.

"I always wanted to dance with you," he said, "but we could never do anything in public." They swirled all around the furniture, Hugh twirling her, moving her in that magic way that men who can dance well can. Why, Nina thought, such is love itself, isn't it? That which holds you tight within its embrace while setting you free to soar. To Hugh, she only called out gaily, "My God, you do this so well, too!"

He stopped right in the middle of "Tales From The Vienna Woods," but holding her still in the tableaux of the dance. "I do this well *with* you," he replied.

He swept Nina off her feet then, literally, and carried her into the bedroom.

As Bucky lay near sleep upon her bed, Constance drew her fingers down his back. At first, she did not consciously realize what she was tracing, but then it occurred to her. She was making, diagonally, from the left of his neck to the right of his buttocks that zig-zag pattern of the red and black diamonds. It did not surprise Constance, though, for so often this evening as she and Bucky made love, the silver would be so bright, but then it would fade before the vision of the red and black.

She drew another line of reds down over his spine. "We must go to Antwerp together, darling."

Bucky only murmured, "ummmm," for he was barely awake.

"How wonderful that would be! We'll go to Rubens's house and to the one on Hopland Street and to all the other places where we were in love before. Ollie and Margareta, you and me."

Bucky stirred. "Do you think?" he asked, rolling on his side to face her.

"Think?"

"Think that would be wise?"

"Of course! To be back where first we loved—together! Again! Did anyone else ever experience that before? Anyone? Ever?" She leaned down and kissed him on the forehead. Then gently, she pushed Bucky onto his back and kneeled above him, placing him within her. Sweetly, easily, Constance began to rock herself back and forth, pausing only to lean down and kiss his nipples. "Ah, my Margareta," she sighed, moving her lips up, closer to his. "And I am your Ollie." She kissed him. "The way we were in Antwerp. Man and woman, woman and man."

Bucky swallowed, a little disturbed, a little baffled. It was so strange. But Constance was right. There was a oneness to them, a seamless circle joined, so that as she rose up again on her knees, riding him, tossing her hair, in their joy it all blurred, and he was unsure of who it was he was looking at or where they might be.

Still, when they fell off to sleep, both felt more in Antwerp in Rubens's time than in New York now, and Constance knew she had to go to Antwerp—must go to Antwerp—as soon as she possibly could.

Nina lay there with her head upon Hugh's great chest. She could feel his hair tickling her. The fact is, she'd never liked a man with a hairy chest until she'd fallen in love with Hugh. Then she'd decided that he had just the proper amount of foliage there. It was like the way Christopher Robin had defined the dimensions of his little friend: "My favorite size, about the size of Piglet." So, she thought of Hugh's chest hair as "Piglet's Patch." Her favorite size.

And lying there, nestled into Piglet's Patch, Nina's whole being glistened—not only that she had Hugh back, but this time, without guilt or sin. They even began to talk, fluttery, about getting married—maybe at Nina's daughter's summerhouse on the beach in Delaware. Hugh liked that idea, so she drew herself away from Piglet's Patch, kissed him, and they made love again, quite gloriously.

Afterwards, as Nina lay beside him, she said idly (and she thought, quite humorously), "My, my, a lot of people are fornicating in New York tonight."

Hugh found that neither idle nor humorous. She could even feel him stiffen next to her, before he snapped, "So, even as *we* make love, you're thinking of *them*."

"Oh come on, darling, I wasn't thinking of them *while* we were making love."

"I merely diverted you for a moment, did I?" He was surprisingly snappish; he withdrew his arm from underneath her, and instead, placed both his hands behind his head, staring up to the dark ceiling.

"Really now, Hugh, if we're going to have our first spat as fiancés, let's pick a better subject." He only grunted. "I mean, their whole story is so incredible that it's difficult for me to—"

"That's exactly what I mean, thank you. This thing simply isn't healthy for you, Nina." He paused, considering whether he should say something. Then he went ahead. "I'd like you to promise me something."

"Is this a *quid pro quo*?"

"Well, more of a *quid pro semi-pro*. I want you to stop seeing them."

Nina was taken aback. "I don't meddle in your professional life."

"If something in my professional life was upsetting the rest of my life—and upsetting you—I would *expect* you to meddle...if you loved me and cared for my well-being."

"That's not fair."

"Isn't it? This crazy wild goose chase through the ages—excuse me: *alleged* through the ages—has discombobulated you, Nina." What light there was coming into the room crossed his face, so she could see how serious he really was. "In fact, you probably have no idea to the extent it has discombobulated you."

"No, I do know."

"Good. Then you know it's certainly not any typical doctor-patient relationship. You're not along for the ride anymore. This guy Bucky is driving the train. And I want you to get off."

Interesting, Nina thought. Constance wasn't part of Hugh's complaint sheet. Just: *this guy Bucky.* My, my, my. Surely, Jocelyn had sung Bucky's praises to Hugh. Might the good parson be just a wee bit jealous? But, she knew this was no time for teasing. Instead, Nina said, "Okay, you'll be relieved to know that I told them both that they might be advised just to let things go, not to pursue the matter further."

Surprised, Hugh smiled and said, "Good."

"But, whatever you think of my involvement, I am the doctor, these people trust me, and I can't abandon them if they don't want me to. Now, you may think it's a whole lotta nonsense—"

"Hokum. Humbug. Just the best excuse for hanky-panky I've ever heard. Oh, sweet lady, it's okay to drop your drawers now because we were rolling in the hay a few centuries ago, so we can screw to our hearts' content for old times' sake."

"You're entirely too cynical, Hugh. That's not their game at all. In fact, they put off any sex for months just to be sure. They seem to genuinely love each other."

"Fine. All the more reason for you to stop being the seventeenth-century Dear Abby."

That irritated Nina. She sat up, pausing to grab a pillow and hold it firmly before her chest in some manner of symbolic state-ment. "Now, listen to me. Whatever has happened to Bucky and Constance, they sincerely believe they lived back in—"

"Do you?" He spoke that so sharply it shocked Nina. He repeated, "Do you?"

"I don't know. It's very confusing, Hugh. It's very compelling stuff."

"Good God!" He shot up. "Nina, are you actually telling me you've bought into reincarnation?"

"Cheap shot," she replied, poking a finger into Piglet's Patch. "How'd you like it if some Hindu said to you: 'Oh, you've bought into Jesus, have you?'"

Hugh took that fairly, sort of. "All right," he said. "Bad form. I apologize...to the Hindus."

Nina said, "Reincarnation. It does scare you, doesn't it?"

And Hugh said back, "You believe in all that Double Ones stuff too?"

"Maybe."

He sighed in studied amazement when she said that, and changed the subject. Like a lot of preachers who can bounce around to chapter and verse, Hugh was very good at changing the subject. "Look, Nina, I just got engaged—for the *last* time in my life—and I know this, uh, thing upsets the woman I'm engaged to, and I don't like to see her upset." Sweetly, now, he touched her cheek. "So okay, I understand your responsibilities. But I just want you to promise me that you will not, under any circumstances, initiate anything more with either one of them. Now, that squares with Dr. Hippocrates, doesn't it? You can promise me that?"

Nina took awhile to respond, but she did nod and she did say, "Yes." Then, to make sure the subject was closed, she threw aside the pillow and shuffled her body across to him. For a long time, they simply held each other tight, and then they pledged their love again, kissed goodnight, and closed their eyes in happiness. Even then, though, even as Nina began to fall asleep beside the man she adored, even then, on this most joyous night, she could not stop thinking about Bucky and Constance on their most joyous night.

It made her mad, too, that they so enthralled her that they could distract her from her dearest exhilaration. Why, on this very evening that she had pledged her life and love to this most magnificent of men, she knew that she had lied to him. But Nina believed in Ollie and Margareta, and she could never permit Hugh to force her to give up her quest, to stop her from trying to understand this mystery that overpowered her more than her own greatest love.

Bucky awoke in the middle of the night. Constance lay sound asleep next to him, with a sliver of light that came through a crack in the curtains cutting across her in the way a great master like, well...like Rubens would have painted in a picture. The light. The dark. The shadows. The beauty.

Gently, so as not to disturb her, Bucky raised up to look upon Constance. She had the sheet over her, pulled tight across her chest from how she had rolled over to face him, so that her form was per-fectly outlined for him. He marveled at her whole appearance. First, her face. He remembered it as so intense, but now in repose, it was soft and sweet. From her ears dropped the two Venus earrings that Nina had given him, which he, in turn, had given Constance a few hours earlier. He touched the one, and he thought it brought the hint of a smile to her lips—dull as they were in the dark and from all the lipstick that had left them for his own lips. Anyway, Bucky smiled back at Constance, certain that whatever dreams played in her mind were of him now—or of whom he'd been in 1635.

Next, his eyes traced the rest of her form, past the arc of her bust, down the elegant arm that lay outside the sheet, along her legs to where he could even see where her toes curled, at the last of her every golden inch.

For twenty years he had dreamed of this night with this woman. For the last few months, the idea had consumed him. But never had he dared imagine that it—sex...love...passion...a woman—could be like this. Surely, only feelings that had lay restrained for centuries could account for such a raging surge of rapture. And surely, there was more even than that, for had not he and Constance both been the other—she the man, he the woman? Surely, that is what made it so perfect and exquisite, beyond what any mere man could ever feel, beyond what any mere woman could ever know. Only they, together, could experience the fullness of time and person. Only they, reincarnated in love, could be closest to God.

So, Bucky stared at Constance in wonder, reveling in the even grander dream that soon enough, she would be his forever, as he hers, as they theirs. His heart raced, and all around, the world was silver again.

But then as he kept his gaze upon her, contemplating these

wonders, one more feeling crossed Bucky's mind, one that surprised him and baffled him all the more that it could possibly crowd into his radiant consciousness. And that feeling would not go away. But how? How did it linger, even in the midst of this incredible ecstasy? But it did. Bucky would not even allow himself to give the feeling a name, even as it kept nagging at him. But he could not deny it, could not dispute that, deep within him, in some place that Constance could not reach, it was there.

And that feeling was doubt.

And now the silver was gone.

·27·

Constance, the next morning, talking to a cab driver: "Do you know this address?" She shows him a slip of paper that she's copied out of the phone book.

The cab driver takes her downtown to the address that is Jocelyn Ridenhour's apartment. Constance rings the bell by Jocelyn's name, but Jocelyn isn't there because she is at work. Constance, to herself, curses, "The nosy bitch."

She walks about in the heat, this way and that, purposelessly. This is so unlike Constance. At last, she returns to the Sherry-Netherland, packs, and goes back to Chicago. And back to trying to be Constance, altogether, once again.

Constance, a few days later, talking from Jackson Hole on the phone to Bucky at his office: "I love you." Constance's daughter, Elise, is working this summer at a resort in Wisconsin. Carl plays golf every morning. This is when Constance is all alone and calls Bucky. They are billing and cooing over the phone. It is driving them both crazy.

Unlike Bucky, Constance at least has the opportunity to get some of the frustration out of her system. She can ride all day. She's found a favorite horse at the stables, named Paradox. He is a huge stallion, dark bay (almost, in fact, black), powerful and independent. The stable hand, Simeon, didn't want Constance to ride him. Simeon saved Paradox for men—for strong, experienced men. But Constance demanded Paradox, and she showed Simeon that she could indeed handle the stallion.

So every day now, she rides him over the range and trails, galloping full out across the wildflowers. And Constance herself grows steely, stronger. Paradox can feel this domination upon his back, the sure control of the rider.

Always, too, back in the stable where there is a beam about seven feet high, Constance jumps up and grabs it and does pull-ups. Then, when she returns to the cottage, she strips before the bathroom mirror and studies herself. Curiously, though, Constance does not look at herself as a woman usually would, as she always has before. She does not peer in to study the beauty of her face, or to check and see how firm her breasts, how trim her waist. Instead, Constance seeks evidence of her new strength. Sometimes, even, she makes a muscle and flexes, reveling in her greater power.

Behind her own body, there in the mirror, she also sees Ollie. It isn't quite Ollie himself, for Constance can't fully realize a vision of him. But, she can see Ollie as Adonis, as Rubens painted him, draped in orange; she can see that magnificent form, that great rippling back, the tensed, powerful calves, the whole glorious body. And that lapidary handsome face upon it. Oh yes, Constance can see Ollie in the mirror—almost as well as she sees herself.

Bucky, talking on the phone to Constance, telling her: "Hey listen, sweetheart, you can't call me for a few days because I'm taking the kids on a sailboat trip." He is concentrating on spelling out the itinerary to her—up the Long Island Sound, stopping first at the Thimble Islands, then Fischer's Island, over to Block Island, then across the ocean to Cape Cod—because, of course, it is not just "the kids" he is taking. Rather, it is also Phyllis, the whole Buckingham family. Just like old times. But he doesn't have to be distracting, because Constance is barely paying attention. She has a different destination in mind. For them.

Constance, whispering, breathlessly, "Antwerp, darling. We must go to Antwerp and see where we were."

"As soon as we can, Connie. Promise." And just hearing him agree, Constance touches her nipples and she is all Constance again, all woman, all Bucky's.

Constance, dialing Jocelyn's number. Again. She never reaches Jocelyn, but this time, there is a message on the phone machine. Grimacing, Constance listens to: "Hi, it's Jocelyn. I'm gonna be away for, oh, a coupla weeks, and I will *not* be calling in for my messages because that's why I'm taking off, to get away from my messages. And look, if you're a gangster, don't try and rob my place. One of my friends, who was Bluebeard in a prior life, is staying at my apartment with some other bloodthirsty pirates, and he'll run you through, matey. Okay, till then...love ya."

Constance makes a very sour expression and hangs up.

Constance, the next morning, speaking politely to her travel agent, back in Chicago: "I need some help with a quick trip." Afterwards, she rides Paradox further than ever, way up on mountain trails that Simeon specifically warned her to avoid. The horse has total confidence in his rider by now, though, and he manipulates steep, dangerous terrain with confidence. Far from the resort, Paradox and Constance come across a small lake.

As Paradox munches on some grass, Constance strips and swims in the icy water, then lies naked in the sun, drying herself and dreaming of Bucky, of the two of them in Antwerp.

That evening with Carl, Constance telling him, "I got a call from the office today, and Schulbach wants me to attend an analysts' convention in Vegas the day after we get back. I made the reservation." Carl looks up from his paper and says he certainly understands these things. He is doing very well in his baseball Rotisserie League, and is studying the statistics of his players in *USA Today*. Altogether, it has been a good vacation for Carl, even if Constance has stopped giving him blowjobs. But he will return to the operating room with renewed energy, and although Elise will still be working in Wisconsin, he certainly can manage a few days alone at home while Constance will be stuck at that convention in Las Vegas.

That is not, however, quite where she would be.

Nina, sitting alone, despite herself, in gallery twenty-seven. She feels odd and helpless, but duplicitous too, because now she is absolutely cheating on her promise to Hugh. Often. She comes so regularly that all of the guards in European Paintings know her so well that they cast a wary eye upon her even as she merely sits on the bench. Nina looks left and right, staring at Adonis and then at the Madonna, wincing as she hears Bucky scream "...*owwwllllleeeeeee*..." in her head, always glancing back then at Adonis, knowing that incredibly handsome man was a murderer. A serial murderer, we would say now. What did they call such men then? A demon? An ogre? A monster? Words were better then, when they were more visceral and not so damned technical.

Ollie was a monster.

Nina needed to tell Bucky that. But how could she, if she didn't tell Constance, too? And she couldn't bring herself to tell her that she'd been a monster in another life. And it was wrong to conceal that truth. It was professionally wrong. It was ethically wrong.

But now Nina accepts the good news: Bucky obviously has taken her advice and isn't going to call again. And since she'd promised Hugh that she'd never call Bucky, then there's no more problem, is there? Well, she'd also promised Hugh she'd put the whole matter out of her head, but here she is once again, sitting in gallery twenty-seven. So, there still must be a problem.

Nina, returning from the Metropolitan, asking Roseann, "Are there any messages?" Asking much too anxiously, *are there any messages?* Hoping it is Bucky. That one message. So, yes, there is very much a problem.

Nina, late one afternoon after Roseann has gone, speaking on the phone to a receptionist (so very casually): "Is Mr. Buckingham there?" But the receptionist explains that he's still on vacation, till August 3rd. Nina gives her name and asks if he might call, at his leisure, whenever it is convenient, because it isn't important, and when he has the time, etc., etc.

Nina, in Washington, showing her ring to Lindsay. "Ohhh, Motherr!"

They talk about a wedding on the beach. Nina's office is closed so Roseann is on vacation, but still, Nina calls the answering service every day. She goes to the National Gallery, and even though there is a special Velázquez exhibition, Nina is only interested in the Rubenses. The drapery in his portrait of the Marchesa Brigida Spinola-Doria is more of a scarlet than Adonis's orange, but it is so reminiscent. Nina just sits in the National Gallery, staring. It makes her feel at home. And, sitting there, looking up at the Marchesa, it gives her an idea.

Nina, having taken a Metroliner Club Car back to New York, is taking a cab crosstown, to an address in the thirties, on Third Avenue. It is the Belgian Tourist Office, where Nina speaks to a young woman named Paulette, saying, "Would you be interested in making some extra money translating?"

Paulette would, so Nina gives her a list of questions which she asks her to translate into Dutch. She also asks Paulette for a few everyday expressions—hello, how are you, thanks; that sort of thing—and she asks how much difference there is between Dutch and Flemish. Paulette says, "Really, only the accent. At the extreme, it's like someone from Maine talking to someone from Mississippi."

"And how much has the language changed since, oh say, since Rubens's time?"

Paulette answers, "Certain constructions, a few words, some spelling. I suppose about as much as English has changed since Shakespeare." Nina nods, thinking, not all that much. But Paulette adds, "Funny you should ask. There was another lady in here not long ago, asking the same sort of questions. I gave her all the pamphlets on Rubens and Antwerp."

"Do you remember what she looked like?"

"Oh yes, very distinctive." Paulette screws up her nose, recalling the outfit that didn't quite work. But, politely, she only says, "Lovely pearl earrings. I remember. Rather tall lady. Intense. Very pretty, and big busted, too, you know."

Nina nods. "Yes. A colleague. We're involved in the same project. It's a historical, a, uh, history."

"Yes," says Paulette. She promises to get the questions translated quickly. In fact, Paulette gets the questions translated too quickly.

Nina, walking into her apartment that evening, cooing, "Oh, darling" at Hugh.

Her arms are full of groceries. Hugh has not moved in because Nina's place isn't quite big enough, but most nights, he comes here or she goes there, and then he stays here or she stays there. Tonight, back from Washington, she is going to fix him a terrific dinner and tell him all about the plans for the wedding on the beach at Rehoboth.

Hugh, brusquely avoiding a kiss, only takes the grocery bags, and brandishing a slip of paper, snaps, "I have two messages for you that your answering service thought were important."

Nina's body slumps. She can imagine. "You know, Roseann's away," she begins, as if that matters.

Hugh only reads off the paper. "A Paulette, from the Belgian Tourist office, has faxed over that translation you requested, and she also said you'd be pleased to know—*you'd be pleased to know*—that she included some alternative translation, as it might have been in—surprise!—Rubens's time."

"Hugh, I—"

"My, how helpful." Nina steps toward him, but he holds up a hand. "No, no, just a second. I said *two* messages, Doctor." Never has Nina heard his voice drip with so much sarcasm. "The other is quite simple." Long, long pause. "Mr. Buckingham returned your call." He holds out the slips. "Is that correct, Nina? You called him?"

"Yes, I did. I'm sorry."

"I want to make sure I understand. You initiated this?"

"Yes, I did."

Hugh says, "Jesus H. Christ."

Nina says, "Isn't that a lovely thing for a minister of the Lord to say?"

"Oh, I coveted my neighbor's wife. I committed adultery with her. I might as well take the name of the Lord God in vain, too.

Three commandments down, seven to go—"

"All on the Jezebel's behalf."

Hugh simply drops his head, pinching the top of his nose to contain himself. When he looks back up, he merely says, "I don't know whether I wrote it down. Mr. Buckingham will be in his office till six." He knows exactly what time it is, but he glances at his watch for effect. *Cheap pulpit trick,* Nina thinks. "You've still got twenty minutes." Then he walks past her to the door.

"Are you really *that* angry?" Nina calls after him.

"No, Nina. Worse. I'm disillusioned."

"You can't cut me some slack?"

Hugh turns back. "Oh come on. This isn't some situation comedy just before the first commercial, and we're gonna wrap it all up by the half-hour. You broke your promise to me, Nina. This damn nonsense has consumed you. This Bucky sonuvabitch is driving you crazy, so I asked you to promise me for your own good to give it up, and you willfully broke that promise."

"'Willfully,'" says Nina. "Jesus H. Christ."

Hugh lets that go. "Try to understand me, Nina. When we met, I very quickly cheated on my wife, as you very quickly cheated on your husband. And for all the love, all the passion, all the romance between us, I know you as a liar, and you know me as a liar. I wanted to believe that we deserved another chance, because I hoped, I prayed—I prayed to God—that your fall from grace was as aberrational as I knew mine was, that we bewitched each other, so that we acted in a way that was not consistent with the rest of our lives. And finally, finally, I convinced myself that that was so. Only now"—he shrugs—"I don't know, Nina. I just don't think I can ever trust you again."

Nina almost cries because maybe he doesn't love her anymore. And because certainly he thinks she's a liar. But, damn it, Nina won't cry. Instead, she crosses her arms over her chest and (sort of) counterattacks. "Is that it, Hugh? Is it really that cut-and-dried? Me?" He only puts his hand on the doorknob. "Or is it maybe you don't know if you can trust yourself?"

"Is this the Dr. Nina Winston one-size-fits-all analysis?"

"No, I leave that for the clergy. This is cut strictly to your own pattern. Because you seem scared to learn anything more about Bucky and Constance—afraid that if you listen to me, it might leave you no choice but to reconsider your faith and consider reincarnation."

"Ridiculous."

"Yes. Excuse me. Leave you no choice but to *believe* in reincarnation."

"No, you're the issue here, Nina—you and your wide-eyed gullibility." She starts to protest, but Hugh makes a T with his hands—the time-out sign. That certainly serves the purpose of shutting Nina up—although not because he is requesting her to do so, but because she finds Hugh so damn patronizing that it shocks her to silence. But, pleased, he continues. "So, if I mean nothing to you: go on, call this Bucky. Go see him. Hang out up at the museum and swoon, the two of you." And, turning away, he opens the door.

Nina is furious now, shouting, "You want your ring back?" She even holds up her hand—assuming, naturally, that he will tell her not to be a silly goose.

Instead, coolly, Hugh replies, "Yes, maybe that's a good idea." He is so dismissive, it hardly seems to matter, like if somebody at the grocery store has asked him if he wants a receipt. Nina doesn't have the opportunity to holler back at him, though, for just like that, he is gone.

Nina is devastated. But as soon as she composes herself, she knows exactly what she is going to do. Maybe if Hugh could have seen her now, maybe he would have understood how obsessed she had grown with it all. Certainly he could have understood then that Nina's involvement with Bucky and Constance had nothing to do with her love for him. Maybe. Certainly.

Nina, tingling with anticipation and wonder, dialing, waiting just two rings, then talking and planning. "Wonderful, Bucky," Nina sighs. "Just come by after work tomorrow." She says that, even as she plays with Hugh's ring that is still on her finger.

No, Hugh couldn't understand how much Nina wants to meet Margareta.

·28·

Bucky was not his old stuff. He was, in fact, almost timid. "Maybe we shouldn't try this again, Nina," he said.

She was the adventuresome one now. "No, I'm sure—we gotta see this through."

"I guess," he said in resignation even more than in agreement. He took off his jacket and moved to the couch.

As for Nina, she picked up the papers off her desk—the translation to her questions that Paulette in the Belgian Tourist Office had made for her. Briefly, then, she opened the drawer, glancing in at Michelangelo, his hand of God. "I told you," she said. "I think I've figured out a way to take you back—if, of course, you were ever there."

"Oh come on, Nina, I was there. You know that."

And well, yes, she did know this: if Bucky responded in Flemish to her Flemish questions, then what other explanation could there possibly be? "How's Constance?" Nina asked idly, stepping around the desk.

That brushed some of his nervousness away. "Oh, great, thanks. Just about ready to leave Jackson Hole." Nina darkened the lights, then sat in the chair opposite him. "Constance'll be here next month," he went on, "and she wants you to hypnotize her again. In fact, that's all she talks about. Well, that and us going to Antwerp."

"Okay, we'll see if we can take you back to Antwerp now," Nina said—and quickly then, just as before, she put Bucky into a trance, escorting him on that same simple journey back to his childhood.

She flicked on the tape recorder, as he carried on as a child, spoke as a child.

But now came the tricky part, and as he chatted on in his little-boy voice, Nina studied the questions in Flemish and prepared herself to try and make that leap in time with him. In the session before, Nina had been stopped cold by Bucky's scream—his death? Now, her task was to see if she couldn't reach around that block and bring Margareta back to life at some earlier point in her life.

The exercise would be complicated by the fact that if Bucky—if Margareta—did respond to Nina's questions in Flemish, Nina wouldn't understand the answers. She wouldn't be able to follow up naturally, but could only go through the list of questions, one by one. Nina had considered bringing Paulette into the session to conduct the interrogation, but she'd rejected that. This was all too strange and too private to involve some outsider. At least the first time, Nina wanted to try it this way.

So back into time now, Nina herself took Bucky back to "Antwerpen," she said, using the native pronunciation. And then, *"Hallo, Margareta."* Nina tensed, unsure, brimming with curiosity.

But wait—yes, she saw Bucky shift, saw him drop his hands into his lap, the left upon the right. Yes, as a woman would. And when he raised his face to her, Nina had no doubt that it was, somehow, a softer, sweeter countenance, with the eyes searching about in surprise, as if Bucky had walked into a new room. Nina said it again, *"Hallo, Margareta."*

Bucky replied, tentatively, *"Hallo."* But Nina thrilled. Just with that one word, she knew it was another voice, a more velvety tone to go with that gentler face that shyly eyed her now. And there was no doubt, either: the *hallo* was *hallo*, not *hello*.

Quickly then, Nina looked down at what was next on Paulette's sheet. *"Ik ben 'n vriendin van Ollie,"* she said. "I'm a friend of Ollie's."

Bucky's head tilted. Was it because he was so surprised? Because he didn't follow what Nina was saying with such an unfamiliar pronunciation? Whatever, Nina had anticipated such a possibility, and she rushed to read him this: *"Verontschuldig mij, maar ik spreek slecht Vlaamasch.* I don't speak Flemish very well, so please excuse me."

Bucky nodded. And Nina thought, surely he must understand Flemish, because I can see that he's straining to understand my poor pronunciation. If he didn't speak the language, he'd just sit in confusion. Surely, she thought, surely. And then, Bucky spoke again. Only this time it was more than just *hallo.* It was unmistakably foreign, and it certainly sounded like Flemish. What he said was: *"Fijn U to ontmoeten."*

Of course, Nina hadn't the foggiest idea what he'd said, and she wouldn't know until Paulette translated the tape for her. But, in fact, what Bucky had uttered in perfectly inflected Flemish was: "It's nice to meet you." And it was all completely different from the way Mr. Floyd Buckingham of Darien, Connecticut spoke. Why, Nina thought: even his mouth moves differently. And, just as Constance had taken on male mannerisms when she went back and became Ollie, now Bucky not only held his hands in a feminine fashion, but he crossed his legs to the side, at the ankles.

Nina tried to control her breathing. She couldn't lose her concentration. Ollie had been an easy subject, even if he did make a pass at her. But she had been able to fence with him, deal with him in English. But now, with Bucky—with Margareta—there could be no freelancing, no back-and-forth. Nina had to focus on speaking clearly—phonetically, in Flemish—and moreover, since she wouldn't be able to understand Bucky's answers, she had to study his expression, so that she could at least gauge whether his reply indicated agreement or dispute, or perhaps just some simple narrative. *"Ik heb Ollie in Engeland leren kennen,"* Nina said. "I knew Ollie in England."

But this time Bucky didn't respond. He glanced down, brushing nervously at the hair by the ear in a manner that only women do. Yes, Nina thought. She'd anticipated something like this, that Margareta might very well be ashamed to talk about Ollie; he was, after all, an illicit lover. So, Nina had prepared for this eventuality, and, glancing down at the sheets Paulette had given her, she read: *"Ik ben ook eens ontrouw geweest aan mijn echtgenoot.* Once, I was unfaithful to my husband, too."

And Bucky looked up. But no, it wasn't Bucky. Not any longer. Now Nina had no doubt. It was Margareta, absolutely and completely. She even smiled in some sort of conspiratorial, sisterly fashion at Nina, indicating she was pleased to have found a kindred spirit. *"Oh, waarom nam U 'n minnaar?"* Obviously, it was a question, and it frustrated Nina horribly that she didn't know what Margareta had asked her. (In fact, as she would learn later, it was: "Oh, why did you take your lover?") Quickly, then, Nina again sought out those phrases which apologized for her lack of Flemish and pleaded for Margareta's forbearance. And Margareta nodded at the stranger, understanding.

Hurriedly, then, afraid to lose her interest, Nina asked Margareta another question: *"Waarom houdt gij van Ollie?* Why do you love Ollie?"

That was the right question. Jackpot. Margareta broke into what can only be described as an adorable smile. It burst through all her shyness. And now Nina was carried along by the persona before her and no longer saw the person. She was talking to Margareta, and she could even see the Madonna, exactly as she had been posing with St. Francis. It was uncanny. And Margareta gushed an answer: *"Hij is 'n echte gentlemen, zo zacht in de omgang en zo lief. Sinds ik hem voor het eerst ontmoette, poserend voor Adonis in het Rubenshuis."*

That made Nina tingle all the more. She had heard the word *Adonis* clearly, and *Rubenshuis,* and what sounded very much like the English "posing." Hadn't she? Nina had to contain herself, to keep her eyes on her sheets before her, to keep asking the questions she had there. But she seemed to have Margareta's confidence, because she replied to Nina's every question. Sometimes, even, she answered at length, often with animation, about her growing up, and her husband (whose name clearly was Jan; it came up again and again) and about their marital difficulties (frowns) and about their two children (smiles). And oh, did she gush on about Ollie whenever Nina asked the simplest question about him.

God, but she loves that man, Nina thought. She didn't need to know the words. It was very much like when Lindsay first started telling her about Ted. Nina knew Lindsay was going to marry him long before Lindsay told her—maybe even before Lindsay knew herself. Just the way she talked about him, her eyes glittering. That was the way Margareta talked of Ollie. And her smile. It was that same warm Madonna smile that Nina knew from the painting. Rubens hadn't created it. No, his genius was that he could have so perfectly captured it.

But then Nina began to fret: Margareta's too much in love with him. Like all of Ollie's women, she's blinded by his charms. The poor thing. He's going to kill her, too, and I can't stop it.

Wait! Nina grabbed her biceps with her opposing arms, and shook herself. *Stop it! Stop it, you jackass!* Hugh is right. You're not being rational. This person talking to you lived three hundred and fifty years ago. This is not happening now. It *has* happened. Already. Past tense. It is over. Ollie *has* killed her. You can't climb into a time machine and go back and stop it. Nina shook herself back into reality.

But the questions on the sheet were running out. Hold to the course. Ask them all. One by one. And: just as well it's almost over. This is too intense. Too much concentration. And worse, now Margareta grows very upset. She is talking about someone. Who's that? Elsa? Is that the name? Wasn't that the name of the whore Ollie mentioned to her? Maybe, Nina thought, maybe Margareta has found out Ollie is sleeping with this other woman, and this is what's troubled her. Anyway, Margareta even sniffled some.

Nina kept asking questions, but it was getting more difficult. When finally she asked when Margareta was going to see Ollie again, and she shied at that—only responding reluctantly after a long pause—Nina knew it was time to end the session. Still, she could not help but add one more thing she had asked Paulette to write down. "*Wees voorsichtig, Margareta,*" she said. "Be careful."

"*Voorsichtig?*" Margareta replied, unknowing, more confused than disturbed.

"*Ja, ja, Margareta. Wees voorsichtig.*"

Margareta only looked up, puzzled, and so Nina knew: enough. She told her to look deeply into her eyes and they locked gazes, at first in friendship and trust, and then in a trance, until right before her, Nina saw Margareta's body shift—the hands, the legs, the posture—until suddenly Bucky emerged again, fresh and buoyant.

"Hey," he piped up in his old familiar voice, "how'd I do?"

Nina didn't answer right away. Instead, she only rose from her chair; she had to control her shaking. Then, instead of responding, she just picked up the tape recorder, pushed the rewind button, stopping it at random. Margareta was speaking. Bucky listened, baffled. "That's not...?" he began.

"Oh yeah, that's you."

"But it sounds just like a woman, speaking—"

"Flemish. It's Margareta speaking. But it's you...speaking."

"Oh my God. What am I saying?"

"I don't know. I'd catch a word now and then. But it's Flemish. I mean, I'm sure it's Flemish. I'll find out exactly when this woman from the Belgian Tourist office comes back from vacation Monday. She'll translate, so let's you and me make an appointment the next evening."

Bucky glanced at his little appointment book. "No, I'll be away that day. Boston. Big Reebok presentation. Wednesday," he said. "I'll come around. Four o'clock?"

Nina nodded. She wrote it down in her own calendar: August 14th. She tried to be matter-of-fact. But all of a sudden, she was overwhelmed with the thoughts of what had just happened, and she fell into Bucky's arms as once in Central Park he had fallen into hers. Nina didn't cry, but she asked him to hold her—"No, hold me, Bucky, really hold me!"—so that he could pull her back together, restore her senses, make her whole, so she would stop worrying about trying to stop a murder that happened many centuries ago.

·29·

As amazed as Nina was with herself, she reached for the phone book and started dialing. She was bouncing off the walls, and so ethical or not, she had to discuss Ollie and Margareta with someone. And who else? But, of course, Jocelyn had already left for Europe, leaving Nina to chuckle at the Bluebeard message as surely as Constance had turned up her nose at it.

You know, Nina thought, I could really like Jocelyn—even if she did scare the hell out of me in various ugly ways. But any woman who could seduce the two men I like most in America must have a great deal in common with me. So, she chirped, "It's Nina Winston, Jocelyn. Call me as soon as you get back from Antwerp. I'm dying to hear."

Back to bouncing off the walls. So, no other choice. Got a cab, went to Hugh's. This'll be a twofer: she'll convince him about Bucky and Constance, and then they'll make up. So, she let herself in and made a Scotch. Tried to read the newspaper. Couldn't. Too distracted. Same with *Talk* magazine. Ditto *The New York Observer*. Finally, mercifully, the key turned. The door opened. "Fix you one?" asked Nina, cheerily raising her glass.

"I'll get it," Hugh replied, without any particular acknowledgment of her presence—let alone any warmth.

Oh well. Nina followed him over to his little makeshift bar in the corner. "I have to tell you what's going on so you'll understand better."

"What's going on about you?"

"No, it's really what happened today with Bucky."

Hugh just said, "That's none of my affair," over his shoulder, as he went into the kitchen for an ice tray.

Nina called after him. "Yes, it is your affair because it affects me, and it's still my understanding that we're engaged to be married."

Hugh didn't respond, only dropped some ice cubes into his glass.

Gamely, Nina went on. "Besides, it isn't exactly like I'm giving away confidences, because all this happened three hundred and fifty years ago."

"Sez you: three hundred and fifty years ago." He sipped his drink, falling into his favorite chair. Nina went to her pocketbook, took out her tape recorder, and flicked it on. Loud. "So, okay, I give up," Hugh said after awhile, affecting disinterest. "What the hell is that?"

"That is Mr. Buckingham talking, hypnotized, in my office about two hours ago. He is speaking seventeenth-century Flemish in a woman's voice, which is especially interesting, inasmuch as he is not a woman and never even knew Flanders existed."

"Whatdya want, Nina? An argument? Is that the purpose of this little show-and-tell? I just don't know. Okay?"

"So, okay, I'll tell you. Her name—Bucky, speaking—is Margareta, and she's in love with a sailor named Ollie, who she doesn't know is a murderer."

"Blinded by love for the cad?" he said, facetiously.

"Yes, yes. We silly female vessels are sometimes blinded by love. Personally, fragile li'l thing though I may be, I still wouldn't know the feeling. But Margareta is so taken in, she doesn't realize he's going to kill her."

"Let's see now," Hugh said, holding up his glass, pretending to peer into it. "This is the twenty-first century, but he is *going* to kill her in the seventeenth century. Damn it, Nina, you're getting as goofy as Jocelyn."

"Maybe only goofy women deign to screw you, Hugh." She sat in the chair across from him, plopping down hard to punctuate her remark.

It was a long time before he said anything, and then he spoke wearily, "You know, Nina, I'm really tired of this. I forgot something in our past in order to give us a future. Now, tit-for-tat: you've gotta forget this...for us."

"Okay, if it was just the past. But somehow I have the feeling that what happens then connects to now—maybe even us."

"Damn it, the only people in the seventeenth century who have any effect on us today are Shakespeare and Galileo and maybe—"

"Oh, Bucky, you're not listening to me." She stopped. It took a delayed reaction for her to realize that she'd called Hugh by Bucky's name. "I'm sorry, I—"

He sipped his Scotch. Then: "All right, it's out. So tell me the truth. This has nothing to do with reincarnation or Rubens or any of that who-shot-John. You're just sweet on the guy, aren't you?"

"Oh Hugh stop, a slip of the tongue."

"Hey, it's okay. I wouldn't be the first old fool who got passed over for a better, younger, reasonable facsimile."

"Oh, come on."

"'Oh, come on doesn't constitute a denial, does it?"

"All right, a declaration: I'm in love with you, and you know it. And I'm not in love with Bucky."

"Were you? Did you two have an affair?"

"No and no. But yes, I am terribly fond of him, and yes, I feel obligated to help him and Constance to sort out this mystery in their lives."

Hugh shook his head. "I wish you had had an affair."

"What the hell does that mean?"

"It means that is something I could understand. *That* makes sense. But this insane determination of yours, to buy into a fairy tale."

"Will you just listen to me, Hugh?"

"Well, thank you. You got your fiancé's name right that time."

Nina let the steam escape through her ears, and then patiently stood up and approached him. "Now, for the last time—"

"Hey, that's the best news I've heard."

"Will you please?" He nodded. "First, Jocelyn played you that awful scream. Unforgettable." He nodded again. "And now you've heard Bucky talking in another language, and like a woman. And Constance tells me she was a murderer. She's a man, Hugh! A total womanizer. Even made a pass at me."

That got his attention. "You're kidding."

Nina pawed at her chest. "Oh yeah, like this. Reached out to give me a feel. And know what? Stopped because she didn't know what a bra is. Because they didn't have bras then." She was rolling now. "Know what a boyer is, Hugh?"

"A what?"

"A boyer. B-o-y-e-r. I had to look everywhere before I finally found out. It's an old English word that means a sailing ship that stays close to the coastline. And Constance—Ollie—used that word. Just tossed it off. She can speak a few words of Flemish, too, and when she's speaking English, she sounds just like Shakespeare."

"Well, maybe that's it. Maybe she was in a Shakespeare play in high school or something like that."

"Yeah, I know. I know all about Bridey Murphy. I know all about all those people who seem to have lived in the past, but were exposed. They learned a language as a child and forgot they had, or something they read in a book stuck in their head long after they forgot about reading it. I know all that stuff. But nothing explains this."

"Why is this different?"

"Because," Nina said, leaning on the arms of his chair, staring into his face, "because never—*never*—have we had two people independently collaborate on a past life. Can't you see? Jocelyn is right. That's what sets this apart from even the most serious evidence of reincarnation, ever."

He held up his hands, and she—well, she got out of his face. But Nina kept looming over him, arms akimbo. Finally Hugh replied—calmly, unmoved. "Look, Nina, maybe we can't see it, but there's a logical explanation."

Nina shook her head—too deliberately. (Two could play this game of overacting.) "You know what, Hugh, if you'd been back there two thousand years ago, and Jesus came up to you after the crucifixion, and you stuck your fingers into his wounds, you'd have said, well, there must be a logical explanation. And you know what: it'd be Doubting Hugh now, not Doubting Thomas."

Hugh rolled his eyes, infuriating her even more. "Come on, Nina, you profess to be a devout person. A faith is not a buffet where we just pick out what we want to. There must be a coherence to what we believe."

"Our beliefs can't grow like our knowledge?"

Hugh squirmed a bit. "I didn't know this was going to be a theological discussion."

"Hey, you won't listen to what's actually *happened* to me, so I have to move into your realm—faith." Nina was getting very frustrated, both at his refusal to give her any credence, and his condescension. "And no matter how deeply you believe, or I believe, or millions of Hindus or Buddhists believe, no matter how much anybody believes, none of us *know*." She leaned down then, and jabbed Hugh with her forefinger—right smack in his chest, right in Piglet's Patch. "None of us *know* Jack shit."

Well, that certainly took them both aback. *Jack shit*, Nina thought; for years I've wanted to say "Jack shit." (Maybe this wasn't quite the right moment.) She smiled weakly. "I mean, Hugh, when something new and inexplicable appears, who's to say that we can't believe that, too?"

"Maybe I'm just a hard sell, Nina. When a likeness of the Virgin Mary appears in a pepperoni pizza over in New Jersey, I don't fall down and worship it right away."

"Oh, that's so easy, Hugh, so glib. But let's forget the abstract. Let's forget Virgin Mary pizzas and Bucky and Constance. What's the explanation for *us*?"

"For us?"

"Yeah, that's not so easy. But you know damn well that the only thing that accounts for us now is that somewhere, sometime we were lovers before."

Hugh got up and walked away from her. "Oh, knock it off, Nina. People fall in love all the time, inconveniently, for the same reasons we did. Because we're all very human. And because there's a physical attraction, and because we share the same interests and humor and temperament, because of all that. It happens. And it doesn't mean that we had to have been sweethearts back in the Ming Dynasty."

"Oh no, Hugh, it's not that simple. I know you saw it, just like I did. I know you saw it when you touched me, when we—"

"Oh God yes, Nina, it was wonderful. Every time."

She shook her head at him. "Oh come on, Hugh. I'm not talking about the Earth moving beneath us. I'm not talking about orgasms. Orgasms are dime a dozen. Orgasms are on magazine covers. You can send away for orgasms in videos. I'm talking about the color, Hugh. Every time I kiss you. Every time you touch me. Every time we make love. It's our color. It's what identifies Double Ones. Right? And I know you've seen it, Hugh. I know."

Hugh didn't reply. He only stood there, looking at Nina with a certain bewilderment. Nina walked over and took the doorknob. "You know you saw it, and you always do see it with me, and that scares the holy hell out of you, doesn't it?"

When he still didn't answer, Nina made him react fast. Quickly, without warning, she snatched his engagement ring off her finger, and underhanded, lofted it to him. The flip was a little to his right, and since he still held his drink in that hand, he had to twist some to snare it across his body with his left hand. Even with just that brief an extra motion, though, Nina had time to open the door and depart before he could say anything else.

Instead, Hugh simply stood there, looking at the ring. Only softly then—but out loud—did he murmur: "Oh God, Nina, you're right. Every time with you, every time it was always so silver."

•30•

The bells, the bells. From the moment Jocelyn had arrived in Antwerp, it seemed to her that it was all bells, tolling all the time. The bells on high even made her instinctively look up. So, she studied Antwerp from the top down, starting with the magnificent gothic tower of the Cathedral of Our Lady, soaring above all of Antwerp, all of Flanders, all of Belgium.

Down some then, Jocelyn lowered her gaze to the familiar stepped roofs, their perpendicular lines so different from the slanted roofs of other houses the world over. And then, below them, her eyes fell upon the statues of Antwerp—the Madonnas especially. Everywhere. *Is this a city or a convent?* Jocelyn asked herself, laughing. But the answer came quickly enough as she dropped her sights to her own level, to the happy people milling everywhere about her, plunking themselves down at the cafés that spilled over into the sidewalks—snacking at chocolates, wolfing down mussels and pastry and pasta, quaffing beer upon beer, laughing and flirting, and altogether, being very, very secular.

How glorious is Antwerp, Jocelyn thought. Oh, to be a Double One here with the bells and the gaiety ringing in your ears. She took a seat near a strolling accordion player and when the waiter approached, Jocelyn Ridenhour, the first lady of coffees, slammed her fist down on the table and hollered out, "Gimme a beer!"

It was hardly that Jocelyn needed the special sparkle of Antwerp. On the contrary. Her visit with Sergei and Ludmilla had been exhilarating. For their part, too, the Mironovs had been absolutely thrilled by Jocelyn's revelations about Bucky and Constance. "You must speak with them again," Sergei had exclaimed. "Why, it may be centuries before we have such perfect Double Ones specimens again—until people start seeing their former selves in old photographs."

Jocelyn winced a bit when the translator explained that Sergei had used the word "specimen." That was a bit too scientific, even rather un-American. Still: "I'll do my best," Jocelyn promised. When she left on the train for St. Petersburg, laden down with the Mironovs's blessings and with all the notes she had taken, Jocelyn was more determined than ever to publish their work.

For now, though, all she wanted was to immerse herself in Antwerp, to revel in the city where Bucky and Constance had cavorted with Rubens so many centuries ago. Jocelyn had, in fact, chosen to stay at the Alfa Theatre Hotel, precisely because it lay so near Rubenshuis. By the time she'd arrived in Antwerp, though, it had already been a long day from St. Petersburg: an SAS connection through Copenhagen, then a good hour's bus ride from the airport at Brussels. So Jocelyn decided to put off visiting Rubenshuis immediately, saving it for tomorrow when she'd be more rested. Instead, that was when Jocelyn had ventured into the very heart of the old city to soak up the atmosphere. And she soaked up that beer, too. And another. With the bells ringing. Ah, the bells. Ah, Antwerpen!

Well, she thought, glancing at her watch, she could still manage visits to a couple of Rubens attractions before dinner. So, she wound around the twisty streets to the entrance to the Cathedral. It was thronged. "Is it always so crowded?" Jocelyn asked the ticket taker.

"But, of course, madam, tomorrow is August the fifteenth, Our Queen of Heaven's own special day, when she was taken up to heaven." Assumption Day was even, in fact, an official holiday in Antwerp. So, inside, Jocelyn moved directly to the altar to stand there before Rubens's rendering of that very occasion. *The Assumption of the Holy Virgin*, perhaps his most acclaimed baroque work, had been finished in 1627. Jocelyn was no particular fan of religious art, and she surprised herself that she studied it for so long. But she was enthralled by the huge painting's energy and movement, those glorious colors, the shades, the light—Mary, lifting off to heaven, convoyed by a bevy of cherubs—and she stood in front of it for several minutes before she went back outside again to the worldly chaos of Antwerp. There, Jocelyn brought an ice cream from a vendor and watched a mime posing as a clown before she pulled out her tourist map and decided to stop at the Plantin-Moretus House on the way back to her hotel.

So, down the Blomstraat she wandered, into the Groen Plaats—the Green Place—the great park that was dominated by the massive bronze statue of Rubens himself, looking out over his city. Of course, Jocelyn went out of her way to stand before the sculpture, and that diversion got her turned around (which is easy to do in old Antwerp) so that Jocelyn had gone the other way out of the Groen Plats, around the Hilton Hotel, before she got back on track and came down the Lombardenvest toward the Plantin-Moretus House.

Balthasar Moretus, one of Rubens's closest friends, had been recognized on his own merit as perhaps the finest printer in all of Europe. And now, inside the huge, rambling house—a residence and shop alike—Jocelyn felt herself transported back even more to the time of Rubens—especially since the master's work adorned the halls, his portraits there, it seemed, in every room that Jocelyn walked through. My God, she thought, if this house where Rubens was only a guest can affect me so, then surely Rubenshuis, where he actually lived, where he slept with Helena and painted Ollie and Margareta—surely, that will overwhelm me.

Yes, tomorrow she would go there, to Rubenshuis itself. And then to Saint James, Rubens's parish church, where the guidebooks said he had married Helena, where their children were baptized, and where—under his own magnificent painting of *The Madonna with the Christ Child and Saints*—Rubens himself lay, bracketed forever between the bones of both his beloved wives, Isabella and Helena.

But now, finishing her tour of the Plantin-Moretus House, Jocelyn was through with her sightseeing for the day and she only paused at the souvenir stand, perusing the Rubensianna there. The clerk, noting her deep interest, said, "And surely tomorrow you will be visiting the Rubens Fair."

"The what?"

"Ah, didn't you know? Every August 15th, on Assumption Day, in the Grote Markt, everyone dresses as they did in Rubens's time, and there is a wonderful fair all day long."

How perfect, Jocelyn thought, how lucky that I have, by chance, come to Antwerp on this one most appropriate day of the year. She thanked the clerk, but then as she turned to leave, she noticed the guest book. Jocelyn picked up the pen, signing her name beneath the signatures of a visitor from Munich and a family from Turin. Idly, Jocelyn looked back through the signatures to find the name of a tourist from the United States. There was none on this page, so she had to flip the sheet back.

Three up from the bottom, she saw it. The name was in a feminine hand, standing out in a soft, blue ink that contrasted with the other thin, black signatures. Jocelyn could not believe it. Her mouth flew open. This is what she read:

8/14	Constance Rawlings	Lake Forest, Illinois United States	So perfectly restored. I felt as if I had been here before!

·31·

At this same moment, Constance was lingering on Hopland Street, staring at the house which she had decided was the one where Ollie and Margareta had made love all those times. Then, she went round the corner to Wapperstraat, the old canal that was now a broad promenade. At first glance, Constance was put out, for Rubenshuis had been surrounded by modern buildings. She screwed up her face. Why, there was even a music store on one side, a café on the other, an ATM directly across. How could this be done to Mr. Rubens's house?

Besides, most everything else in the vicinity seemed to have appropriated the master's good name. The Rubens tavern, inn, café—God knows what. Only if you narrowed your vision to the house alone, did it stand as magnificent as ever it had. Constance walked by it, down toward The Meir, past where some huge shrubbery islands made of concrete had been constructed in the middle of Wapperstraat. She rested on one of the benches there, lost in reverie, drifting further and further back, before she arose and returned to the Rubenshuis before her.

She stepped inside, handing over her seventy-five Belgian francs. The ticket taker said, "We'll be closing in less than an hour. Perhaps you'd prefer to come back tomorrow."

Constance replied, "Thank you, but I just want to visit the garden now. I'll return tomorrow to tour the house."

"All right, but I'm afraid I still must charge you full tariff."

"I understand, but I'll be quite happy in the garden. I remember how beautiful it is."

"Ah, you've been here before?"

Constance did not answer. Instead, she only stepped away, cutting through the main studio, then past the shop, out under the portico, and on to the garden. There, her knees almost buckled. It was all so incredibly familiar that Constance really wasn't even cognizant of a whole covey of Japanese tourists. Rather, it was as if she was alone, wandering amidst the flowers, under the great fur tree, now looking at all the statues that adorned the rear of the mansion, then almost collapsing onto her favorite bench, the curved stone one at the northern end.

The arbor! The honeysuckle arbor was before her—just as always. God, how she remembered all this. Why, she remembered it even better than she remembered being Constance. But suddenly, then, as she looked out over the garden, it disappeared before her. Instead, all that flooded her vision were the red and black diamonds. That same old pattern. It was overwhelming—more vivid than ever. And now Constance was gone. It was only Ollie sitting on the stone bench. Ollie, alone, listening to the bells. How well Ollie remembered all the bells of Antwerp.

But then, a voice: "I'm sorry, madam, but it's five o'clock. We're closing for the day."

Constance looked up blankly at this stranger. And all of a sudden, she was aware how cold she was. The sun was gone, behind black clouds, and here she was in her short-sleeved, teal blouse. "Oh, yes, of course," Constance mumbled absently, fingering one of her Venus earrings. "But where are the peacocks? There were always peacocks here."

"I don't know, madam. I've been here fourteen years myself, and we've never had any peacocks in the garden."

"Oh, they were here," Constance persisted. "Mr. Rubens adored peacocks."

"Did he?"

"Oh yes. He told me once—" Constance caught herself, nervously toyed with her earring again. The guard was looking at her curiously. "I mean, of course, I read that he wanted peacocks about for his wife, for peacocks were the emblem of Juno, the goddess, the guardian of domesticity."

"Yes, well, I'm sorry, but we don't have any here now."

"Well, you should. If this is Mr. Rubens's house, you should have peacocks."

"Of course," said the guard. It had been a long day. "And thank you for visiting us."

"My pleasure." The bells began again—even clearer, it seemed to Constance.

Jocelyn heard the bells, too, and even louder, because after encountering Constance's name at the Plantin-Moretus House, she had to regroup. She found her way back near the cathedral, to another café at the Groen Plaats, another beer. There were so many beers to choose from in Antwerp. The waiter suggested a Kriek—a brew tinged red, with kind of a bitter cherry taste—and Jocelyn savored it as she pondered her next move.

Well, it must be obvious, she thought: Constance and Bucky had snuck off to Antwerp to be there on the city's day of days—Assumption Day. How appropriate! But she would find them. There weren't that many top hotels in Antwerp, and Jocelyn knew Bucky well enough to know that he wouldn't be going downscale. Maybe Constance and Bucky were even staying at her own hotel, the Alfa Theatre. She'd ask there first, at the desk.

But then, after she tossed down the last of her red beer and started walking back, Jocelyn passed by the Hilton and decided she might as well inquire there. She went across the large lobby to the house phone. A Floyd Buckingham, please? Sorry, the operator told her, no one registered by that name. Jocelyn started to put the phone down, when she spoke up again. "Well then, perhaps a Constance Rawlings?"

"Oh yes, indeed, Mrs. Rawlings is here." Excited, Jocelyn listened as the phone to her room rang. But: no answer. Should she call the operator back and leave a message? No, Jocelyn didn't know Constance, and if the lady was traveling alone, she decided it'd be best to confront her directly.

So, Jocelyn headed out of the Hilton, and following her street map, she turned this way and that until just before she reached The Meir, she took a right on Huidevettersstraat. Too bad. Had Jocelyn gone the other way, up The Meir, she and Constance would all but have collided a block or so on.

Constance was walking so fast now that she wasn't even chilly anymore. And without looking at her map, she knew exactly where she was going. Constance didn't even slow up as she came to the Hilton. Strode right past it. Through the Groen Plaats, then around the little streets that took her to the Grote Markt where soon the stalls for the Rubens Fair would be set up. Above her, all around the square, the magnificent guild houses stood as sentinels, all with their stepped roofs and the shining figures on top that symbolized their patron saints.

And now, off this way, Constance strode toward the river, toward the Schelde. Instinctively, she was heading down the Zilversmidstraat toward Bloed Berg, Butchers Hill. On she hurried, even faster. And she thought: what a wonderfully modern city this Antwerp is. Why, all these fancy statues, abutting out from the buildings on every corner. And all the streets are paved, the gutters running down the middle. Not like that muddy sewer of a city, London. And Amsterdam wasn't much better, was it?

And then, when Constance came round the corner on little Burchtgracht, it all mixed together, the past and the present, that old Antwerpen and this Antwerp, Ollie and Constance, man and woman, and she really couldn't fathom anything anymore. But wait...yes, surely this was Burchtgracht. There was the butcher's hall, the tower. And here was Bloed Berg. But then, where is the cattle market? That's always been here. And the smell. There is *no* smell. How can that be? And the *vliet*—the canal? Where has that gone? A canal cannot just disappear.

Constance kept looking around in confusion. And now the bells were ringing. Yes, yes. That helped. And now: I do smell it. As always here: the odor of carnage, of hides and bowels and blood. And yes, this time when she peered back to the Burchtgracht, it was the canal and she could see Elsa in it, flowing away under Blood Hill, out to the Schelde.

Well, that was as it should be. But suddenly, that memory reminded Constance that she better leave. The *scutters* were surely on the alert. Hadn't Mr. Rubens posted a reward? Damn him. Who would have ever imagined he would have done that for a common whore? And hadn't too many people seen Ollie with Elsa? Yes, it would be wise to get away from here, from where Elsa had been strangled. So, quickly now, Constance stepped off, toward the bank of the Schelde.

There in the river was a massive, spanking clean white cruise ship that had just disgorged its tourists. But Constance didn't even notice this leviathan. What Constance did see, though, was the dull, redbrick old Steen. There, by the river, was the jail where the prisoners were kept. She'd heard plenty about the Steen. And Ollie certainly didn't want to end up there. Yes, maybe better to take off for Dunkirk right now, find a privateer to sign on with and be gone for good from Antwerpen.

But leave Margareta? Her stupid husband is off to Liege tomorrow, and we'll have a whole week together at the house on Hopland. I want that. I must stay. But how strange. It is not just to poke this woman. There are others far prettier than Margareta. Bess was simply gorgeous. And others more sumptuous, more alluring. But Margareta is the one I want.

So, yes, I'll risk staying just to be with her. Even if I may be caught, imprisoned in the Steen, put to my death. Because: I...love... her. At last, I really do *love* a woman.

So Ollie would not leave Antwerp. But now, when he looked out toward the Schelde, not only was there no cruise ship, but no Steen, either. In fact, no river. No city. All that was there, in Ollie's vision, was that pattern of red and black. Ever since he'd arrived back in Antwerp, it was brighter, sharper, the red and the black, tracing away for as far as his eyes could see, out into space, out into time.

·32·

Nina held up the transcript that Paulette had just sent over from the Belgian Tourist Office. "It's all here," she said. "We'll go through it together." Nervously, Bucky took a seat across her desk. First though, for a few seconds, she turned on the tape recorder. "I just want to remind us how you sounded," she said. "Margareta, in 1635, in the Antwerp of Peter Paul Rubens."

He only nodded. Bucky was, in fact, terribly subdued. His reaction to hearing himself on the tape had been different, an even more bewildered amazement than when he had first encountered Constance or *Venus and Adonis*. Those, after all, were external incidents—bizarre and inexplicable, to be sure—but this was more confounding because it was just Bucky all by himself astonishing Bucky. He was still sitting there, in something approaching numbness, as Nina flipped off the tape and started reading from the transcript.

"I began by just saying, *'Hallo, Margareta,'*" Nina said, "and you replied *'Hallo.'* It was instantly clear to me that you were speaking in a different voice." Bucky nodded. "Then I tried to make you comfortable. Paulette had written out: 'I am a friend of Ollie's,' in Flemish. And when I said that, boy, did that get your attention. You gave me a big smile and said, 'It's nice to meet you.'"

"Of course, I didn't understand what you said, but I gathered it was just something polite and conventional, so I told you: 'I knew Ollie in England,' and you smiled again—but somewhat sheepishly."

"Why?" Bucky asked.

Nina leaned back. "There was something I learned from Constance when she was hypnotized that I never told either of you."

"What's that?"

"You—Margareta—were married. Your love affair with Ollie was extramarital."

Bucky was a little annoyed. "Why didn't you tell us?"

"I just thought there was enough on your plate at that time. Okay?"

Bucky said, "Okay," but in a cursory fashion.

Nina went on. "Anyway, I assumed that you—that Margareta—might be a little troubled that I knew she was cheating on her husband, so, quickly, I added"—Nina looked down at the transcript—"something to gain her confidence, just-us-girls stuff. I said: 'Once, I was unfaithful to my husband, too.'

Nina kept her eyes on the paper when she said that. And she didn't raise it, either, when she went on: "And so you asked me: 'Oh, why did you take your lover?'" Only now, and tentatively, did Nina glance up to see Bucky looking at her. He arched his eyebrows, as if to say *Well, did you?* Nina ignored him. "Of course, since I don't understand Flemish, I had no idea what Margareta had asked me, so I just replied: 'I'm sorry. I do not understand.' I'd had Paulette write that phrase out for me, too." And quickly, then: "So next I asked—"

But not quickly enough. "Wait a minute. Why *did* you take a lover, Nina?"

"That was for Margareta's consumption," she snapped.

Bucky smirked. "Okay, Doctor. And your secret is safe with Margareta."

"Thank you. May we go on?"

"Please."

"So then I asked Margareta: 'Why do you love Ollie?' And she answered: 'He is so gentle, so sweet to me. And so handsome. Since first I saw him at Rubenshuis, posing as Adonis, I couldn't take my eyes from him.'

"And so then I asked: 'And do you love your husband...at all?'

"'Once I did. I loved Jan greatly when first we met. But after the children came, he didn't seem to care for me much anymore. And I'm sure now there are other women. He finds them when he travels, or he pays for the whores on the Burchtgracht. Do you know the Burchtgracht, by Blood Hill?'"

Nina annotated the text for Bucky again. "I knew Margareta was asking me another question," she explained, "so once more, I had to say: 'I'm sorry, I don't understand Flemish well.' But quickly, then, to keep her interest, I asked: 'Do you like being a model for Rubens?'

"And Margareta answered me: 'Oh yes, it is wonderful, for now I have new friends and a job where I can earn a few guilders for myself. And, best of all, that was where I met Ollie, when Mr. Rubens chose him to be Adonis.'"

Nina looked up again. "I remember that well. I heard Margareta say 'Adonis' again, so I took a chance and I pointed at you—at Margareta—and I said, 'Venus?'

"And you laughed a little, and"—Nina looked back down—"and you said: 'Oh no, not me. I haven't enough—'

Nina laughed herself. "Of course, Paulette only had the tape. She had no idea what was transpiring, so there's nothing descriptive in the transcript. But what happened was that you'd gestured to your chest then and shook your head. And that's what you meant when you said you didn't have enough to be Venus."

Bucky shook his head sadly. "I wasn't stacked, huh?"

"Well, not enough for Rubens. But don't take it too hard, Bucky. Remember, Rubens was pretty demanding in that category. In fact, since I was pretty sure what Margareta was gesturing about, I pointed to my own chest, like this, and said, 'No, me too'—you know, in English, but Margareta understood and we laughed together."

Bucky shook his head. "*We* laughed together. You and me. Our little hen party—our affairs, our boobs."

Nina didn't take the bait. She only said, "But you must understand, Bucky. You *were* a woman—completely. The way you spoke. Your manner. The way you held yourself. It was every bit as disconcerting as when Constance became Ollie. You have to believe me: she was totally masculine. And you: feminine."

Bucky only sighed and mimicked a woman's wave. "Go on, dearie."

Nina continued reading the translation. "So Margareta told me: 'Helena, Mrs. Rubens—she is Venus. I am the Madonna, but in another painting. You see, the master thinks I have such a sweet face. All my life, in fact, everyone has said: Margareta, such a sweet face you have. Ollie is the first to tell me how beautiful I am...as a woman. I know I am not beautiful, not really, but to hear such a little lie from him makes me happy. But you know? Ollie is prettier than I. He's the prettiest man I've ever seen.'"

Nina stopped. "I remember that, Bucky. You kinda hugged yourself then. Just thinking of Ollie."

Bucky said, "Doesn't my husband suspect at all?"

"I asked her that. Margareta said: 'Jan pays so little attention to me. He is in the cloth business. And he is often away to buy or to sell—and that is when he is with his other women, with his whores. So, after Mr. Rubens asked me to pose, I hired a woman to take care of the children while I am at Rubenshuis. Now Clarissa stays the night, too, when I am with Ollie.'

"So then I asked, 'Where do you stay with Ollie?'"

Bucky interrupted. "But you already know that. You told Constance and me that they met in that house that Rubens let Ollie stay in."

"Yes, on Hopland Street. But you see, I wanted Margareta to tell me. I wanted validation. And not just the house, Bucky. There was a lot of stuff that I'd already been told by Constance—you know, as Ollie. But that's exactly why this is so extraordinary. It matches! Exactly. What Ollie said and what Margareta said is all the same—different viewpoints maybe, but same facts."

Softly, Bucky whispered, "Double Ones."

"Nothing else makes any sense to me. Look," Nina said, "here it is. Here's Margareta's answer: 'Oh, Mr. Rubens is so anxious to keep Ollie here as his model that he's given him the use of another house he owns, around the corner from Rubenshuis, on Hopland Street. We have it all to ourselves—our love house.'

"And then I asked Margareta: 'Does Ollie ever get mad at you?'"

Bucky broke in again. "Why would you ask that?'

Nina had to think quickly. She'd revealed to Bucky that Margareta was married, cheating on her husband with Ollie, but even now she still wanted to keep it to herself that Ollie was a murderer—and probably would be Margareta's murderer. "Well," she ventured, "Ollie's a tough guy, a sailor. He's made it plenty plain to me that he's no warm and fuzzy millennium kinda guy with the ladies. But he's also sworn to me that he's a pussycat with Margareta, that he truly loves her in a way he's never loved anyone else."

"Double Ones," Bucky said again.

"Yes, and sure enough, Margareta goes on and on about how sweet he is to her." Nina ran her fingers through the words on the page, the loving response—all the time, in her own mind, remembering the beautiful Bess back in Norfolk, the unsuspecting Caterina in Amsterdam, and all the other flashy dolls he took advantage of—one way or another. Could it really be possible that Ollie had truly fallen for the soft, sweet, Madonna-ish Margareta? Now Nina resumed reading out loud again. "'I swear by his love. Why, even as I go to Saint James to confess my terrible carnal sins, I will not allow the priest to admonish me, for I know our love is pure and that I will love Ollie—'"

"*Altijd,*" Bucky suddenly said.

To Nina, it sounded like "al-tied." "What'd you say?" she asked.

"*Altijd.* I'm sure it means 'always.' You know: 'I will love Ollie, always.'"

"But what in the world made you say it—that word, in old Flemish?"

Bucky shrugged hopelessly. "I don't know. I was just listening to you, and it just...came to me. From somewhere. Just listening to Margareta's words, and suddenly, it was there. *Altijd.*"

"Like you said the name Ollie once without even knowing."

"I guess." He waved at the transcript. "Well, look. Is the word there?"

Nina looked down at the translation. Yes, there it was. The next word: *always.* She nodded and sighed. "Okay," she said then. "This is where I started asking Margareta about herself."

"So now I find out who I was?"

"Yes," she answered, looking back at the transcript, introducing Bucky to the woman he had been.

·33·

"'Are you from Antwerp, Margareta?'"

"'I think, but I cannot be sure. I may have come from nearby, but outside the Spanish fortifications. You see, I never knew my parents, because when I was a baby, someone—my mother, I suppose—left me in the wall at the Maidens' House on Lange Gasthuisstraat. Do you know that?'

Nina shrugged, so Margareta had gone ahead and explained. Nina read to Bucky. "'Well, there in the middle of the wall, the sisters had made a hole so that babies who are not wanted could be left there at night. Only my Christian name was pinned to me. That and half a playing card.

"'It was the eight of diamonds—although I don't know why my mother chose that card. Anyway, she left the top half of it pinned to me. Then the sisters chose a last name for me. Engelgraef. They chose names for the orphans by the alphabet. The baby before me had been given a name that started with a D, the one after would be an F, and so on. So, I was Margareta Engelgraef thereafter, and my only home was the Maidens' House.'"

"Poor kid," said Bucky.

Nina read on. "'My favorite nun was Sister Magdalena, and she wanted me to stay there, to be a nun myself when I grew up. But I was sure my mother would return for me. I was so certain. That was, after all, so often the case. When the child was old enough to work, to help the family, the mother would come back to the Maidens' House, show the other half of the card, and take her child home with her.

"'Perhaps, since you are not from here, you cannot imagine how difficult it was just a few years ago. Always war, all the time. So many of the Protestants had left Antwerp, gone north to the Netherlands, and although, of course, they are heathens, they had so much money, and they took that with them. And then the Schelde was closed, and the great trading ships could come here no more. The sisters would tell us of the glorious times past, when Antwerp was as rich as any city in the world, but now it was hard, and we needed the *scutters*, or otherwise there would be so much crime and murder that no one could be safe.'"

Bucky asked, "What's that—scooters?"

"Well, Paulette didn't translate it, so obviously she didn't know what it was. But it was a guild, and since there weren't any police forces back in the seventeenth century, I guess the *scutters* were sort of a private security force you could hire."

"Okay, I got it."

Nina resumed reading Margareta's account of her life: "'Often, at the Maidens' House we were hungry. I remember how rare was a smoked fish or a meat pie. Usually, it was just the same old porridge, made of bread and beer. Over and over. Well, maybe some dried figs.

"'Why, I remember once, not long ago, when I was sitting on the floor of Mr. Rubens's private studio talking to Ollie while the master sketched him. Ollie asked Mr. Rubens why he preferred painting such chunky women. Mr. Rubens had replied, "Why, my English friend, those are the ones you are wisest to love, for they are most likely to survive." And then he said, "My first wife, Isabella, was not so stout, and alas, the plague took her."

"'Then he looked down to me and he told me in *Vlaamach* what he had said to Ollie in English, and then he added: "But I do not worry about you, dear Margareta, for even though you are not so stout, I know you lived through all those hard years at the Maidens' House, so you must be very healthy."'"

Nina paused, smiling. "Now," she said to Bucky, "I know why Margareta pointed at me then."

"Why?"

"Because here's what she said: 'You should eat more yourself.'"
Nina laughed. "I guess I look downright starved to some healthy
person from the seventeenth century."

Then, once again, she resumed reading the translation of Margareta's narrative. "'Anyway, I awaited my mother, every day. My
best friends had their mothers come for them, showing the other
half of their card. Anna—the four of clubs. Her mother came. Cor-
nelia—the ten of spades. Only then did I begin to realize that my
mother was never coming. No one had the lower half of my eight of
diamonds anymore. I believed my mother must have died. For otherwise, she surely would have come for me, would she have not?'"

Nina, guessing it was something of a rhetorical question, had
nodded, *"Ja."* She glanced up now and saw that Bucky appeared
very somber. "You okay?" Nina asked.

"Well, it's sad. Hey, that's me. That was my life."

Sweetly, Nina reached cross the desk and patted Bucky's hand.
Then she read on: "'So, Sister Magdalena pleaded with me to take
up the vows myself, but even then, even though I knew now that the
sisters were my only family, I feared that I could never give myself to
Christ. Already, I had allowed Pieter, a boy I liked, to kiss me and to
touch me where he should not, but I had enjoyed that, and so I
understood that I was possessed of too much lust ever to be a bride
of Christ.

"'But then one day, at last, I was granted a measure of good fortune. It was on Assumption Day, the fifteenth of August, when we
celebrate Our Lady's return to heaven. Some of the older girls at the
Maidens' House were taken to Saint James Church. There we were
seen by the prominent members of the parish who were gracious
enough to allow us orphans to worship there. That was, in fact, the
first time I had ever seen the great Mr. Rubens. But it was Mrs. Gansacker who noticed me. She would tell me later that it was so much
because of the sweetness of my face. You see? And so, she asked the
sisters if she and Mr. Gansacker might not take me home to their
great house on Keizerstraat, where I could be a servant.

"'Oh, how blessed I was. What else would have become of me?
There was so little work for a girl, except, perhaps, to go to the

Burchtgracht and whore for the sailors and the Spanish soldiers and the other men. Many of my older friends at the Maidens' House had left for the brothels. They are not sinful by nature, only given no choice, and—'"

Nina stopped her reading and leaned back, telling Bucky, "This was where Margareta became very emotional. Of course, I had no idea what she was talking about—except I heard her mention a name: Elsa."

Nina didn't reveal to Bucky that Ollie had known Elsa, too, that she was the plump whore who had serviced him for free in order to enjoy the fine accommodations of his house on Hopland Street. But it was only now, as Nina resumed reading Margareta's account, that she understood why she had become so upset.

"'Why, just the other day, one of my old friends from Maidens' House, Elsa, was murdered. Yes, Elsa was a whore, but she had also become one of Mr. Rubens's models, and she was so dear, and always so much fun. Why would anyone kill her? Elsa pleased every man who ever paid for her. I know. For she also told me secrets of what men desired, and I used them to better satisfy my husband...and Ollie, too. And yet someone killed my dear Elsa. Not only strangled her, but threw her body into the little canal that runs by Blood Hill.'"

Nina had to stop, chilled. For she knew, surely, who had killed Elsa. One more woman Ollie had slept with—then murdered. And certainly, Margareta would be next. Luckily, however, Nina's distraction did not register with Bucky, for something had triggered in his own mind. "Wait...Elsa," he said.

"What?"

"I don't know. It's just that she's back there, somewhere. Margareta must have been very upset."

"Yes, she was," Nina said, turning the page. "But now I asked her how she met her husband, and this is what she told me:

"'In that too, I owe blessings to Saint James. You see, not long after the Gansackers took me in as a servant, Mrs. Gansacker promoted me, trusting me to become a nanny for their youngest daughter. And so it was that every Sunday, I would accompany the family to church, and it was there at Saint James on Whitsunday, in the year of Our Lord, 1628, when I, nearly a spinster, already past my eighteenth birthday, was spied by Jan De Gruyter.'"

Bucky mused, "So that's who I would marry. I would become Margareta De Gruyter."

"Well, let's see," Nina said, and she resumed Margareta's oral autobiography.

"'Oh, Jan was most pleasing to look upon, well attired in a fine vest, with gold buttons. He seemed an honest man, and we knew him to be a good Catholic, because he had fled the Netherlands to come south to be amongst true believers. But Jan didn't know the better women of Antwerp, so when he saw me with the Gansack-ers—I dressed in much finer clothes than my position called for because Mrs. Gansacker would pass onto me her older dresses—Jan was very impressed. He presented himself to Mr. Gansacker and asked if he might be allowed to see me, and with time, our courtship blossomed. We were married at Saint James the autumn following, on the Sunday prior to All Saints Day. Jan prospered, and soon we moved into our handsome house on Schuttersshofstraat.'"

Bucky said, "Hey, great story. Little orphan girl breaks into society."

Nina agreed. "Then," she said, "I asked Margareta about her children."

"'Adrien was born first, barely nine months after our marriage. Well—'"

Nina commented, "I remember the blush here. Now I know why."

"'Well,' Margareta admitted, 'really seven months on.'"

"Naughty me," said Bucky.

"'And two years later came our beautiful daughter, whom I named for Magdalena, my favorite sister at the Maidens' House. I want no others, for Jan has grown so cruel toward me, and I even pray that I might take my darlings should Ollie ask me to leave Antwerp with him. But then, I fear that he will someday go without me. He is a sailor, and he talks even now of a place called Dunkirk, where he hears there are great riches to be made by brave men.'"

Nina said, "Next, I asked Margareta: 'So, when will you be alone with Ollie again?' And I remember, Bucky, she paused a long time before she decided to answer that. Then she kinda shrugged, a sort of what-the-hell, in-for-a-penny, in-for-a-pound expression, and she answered at great length."

"Probably told you about the green dress."

"What?"

"Oh, I'm sure Margareta told you about the green dress. I can almost see it, Nina. It was by far the most beautiful dress I ever had." Bucky stopped himself then. For just a second, it didn't seem as if he was sure who he was. He was still speaking English and his voice and his manner were masculine, but something of his consciousness had drifted back to join with that woman in Antwerp, long ago. But then just as quickly, he returned and gestured for Nina to go on. "I'll let her tell you about the green dress."

"All right," Nina said, and she picked up the final sheet of Paulette's translation. "Here's what Margareta told me: 'Tomorrow, after Jan and I attend a service in honor of Our Lady's Assumption, afterwards he will depart for Ghent, and then Liege. He'll be gone from Antwerp a whole week. So I can be with Ollie every wonderful night!'"

Nina looked up at Bucky, as if to say: *where's this green dress?* He just waved to her confidently to go on. And sure enough, Nina read next:

"'I must tell you something else. With the money I've made posing, I've bought the most magnificent gown.'"

"What'd I tell you?" Bucky cracked, with a good old buckysmirk.

Nina just read on: "'...and I've saved it for tomorrow, for Ollie. Oh, if only you could see it. It's green—'"

"Bingo!"

"'It's green with gold trim, and it's cut low, square across my bosom.'" Nina remembered now how Margareta had drawn her hand that way, smiling devilishly. "'And with it, I'll wear a pendant Mrs. Gansacker gave me when I left, and the most gorgeous new hat that I just bought in the Grote Markt. It's also green, but a darker shade, and it has one gold feather flying up from it.'"

Margareta had seemed so incredibly happy as she explained all this, that Nina had decided it was a good place to conclude the session. Right away, as soon as she told Bucky that, he got up and said, "You gotta hypnotize me again. I gotta find out what happens to her."

"In time. When Constance comes back to New York."

"All right. But I worry about her."

"Constance?"

"Oh no. Connie can take care of herself. Margareta. I just have this feeling."

"What?"

"I don't know. Just...something's gonna happen." Suddenly then, as he was pacing about, Bucky pulled out his little appointment book. "Look—I thought so."

"What?"

"August 14th. Today. The very day in 1635 when Margareta was talking to you. Remember?" Nina nodded. "Eerie. Tomorrow, she said, tomorrow—Assumption Day—is the day Jan goes away and she shacks up with Ollie. The fifteenth of August. Tomorrow. For Margareta then, for us now. Wow."

"You all right, pal?" Nina asked him.

"Yeah, under the circumstances." He glanced at his watch. "And also, I can still get out of Antwerp and make the 5:56 to Darien. Better do that." So, he headed to the door, but just before he got there, he turned back. "Ask you a question?"

"Personal?"

"Very."

Nina knew what was coming, but she also damn well knew she'd set herself up for this and there was no way she could take refuge behind any doctor's shield. "Okay."

"You *were* unfaithful once? You didn't just tell Margareta that?"

"No, I was."

"Feel guilty?"

"I coulda killed myself."

"But you kept on going back?"

"As you can see: I didn't kill myself." Bucky just sort of nodded.

"Okay?" Nina asked him.

"Yeah, thanks. It's good to know we're alike—you, me, and Margareta."

For a long time then, Nina sat alone at her desk, the lights still dim. Finally, without really knowing why, she reached into her bottom drawer and pulled out a forgotten pack of Salems. How long had they been there? Months, maybe a whole year—tossed away by Mr. Grady, one of her patients, in the midst of a session. He said he'd never smoke again. Did he? Anyway, Nina dropped his pack down there with some old photographs, a letter or two patients had given her, various other abandoned accouterments of changing lives.

Nina hadn't smoked in—what?—twenty years. So long, she'd stopped being proud of herself. But now she hauled out one of Mr. Grady's stale old Salems and lit it. To help the thought process. Isn't that what everyone used to think cigarettes did? Nina didn't dare inhale, though. She knew that would leave her dizzy. Instead, she just drew the smoke into her mouth and whooshed it out, leaning back, watching it rise above her. And maybe it did help the thought process. There, daydreaming, just watching the smoke, Nina imagined seeing Margareta coming through the swirls.

It was tomorrow, Assumption Day, August the fifteenth, but it was 1635. Nina saw her clearly now, going to Saint James with her husband and her two children, knowing all the while that, as soon as she finished praying, she would bid Jan good-bye, leave the children at home, put on her fetching green dress, and rush off to fall into the arms of her lover.

Nina blew more gusts of smoke, then laid the cigarette down in a forgotten old ashtray. She watched the smoke swirl higher, and now she saw Margareta again, only now she was in the green dress—and the green hat with the tall gold feather—and she was rushing along by the side of the Wapper Canal toward Hopland. And her face. Nina could see her so clearly—that precious, wholesome countenance she knows so well from the Madonna in gallery twenty-seven. But now, where that gentle peacefulness had rested, there is a sparkle to the eyes, a tension of anticipation. There is even, yes, a passion evident in the Madonna's expression. She steps faster. For now Margareta has spied Ollie.

Nina looks to see what Ollie's wearing. Well, surely, exactly what gentlemen wear in Rubens's portraits. Ollie is a dandy. Yes. The fashionable flared sleeves, of course, slashed with cuts, lace at the wrists, with knickers for pants, so that his high socks bulge above his magnificent calves. Hmm, Nina thinks, what a delicious package.

And he whistles at Margareta, and they rush faster toward one another down Hopland Street—and never mind that someone might see them together in public. No, surely Margareta won't kiss him there. She must show some discretion. But she can't stop herself from staring into that impossibly handsome face with the dark button eyes. Nina knows she will kiss him as soon as they enter the house. The door closes.

Quick, quick. The smoke is gone. Nina picks up the Salem, blows some more. It is swirling again, all around, and once again she can see Nina and Ollie in the middle of the cloud. Now, they're entering the bedroom—the *slaapkamer*, Paulette had told her it was called. Silly word. But Nina is a voyeur now, and she is inside the *slaapkamer*, unashamedly watching Ollie and Margareta together upon the bed. The feathered hat has been tossed aside, way over in the corner, the gorgeous green dress crumpled in disarray on the floor, so all she sees is that fabulous body upon Margareta, rising and falling.

Nina turns away, ashamed, waiting for all the smoke to fade. She cannot bear to see them together anymore. She knows he will kill her. Probably this very night, of Assumption Day, 1635. Doesn't Ollie grow angry and kill all his women? What will Margareta say that will set him to violence against her? Maybe nothing. Maybe it will just be his whim.

Nina must close her eyes. But she still smells the smoke, and then one more terrible time, she hears Margareta scream out: "...*owwwlllllleeeeeee...*" That awful, keening sound.

And already she wishes she had not let Bucky leave. She should have hypnotized him again, this evening. She must hypnotize him again. She must find out. Sometimes, in fact, Nina doesn't even care about Hugh anymore. All she wants is to be with Ollie and Margareta in Antwerp. That is all that matters in her world now.

That world.

·34·

At the Hilton, Constance awoke to the bells from the Cathedral of Our Lady on Our Lady's very own Assumption Day. All today, even more than usual, the bells would ring over Antwerp. Their sound stirred Constance. The whole city did. She knew she belonged here. She was so glad she had come to Antwerp, even if she had had to come alone, without Bucky. There were so many places to go today, so much to see. The Rubens Fair, to start with. Then back to Rubenshuis—and today she would go inside, even up to Mr. Rubens's private studio where Ollie had posed for him. Where Ollie had been with Margareta.

But also, she would go to Saint James, where the master lay in eternal rest. Ollie himself had never been there, but the place meant so much to Margareta. Such a grand day this would be! Constance even liked it that the skies were gray, the air heavy, for in a way, that kind of misty atmosphere made it all the more evocative. Oh, if only Bucky were here to relive all this with her!

So Constance dressed quickly, then went directly to the Rubens Fair in the Grote Markt. Hardly had she stepped out of her room, though, when her phone started ringing.

It was Jocelyn, calling from her room at the Alfa. She let it ring again and again before she finally hung it up. Well, Jocelyn decided, she would try Constance one more time before she left her room to start her own day at Rockoxhuis.

Constance, though, was herself already at the Fair having a roll and coffee. Oh, but the bells were ringing and the stalls were thronged, all the salespeople faithfully dressed in their colorful Rubens attire. Constance began to move about, enthralled. She thought of Bucky. Or, even more, she began to think of Margareta. Especially, she thought of Margareta when she saw a woman in a candy stall wearing a green and white dress with a green cap that had a tall gold feather. Constance stopped dead at the sight. It was too vivid. She must leave the Rubens Fair. She must go straight to Rubenshuis.

She walked down Kaasrui toward Wingaardsstraat. The streets not only bent and twisted, but often enough, they would arbitrarily take on new names every few blocks. Constance hadn't even brought a map with her, but how easily, how intuitively, she moved along.

And once again, Jocelyn and Constance almost crossed paths. They were both on the Keizerstraat, but Jocelyn had ducked into Rockoxhuis and Constance had visited there yesterday, so she walked by.

Jocelyn had just stepped inside and paid for her admission ticket. She looked around. Nicholas Rockox had not only been a prominent politician of Antwerp—even, for a time, the *burgomeister*— but he was also another great friend of Rubens's. And, like Rubenshuis and the Plantin-Moretus House, Rockox's own magnificent home had been restored. Jocelyn studied the two original Rubens there. One of them was of the Madonna, the model almost surely Isabella, his first wife. "Our own Virgin, by the master, on Assumption Day itself," said the guard.

"Yes, how perfect," Jocelyn replied. And then she wandered through the interior redbrick courtyard with the baby box bushes. But she was distracted. She kept thinking how she really must go to the Hilton and leave a note there for Constance. She couldn't wait any longer. She had to make contact.

So it was, that wrapped up in these thoughts, Jocelyn at first didn't even notice the guest book. But as soon as she saw it, she rushed to it. Didn't even bother to sign her own name. Instead, only searched the pages for—yes, yes, there it was. The same blue felt pin. The same handwriting. But wait. Jocelyn read it again, in shock. It did not say, "Constance Rawlings, Lake Forest, Illinois." But now, instead:

August 14th   Constance Buckingham   New York City,   How memorable!
                                            U.S.   I must return
                                                          with my husband

Meanwhile, Constance: just now she was herself entering Ruben-shuis again. But no, no thank you, she did not want to rent an audiocassette. "It'll all come back to me," she declared almost dismissively, entering into Rubens's main studio. This time, Constance took a seat, looking around, breathing in the place, feeling at home again.

She closed her eyes in reverie. And suddenly, she could hear Cornelis reading the classics to Rubens as he painted. Probably something from Seneca. Rubens preferred most to hear Seneca. In the original Latin, of course. So Ollie had been told. Oh well, Constance thought, opening her eyes, it wouldn't be a whole lot different from some painter today, listening to Rush Limbaugh or NPR as he worked.

She looked around the room. She studied *Adam and Eve*, an early Rubens. But then, far across the way, her eyes lit on another painting. She knew this one wasn't a Rubens, but she did like it. It reminded her of something. So Constance stood up and stepped as close to it as she could—blocked by a rope barrier. She squinted. It was a picnic scene, men and women drinking and cozying up. *Pastorale*, the card said. The name didn't mean anything. But the painting. She leaned closer to see who had done it. Jan Wildens and Frans Woulters. Oh yes. Wildens didn't register, but Woulters....

Constance closed her eyes again, and yes, the vision of a stout young painter began to form. Frans, with his hearty laugh. And now Constance can also hear a voice. "Frans did the figures," it says. "You like them?"

She knows, right away, the voice belongs to Mr. Rubens, speaking in English. And now, in her mind, *Pastorale* is not on the wall. It is not even quite finished yet, but sitting on an easel. And it is Ollie standing there, admiring it, as Mr. Rubens comes up beside him.

Constance hears him. "Do you like the painting, Ollie? It's based on an old proverb that goes like this: 'Without Bacchus, the god of wine, and Ceres, the goddess of the fruits of the earth, then Venus, the goddess of love, is left out in the cold.' So you see—"

"Sure," says Ollie, "the fellows are plying the wenches with the grape and a pleasant time that they might come away with a good poke."

"And do you believe that, Ollie? I hear you're quite the ladies man, but do you believe that love can only come after a good time and a good wine have reduced a lass's defenses?"

Constance turns to her side, as if Peter Paul Rubens is surely standing there, as sure as she is hearing Ollie talk to him. And if she doesn't quite see the master next to her, she does speak out loud, exactly as Ollie did: "No, Mr. Rubens. Once I thought that, but now I believe there can be real love—and without such blandishments."

"Good, good Ollie. It is my belief, too, that every man has within him a true love to pour out, if only he finds the right woman to be that vessel. With me, 'tis my dear Helena. And I only hope you should be so lucky to find your lady love."

"Perhaps some day," said Ollie, keeping his counsel, for Margareta was a married woman and he would not disparage her reputation in the eyes of such a good Christian gentleman as Peter Paul Rubens.

"Well, 'tis only proper," Rubens exclaimed, "that the man I chose as my Adonis, who won the heart of Venus herself, shall find his own true love upon this Earth of ours." And Constance remembered well how he had clapped Ollie upon the back before he turned away. And then Mr. Rubens was gone, and *Pastorale* was no longer a work in progress upon an easel in the summer of 1635, but a finished masterpiece back upon the wall this summer's day in the here and now.

Quickly, Constance hurried away from the studio, through the antechamber with the gold leather walls, into the kitchen with its Delft tiles, and on to the serving room. It was all so familiar, and Constance could even hear the names being called out: Jan and

Frans—yes; and Danelis and Willem, Susanna, Cornelis, Basilia, Elsa. She stopped with Elsa. What was it about Elsa?

But she had reached the dining room and there was the master's own portrait, staring at her. Those pitch-dark eyes, the pointed nose with the pointed chestnut beard to match, the hat and the white collar tilted in such a way that seemed so reminiscent...of what? Could it be that Mr. Rubens held his head just that way when he painted? Of course. Now Constance could visualize him. And, after all, he'd been painting when he painted himself here, hadn't he? She could see him so clearly now, head tilted just so, sketching her. Him. Ollie.

Finally, when a group of Walloons from the south of Belgium came by, their guide chattering to them in French, Constance left the Rubens self-portrait and went upstairs where the great man died on May 30th, 1640. She glanced about his bedroom, then doubled back to another, smaller bedroom where Helena slept. Such a short bed. Constance thought: how did Margareta and I make love comfortably in such short beds? Were we that much shorter ourselves in that life?

Down the hall she moved, to a portrait of a young woman. "Traditionally identified as Helena, Rubens's second wife," the card said. "Attributed to Jan Boeckhorst." Oh yeah, Constance remembered Boeckhorst. A wiseass. She studied the portrait closer. Well, the woman did look somewhat like Helena, but Mr. Rubens himself had done so many much better renderings of Helena. Hardly knowing she'd spoken out loud, Constance had mumbled, "Didn't quite get her."

A German couple standing close by glanced at Constance, then quickly moved away. Well, Constance thought to herself, that jerk Boeckhorst *didn't* quite get Helena. That was Boeckhorst's trouble. He didn't quite get anything. Constance was sure Mr. Rubens would be furious if he knew that some curator had stuck a Boeckhorst—a Boeckhorst *of his wife*—up in his own house.

She shrugged and moved on, past the linen room and the corner bedroom to Mr. Rubens's famous portrait of Michael Ophovius. Funny place to keep it, Constance thought. Mr. Rubens had it hung downstairs where more people could see it. God, she was remembering everything now. It was all flooding back. And yet, something was driving her forward, too. She rushed past some Italians and that German couple, dashing up the stairs to the top floor to the private studio. But it was only worse there. Constance was sweating, her heart pounding as terribly as those times when she had encountered Bucky or the Madonna.

She needed air. She rushed to the window that opened onto Wapperstraat and that purchased Constance some relief, for the window afforded a peek into the twenty-first century—with Coca-Cola and Palm beer umbrellas outside the cafés below. They were her salvation, a glimpse of modern civilization. Thank God for Coke. Constance sucked in her breath and looked all the way down Wapperstraat, past the huge shrubbery islands to the intersection with The Weir, where a bunch of African musicians were playing a melody heavy on drums and chants.

So, composed as best she could be, Constance was ready at last, and she drew her head back into the studio. But instantly it happened again, and she was completely swallowed up by that place and time. She didn't even realize what she was doing. But without warning, while the other tourists stared in fear and wonder, Constance contorted her body, facing back, her one hand down, her other raised high. She was Adonis again—Adonis without the spear, but otherwise Adonis. And of course, she was looking down, looking to where Venus would have been. Only:

Constance was staring at the red and black pattern.

But she wasn't just imagining that she saw it. No. It was right there. The pattern was before her eyes. It was on the floor.

The pattern that Constance had always seen was the design on the floor of Mr. Rubens's private studio.

All these years, this is where the vision had come from. It was not something she had just imagined. She saw it for real, right now. Exactly the way it had always been, the black and the red diamonds, clustered just so. Of course! No one could have dreamed up such an odd pattern. No, no: Constance had seen it. Well, Ollie had seen it. And she held her Adonis pose, staring at the red and black diamonds.

The other tourists gave her a wide berth. Constance only smiled, relieved. And then, closing her eyes, she isn't just seeing the red and black pattern, but she envisions Margareta sitting upon them—sweet and precious, looking up at her with that same heavenly smile that made her Mr. Rubens's Madonna. And now Constance also hears a voice. It is Mr. Rubens himself. After all, he is right here in his studio painting Adonis, isn't he? *"Ah, bemint zym,"* he says, making Margareta smile.

"What?" Ollie asks.

"I said: ah to be in love," Rubens replies. "As we discussed downstairs the other day, Ollie. To be totally in love—as Adonis and Venus."

Ollie winks at Margareta because they attach the master's words to themselves. Then, in his best, bad Flemish, Ollie repeats it: *"Ja, bemint zym."* And he grins at Margareta until at last that vision of her is gone and it is only Constance again, standing alone by herself in the middle of the private studio.

She abandons the Adonis pose and just stands there, limp. At last she knows where the red and black has come from. And then, just like that, the other awful visions start to present themselves. Bess upon the pebbles, Caterina lying on the bed, and Elsa floating along down the dirty canal. Constance can't get them out of her mind. And she realizes that if the red and black pattern had once been real in life then these awful other visions must also be based in the actual past. Who are these women? Why are they dead in Constance's mind's eye? Why are they...murdered?

"Oh no," Constance screams out in despair, as she falls upon the floor. There, on her knees, she draws down her face to where Margareta sat, where she can only see the floor, only see the red and the black—her eyes wide, staring at the pattern until it fills her whole mind, every nook and cranny, so that nothing ugly can intrude.

·35·

Jocelyn was moving in the other direction now, away from Ruben-shuis, toward the Grote Markt. When she passed the Hilton, she went right in. There was no answer when she rang Constance's room, so this time Jocelyn wrote out a message identifying herself, and asking Constance to call her at the Alfa Theatre Hotel, room 554. Leaving that note at the desk, she proceeded on to the Rubens Fair.

She was instantly enchanted by it, transformed by the spirit of the period costumes, hardly less than Constance had been. And soon, like Constance, Jocelyn's eyes fastened on the pretty young clerk in a candy stall, wearing a green and white dress with a green hat and the tall, gold feather. "How much?" Jocelyn inquired.

"Oh, the hat's not for sale. I have to wear these clothes all day."

"Well, will you sell it to me at the end of the day?"

The salesgirl demurred. Jocelyn offered an outlandish price—three thousand Belgium francs, about ninety dollars. "Well..."

"And I'll throw in my hat, too," Jocelyn said, touching the one on her head. It was a very fashionable chemille that she'd just bought in St. Petersburg. That clinched the deal, so happily, Jocelyn moved on, finding her way next up to Saint Paul's Church where she studied the three Rubens paintings there.

Then, she walked over to the Royal Museum, where a full two dozen of the master's works were hung in special, great, high-ceilinged rooms with red velour banquettes. There Jocelyn sat, drinking in all the paintings: the men in their great broad-brimmed hats, their lacy millstone collars, and their fancy doublets. And the pretty women: bodices opening over chemisettes, beautiful skirts, petticoats, and aprons, feather fans, and pearl necklaces. Jocelyn beamed, too, as she saw more than one gorgeous hat much like the very green one she'd just arranged to buy.

So now, altogether imbued with the spirit of Rubens, Jocelyn decided that she was ready to go into his house. She headed that way, up Arenbergstraat. And how close she came there to crossing paths again with Constance. It was almost as if the two women were destined to move about the same places in Antwerp, but always at a slightly different pace, in a slightly different direction. Now, even as Jocelyn approached Rubenshuis, Constance was leaving there for Saint James Church, for Rubens's crypt.

Saint James is located on Lange Niewstraat, an altogether undistinguished street just outside the charming reach of the old town. Streetcars run down Lange Niewstraat, with neighborhood shops and residences that are neither remarkable nor reminiscent. Notwithstanding, once Constance stepped inside the dark old Gothic church, she was immediately rushed back to Rubens's time and she walked softly through the shadows, pausing reverentially to examine the statues and paintings that lined the walls and filled the chapels.

No, Ollie had never been here. He'd never set foot inside any church in Antwerp.

But Constance felt comfortable in Saint James. After all, this was Rubens's parish church. He'd married Helena here, seen their children baptized here, confessed his sins (such as they were) here, risen every day that his gout permitted it to come here and worship. And, of course, it was here that he had chosen to be buried.

But even more: this was Margareta's church. And this place was her salvation. It was here where the Gansackers had found her, and here where Jan De Gruyter had spied her. And here he married her and here their two children were christened. Moreover, it was here, too, that the master had first spotted Margareta, visualizing in her countenance a Madonna's face. Yes, in a way, all that Margareta had become was thanks to Saint James, and it was impossible for Constance not to feel that power, that warmth.

But now, it was time for her to pay her respects to Mr. Rubens where he lay for all time behind the high altar. Constance walked softly upon the marble floor, gently now, approaching the tomb where the master rested, on either side a wife—Isabella to the left, Helena the right.

Helena, of course, had survived him by many years, but Rubens himself had approved of this site for his earthly rest, even stipulating which one painting of his should be displayed above his tomb. "The one I choose to hang above me," Rubens had whispered in agony, "would be the recent one of Our Lady—with the Christ Child upon her arm, surrounded by the company of divers saints." And, of course, his request was upheld. After the Fourment family completed the chapel, that painting was taken from Rubenshuis and raised above his tomb where it has remained until this day.

Constance drew closer, but with each step her emotions changed. She had begun to approach with reverence, in solemnity, but now as she moved nearer, there was excitement and wonder—sensations very much like those she had experienced when first she had come into gallery twenty-seven with Nina. Suddenly, in fact, her knees wobbled, and cool as it was, Constance found herself sweating.

And if at last before her was the tomb, her eyes were drawn immediately to the painting above, to *Our Lady and Child with Saints*. Constance noticed St. George first—hard to miss him with the slain dragon at his feet. And then she saw some other saint (in fact, it was old Jerome) kneeling on a lion, and Mary Magdalene, ever in her ambiguity, and also here, well...Rubensesque: chubby and bare-breasted. Everywhere, too, there were angels because the Virgin holds the Christ, and the cherubs are smiling upon the happy little child.

But now Constance is pulled nearer. She suddenly even has this urge to climb upon Rubens's tomb, to touch the painting, to kiss it. She manages to stop herself, baffled at why she is so overcome. She looks closer. She stares at the painting. And now she doesn't see St. George or St. Jerome or the Magdalene or the angels anymore. No, she only sees the Virgin and the Child. Because she knows Mary.

Mary is Margareta. Margareta is Mary. Ollie's Margareta. My Margareta. There is no doubt. Once again, Rubens has used Margareta as his Madonna.

Constance keeps her eyes fixed on Margareta. She is alone in the chapel, no guards nearby. Only now that Constance is all by herself, she is no longer Constance. Constance Rawlings has again fallen into a trance, transformed. It is Oliver Goode now standing before the tomb, before the painting. And there is one other thing that makes Ollie's skin tingle. It is not only Margareta in the painting that enraptures him.

It is the baby. The child who is Jesus. Ollie somehow senses that child. He is drawn to him. He presses his fists to his head. *Yes, yes, I know.* The child posing in Margareta's arms is Margareta's own baby. And yes, it is Ollie's child. It is their baby. *My god, we had a baby,* Ollie thinks. *Margareta and I had a baby.*

Ollie kicks off his shoes—Constance's clogs. He climbs upon Mr. Rubens's tomb, and standing up there, crying now, he leans forward. First, he kisses the lips of his love, and then the forehead of their child.

So, Nina must have had it wrong. If Margareta had Ollie's baby, then Ollie did not kill her. Could he? Why then? Why then did Margareta scream "...oowwwwllllleeee...?"

Ollie finally tore himself away and left Saint James, wandering over toward the Schelde, stopping for a couple of beers. After all, it wasn't really Constance anymore. In fact, it was late in the evening before Ollie began to find his way back to Constance's room at the Hilton. She is supposed to fly back to Chicago in the morning. If she can become Constance again by then.

As for Jocelyn, she had left Rubenshuis and arrived at Saint James shortly after Constance had departed there. As soon as she entered the church, Jocelyn saw the guest book, and her curiosity was too great for her to wait. Even before she headed to the tomb, she turned to look at the book.

Surely, Constance would have come to Saint James. But Jocelyn failed to see Constance's familiar script. So, she started to sign her own name. As she wrote it, something caught her eye. It was only three lines up, a scratchy, thin black writing far different than the soft blue words that Constance had written at the Plantin-Moretus House and at Rockoxhuis.

Jocelyn focused on that line, and her eyes bulged out as she read:

15 Au'st. Cecil Wainwright   Norfolk, Englande   With my deare
                                                   Sweetheart
                                                   & Childe

·36·

Now, of course, Jocelyn was almost frantic to reach Constance. She had come to Antwerp simply to experience the feel of the place where the Double Ones had lived and loved. But now she had discovered that one of them had actually come back there herself. And on top of that: these bizarre, fascinating, public notes from Constance. Jocelyn was beside herself with curiosity and excitement. Twice that night she tried Constance's room, but neither time was there an answer. She thought about going down to the Hilton, waiting in the lobby, confronting her personally. No, too pushy. She tried the phone again. Nothing.

In fact, Constance had been sitting there by the phone, all along. She'd read Jocelyn's note. She knew it must be her calling, too. Meddling. *The nosy bitch.* After all, no one else knew that Constance Rawlings was in Antwerp—let alone at the Hilton Hotel. Mrs. Rawlings was at a convention in Las Vegas. Wasn't she?

Frustrated, Jocelyn looked at her watch. A quarter to eleven. Only a quarter to six in New York. She pulled out her address book and dialed Dr. Winston's home number. No answer. Damn. Oh well, she'd leave a message on the phone machine: "Nina Winston, it's Jocelyn Ridenhour. I've got so much to tell you. Sergei and Ludmilla were terrific—Double Ones!—and now I'm in Antwerp. And you'd never guess who's here. Surprise! If you get back by seven, call me. I'm at the Alfa Theatre Hotel for two more days." Then Jocelyn gave the country code for Belgium, the hotel number, her room.

Quickly, as soon as she hung up, Jocelyn looked down to see if the little message light was blinking. Just her luck, Constance would finally call her back while she was on the phone for a few seconds. But no. She fidgeted. She fixed a cup of decaf at the little coffee maker across the room. And finally, approaching eleven o'clock, Jocelyn decided to try Constance one last time tonight.

Constance gritted her teeth when the phone rang. She was standing there, almost done packing. She knew who it had to be. That woman. That woman who had known Bucky, who had...*fucked* Bucky. That woman. Miss Buttinsky. That woman who is after me, sticking her nose in. After Bucky and me. After Margareta and me. One more ring.

And now, suddenly, Constance's angry eyes were dead, and she saw Elsa in the canal again. She shook her head vigorously, trying to blur over that vision, to replace it with the red and the black diamonds. And she did! With Margareta sitting on them, smiling up at her. Now it was all so clear. And look! Their baby! This time, Margareta was sitting on the red and black diamonds nursing their baby.

But: one more ring.

Constance swirled to glare at the phone. That woman is going to tell about Elsa. Report me to the *scutters*, get the reward. I will never again be with Margareta. Instinctively, Constance snatched up the receiver. "Yes?"

Jocelyn had all but given up. She was so shocked that she'd actually finally reached Constance that it was all she could do to stutter, introducing herself.

"Yes, what is it, then?" was all Constance replied, icily.

"Well, I'd just love to see you sometime tomorrow, to talk about what I've learned about you and—"

"I'm returning tomorrow," Constance said. "But..." There was the longest pause. "We could meet tonight."

Jocelyn was flabbergasted. "Now? It's eleven o'clock."

"Well, it must be now."

"Of course, of course. I'll come right down."

"No," said Constance emphatically. "I'll meet you by Rubenshuis. There are places nearby for coffee, a drink."

Jocelyn hung up in excitement. She couldn't believe her good fortune. There was so much she wanted to tell Constance about Double Ones. So much Constance could tell her. Jocelyn grabbed her shoulder bag, then her long raincoat. If it wasn't raining yet, it was already chilly enough. And of course, she put on her new Rubens-era hat, the green one with the tall feather.

She hurried down the hall to the little elevator. Hardly had she pushed the button, when back in her room, the phone rang. It was Nina. This was the message she left: "Oh, Jocelyn, this is Nina Winston. How perfect! I was going to call your office tomorrow to see how to reach you. Here's a name I want you to check out: Jan De Gruyter." She spelled it out. "Can you find anyone by that name living in Antwerp in 1635? Are there town hall records from back then? Or any registry at Saint James Church? And not just Jan. Also Margareta De Gruyter. Okay? Call me."

Jocelyn, though, was gone from the room and soon walking down Wapperstraat, then passing by Hopland, onto Rubenshuis. All the Palm beer and Coca-Cola umbrellas had long since been folded up on this dreary evening. So about ten minutes later, when Jocelyn could hear footsteps approaching down the side street by the ATM, she was certain that it could only be Constance Rawlings. And yes, when the figure emerged under the street light, Jocelyn knew that it was her.

There was a certain irony in that, too, because by then, at that moment, Jocelyn Ridenhour knew better who Constance Rawlings was than did Constance Rawlings know herself.

In fact, the whole way, walking briskly from the Hilton, the person who was Constance Rawlings kept wondering whether Jocelyn had already contacted the *scutters*. Maybe it was a trap.

"I'm sooo glad to finally meet you," Jocelyn cooed, sticking out her hand. And now Constance was even more discombobulated, because there in the dark by the Rubenshuis, Jocelyn—in her hat with the feather and in the long raincoat that seemed so like a gown—appeared even more to be a figure from the past. Constance's eyes darted about.

"They're still open over there," Jocelyn said, cheerily, pointing to the bistro on the corner of The Meir, catty-cornered from where they stood on Wapperstraat.

Now, for the first time, Constance spoke, and if Jocelyn had been listening carefully, she might have taken note of how oddly she talked—deeper of voice, different in tone and cadence than the voice on the phone. "No," the new voice said, "I know a place further down."

"Terrific!" Jocelyn said gaily.

The two of them were standing by some conical trees, arrayed for decoration in the middle of Wapperstraat. Just beyond, toward The Meir, were the large concrete bins, maybe three-and-a-half or four feet high, that held thick shrubbery. As they passed by the first one, Constance made sure to glance around. There was still no one about in the street, and what few people were finishing up their drinks across the way in the bistro were shielded from view by the bushes on the promenade. So, here they were, the two of them alone, just the way it had been the other day with Elsa on the Burchtgracht. "Wait," Constance said, as soon as they were behind the island of shrubbery.

Jocelyn stopped. Without warning, Constance stepped forward and slammed a fist into the raincoat, into her midsection. In the dark, Constance couldn't see the utter shock on Jocelyn's face. She only heard the involuntary *whoosh*, as Jocelyn doubled over, the wind and the wonder gushing out of her. Her hat flew off her head, and her purse fell off her shoulder. It was easy, then, for Constance to take her powerful forearm and bring it up solidly into the crook of her neck. Now she gasped for any breath. But that was really only a brief panic, her startled eyes wide, for then Constance banged her head against the concrete wall and watched Jocelyn, unconscious, crumple to the pavement.

It was easy enough for Constance to fall upon her, and placing both hands around her neck, squeeze until there was no life left in Jocelyn Ridenhour.

Quickly, Constance looked around. Still, no one in sight. Sure, it'd been easier just dumping Elsa in the canal, or leaving Caterina right there in the bed, or letting Bess slip down upon the pebbles. It would be more difficult here, and it had to be done with dispatch, too. She had to raise the body up the four feet or so and dump it—dead weight—into the shrubbery. Jocelyn was no petite woman, either. But Constance was so strong from her riding and her other exercises, and she was so galvanized by the urgency required of her, that swiftly enough, she lifted Jocelyn up upon the concrete edge and then plopped her over into the dirt.

Constance snatched up the hat and the shoulder bag and one shoe that had come off. Just then, she heard voices to her left, coming down The Meir. Quickly, she tossed Jocelyn's effects up into the bin then hoisted herself up to lay still beside Jocelyn, listening breathlessly as the footsteps approached the intersection of Wapperstraat...and then kept on, receding down The Meir.

Constance peered out and was just about ready to rise up so that she could yank Jocelyn back, more into the cover of the bushes, but she saw someone arriving at the ATM. So, she lay back down, still, staring up at the dark skies and then over through the bushes to the upper floor of Rubenshuis.

There were no candles lit inside, but she knew that was Mr. Rubens's private studio, and she knew, on a night like this, that if the master should leave his bedroom and go up to the studio and peer out, he could spot her from there. But the windows were not open now. Perhaps the master's gout was not bothering him this night. Stay with Helena, Mr. Rubens, she thought. Try to sleep.

Constance turned her head to the side to look toward the ATM where the man took his francs and departed back down the side street. And now she and Jocelyn were alone again, so Constance rose up on her knees and pushed the body over, deeper into the shrubbery. She couldn't hide it completely, but she could conceal it enough so that unless someone came very close to the island and actually peered in, no one would see the body.

Then something else occurred to Constance. She reached under Jocelyn's raincoat, ripped open the buttons on her blouse, and then yanked at where the bra hooked in front. With her right hand, then, she pinched one of Jocelyn's breasts hard. She did not have to see to know she'd made a bruise. Good. It was a crime of passion. Once again, a lonely, middle-aged woman had ventured out at night on vacation and met the wrong...man.

Constance prepared to depart, shuffling over to the edge of the bin. But just at that moment, she heard people leaving the café across the Wapperstraat. They couldn't see her from that vantage, but perhaps they'd come round this side of the island. Be patient. Constance threw herself back down on the dirt, flat out on her back.

And sure enough, they were coming toward her, chatting. All men's voices. Germans, she was positive. Damn Germans will drink beer all night. They were laughing. They were right by her. Suddenly, one spoke loudly: *"Warte.* Wait." They all stopped. Constance held her breath. Out of the corner of her right eye, she could see them, which meant that, if they but glanced over, they could see her.

Luckily, they'd gone two steps past her. But now the one who'd called out turned and faced the shrubbery bin, and Constance realized he was going to relieve himself. He was so close, she even heard the little noise his zipper made going down. The German never looked to his left where Constance lay, but instead, only kept his eyes on the endless stream he made against the wall. When he was finally finished, he took out a cigarette and lit it, tossing the match into the bin. It landed, spent, next to Constance's legs where she lay all this time side-by-side to the woman she'd just murdered.

At last, the Germans moved off and the streets were empty again. Constance peeked out. She left Jocelyn's feathered hat behind with the body, but she made sure to grab the shoulder bag, and with it, leapt down nimbly out of the shrubbery bin then hurried away, past Rubenshuis. Only when she was well beyond did she duck into the shadows and brush off the dirt that clung to her clothes, rearranging herself to be neat, undistinguished by any disarray.

Moving through back streets, Constance stopped under a streetlight, where she searched through Jocelyn's bag. Quickly, she laid her hands on what she wanted: that little plastic card key that would let her into room 554.

Constance cut over to Arenbergstraat, paused briefly before the Alfa Theatre, and then strode casually into the hotel, straight ahead to the elevators. If the clerk at the front desk had seen her, Constance certainly hadn't occasioned him to take any special notice of her. Besides, night clerks have no idea who's checked in during the day.

Constance opened the door to 554. She found the room neat enough, with a few tourist maps and guidebooks tossed about. She made sure not to touch anything without using a handkerchief as a glove. No fingerprints—she knew that. Quickly, then, she started rifling Jocelyn's briefcase. And there it was: a manuscript. She read the title. *Double Ones.* Furious, Constance flipped through it. Most of it was in Cyrillic, meaningless to her, but there were also whole notebooks full of Jocelyn's own beautifully ornate script, including—yes, there it was—a large section entitled "Bucky & Constance." Constance's eyes flashed as she read that. The names jumped out. Cecil Wainwright. Oliver Goode. Margareta.

That was enough. Constance trembled with fury. She had to sit down on the bed. The intrusive bitch. She got what she deserved. Constance would take the briefcase and destroy it. She and Bucky would be safe from prying. Dr. Winston might know about them, but as a doctor, she was obligated to secrecy.

Next, Constance dumped the contents of Jocelyn's shoulder bag onto the bed. What else might be in there? The usual, mostly. Cosmetics. Some Polo mints, a tin of Excedrin. Some old grocery receipts from New York, new ticket stubs from Antwerp. But, uh oh, what's this? Two condom packages. Constance picked them up, bemused. Jocelyn came prepared. It gave Constance an idea, though.

Jocelyn had been killed by a man, had she not? So, let's make that even more obvious. The man had been in her room, too. Constance tore open the two packets, then threw the rubbers into the toilet. She took the wrapping paper from the first one and pitched it into the wastebasket, but the second she dropped next to that receptacle—bad shot. Also: easy to notice. Then she put up the toilet seat, and squatting over the bowl, made sure to pee some on the top of the commode. Just like a man. Bad shot. She flushed the toilet and returned to the bed, where she rolled about, messing up the sheets, leaving no doubts but that there had been considerable passionate activity there.

That was when Constance noticed that the message light was blinking. She considered that for a moment, then picked up the phone, punched the message button, and listened. There was only one call. From...Nina Winston. "How perfect!" Constance's jaw clenched. *She has no business passing out our secrets.* At the mere mention of Jan De Gruyter's name, Constance slammed her fist hard into the bed. She hated Jan De Gruyter, even if she wasn't altogether sure why.

Now, too, she hated Nina Winston. For cause.

Constance returned the phone to its cradle and took deep breaths, regaining her composure. That was when her eyes fell on Jocelyn's coffee cup across the way, sitting half-finished on the desk. That gave her another idea. However, it distracted her and made her forget about the message light. She did not push star-three to eliminate the message. The little red light didn't blink anymore. But it did remain on, signaling that the message, once heard, remained there, able to be summoned up again.

Constance went across to the mini-bar. It opened without a key. She withdrew a bottle of Stella Artois, poured about three-quarters of its contents down the toilet, flushed that again, then put the beer bottle next to the coffee cup on the night table, so that it appeared as if Jocelyn and her lover had enjoyed a little post-coital drink before they'd gone out strolling down the Wapperstraat, until maybe a little lovers' spat and...

Constance gave one last look about the room, picked up the briefcase with the *Double Ones* manuscript and notes, snuck a peek down the hall to make sure no one was about, affixed the Do Not Disturb sign to the door handle, closed the door to 554 softly behind her, strolled down the hall, caught the elevator, departed the Alfa Theatre Hotel, and returned to her room at the Hilton where she left a wake-up call for eight so that she could make the nine o'clock Sabena bus to the Brussels airport, which she did.

Constance was dozing off well over the Atlantic on Delta/Sabena 2703 that afternoon, when in Antwerp, along Wapperstraat, a young man, laughing, backed his girlfriend up against one of the shrubbery bins so that he might give her a playful kiss. Almost simultaneously, she smelled something awful, and he caught a glimpse of Jocelyn's body.

·37·

Inspector Gijs Stoclet, assigned to head up the case, assumed at first that the murdered woman was a local resident who had worked at the Rubens Fair. Why else would she have had the Rubens-era hat with the gold feather? Perhaps she'd even met her killer there, in the Grote Markt.

But naturally, the murder received considerable attention, and the clerk in the candy stall who'd sold Jocelyn the hat read about the crime in the *Gazet Van Antwerpen*. She notified the police that she'd sold exactly the kind of hat mentioned in the press account to an American who seemed to fit the victim's description. After that, it did not take Inspector Stoclet long. Soon enough, three employees of the Alfa Theatre Hotel positively identified Jocelyn's body.

The hotel maid, an immigrant from the Congo, had long since made up room 554, but she recalled the scene there. She distinctly remembered the condom wrapper on the floor. Likewise, the employee in charge of mini-bars reported that whereas the guest in 554 had not previously purchased anything but one Orangina, on the night she was killed, a Stella Artois beer had also been removed. Nonetheless, while all the circumstantial evidence pointed to a male acquaintance, the Antwerp police were unable to find a single witness who had seen Jocelyn Ridenhour in the company of a man (or a woman, for that matter). Stoclet grew fearful that the American had been the victim of some chance encounter that had left no clues of any consequence.

The inspector had, by now, already contacted New York. A card in Jocelyn's wallet identified her employer. That had led to a call to Jocelyn's nearest kin, her brother, Randolph, who still lived in southwestern Virginia where Jocelyn had grown up. Next, Stoclet phoned Nina. It was early evening in New York, and she was at home, to be absolutely floored by the news.

"I'm sorry, Dr. Winston," Stoclet said, in an English that was largely free of accent, "but it seems that you were the last person who tried to contact her."

"I see," Nina replied, collapsing onto her sofa. She told him about the exchange of messages. "I was in the shower when she called me."

"Do you recall what time that was?"

"Oh, exactly. I'd just gotten back home. Around six—my time. That's why I was so surprised when I called Jocelyn back and she didn't answer. That would've been past eleven, your time. That's awfully late to go out."

"Yes. And you called her as soon as you got out of the shower?"

"Well, yes and no. I called her back right away, as soon as I found the message. But the line was busy." Stoclet jotted down that information. It jibed. The hotel record showed that Jocelyn had made a local call at that time. "So I waited awhile," Nina went on, "then called her back. No answer. That's when I left the message."

"Yes. So now, Dr. Winston, may I ask you: who are Jan and Margareta De Gruyter? There are no such persons we can find. And why 1635?"

Nina was frazzled enough by the shocking news. She was hardly prepared for any interrogation. She mumbled—probably not very convincingly, "Oh, uh, Jocelyn was involved in some sort of genealogical search. But it couldn't have anything to do with this awful thing."

Stoclet could hear Nina's voice starting to break. "I'm sorry, but just to be sure I understand: neither Jan or Margareta De Gruyter could possibly be involved?"

Nina inhaled her sniffles. "Inspector, there is no Jan or Margareta De Gruyter. Not now." But Nina couldn't hold back the tears any longer, and Stoclet surmised it was a dead end. Too bad. The next question he was going to ask was whether Nina was aware of anyone Jocelyn knew in Antwerp. That, surely, would have reminded Nina about Jocelyn's teasing remark about a most "fascinating" person who was also there. But for now, in her distress, she'd forgotten that, and she barely managed to scribble down the inspector's name and number.

Jocelyn's murder was reported in all the New York papers the next morning. It was the same Associated Press account. *The Times* headline read, "Advertising Art Director Killed in Belgium;" *The Post,* "Police Say N.Y. Femme Exec Euro Sex Crime Murder Victim;" *The News,* "Manhattan Ad Beauty Slain in Belgium Mystery." Jocelyn's death was front-page in *The Times* and *World News* of Roanoke, Virginia, for the Ridenhours had long been a prominent family in Bedford County. Jocelyn's body was being shipped there to lie in the family plot.

In Chicago, however, without a local angle, an unknown American's murder abroad did not merit inclusion in either *The Tribune* or *The Sun-Times,* so Constance read nothing of the killing. Anyway, it had already been shifted in her mind, back with all those other unfortunate murders of long ago, to Bess and Caterina and Elsa.

Besides, Constance had things to do, helping Elise prepare to go off to Oberlin. She did tell her—and Carl—what a bore Las Vegas had been. By now, in fact, Constance had long since disposed of the *Double Ones* manuscript and Jocelyn's notes, as well as all the other papers and receipts that might associate her with Antwerp. But, oh, how she thought about returning there with Bucky, to relive together what they had lived in the past, to—above all!—see their beautiful love child in the painting above Mr. Rubens's tomb.

Constance yearned again to be in Bucky's arms. She couldn't wait any longer. As soon as she and Carl had taken Elise to Oberlin, she would go to Bucky. And this time, Constance would not ever leave him again.

Thursday the twenty-third was the day she would arrive in New York.

After Jocelyn was buried in Virginia, Randolph Ridenhour called Hugh. Evidently, he said, the Reverend Venable was the only clergyman Jocelyn had been acquainted with in New York, so would he conduct a memorial service for her there? Hugh said he would be honored, and arranged for a nondenominational service at his old church, Holy Trinity, on Central Park West, for the next Wednesday, August 22nd.

That day arrived rather cool, containing as much a hint of the autumn ahead as the heart of the summer behind. New York could be like that for a few odd days every August; it was, Nina thought, sort of like the January thaw in reverse.

She dressed in a dark suit which was, of course, very much like what Bucky was wearing when he came by her office to pick her up. He'd asked Nina if she'd go to the service with him, and she was pleased to accompany him. They took seats on the aisle about halfway down, and soon after, saw Hugh enter from the side to stand before the crowd. He wore a business suit with his clerical collar, and in his lapel: a small pink rose. He spoke briefly:

"Hello, my name is Hugh Venable. I was pastor here for several years, but today I join you only as a friend of our friend, Jocelyn. We are all still in shock at her brutal death, but I ask you to put that horror from your minds, and to think only of her when she was with us. Now is the time for us to celebrate this person we loved so...who so loved us, so loved life...Jocelyn Louise Ridenhour." Hugh paused. "We'll sing together now. The words are in your pamphlet."

As they all rose, Bucky whispered to Nina, "Who is this guy? He's good."

"Uh huh," she said.

They sang "Morning Has Broken." Then, in turn, three friends came forward and spoke of Jocelyn. There were fond reminiscences, humorous recollections, sweet stories, and the poem:

Go, Lovely Rose

How small a part of time they share,
That are so wondrous, sweet and fair.

Hugh himself then read Psalm 17, verses three through eight. He said that he'd recited it once to Jocelyn "over coffee"—that brought a big laugh—and she'd liked it a great deal. There were a lot of sniffles when he spoke the last verse: "Guard me as the apple of your eye, hide me in the shadow of your wings." Bucky teared up and Nina grasped his hand.

Next, Jocelyn's brother paid tribute. Randolph said that as a child, Jocelyn's favorite hymn had been "Rock of Ages." So, they all sang—and quite lustily, too.

Hugh stepped forward again. He said, "It would irritate Jocelyn mightily if I hid behind this collar and did not speak to the full extent of our acquaintance. We were not, you see, merely friends. We were very good friends. For a time, in fact, we had what people nowadays who are afraid of love call 'a relationship.' Well, Jocelyn and I did not have a relationship. We had a romance. And it was wonderful." Nobody in these pews shocked easily, but that revelation from the preacher did produce something of a murmur. Smiling, Hugh played to the crowd. "As you know, Jocelyn was nothing if not eclectic." Some laughter. "And she was terribly sweet. It's funny. Although we argued about everything, I never met a person whom I could trust so well as Jocelyn Ridenhour."

Nina shifted in her seat uncomfortably. Was it just her imagination, or had Hugh looked directly at her when he emphasized how much he could trust Jocelyn?

He continued. "And surely, you know that Jocelyn was a whale of an advocate for whatever she believed in. Specifically, of course, Jocelyn believed in reincarnation. Make no mistake, she was a deeply spiritual being. And if Jocelyn believed that she will return to walk these streets again but I believe that she already watches over us from somewhere else, it really does not matter who may be right, for all that is important is that she is with us...in all our hearts...and will remain so, forever."

Hugh held out his hands, open, to either side and glanced up. Many more people began to sob. That included Nina. She was angry, too, because she really didn't know if she was truly weeping for Jocelyn—whom she had hardly known—or because Hugh had moved—manipulated?—her so. It infuriated her to think that she was susceptible to almost every damn thing the man did. And she grew even angrier to think that she had allowed herself to think about Hugh at Jocelyn's memorial service.

"We will rise and sing together one more time," Hugh went on, "and then I would ask each of us to think...pray...remember in whatever silent way we choose to, before we go out again into this world that has now been so diminished for us."

The mourners sang "Blowin' in the Wind," and then there was silence and more tears and those tentative moments of disassociation when nobody quite knows what to do next. Nina did. "Come on," she said, yanking Bucky's hand, "let's get outta here."

The two of them walked around, aimlessly, up Central Park West, over by The Tavern On The Green. It was amazing how little they said the whole time. Once, more to the breezes than to Bucky, Nina sighed, "I wish I'd known Jocelyn better."

Bucky said, "Yeah, and I feel guilty. You know, that I didn't return her calls there at the end."

Nina touched his shoulder. "No, Bucky. Jocelyn wasn't being fair with you. And she knew that. She just...cared so damn much about what she believed."

Then they walked on some more in silence, cutting back away from the park. When they stopped for a light at Columbus, Bucky felt almost obligated to say *something*. "I really was impressed with that minister."

"That's his job," Nina replied, but when she realized, right away, how sharp she'd been, quickly she added, "Anyway, I'm hungry. I didn't have any lunch."

"Yeah, sure," Bucky said, and since there was a little Italian restaurant right there, Il Violino, they went in and took a table. "Wanna start with a martini?"

Nina shook her head. "No, we'll save martinis for some happier time."

"Well then, just coffee for me," Bucky told the waiter. "In honor of Jocelyn, Our Lady of the Coffee Bean."

Nina smiled and said, "The same." In time, they had a little pasta, too, but it was amazing, really, how little Nina and Bucky talked—they who normally couldn't stop talking to each other. Of course, it really didn't matter, inasmuch as they were both thinking of the same thing. Finally, in fact, when the espresso and the bill came, Bucky cleared his throat and said, "Okay, I'm ready, Nina. Anytime."

"I know."

"So, let's do it now."

"You mean now? Right now?"

"Why not?" Bucky asked, handing his credit card over to the waiter, who pretended not to hear this rather blunt exchange from the stylish lady and the younger gentleman in their somber black suits.

She shrugged. "I suppose." Nina almost whispered that with resignation. Then she leaned forward and added this, "I just want you to understand—"

"I do."

"You do?"

"Yeah, I know that after I've done one more session with you, and then Constance does hers, then that's it."

"Right. I gotta get out of this then, Bucky. You and Constance'll be on your own."

"I know," he said. Purposely, though, he didn't volunteer to Nina about his doubts, about how even though he dwelt on Constance all the time—dreamed, fantasized about her—he just somehow wasn't sure anymore. He'd decided he wouldn't tell Nina that. How can you be Double Ones, destined for each other forever, and yet somehow be unsure?

Of course, what's good for the goose.... Nina had never told Bucky that she was positive that she and Hugh were also Double Ones. She'd never told him about the silver. In their own way, then, Bucky and Nina were sort of cheating on each other. On the other hand, Jocelyn's murder and their shared grief had only brought them closer than ever before. Nina put down her cup. "This whole thing with Jocelyn..." Her voice trailed off.

"Hey, we don't have to talk about it."

Nina sat up straight so that the physical parts of her came aligned and gave her the strength to speak. "No, I have to tell you something." Bucky tilted his head in anticipation. Nina spoke directly, trying to leave out any emotion. "Look, I don't believe Jocelyn was killed by some guy she met in some chance encounter."

"But—"

"Listen to me, Bucky." He nodded. "The first time the Antwerp cops called me—an Inspector Stoclet—I was so shocked I wasn't thinking straight. I forgot all about this sort of teasing part of Jocelyn's message."

"What's that?"

"It was something to the effect that I'd be fascinated—that was the word: *fascinated*—at someone who was also there in Antwerp. Jocelyn wasn't being mysterious. Remember, we figured to talk again, so she was just being mischievous." Nina leaned forward. "But if she'd met some man, she wouldn't have put it that way. It'd been something like: 'I've met an old beau, Nina' or 'I might've gotten lucky'—that sorta thing."

"So, whatdya think?"

"Well, when I remembered this part, I called Inspector Stoclet back. And then he told me something that kinda bugged him. The telephone message light in Jocelyn's room—it wasn't blinking. It was just on."

"Meaning?"

"Meaning, you see the light blinking, you play the message. Then, if you don't get rid of the message—punch star-something or pound-something—the light just stays on. If Jocelyn had gotten the message, she would've erased it and called me back."

"Maybe she was in a hurry."

"Maybe. But listen now. When the inspector told me that, it suddenly hit me. I said, 'When you searched her room, was a manuscript there?'

"He said, 'What manuscript?' I told him that the whole reason for her going to Europe related to this research project, that she had hundreds of pages, probably a lot of it in Cyrillic, plus all sorts of her own notebooks—he couldn't miss it. There had to be a whole briefcase full. But no, Inspector Stoclet said nothing like that had been found. No papers. No briefcase. Nothing. Just clothes, personal stuff."

"So, what's this mean?"

"It means—I *think* it means—that somebody lured Jocelyn out of her room, killed her, returned to her room, found the notes and the manuscript on reincarnation and Double Ones, made it look like there'd been some sex, then took the stuff and left—incidentally listening to my message."

"But who would do that?"

"I've thought about that. Maybe somebody she'd met in Russia. How *fascinating!* But maybe that was some religious fanatic who really didn't like what Jocelyn and Sergei and Ludmilla were coming up with—somebody like that who she trusted, but who turned on her. Or maybe somebody from the United States who she'd told all this stuff to. Some screwball who figured the material could be valuable—spiritually or commercially. Remember, Jocelyn had a wide circle of strange acquaintances."

Nina kept on, filling out the hypothesis, but Bucky wasn't listening anymore. The most awful thought had popped into his head. Of course: Constance. He was horrified that the thought could have emerged, if only dimly. But he couldn't help it. There was the vision. There was the possibility. There she was, alone with him at The Sherry-Netherland, when Constance was angry, when Constance was calling Jocelyn "wicked"—so furious in her wrath that the memory had never left him. No, no. Bucky physically shook his head, as if somehow he could throw off that awful thought from his mind, as he could shake water out of his head after a shower.

Nina said, "You think I'm crazy." He looked up, distracted. "You're shaking your head at me."

"No, not really, Nina. I'm just so confused." The waiter left the bill, and Bucky signed his name. "What's the inspector think?"

"Well, it certainly interested him."

"What's his name?"

"Stoclet. Gijs. G-I-J-S. I guess that's a good old Flemish name."

Bucky scribbled on the receipt. "Damn it," he muttered. "I'm so screwed up, I can't even figure the tip." He scratched out something, then threw the pen down. All he wanted was to clear his mind—and what better way than for Nina to hypnotize him? "Come on, can we do it—right now?"

She only paused to consider it for a moment more. "Yeah, what the hell, let's get it on." The waiter, who'd come back to pick up the receipt, briefly looked at them askance again. Neither even noticed. "The only thing is," Nina said, "the new questions I have to ask you—the ones in Flemish that I got the lady in the Belgian tourist office to make up for me—"

"Yeah?'

"They're back in my apartment. We'll have to swing by there to pick 'em up."

Bucky had gotten to his feet. The waiter helped Nina with her chair. "Well, let's do it there."

"My apartment?"

Oops. Another raised eyebrow from the waiter.

"Why not?" Bucky asked. "It's so much more...real. It might even help me relax more, make it even easier for me to go back in time."

Nina pondered that thought, but only very briefly. Why not? "All right," she said, smiling. "My place. Your century."

·38·

Jaime eyed Nina suspiciously as she entered the lobby with Bucky. He'd already noticed that her new engagement ring had disappeared. And now, here she was bringing home a younger, flashier fellow. Why, Dr. Winston was turning into a regular tramp.

Nina could feel the doorman's censure, but what the hell? She just continued on, escorting Bucky up to her apartment. She showed him where the guest bathroom was, then went into her own bedroom, closed the door, and turned on the phone machine.

Nina always did that now. Reflexively. Hugh would call again. He would. This evening, after the terrible emotions of Jocelyn's service, he surely would call. And there were four messages. Four! So one must be from Hugh. But the first was a girlfriend: "Let's have lunch after Labor Day when I get back from the Hamptons." Zap—Nina pressed the FORWARD button. Next, Roseann: "A report since you left the office early for the service." FORWARD. Third, "Please call for a free esti—" DELETE. And finally: "Hello, Dr. Winston. I hope you don't mind that I took you at your word and am calling you at home." STOP. Nina knew that voice, instantly. She listened to hear if Bucky might have overheard. Nothing. Still, Nina turned down the · volume before she pushed REPEAT.

"...but this is Constance Rawlings, and I have decided that I *will* come to New York tomorrow. I'll call you when I arrive so that we might arrange our final session, but I would ask you to keep this on the Q-T from Bucky, as I'd like to surprise him. So, until tomorrow."

Nina sat still, composing herself. Well, good, she thought. I'll hypnotize Bucky tonight, Constance in a couple of days, and then I'll be done with them. Good...and good riddance.

Nina went into the living room then, nodded to Bucky, and proceeded to her desk where she picked up Paulette's folder. Nina had gone over it with her very carefully, having her draw up new questions in Flemish. But it was tricky. If, as Nina was so sure, Ollie had killed Margareta, then there was obviously no way that Margareta could talk about that event after the fact. No, somehow Nina must lead Margareta right up to the very moment before her death.

Nina picked up a votive candle. "Let's do it in the guest bedroom," she said, and when Bucky's eyebrows raised a little, quickly she added, "It'll be the most natural place." Of course, Nina didn't reveal to him that it was a particularly natural place because it was to another bedroom, the one in the house on Hopland Street, where Ollie and Margareta were headed that evening of Assumption Day, on August 15th, 1635. "Sit on the side of the bed," Nina ordered him, as she drew up a chair before him. Then lighting the candle, turning on the tape recorder, speaking softly, and putting him into a trance, she took him back to Antwerp, back into Margareta.

Nina looked down at Paulette's questions and, as best she could, phonetically read the first: "You remember me, don't you, Margareta? I'm Nina." She paused, and for emphasis, "Ollie's friend."

"Ja. Vriendlin van Ollie." Incredible. Just with those few words, and it was obvious that Bucky had receded before Nina, folded into a woman, into Margareta. He had taken off his jacket and tie, revealing suspenders—and now, as he speaks, looking to her, it is as if the suspenders are straps to a gown. God, how strange. Bucky's suspenders are a standard dark blue, but the more Nina looks at them, the more, in the candlelight, they appear green. With gold trim. Amazing. It's almost as if Nina is as entranced as Bucky.

She smiles. She reads the next question from Paulette's sheet: "It's important that we talk about your time with Ollie after Jan left for Liege on Assumption Day."

Margareta ducks her head—nervous, embarrassed. Well, Nina had expected that. Quickly, she reads what extra she'd had Paulette prepare for her. "We'll make it easy, Margareta. We'll have you pose some, like you do at Rubenshuis. You can act out your time with Ollie, so you won't have to speak a lot to me."

Margareta seems dubious. "I will act?" she asks.

From Margareta's tone, Nina can pretty much guess that she is only being cautious, not negative, so even if she doesn't know what Margareta has said, she nods in the affirmative and plows ahead, following the script. "Yes. Now you are at home on Schuttershofs-traat, and your husband, Jan, leaves—" Margareta nods, but with something of a shamed look. "—and you put on your beautiful green gown with the gold trim."

Nina holds out her hands as if she is presenting the gown to Margareta, and sure enough, she makes a motion as if she is putting it on. She holds herself more upright and turns sideways, looking as if there is a mirror there, even drawing her hands over the outline of her upper body, as she would smooth out any wrinkles. And then Margareta adjusts the suspenders, as a woman would her straps.

Nina is excited. Yes, yes, she thinks, it's working well this way. So, quickly: "Now you're ready to meet Ollie at the house on Hop-land?" Margareta smiles—at once shyly, but with a touch of the devil in it, too. So now, louder, enthusiastically, looking just to Mar-gareta's side, Nina calls out, "And isn't that Ollie now?" Margareta glances to her left and beams. "Do you kiss him?"

Coyly: *"Wij soctelick koffen ofte fuenen."* Of course, Nina doesn't understand, but from Margareta's tone, she has a pretty good idea. Yes, they kiss. You bet. Clearly, things are progressing nicely. With the hypnosis. With Ollie.

In fact, now Margareta becomes downright expansive. Actually, all she's telling Nina is that inside the house she and Ollie have some beer and they chat. At one point, Margareta even pantomimes picking up a glass, and there are other hints in her breeziness and manner so that Nina can easily imagine what fun Margareta and Ollie are having.

This really is a love nest. The husband's away. Someone's taking care of the children. There's no rush. They can take their time, build to the lovemaking. Nina would like to be able to chat some herself, win more of Margareta's friendship. But, of course, she is limited to the questions she made up with Paulette, so she can only ask next:

"So now, do you and Ollie make love?"

Margareta blushes at first, but then a gloriously happy smile emerges upon her face and she drops back on the bed on her elbows. *"Ja,"* she says. And now she takes her fingers and traces them around her breasts, closing her eyes, moving her head back and forth. Margareta doesn't have to be graphic. Anyway, it is not her nature. But she reveals enough for Nina to understand that it is Ollie's fingers that are really upon Margareta's breasts. And then, when Margareta pulls slightly at Bucky's suspenders, Nina knows that it is Ollie, taking down her straps, and when Margareta lies back, Nina knows she is making love now, Ollie upon her. In time Margareta sighs, and that is enough to indicate the climax of the act. Then, she pushes herself back up again, fixing Bucky's suspenders, grinning at Nina as if to say: there...enough...you are a woman, too. You know.

And Nina nods, in understanding and appreciation.

But she must go on. Of course Margareta made love. But Nina is not a voyeur. It is the scream she wants to get to, the murder. We must reach: "...*owwwllllleeeeeee...*" When does that come? Is the evening over now that they've made love? But Nina hadn't thought to ask Paulette how to say, "So you and Ollie went to sleep?" So improvising, Nina lays her two hands, palms together, up by her cheek in what surely must be the universal sign for sleep.

Margareta only giggles, shaking her head. Then she holds two fingers up. Nina gets the picture. This time, Margareta doesn't have to lie back down and be so illustrative. She merely arches her eyebrows and shakes her head in delight, and Nina lets her revel in those glorious moments.

But Nina must continue. So again, she makes the sleep sign. And this time Margareta nods and peacefully closes her eyes.

Nina collects herself. Is this a dead end? Maybe whatever happened that terrified Margareta and made her scream so did not take place on Assumption Day. Okay, try to move on. She glances down at the questions, struggling to make the next one out in the dim candlelight. But without warning, Margareta interrupts. She opens her eyes, and in Flemish, cries out: "No, no, I must tell him." And then, she looks down, clasping both of her hands softly upon her stomach. She smiles.

Nina still sees Bucky. It is Bucky's hands on Bucky's stomach, but Nina knows it is Margareta. Margareta is a woman, and she is touching a woman's stomach. Of course. Now it is clear. Margareta is having a baby.

Nina holds her arms before her, rocking them. Margareta understands that Nina understands. She beams. But then she looks down to where Ollie is asleep and furrows her brow. She says (almost to herself): "I have to tell him. But not now. In the morning. First thing in the morning."

Nina is frustrated that she doesn't understand. But the last word: *morgen*. She knows that. Morning. Is Margareta saying it's already morning? *"Morgen?"* Nina asks.

Margareta only shakes her head, then looks down where she sees Ollie asleep. "Oh, I love him so," she says. And now, it is as if Nina is gone, and she is alone with Ollie. She reaches down with her left hand and draws it softly through the air, just above the bed. She is caressing Ollie, who is lying there sleeping after their lovemaking. And now the hand moves further down. It stops. She smiles. She has awoken Ollie, aroused him. She smiles down on him then arches her back. Nina thinks: he must have reached up, touched her breasts.

And now Margareta shifts her whole body. She pulls up her legs from where she—Bucky—is sitting, and raises up, kneeling upon the bed.

Kneeling! Nina sees it and remembers. Of course. It is all so vivid. It was just like this in that first session when Margareta came down off the couch to kneel. Just before she screamed. Oh my God. Margareta is kneeling on him. And, Jesus Christ, it is going to happen now. Ollie is going to reach up and strangle her even as they make love. He truly is a monster.

But I must watch. Somehow, I must....

Margareta keeps smiling down at Ollie. She has, obviously, already placed him inside of her, and now she only looks sweetly upon him as if to say: you hardly need to wake up. I will be the one to bring us both to bliss. She moves. She radiates joy.

Nina watches. Despite herself, she is so enthralled.

But then...wait. Margareta doesn't change the way she is kneeling, but she turns her head sharply. Nina is jarred by the action. She sees Margareta cock her head. She's heard something.

And now, Margareta's eyes are full. She must have seen what she heard. Her expression changes. Nina can see her clearly. After all, she is looking directly at her. Only, not really. No, Margareta is looking through Nina. And she is utterly, horribly in shock. No. In fear.

What is it, Nina wonders? What? And then Margareta's lips move. Barely a whisper: "Jan."

Jan! Her husband. He has come here. He has caught the lovers.

Now Margareta's hands fly up and she calls out—screams out: "No, Jan, no!"

But it is too late. Jan must be upon them. In a fury. Margareta's hands flail about. Yes, of course. Jan has a knife. And now, he must be stabbing Ollie. Right before Margareta. My God: not just before her. Under her. Even as they are locked as one.

The blood must be spurting on her. Of course. That is why Margareta is looking in such horror down at herself. Her face is twisted, tormented. Her hands go to her chest. Ollie's blood is all over her. He lies still beneath her. Murdered. Surely. And so now Nina knows what's coming. Right now. But still, she cannot prepare herself. And it is awful. It pierces the night, that dreadful, horrific, keening wail. It is Margareta screaming: "...*owwllllleeeeeee*..."

And yet. And yet, Nina is oddly comforted. She had it wrong. Ollie didn't kill Margareta. No, Margareta lives. It was Ollie who was murdered. In anguish, Margareta thrashes about, crying for her lover.

Nina regains her composure. She reaches over, turns on the light, then falls back onto the bed, grabbing Bucky, taking him into her arms, and softly, sweetly holding him, rocking him, starting to bring him back in time.

·39·

They sat there a few minutes later on the sofa back in the living room. Nina gave him a beer; she took a brandy. Bucky had literally toweled himself off, for he was damp from the experience. Nina had dug up a man's plaid shirt for him—her husband's from years ago. They both were very subdued. Finally, he said, "It was awful, wasn't it?"

"Yeah. You remember?"

He shook his head. "Just that somehow I've been through a wringer. When can we find out what I said?"

"The fact is, I really don't have to wait, Bucky. I had you kind of act it out. Oh, I'll need Paulette's help with a few things, but mostly, I didn't need the words."

Bucky perked up. "You mean you can tell me now?"

"Pretty much." Nina sipped her brandy, then got up. She really felt that she had to. Then, taking a deep breath, standing right before him, she began the narrative. It was all fresh in her mind and just flowed. The green dress, off to Hopland, meeting Ollie, some beers. Nina paused. "You made love then."

"I told you that?"

"Look, Margareta and I have become good friends."

There was a familiar old buckysmirk. "Did the Earth move for me?"

"Your wife should be so lucky." It just popped out. One damn buckysmirk and she was back fencing with him again. "I'm sorry," Nina said. "Uncalled for."

"No, I deserved it." He swigged from his beer can. "And then?"

"Return engagement."

"Did I, like, describe this? Act? Did I, you know, show you?"

"Believe me, Bucky, it was all very discreet. Very classy. And Margareta understood she was talking to another woman. She didn't have to dot the *i*s and cross the *t*s for me." Nina reached down and took another sip of her brandy. "Anyway, more importantly, the lady was pregnant." Unsure, Bucky pointed a thumb at himself. "Yeah, evidently you'd just learned, and—"

"Ollie?"

"Oh yes, no doubt in your mind: Ollie was the father. I sort of gathered that Margareta had decided to tell Ollie right away, but she put it off, afraid he might not like the news. So, she woke up in the middle of the night, pondering her dilemma."

Bucky shook his head. "Damn, I can't believe I let myself get pregnant." He took the cold beer can and drew it across his forehead. "Then what?"

"Well, you were sitting on the side of the bed telling me about this, and you looked over where Ollie would be, and well, let's just say you couldn't keep your hands off him." Bucky blushed. "And then you actually got up on the bed. Oh, what the hell." Nina sank to her knees on the rug. "Like so."

"Oh God, I see. Ollie and I were—"

"Exactly. But suddenly you heard something." Nina pantomimed. "Your head shot over like this."

"What? Who?"

"Yeah, who. Jan. Your—Margareta's—husband. He'd come back and caught you."

"Right in the act."

"Yeah, it was late. Maybe he'd just figured on finding you two asleep. Who knows? Anyway, Margareta sees him come into the room." Nina reached over and turned on the tape recorder. She'd rewound the tape to these last moments when Bucky had been drying himself off in the bathroom. Now she held up the tape recorder before him as she stayed on her knees, still playing the part of Margareta.

The whisper: "Jan." Nina throws her hands up, then opens her mouth as the words shoot out from the tape: "No, Jan, no!" Nina watches in horror, holding her hands up in Margareta's defense.

Bucky catches on. "He's got a knife?" he asks. She nods. He winces. Bucky can almost hear Ollie scream, almost see him writhe, die. Especially Bucky can visualize that as Nina draws Margareta's bloody hands across her chest, holds them before her eyes. And then she looks down and she opens her mouth. She says nothing, just holds the tape recorder by her face and lets Bucky hear Margareta's voice scream: "...*owwlllllleeeeeee*..."

Nina clicked off the tape.

Before her, Bucky dropped his head in his hands. Nina wanted, all too much, to hold the poor guy in her arms and comfort him, the same as she had clutched him at the end of the hypnotic session. But he was Bucky now—not Margareta—and so she stayed there on the floor. At last she asked, "You all right?"

"No, as a matter of fact." But he did at least lift up his head, trying to venture a tiny smile. "I'm not at all all right. I'm a bloody wreck."

"Me too. Spot on."

Bucky shook his head. "Nina, I can't go home. Please. I can't do it."

"I understand."

"Would you mind. I mean, is it possible for—"

"Of course you can stay here." Nina heard herself say those words in compassion and convenience, but still, they scared her just for the implication they carried.

She was glad when he picked up the tape recorder himself and said he'd like to hear it again, because that gave Nina an excuse to get away. She went through her bedroom into her bathroom, closing both doors, shutting out the sounds of 1635, and she peered at her face in the mirror. It looked very drawn. But, she thought, it did look pretty, too. It looked pretty *enough*. The laser job really had been a dandy. Nina drew a brush through her hair, and then, quite intentionally, she picked up a lipstick.

Now, she really stared at herself. Why would she be doing this? Why, of all times, would it matter that she look nice to...a patient?

Walking back into her bedroom, she could hear the tape again, faintly. The scream would come soon enough. She waited till it was over. Then she opened the door. Bucky was still on the sofa, lying back, his legs spread out before him. He looked quite as if someone had slugged him. The tape was whirring soundlessly. Nina turned it off. She said, "Maybe you ought to get some sleep."

Vacantly, he raised his head and looked straight at Nina. "I can't believe it. He killed Constance."

Nina, bending her knees, sort of squatting before him, took one of his hands. "No, Bucky. Come on. He killed Ollie. He killed a man named Ollie—and that was almost four hundred years ago." She paused before going on. "In fact, you should know: he wasn't really even Ollie. He was actually a man named Cecil Wainwright."

Bucky's face scrunched up. "Oh? Why?"

Nina raised herself up to sit next to him on the sofa. "All right, now listen to me. I'm going to tell you everything. Now. And then there's no more. I don't even need to hypnotize Constance again. There's nothing more I can learn from her. I know what happened now. I know you're Double Ones."

"Robbed of love," Bucky said. "I wonder—"

"What?"

"If that's what makes Double Ones."

"You mean, being taken from each other in the very act of making love?"

"Yeah. You think?"

Nina's mind jumped to Hugh. Was that it? Was it all just that simple? Had one of them died in the act? No, please. Then God really was a man. He didn't bring you back for love. No, He just reincarnated you, centuries later, so you could finish up a good piece of ass. No. No, Nina wouldn't believe that. "I'm sorry, Bucky, I gotta think it's more than just...that."

"Maybe Jocelyn had come to some sort of conclusion about that—you know, in her manuscript," Bucky said.

"Yeah, maybe." She looked at him closely. Suddenly, remembering Jocelyn, it appeared as if he might cry. So: "C'mon now, you gotta go to bed," Nina said—and to underscore the point, she got up herself.

Hardly, however, had Nina begun to turn away, when she felt Bucky's hand grab her wrist, pull her back. Please, she thought, don't do this. Largely, she felt this too, because she was scared that she wouldn't stop him. Only Bucky could stop Bucky. She looked back down at him, waiting. And then, plaintively, he merely said, "But you were going to tell me why Ollie was...who? Cecil Somebody?"

"Oh yeah, that." So Nina caught her breath and slumped back down next to him. Then she began. "Okay, Bucky, Ollie wasn't a nice person."

"He wasn't?"

"No, in fact, he was an evil person. A murderer."

"Jesus."

"Killed three women—that he told me about. Elsa—remember?"

"Yeah, the name was lodged somewhere."

"Elsa was another one of Rubens's models. And she was a whore, and Ollie killed her. Just a few days before..." Nina nodded toward the tape recorder.

"God, did I—I mean, did Margareta know?"

"Oh no. Margareta was distraught. Elsa was her friend. But she didn't have a clue about Ollie. Right to the end." She gestured to the tape recorder again. "Margareta never knew that Ollie was really this man named Cecil Wainwright. And the reason he changed his name and came to Antwerp was because he killed a woman in England and was on the lam."

"Was Margareta just more snatch for him, then?" Bucky asked— and with real pathos in his voice. "Didn't he love her?"

"No, honestly, Bucky, I really think he did. I think Margareta must have finally been the one true love of his life. And I think he would have been absolutely delighted if he'd ever learned that Margareta was carrying his child. I'm sentimental enough to believe that even if there's no good in some of us, at least there's the potential for love."

"So maybe that's why we're Double Ones. Ollie found true love, but it was taken from him just when he discovered it."

"I hope so," Nina said. "I'd much rather have it *that* way." She was distracted for a moment, though, because she guessed what was coming next. And it did.

"Does Constance know yet?" Bucky asked. "What Ollie was really like?"

"No. I was waiting to see what came out of our next session."

"We gotta tell her."

"Of course. And it'll be easier now. Because always, before tonight, I thought that Ollie must've killed Margareta. That's why you were screaming. I was so scared of that."

Bucky twisted to face Nina. "Why? Why would you be scared?"

"Well, you know. Because I didn't want anything to happen to you—to Margareta."

Bucky shook his head gently, and for the first time in a long time, he really smiled. "Hey, come on, Dr. Winston, it seems to me that I've always heard you say to be cool, because all this happened hundreds of years ago to a man we don't know named Ollie and to a—"

"I know," Nina said, "but sometimes we don't listen to the doctor—even when we are the doctor." And, with that, Nina laid a hand upon his, where it rested there on his leg, and Nina knew—and she knew that Bucky knew—that the gesture was more rife with personal affection than it was with professional concern, that the hand belonged more to Nina than to Dr. Winston.

He glanced up, then, into her eyes, and without hedging any, he said, "You know Nina, you're wonderful. I've never met anybody like you."

She did not avert her eyes. She was touched and she was proud and she glowed and she said, so softly, "I just want you to be happy again. You mean so much..."

Her last words hung there as she and Bucky stared at each other, their faces only inches apart, in that familiar tableau, just so, where a man and a woman *know* they are about to kiss for the first time. And kiss in a way they both know must only be a start to much more.

That was the moment. Here and now. Just so. Nina fell into his arms. Their mouths opened and their lips touched, and they kissed with sweet force, the both of them. Only after a long time did they pull apart—and then hardly at all, only so much as to admire one another and what they had done together. A *couple* now. Both smiled that dear, warm expression of happy wonder, as if no two people could ever possibly have done this quite so well ever before.

Bucky's hand then moved up toward Nina's breast, and their lips approached again. But just at that very instant where they would meet once more and where their passion would have too much momentum to overwhelm any reason, suddenly something overcame Nina, something turned her face from his.

It was hardly a moment before she looked back at him. It was almost as if it hadn't happened. Just that instant. Bucky's hand was still upon her. Nina said, "I—" and she would have fallen straight back into his arms. But somehow, even as they still both wished for that, they both knew that their moment had come and gone, never to be there ever again.

·40·

Nina lay awake for a long time, thinking, wondering, second-guessing.

Oh well.

It was still pretty early—hardly past ten when Bucky'd gone off to the other bedroom. Suddenly, though, with a start, the phone rang. Now, it *was* late for a phone call, and late calls seldom meant anything but grief. Nina didn't think she could deal with something like that now. First, she would see who it was. So, she waited for the fourth ring, and—

Hearing one word, her heart leapt. The word was "Nina." The voice was Hugh. The second word was "darling." Then he paused. "Let me get right to the point. Since I saw you at Jocelyn's service, I have not stopped thinking of you. Of us. I can think of nothing else. God forgive me, I have not thought of Jocelyn. And suddenly, an hour or so ago, it was almost mystical. Nina, it was as if I was pulling you to me—or yanking you away from something. Finally, I had to call. Please, Nina, call me back."

The intensity must have been too much, because Hugh added a little light change of pace now. "You know, Nina, I have something of yours. I'd appreciate it if you could drop by soon and put it back on your finger, where it's supposed to be." A brief pause. "And while you're at it, well, in the words of that great new country-western song, 'Put Your Ring Back on My Finger and You Back in My Heart.' Okay? Please?"

And gently, then, he hung up the phone. Yes, Nina could tell for certain that it had been gentle. She pushed the REPEAT button and hugged the pillow, listening to it again. ...*it was almost mystical. Nina, it was as if I was pulling you to me—or yanking you away from something.*

Nina threw on her wrapper, went out, and knocked on the guest room door. "Bucky?"

"Nina?"

"The phone wake you up?"

"No, don't worry, I never got to sleep."

"Well, are you decent?"

"I'm safely ensconced under the covers."

So, Nina pushed open the door, letting the light behind her throw just enough of a shaft across him where he lay, his hands on the pillow, propping up his head. Nina came to the end of the bed, leaning onto the frame, looking down on him from above his feet. She said, "We almost made love back there, didn't we?"

"That was certainly my impression," he replied, buckysmirking.

"Funny. I never would've thought that was your style."

"Well, I didn't think it was yours, either."

"Honestly," Nina said, "you're really not the type to fool around, are you?"

"All my big talk, all my flirting—I'm harmless."

"So, why me tonight? All the trauma of this day? Or just a lonely old lady, all too available?"

Bucky raised up on his elbows, which was disconcerting for Nina, inasmuch as it was very much the way Margareta had positioned herself on this same bed in their session. "Ah, lay off the how-could-you-possibly-come-on-to-poor-old-me crap. You wanna compliment, Nina?" She shrugged. "Well, that's easy. You're one terrific lady and you turn me on—and that's a very powerful combination."

"Okay," Nina said, and without further ado, she turned away.

"Hey wait," he called after her. "'Okay.' Just 'okay'?"

Nina looked back at him from the door. She knew she was framed in the light there. "Well, you confirmed what I already thought. I really didn't think I was just another roll in the hay."

"No."

"So, if you really cared about me, then think about it."

"Think about what?" Bucky asked.

Nina stepped forward to the end of the bed again. "Think about it: if you cared about me, then what does that mean about how you think about Constance?" Bucky didn't reply; he just let himself fall back on the pillow. So, Nina went on. "You know, if we had got it on, I don't think you'd've been cheating on Phyllis. I think you'd've been cheating on Constance. That's all. Night-night." She started to close the door behind her. In fact, it was almost shut when he called out to her again. She opened it back up. "Yeah?"

"Are you telling me that as my psychiatrist or as a woman who almost climbed into bed with me?"

"Oh, the latter, Bucky. Very definitely the latter. Psychiatrists are like everybody else. They really don't know a whole lot about love." And this time, Nina winked at him before she pulled the door shut.

The next morning, even before Nina awoke, Constance was already sitting in a boarding lounge at O'Hare. She and Carl had returned from Oberlin only yesterday after safely enrolling Elise there. "Now it's time for me to get on with my lives," Constance thought to herself. That was a good joke; she must be sure to tell that one to Bucky. She'd call him as soon as he got to his office—surprise him. Constance had to tell him that she'd changed her hotel, too. This time, she'd taken a room at the Stanhope—up by the Metropolitan. She'd go there, to gallery twenty-seven, as soon as she unpacked. And now the boarding for American flight 390 to LaGuardia was ready to start.

Nina read the note Bucky had left behind on his bed. It read: "Dear Doctor, Thanks for the best piece of almost I ever had. Always, Bucky."

She laughed and dressed. She had Hugh back; she floated. WNYC said it would start off as another uncommonly cool August day, with a seventy percent chance of afternoon showers. Then: clearing and seasonable. "That's me right now," Nina announced to herself. "I'm clearing and seasonable."

She'd call Hugh later; hey, let him sweat it a little. No, she wouldn't. No games. She called him right then, right that moment. "Hi, I still love you too," she sighed, as soon as he picked up the phone.

"Oh God, Nina, when can I see you?"

"My last appointment finishes at four. How 'bout four-oh-one?"

"Better idea. Meet you at the Tiffany Court at four-fifteen."

"I like that. That's romantic."

"Yeah, it's a good place to get engaged again."

They cooed some more before they hung up. Immediately after that, Nina called Lindsay in Rehoboth. "Hi, is the nuptial beach still available?"

"Oh Mother, is it back on?"

"Better than ever. Hugh and I'll work out the details tonight."

Whistling (which she rarely did), Nina put on her favorite suit, the violet-colored one. Skirt, not pants. And the cream blouse that was too daring for the office...but then: who cared about the bloody office today? Who cared jack shit about the office? Life began at four-fifteen in the Tiffany Court. To top it off, Nina put on her Nike model Picabo Street Air Max Electrify Sneakers, but she also took her new four-inch spike heels with her. Monstrosities, yes. But fashionable again. Made her taller, gave her better legs. Especially if you just happened to be wearing the right sort of sexy violet suit.

"Good morning, Jaime," Nina chirped, heading jauntily through the lobby.

"Oh, Dr. Winston," Jaime began tentatively.

"Uh huh?"

"There's something I'm supposed to tell you."

"There's something you're supposed to tell me?"

"Yes, ma'am." He cleared his throat. "The gentleman who came in with you last night..."

"Yes?"

"When he left this morning, he said for me to tell you..."

"Yes?"

Jaime paused to make sure he had this just right. "He said for me to tell you that *he* had told *me* that he had slept in the guest bedroom."

Nina broke into a big smile. "And do you believe that, Jaime?"

"Oh, yes ma'am, I certainly do."

"Damn, Jaime," Nina said, walking off in her Picabo Streets, "I wish you thought better of me."

The moment that Bucky's secretary, Aimee, arrived at the office, he called her to his desk. There he was fiddling with his American Express receipt from Il Violino last night. He studied it one more time. After he'd worked out the tip, Bucky had written a name down on the back of the slip. Now he copied it neatly on his FROM THE DESK OF... memo pad and handed it to Aimee. "See if you can find this guy for me," he said.

She studied the strange name. Bucky explained. "It's Flemish. It's pronounced like Gees. Gijs Stoclet. He's an inspector with the Antwerp police. In Belgium. That's all I know. But just find him, Aimee. Don't worry about anything else till you do."

"Okay, Bucky." She looked funny at him. She thought he might've been crying right there at his desk. Certainly, he looked like hell.

Over Ohio, Constance reached for the Airfone in the seat back facing her. She ran her credit card through it and dialed Bucky's office.

·41·

Roseann broke smack into Nina's two-o'clock appointment with Mrs. Chen. "I'm sorry, Doctor," she said, but I really think you ought to pick up line one. It's that Mrs. Rawlings."

Nina apologized to Mrs. Chen for having to take the call. Then: "Constance?"

Abruptly: "I'd like for you to meet me at the museum."

"Well, I'm with a patient now." She thought of Hugh. "And then I have a very important meeting. Perhaps we can—"

Rudely, Constance interrupted. "No, I can't wait. I'm going over to gallery twenty-seven now."

Nina could sense the obstinacy in her attitude, the urgency in her voice. She tried to redirect the conversation. "Have you spoken to Bucky?"

For a moment, Nina could almost hear her coo on the other end of the phone. "Of course. We're seeing each other tonight." But right away, the harsh Constance returned. "Yeah, I understand *last* night, you had a little tête-à-tête with him."

Nina was thrown back. And a bit put off herself, Mrs. Chen went into the bathroom. Nina tried to reconnoiter her position; surely Bucky hadn't told Constance all of the events of the past evening. "Bucky was very upset after Jocelyn's service, Constance, and I just—"

"Tell it to the Marines." The phone clicked off.

Nina took a deep breath, trying to figure out what she should do next. Call Bucky. She reached for the address book and actually started dialing his office number: 986-70...No. What good would that do? The problem isn't with Bucky. The problem is that the woman is already on her way to gallery twenty-seven, where she all but lost her composure—her sanity?—last time. And like her or not, Constance Rawlings is still my patient—at least for another day or two—and I must go see her.

Nina snatched up her purse, calling to Roseann as she passed by to try and explain to Mrs. Chen. In fact, Nina was already charging up Fifth Avenue before she realized she had left her sneakers back in the office. To hell with it. She just stopped, pulled off her spike heels, and kept on running in her panty-hose feet.

Only inside the Metropolitan did she remember she was barefoot. She slipped her heels back on as she got the day's admission button. Appropriately, it was silver—although, Nina observed, it was a pretty drab silver: more of a bathroom-faucet silver than a Hugh-Venable, Double-Ones silver.

Scrambling up the escalator, then maneuvering in her heels the best she could, Nina rushed down the corridor and through the European paintings, catching her breath as she turned into gallery twenty-seven. And, yes, there Constance stood. She was only a few feet before the Madonna painting, her eyes fixed on it, on the Madonna. On Margareta.

At least she was able to acknowledge Nina. "Hello, Doctor." But that was all. She stared at Margareta again. And, to herself: "How beautiful is my Margareta," she murmured. With that, she took another step closer to the painting. Nina could see the guard—a different guard, but another very wary guard—eyeing her. She took Constance by the arm, and gently tried to pull her away. But she couldn't budge her. God, she's strong, Nina thought.

So, she tried another tack. "You're gonna see Bucky tonight, huh?"

Constance nodded, but although her lips formed a little happy smile, she kept her eyes fixated on the painting. Nina knew enough to understand that a part of her, at some level, was already Ollie. After a few moments, though, much to Nina's surprise, Constance turned to her and beaming, said, "She had a baby, you know?"

Nina could barely answer. "Who did?"

Constance gestured to the painting. "Margareta." She sighed then. "Ollie's."

"Of course."

"Yes, we had a baby."

Nina swallowed. Constance had said "we." Didn't realize it. But, nonetheless, clearly said it. Nina tried to be matter-of-fact. "Oh," she chirped. "Did Bucky tell you that?"

"No," Constance replied, airily.

"So, then, how did you find out about Margareta's baby?"

"Because I saw the baby."

"You *saw* the baby?"

Constance scowled at Nina, and in a voice dripping with condescension: "Of course I didn't *see* the baby. I saw a *painting* of the baby."

"Of course. And...where was that?"

"Why, the painting over Mr. Rubens's tomb. A wonderful work he did not long before he died. And Margareta is in it as the Madonna again."

"Oh yes, of course."

"And our baby is the Christ Child."

"Oh yes," Nina managed to say. But now her mind was racing. Peter Paul Rubens could only have been buried in one place. In his Antwerp. Nina knew that. She'd read it. There was no doubt in her mind: Rubens lay in Antwerp. And if Constance had seen...

Suddenly, Nina could hardly breathe. Suddenly, she was dizzy.

"Bucky," Aimee said, "I got that guy in Belgium."

Bucky grabbed for his phone. "Inspector Stoclet?"

"Yes, Mr. Buckingham?"

Bucky hunched forward over his desk, grasping the phone as much for support as for merely using a speaking device. Squeezing it hard, he began, "I was a great friend of Jocelyn Ridenhour."

"I assumed perhaps this might be about her."

"Yes. There was somebody who *might* have been staying in Antwerp at that time, and if that person was there—which I don't know—but if..." His voice trailed off.

Stoclet sensed Bucky's discomfort. "And how might we discover if indeed that person was here?"

Bucky sat up in his chair now, his head back, looking up to the ceiling, seeing nothing. "Well, I feel certain that she—that person—would have been staying at some hotel—and, you know, probably a good one."

"I see. And could you tell me, Mr. Buckingham: what is the name of this person?"

Bucky closed his eyes now, as if somehow the dark made it easier to hear himself say, "The name would be Rawlings. Constance Rawlings."

"We have a list of all the registered guests who stayed that evening in the Antwerp area. If you'll give me a few minutes, I'll get back to you."

It was all so clear to Nina now. Now she remembered. Paulette had said that Constance—it obviously was Constance—had dropped by the Belgian Tourist Office. Of course. Constance had then gone to Belgium, gone to—*And you'd never guess who's here. Surprise!*

Now—now—it all made such perfect, simple sense. And suddenly, Nina's whole self was chilled. Constance obviously didn't realize what she had revealed. Maybe she didn't even realize now that she was Constance. Not altogether. Anyway, she just kept her eyes upon Margareta.

Nina snuck a glance over, and her eyes lit on Constance's museum admission button. Silver. Double Ones. But if love can be reincarnated, why can't all else that we are? Love never lives by itself. It's not an independent thing. It's not a bluebird drifting up to the clouds. For all the poems and songs, for all the June/moon/swoon, all the sweet whispers about love—still, love is within us, of us. No less than laughter is us or intelligence is us or character is us or...hate is us. If the capacity to love can jump centuries, why not the capacity to kill?

Nina turned away. Her breathing was coming in gulps now. She must leave, must run, must find help. And somehow, she found the presence of mind to say, casually (well, she thought she sounded casual), "Sorry, Constance, stay right here. I've just gotta go to the bathroom."

"You look peaked. You're not having your period are you?"

"Oh, no, no. I just have to—"

"I didn't think so. I told Bucky I thought you were struggling with menopause." Now that was frosty. Even from a killer, that was out of line. *Struggling.*

Never mind. Nina rushed off, sort of waving, but not daring to look back at Constance. She went out the door to the left, the one by *Venus and Adonis.* That was the last thing Nina saw as she hurried away. Adonis. That great and glorious body, the rosy cheeks, the sexy eyes, the mighty calves, the...hands. Those hands—the one upon the spear, the other reaching over to Venus. The hands that otherwise strangled women.

Nina knew exactly where she was going. She knew there was a back stairs past the next gallery, just before the Rafaels and Titians, that wound down to the main floor. So, without looking back, she ducked onto those steps and almost fell on her face. The goddamn heels. Why did stupid women wear heels? Bloody chastity belts made more sense. Probably more comfortable, too. Nina needed the banister to save her fall; then gingerly, keeping hold of it, she made the last few steps to the landing.

There, she finally forced herself to glance back up to see if Constance might have found these stairs, might be following her. No, thank God, nobody. Hurriedly then, Nina ripped off her heels and taking hold of the banister again, almost using it to vault her way down the stairs, she descended into the medieval armor section. She caught her breath. Damn. She was breathing as hard as if she'd run *up*stairs. She looked back. Good. Great. Still, no Constance following.

Quickly now, she ran toward the front entrance. She knew there were two phones on the right side of the main door. Maybe she would even find Fernandez. No, no. Not that. Not any police. Can't do that to Bucky. Nina had no proof that Constance had been in Antwerp—that she'd killed Jocelyn. Of course, Nina *knew.* But, no proof. No, first she must call Bucky. She must tell him the terrible truth. And he must come and save her.

But: Bucky's number. She'd just seen it at the office. But how did it start: 986? Or was it 896? Damn. She fingered in her purse as she ran. Thirty-seven cents. One quarter. One call. Get it right. Otherwise, that maze of directory assistance, of talking with unknown phone companies, 1-800s, pin numbers. No, get it right. Nine. Eight. Six. That's it, for sure. Ninety-nine percent sure. Well, ninety percent. Okay, *maybe* ninety percent.

By now, she'd reached the Great Hall and she saw the phones. Oh, Jesus. Both in use. But no one else was waiting. Nina glanced back, looking up to the top of the grand staircase. No sign of Constance. She stood there at the phones waiting for one to free up. Please.

In gallery twenty-seven, Constance finally tore herself away from the Madonna and sat down on the bench, smiling to reassure the guard. But then she began to wonder. Did I say something I shouldn't have? Maybe the woman knows you were in Antwerp. Not Ollie. You. Nina left so quickly, so nervously. Maybe she hasn't gone to the lavatory. Maybe she's gone to tell Bucky. She loves Bucky, doesn't she? She wants Bucky. Constance jumped to her feet and dashed out of gallery twenty-seven.

·42·

Constance hurried through a couple more galleries. No Nina. No ladies room, either. She didn't see the back stairs, though. And finally, she did find the ladies room—way in the opposite direction. But, no—no Nina there, either. So Constance ran back to the top of the grand staircase and looked down into the Great Hall.

Just then, the phone closest to the door opened up, and Nina stepped up to it. Now she was in the shadows. At least she couldn't be seen from the top of the staircase. But, especially in her bright violet suit, anybody who came toward her couldn't miss her. Constance started to descend.

Nina dropped in her only quarter. Please: it's 986-...isn't it? She dialed that. And the other four digits. Please. Ring. Ring. "Good afternoon." Please. "*Summer Sailing* and *Snow Ski* magazines." Bingo! "How may I direct your call?"

"Floyd Buckingham."

Aimee said, "Mr. Buckingham's office." Nina identified herself. "I'm sorry, but Mr. Buckingham is in a meeting."

What to say? How many times had Nina called his office? Twice? Maybe three. Hardly ever. Did his secretary even know he went to a psychiatrist? "Listen," Nina ventured, "I know you don't know who I am, but this is really important. Can you please just tell Bucky it's Nina, and I must speak to him now, this instant?"

"I'm sorry, but if you'll just leave your number, I'll have Mr.—"

Nina threw back her head in exasperation, and as she did, she saw Constance out of the corner of her eye. She was already much of the way down the stairs, her eyes glaring, set straight ahead. Nina pulled the telephone cord taut, moving over as far as she could into the shadows of the wall that formed the side of the front door. "Please," she whispered into the phone. "I have never said this before in my life, but I swear to you: this is a matter of life and death."

Aimee could sense the fear in Nina's voice, but she saw that Bucky's phone light was still on. That inspector from Belgium had just phoned him back—and she knew how anxiously Bucky had awaited that call, how he had even closed his door when he got it. Aimee held the phone away from herself, looking from it to the red light. Finally, she brought the phone back to her mouth. "Just a moment," she said, and she got up and knocked on Bucky's door. There was no answer.

That was because Bucky didn't even hear the knock. Just now Bucky had heard Inspector Stoclet say, "Yes, indeed, Mr. Buckingham, we have it. A Mrs. Constance Rawlings of Lake Forest, Illinois, was registered at the Hilton the fifteenth of August."

Then Stoclet had begun asking questions. But Bucky didn't hear them either. And then the phone even slipped from his hand. Aimee heard the receiver clatter as it hit the desk. And then she heard a low, awful moan. She didn't stand any longer on office protocol. She threw open the boss's door. She saw that Bucky had fallen back in his chair. She thought maybe he'd had a heart attack. She ran to him.

Nina couldn't hear any of this. Besides, by now, all her concentration was upon Constance. Nina was trapped. She scrunched down, still holding the phone, but hiding as best she could in the shadows. Would it even matter? Constance had reached the bottom of the stairs by now and was heading directly toward her. Only the large information booth lay between them, in the middle of the Great Hall. Nina saw how simple it all was. If Constance came round to her right, she would be striding right toward her. She could not fail to miss seeing her. But, if by chance, Constance rounded the booth to the left, then maybe Constance wouldn't spot Nina as she angled to the door. Nina froze against the wall. Here we go: left or right.

Nina held her breath.

Constance bore to her left.

Aimee took her boss's hand. "Are you all right, Bucky?"

He managed something of a nod. Aimee heard Stoclet's voice coming through the receiver dangling there, so she snatched it and pressed the mouthpiece to her thigh so that the inspector couldn't hear. Then, kneeling there before him, Aimee said, "Bucky, there's a Nina Something—"

His head shot up. "Nina?"

"She's on the other line. She says it's a matter of—"

Immediately, Bucky came back to life. He grabbed the phone from Aimee. "Nina?"

But, of course, the man's voice replied, "Mr. Buckingham, it's Inspector Stoclet here. Are you all—"

Bucky didn't even say I'll-call-you-right-back. Instead, his hand reached over to his console and he pushed the button on line two. "Nina?"

"Oh God, Bucky! Help me!" Nearby, not five feet away, Constance flew out the front door to stand at the top of the Fifth Avenue steps, there to search the horizon for a retreating figure in violet.

"Where are you?" Bucky asked. But before Nina had any chance to reply, he moaned again, "Oh, it's the worst."

"What is?" But she only heard him groan again. Nina couldn't wait any longer. She had to tell him. She tried to get a hold of herself, and, finally speaking clearly into the telephone, she said, "Bucky, I hate to tell you this, but I'm pretty sure it was Constance who killed Jocelyn."

She waited, then. She expected to hear raging disbelief, curses, ugly accusations. In fact, nothing could have prepared Nina for the quiet little beaten voice that merely said, "I know."

"You know?"

He sat up straight in his chair. "We gotta talk, Nina."

"I know."

"Where are you?"

"I'm at the museum."

With that, he shot to his feet. "Good God, is Constance—?"

"I just met her here. That's how I found out. I got away. She just ran outside looking for me. She's probably on the way to my office."

"Get a cab, Nina. Come here."

Nina shook her head. "No, Bucky, she's out there."

A recorded voice came on and announced that this was going to cost more money.

"All right, all right," Bucky said. "I'll be right there." He was galvanized now. Yes—still in shock on one level, in despair on another. But he knew he had to act. Well, it was easier to act. To do something. "Wait for me, Nina. Don't move. Look, I know what. Go up to the Roof Garden and stay there. Don't leave."

Nina whispered, "I'm so sorry, Bucky." But he'd already hung up and was grabbing for his jacket. Nina simply held onto the receiver, and then leaning back against the wall, she closed her eyes and tried to breathe like a normal person.

By now, outside, Constance had rushed down the steps looking for Nina. She must be heading for her office. But, though Constance peered far down Fifth Avenue: no bright violet suit. She ran along for a block or so, dodging pedestrians who were examining the sidewalk art. But still: no Nina in sight.

At last, Constance stopped. Maybe Nina didn't go to her office after all. Maybe she caught a cab. Or maybe—maybe she didn't even leave the museum. Maybe I overreacted. Maybe Nina's none the wiser and is back up there in gallery twenty-seven, wondering where I am.

Constance turned around, and her Venus earrings bobbling, she rushed back towards the museum, back up the front steps. In fact, at the top of the stairs, she rushed past an older man, actually brushing him aside as she burst back in to the Great Hall. That was Hugh. He simply hadn't been able to wait any longer in his office, so he'd come to the museum early. Before it was time to meet Nina, he'd rent some earphones and go upstairs to the major new exhibit: Velázquez: The Years in Italy. He ambled in, heading toward the admissions booth.

Ahead of him, Constance hurried on, dashing around the information desk toward the grand staircase that would take her back up to gallery twenty-seven. Wait. She stopped. Who was that in purple just disappearing around the corner up ahead? She was gone now. But it had to be Nina. Constance started to run after her.

The guard stopped her. "I'm sorry, ma'am. You have to have a button."

Constance glanced down. Her little faucet-silver button was gone. "It must've fallen off," she said, but the guard had heard that one too many times before. Constance fished into her purse and came up with the receipt. The guard gave her a new button and she hurried in, down the hall, toward the statue of the Virgin reading to the Baby Jesus. Constance momentarily paused to look. Margareta made a far better Madonna, she concluded. She glanced to either side. Nothing. But instinct guided her left, toward the European Sculpture Court. Frantically, her eyes searched about.

Wait. Up there. In the Kravis Wing. Wasn't that a bright flash of purple? Yes. It could only have been Nina. Constance almost bowled over a couple of old Asian ladies in her path. But when she looked up, the purple was gone.

She ducked to her right, into the maze of eighteenth-century palace rooms. Salons. Dining rooms. But no purple. No Nina. And next, absolutely as it had been, the formal reception hall of the Hotel de Tesse, Paris. But no Nina. So Constance scrambled away to her right: The Arts of Africa. Rushing there. But what's that? Out of the corner of her eye, she saw a door open. She whirled back. It was an elevator, the door just closing now.

Constance stared at the elevator. But soon enough, she didn't see the blank doors shut there. Instead, what she saw so very clearly in her mind's eye was the painting over Rubens's tomb at Saint James. And there—there was her beautiful Margareta. Holding their baby. Constance saw that dear painting all so vividly that she didn't even notice that the doors had opened again before her and the elevator operator was saying: "Roof Garden."

·43·

It wasn't a roof garden kind of day. Rather, it was still gray out and even windy, too, up at this height. Certainly, there was almost no one on the roof, save for a couple employees grabbing a smoke and a handful of visitors scattered about. Off the elevator now, outside the glass doors on the roof itself, Nina paused at the portable bar.

Her throat was dry. She asked for a glass of mineral water, and the young bartender cut off a slice of lime for the drink. Then Nina realized her damn feet hurt. She took off her heels again, and carried them with her under the arbor, past the statue of the *Standing Woman*, into the lee of that big, fat bronze lady. "My dogs are barking," she said to herself. Her grandfather had always said, "My dogs are barking." Remembering, she laughed, and sat down there at the far south end of the roof in that little extra square area that jutted down off what was otherwise the neat rectangle of the garden.

Nina sat there, sipping her drink, trying to imagine what would happen next. She glanced at her watch. If Bucky had gotten a cab, he should be here soon enough. Now that she was safe from Constance, she felt more sorry for him.

After all, he would have to confront his one great love of the ages who was a murderer. Poor Bucky.

Bucky was, in fact, already in a cab speeding up Madison. He was trying not to cry.

Hugh started up the escalator to the second floor to go to the European paintings section where the special Velázquez exhibit was on display.

Constance got off the elevator, a bit unsure where she was. She stepped outside, and standing by the little bar, caught her bearings. Nina wasn't visible to her because the massive *Standing Woman* statue hid her from Constance's view. When the bartender asked Constance if she wanted anything and she said no thank you, he turned away to rearrange some glasses. But just in that instant, Constance had seen it lying there. Now, with his back to her, she snatched up the long knife he used for cutting lemons and limes and casually ambled away toward the western side.

There, Constance gazed out over Central Park to the Obelisk and beyond. She turned back then, and facing in, she put one foot up on the rail behind her and idly scanned the garden. Still, she couldn't see Nina because now another statue blocked her view. This one was called *Becca*; it was a bunch of large steel plates welded together.

Constance pushed herself off the rail. Nina must not have come up here. By now, she'd adjusted the knife within her grasp so that it would be impossible to notice. She held it with her fingers pointing back to her palm so that the handle rested there, the blade laying flat along her wrist, all but hidden by her sleeve.

Bucky's cab was making pretty good time coming uptown. The driver pretended that he didn't see his passenger crying a little.

Constance walked to the south, giving the garden a final once-over. And there, her sight line changed and she spotted Nina around the side of *Becca*. There she was. Constance quickly drifted left to put the statue back between Nina and herself. She kept moving closer until she reached the statue. Then she stepped to the side. And now there was nothing between herself and Nina, just a few yards away.

At last, Nina sensed something. Slowly, she raised her head, and turning it slightly, saw Constance. She was looking down at Nina with a smug, almost bemused expression. "Hi," Nina managed to say, as if two old pals had just happened to run into each other.

"You left me," was all Constance snapped back.

"I know. I'm sorry." Nina tried very hard, without success, to appear cool and casual. "My feet hurt from these heels." She rubbed them. "My grandfather always used to say, 'my dogs are barking.' I had to sit down, Constance. My dogs were barking." She forced a chuckle.

But Constance did not respond to the family reminiscing. Instead, without a word, she closed the distance between them, laid her shoulder bag down next to Nina, then leaned back up against the rail that, with the hedge, lined the area. Nina looked up. Constance was glaring at her.

Nina squirmed. She saw a few people at the other end of the Garden. She thought about running to them. Or screaming for their help. But she was still confused and self-conscious. Anyway, it's gonna be okay. Bucky would be here any minute.

In fact, the traffic had piled up some just north of 79th Street. Delivery trucks.

Hugh went into the Velázquez exhibit, but his mind was so much on Nina that he didn't rent an audiocassette after all. What would be the point? He couldn't pay attention to all that information. Instead, he just started to stroll along, looking at the paintings, thinking of Nina. It wouldn't be but another half-hour before they'd be together in the Tiffany Court.

Constance came off the rail then, and like a man, placed her one leg on the bench, leaning forward on her knee. That was when Nina noticed her Venus earrings for the first time—*her* Venus earrings, that she'd bought for Bucky. It was all so confusing. Constance seemed so much like a man. Except now, it was a jealous woman who snarled, "You're trying to keep Bucky away from me, aren't you?"

Reflexively, Nina leaned back, away from her. "That's not my job, Constance. I don't advise. I only seek to show my patients their options." She started to get up. "Anyway, I don't think right now is the time to—"

But in a flash, Constance reached out and with her left arm, pushed Nina's shoulder, shoving her back down hard onto the bench. And then without fanfare but with calculated deliberation, Constance removed the knife from her sleeve and brandished it.

Even before Nina could be scared, she was amazed. Never in her life had anyone threatened her. Oh yes, Jocelyn. But, primarily, she'd been a mystery—only a potential menace. Jocelyn had never confronted her. No one had ever put Nina in real jeopardy before. But now, right here, a crazy woman who might actually feel more like a man, was waving a knife under her nose. And there was no one close enough to see her in trouble. Even: was that a drop of rain she just felt? Now would everyone go inside? Leave?

Nina's mind raced through what few alternatives she still did have. Scream? Constance would slit her throat at the first shriek. Try and wrestle the knife away? Constance loomed as overpowering as some monster football player. No, I have only one hope. I can only try and run away. Quick. Surprise her. Before she can grab me. Thank God, my spike heels are off. Wait. My heels.

Nina laid her cup of water down on the bench. Her shoes were there. Slowly, she let her hand crawl the few inches down from the cup to where she felt a shoe. Nina wrapped her hand around the toe as she talked. "Please, Constance. Bucky won't like it if you do anything like this."

"You really think he loves you?"

"No. He loves you. But I just mean Bucky won't like it if you hurt *any*body."

Constance sneered. "I know Bucky best of all." She leaned forward, bringing the blade even closer to Nina's face. "And I know he doesn't want anybody coming between us."

Nina thought: yeah, like Jocelyn. She only said, "Yes, of course."

Bucky got out of the cab along 83rd Street as it waited for the light up ahead at Fifth Avenue. He hustled down, then dodged the traffic to get across Fifth. But only ducking nimbly, not running. He didn't know there was an emergency. Besides, now what suddenly occurred to Bucky was that Fernandez or one of the guards would spot him.

So, he came into the Great Hall, greatly feigning nonchalance. But, no. Even as he stepped into the ticket line, it was all there again, the same powerful emotions, and Fernandez and the cops faded from his mind before Ollie and Margareta. Nothing had changed. Nothing ever would. Thank God he didn't have to go near gallery twenty-seven, but could head away to the Roof Garden. Bucky put on his little silver button.

The young man operating the portable bar thought he felt a sprinkle. He decided he better push his cart to cover. That was when he noticed his knife was missing. He searched all around the counter, on the shelves underneath. Damn it. Where did that thing go?

The only visitors left who were at all close to Nina and Constance were two men over in the southwest corner, but with the touch of drizzle, they started to head diagonally away, back toward the elevators. One of them happened to glance back. To his friend, he said, "What is that, Bruno? Is that two dykes necking or are they pissed off at each other or what?"

"Or what?" said Bruno, hurrying on to the elevators.

That was the moment when Nina suddenly snatched up her shoe and swung it. The heel dug into Constance's cheek, and she fell back in pain. The force of the blow was so strong that Nina almost lost her grip on the shoe. But she did hold on, and she swung again, this time skimming the heel into Constance's breasts. She staggered back, but she stayed on her feet and she held onto the knife, even so.

Nina sprang up and prepared to run by her.

Just Bucky's luck. Fernandez had to meet someone in the museum offices, which are on the third floor, just below the Roof Garden. He spied Bucky, slightly ahead, as Bucky headed through the European Sculpture Court. Fernandez called out, and Bucky stopped and waited. Fernandez shook his head in disappointment. "Oh, Mr.

Buckingham, I thought I had your promise."

Bucky pleaded, "You gotta believe me. There's a crisis."

"No. I want your butt outta here right now or I'm callin' the NYPD and we're pressin' charges."

"Please. I just wanna go to the Roof Garden. Will you escort me?"

Fernandez was angry. He prepared to call for assistance. But just then, his portable phone rang. "Don't move," he snarled at Bucky, as he listened on the phone. "Holy shit!" he cried out all of a sudden. "Clear everybody off the roof. I'm coming."

"The roof!" Bucky screamed. "What?"

But Fernandez had already lost interest in him. "Crazy woman with a knife," he called over his shoulder. "Now take off."

Instead, Bucky chased after him. "I know her, Mr. Fernandez. I can help!"

Fernandez only shook his head and kept running. Bucky stayed with him. "Hold the elevator," Fernandez screamed.

•44•

Constance was too quick for Nina, though. She collected herself and sidestepped to the left, cutting Nina off at an angle. Nina backed up, then, as Constance began to inexorably close in on her quarry. And now, with no other recourse, Nina screamed, "Help!" at the top of her lungs.

The young man with the bar cart looked up and caught on quick. "That woman's got my knife!" he cried out.

The uniformed roof guard, small and scrawny, picked up the phone and called in the report. But then he stayed by the phone—at a safe remove. Everyone else left on the roof scurried away.

Nina was pretty sure she would be killed. Bess, Caterina, Elsa, Jocelyn. She looked about wildly. The little guard had ventured out a few steps, under the arbor. It was only a token effort, but it did give Nina an idea. Just as Constance prepared to close the last few steps, Nina yelled, "Yes! Grab her!"

Constance turned her head—dubiously, only slightly. But it was Nina's chance. In that instant, she dashed to her right, the few steps to a bench at the east end of the garden. And then, it was like those people who suddenly lift five-thousand-pound trucks off of little children, for somehow, Nina found that magic, that spirit, that adrenaline. She virtually leapt onto the bench, and scrambled— dove—over the hedge behind it.

Constance swung the knife at Nina but just missed, catching the tail of Nina's violet jacket, slashing it. Nina fell hard on the other side of the hedge. There was a walkway there for the museum workmen to use. It ran alongside the hedge, providing access to an air-conditioning apparatus that stuck out to the south end. On the east side of the walkway, toward Fifth Avenue, was the glass ceiling that covered the twentieth-century galleries. It consisted of row after row of stylish, modern inverted Vs.

Constance's knife, snagged on Nina's jacket, had fallen to the ground. As Constance leaned down to retrieve it, Nina pondered, for those few brief seconds, whether to try and escape by crawling out over the jagged ceiling. Maybe the glass was thick enough to support her. Or maybe, like some human fly, she could maneuver along the metal beams.

She glanced back and saw that Constance had picked up the knife and was preparing to come over the hedge. No one else on the roof was anywhere near them. Nina was alone with Constance.

She decided not to risk the glass ceiling. Too dicey. Instead, she turned to her right, to the south end of the building. The walkway came to a dead end there. The drop down was about sixty feet. To the right was the air conditioning unit. But to her left, at the top of the glassy convex wall that shot up from the ground like a modern fortification for an ancient castle, was an unprotected ledge that ran at the edge of the glass ceiling. It could be used by workmen in a pinch. Or by someone running for her life.

Constance had made it over the hedge now, and was stalking Nina almost playfully, holding the knife high. Nina could see, too, the blood dripping down Constance's cheek from where she'd gouged her with her high heel. In fact, when Constance paused to wipe the annoying blood away with her free hand, she looked down at the blood on her fingers then up toward Nina, shaking her head at her as if to say, *naughty girl, naughty girl.*

Nina had reached the end of the path. She realized she had no choice. Sure, it would be easier to climb onto the air-conditioning unit, without any fear that she would fall to her death from there. But to what purpose? Constance could easily follow her where there was no escape, then casually slash her to ribbons.

No, Nina had to take the lesser of the two evils, go left down the ledge. She checked it out. Oh, my God. She really hadn't noticed it before. To even reach that slender two-foot-wide path, she'd have to clear a gap where the two parts of the museum were not quite joined. Between them, it was like a mineshaft sixty feet down. Holy Mother.

Worse, the Roof Garden was about five feet higher than the ceiling path. So Nina had to jump over *and* down to land on that narrow ledge. She stood, poised.

Constance, raising the knife even higher, took one more step toward her.

Nina thought, if I make it...if I do...and then if Constance does come after me, neither of us can move too fast along that tightrope of a ledge. And I'm smaller, more nimble. At least it might buy a little time. Help must be coming. Bucky...where was Bucky?

And so, Nina thought of Lindsay and she thought of Hugh, she said a little prayer, and then she bent her knees and pushed off, trying to fly the gap.

The elevator reached the Roof Garden. The whole way up, Fernandez, furious, bellowed at Bucky to go back down. He even pulled out his pistol, and when the doors opened, the elevator operator took the cue and grabbed for Bucky. Fernandez shoved him back. "Close the doors," he screamed. "Close the doors."

Swiftly, though, Bucky drove his elbow into the elevator man's gut—just enough to make him loosen his grip. With that, he burst through the doors in the instant before they closed. The little guard who'd called for help was there, ready to bring Fernandez up to speed, and as he did, Bucky brushed past them, dashing out into the Garden. "Stop! Stop!" Fernandez screamed, but Bucky ran out ahead.

And there he saw them. Constance. His Constance. His Double One. Waving a knife. At Nina. Nina standing on the precipice. But, no. Now she was gone. Nina had jumped.

Bucky ran closer, trying to see over the hedge.

Nina flew over the gap. But just barely. Her trailing leg banged hard on the edge and cut the top of her foot. She thudded there, fighting to hold her purchase, to keep from sliding off. Nina looked over, down, where she almost had fallen. She saw the park far below her. She saw her death.

But, if she had escaped falling, she had not escaped Constance. So, quickly now, she began her retreat along the edge. At first, she dared only back up on her bottom, feeling the way behind her. In this fashion, she could keep a lookout fixed on Constance. Besides, on top of everything else, Nina had never been really good with heights.

She could see that Constance had reached the gap herself now. She was getting ready to jump. Soon, she'd be on the ledge with her. Nina had to put more distance between them. Slowly, gingerly, she pulled herself up—first to her knees, then to her feet—all the time trying to keep her eyes on Constance so that she wouldn't look down.

And that was when she heard the screaming. She dared turn her head. And then she saw Bucky. And behind him: Fernandez. Chasing Bucky, screaming, waving his pistol.

Constance didn't look back, didn't see Bucky. She was already in a crouch. She pushed off. She made it with a foot to spare, too, falling forward. But in her concern to hang onto the knife, she lost her balance and had to struggle to keep from pitching over the edge.

Bucky screamed, "Constance! Constance, darling! Wait for me!"

Nina thought: *It isn't Constance, Bucky. It's Ollie.* But she didn't say anything, only backed up some more.

Bucky jumped up on that same bench where both of the women had gone over the hedge. Fernandez approached. "Don't do it, Mr. Buckingham. Don't move." And he pointed the gun directly at him.

Calmly, Bucky held his place and answered, "Mr. Fernandez, I'm not the problem right now." Fernandez considered this, but he also kept Bucky in his sights. For an instant, then, Bucky glanced over his shoulder. He saw Constance advancing, Nina shaking, moving back. "Really," Bucky said, "I am not the problem anymore." And with that, even as Fernandez kept the pistol trained on him, Bucky vaulted over the hedge. He landed cleanly on the walkway, and right away, without looking back at Fernandez, he ran to the dead end of the path.

Hugh suddenly found himself at the end of the exhibit. Velázquez in Italy. In Spain? In Saskatchewan? It hardly registered. All he kept thinking about was Nina. And then he came out, past the Velázquez books and calendars and posters, and he turned the corner there. Right away, he realized where he was. Straight ahead, two or three galleries on, was Rubens. Hugh hated himself, but he couldn't stop himself from heading there, directly to gallery twenty-seven. All right, he would look at that damn painting one more time.

Along the precipice, Nina edged back, inch by inch, Constance moving toward her, cutting the difference with each easy stride. But beyond Constance, now Nina could see Bucky. He had arrived at the end of the walkway, and was looking over the gap, envisioning the leap. Instinctively then, Nina yelled out one word. It was: "Margareta!"

Bucky heard it. Of course, he thought. Of course. He called back, "Yes?"

Constance turned back, saw him over her shoulder, and smiled happily. Nina ducked back a couple more steps.

Bucky jumped. He landed well—the skier in him?—only swaying a little. He was, however, crying. He reached up to wipe at his eyes, and that was when he felt the drizzle. It was steady now; it would be all the more slippery. But, slowly, barely lifting his feet, he began to slide toward Constance. And now it was all three of them, birds on a wire, inching along, sixty feet up, sixty feet down.

Nina called out—but gently, "Please, they have a gun. Come any closer, they'll shoot you."

Constance did glance back, but only for a second. No longer could Nina even guess what she was thinking. Or even: what did she see? After all: who was she in her own mind? But beyond Constance, beyond Bucky, Nina could see Fernandez and some other guards massing along the hedge. At last, they'd lost interest in Bucky. It was only the one tall woman threatening the other, smaller woman with a knife.

Nina held up her hand to Constance. "Please, don't move," she said. And to Bucky behind her, "You either, Margareta. Everybody— stay still."

Constance, though, kept coming toward Nina, unmoved even by the rain. By now, she wasn't but about six or seven feet away.

Fernandez hollered, "Don't move, lady. Don't move or I shoot!"

Constance shook her head at Nina: *Naughty girl.* Then she spoke—although as soon as she opened her mouth, Nina knew it was Ollie speaking. "I knew it," said the voice. "I knew you'd call the *scutters.* I knew you wanted Mr. Rubens's reward."

Nina shook her head vigorously. She could see Bucky drawing closer to Constance. Oh, she didn't want that. Don't be a hero, Bucky. But he took another step. Damn, thought Nina, we'll all three fall, all three die. All of us.

Nina did a risky thing then. Somehow she found the courage to stop, to hold her ground. And then she held out her hands to Constance, pleading, "Please, please." She pointed toward the cops. "The *scutters.* They'll shoot. They will! Please." And then Nina added one more word: "...Ollie."

Constance smiled at that. Fernandez screamed to surrender. She glanced back at him. Then incredibly, Constance began to turn herself upon the ledge, twisting her body, oblivious to what little space she had to operate in and how much more slippery it had become. Fernandez and the other officers looked on, baffled. In fact, it even took Bucky and Nina a few moments before they both realized, almost simultaneously, that Constance was taking her pose as Adonis. Her feet planted correctly, she held out her left arm, raising it, grasping the knife as a spear.

Fernandez and the others tensed, their guns all sighted on Constance. "Put the knife down!" Fernandez screamed. To him, of course, it looked as if Constance was preparing to bring it up so that she could drive it down into Nina.

Nina screamed back, "Don't worry. It's okay" —even as the blade pointed straight at her. She knew that Constance had only taken up her pose. And Bucky knew that, too.

Fernandez, of course, didn't know. He didn't know she had been the other Adonis. "Put the knife down or I shoot!" he yelled.

She only held the knife high above Nina, but now she was twisted around so that she was looking back down at Bucky, where he crouched in fear. And now she smiled so sweetly at him, because now Constance saw the red and black diamonds, the patterned tiles upon Mr. Rubens's studio floor. And yes, of course, Margareta was sitting upon them, reflecting the true love that a woman had finally been able to draw from him.

Maybe Constance's arm quaked a little at that moment. Even for one so strong, it was, after all, always such a difficult pose to hold. And this time, too, there was no spear to lean on for balance, but only one arm to hold up free, the knife within that hand shaking.

Fernandez twitched, too. "Jesus," he said, "she's going to kill Dr. Winston." So once more he screamed for Constance to let go the knife, and once more she ignored him. But now she was gone completely from this place and time. Just the red and black tiles. Just Margareta upon them. So now, when her arm seemed to waver just a bit more, Fernandez decided he could wait no longer. He brushed the raindrops from his eyes, then steadied his right arm with his left, sighted the target better, and squeezed off one round.

The shot rang into Nina's and Bucky's ears as no other sound had ever stunned their hearing. Thereafter, had even the greatest hypnotist in all the world tried to hypnotize Bucky, never could he succeed, for all Bucky would hear is the eternal echo of that sound, smashing whatever reverie there might be in his trance.

The bullet lodged in Constance's right shoulder—a fine shot for a pistol in a drizzle. Her body shuddered as the shot pierced her body, and maybe that impact would have been enough by itself to pitch her over the edge. But Bucky was looking at her at that instant—as she at him—and the way he saw it then, and the way he would always remember, was that Constance could have saved herself.

But maybe, she thought, maybe if I reach out for help, Margareta will rise up off the red and black tiles and she'll grasp me, and we'll fall to our deaths together. Ollie could not do that to the only woman he ever loved. Besides, there was their baby to think of. Mr. Rubens would need him for his Christ Child in his painting above his tomb.

So Bucky was certain that when Constance looked at him and so sweetly sighed, "I love you, Margareta," she still could have saved herself. But instead, Constance only held the pose for an instant more, and then tensing her legs, she purposely pushed herself off, even tumbling far enough out to fall beyond the curving wall, to smash, in death, clean upon the sidewalk.

As Constance fell, Nina was sure she heard Bucky call out softly, "Ollie." Not a wail this time. Not a screech. Just a sad murmur.

It was the strangest thing, Hugh thought. Hardly had he stepped into gallery twenty-seven, even before he began to approach *Venus and Adonis*, he was sure he heard dogs barking. Dogs? He would have dismissed the thought, but the one other visitor in the room, an older woman with an English accent, was standing next to the guard and Hugh heard her say, "Might that be a dog I heard?"

The guard nodded, dubiously. "Must be a seeing-eye," he said, peering around the corner into the next gallery .

Hugh nodded himself. But then he thought: a seeing-eye dog? In a museum? What blind person would come to an art museum, where there are only things to see? And anyway, damn it, it hadn't been one dog. Hugh was positive: it had been two—two happy barks, the one overlapping the other.

And suddenly, at that moment, a chill touched him. A breeze? A wisp of something or other? Whatever, in that instant, Hugh couldn't help himself, and he found himself hurrying forward, rushing toward *Venus and Adonis*.

There was no doubt in his mind that he saw it. He couldn't understand it, of course, and he couldn't rationally accept it, but damn it, he saw it happen. Not in a flash, either, but in real time. Suddenly, there before him, where the two hunting dogs had barked, Venus pulled Adonis to her by his shoulder and she kissed him. Nothing long and passionate—but only an affectionate kiss, as you would welcome back someone who had been away. That was the way Venus kissed Adonis, and the dogs barked again.

And then the painting was still once more.

Hugh shuddered. But he had the presence to look around, and he saw that he was still alone in the gallery, that the guard had remained in the adjoining room, looking about for that seeing-eye dog. And so, Hugh reached up and touched the painting. It was solid and it was cold where his fingers rested for an instant on the ground where Adonis stood. Hugh removed his hand and started to back away, but then he had the urge to reach out again. This time, he touched Adonis himself, his left leg, that great, muscular calf.

It was warm. Maybe (Hugh wasn't positive about this) it even quivered a bit. But, yes, it was warm. No doubt.

Hugh stepped back, then, just as the guard returned, and he looked to heaven and murmured a prayer. As he left, he put a smile on his face and said to the guard, "Well, I guess I *will* be that peasant in Bolivia next time." The guard, of course, didn't have a clue.

Some day, Hugh thought, maybe he would tell Nina what he'd seen, what he'd felt. Or maybe not. After all, for how deeply that Nina believed, maybe even she wouldn't believe him if he told her about this experience. Anyway, that decision could wait. For now, it was all too much for Hugh, because he couldn't any longer be quite sure who he was. Then again, he wasn't altogether certain whether that even mattered, so long as whoever he was, wherever in time he might be, he and Nina belonged to God. Wasn't that all that really counted?

On the roof at that moment, the both of them crying, Nina and Bucky crawled back along the ledge where strong arms helped them across the gap and over the hedge to safety. They stood there, then, in the Roof Garden, above all the moist green of Central Park, both of them sobbing in a shared embrace, and never mind that the drizzle had become a real rain, and somewhere distant there crashed the last thunder of that summer.

❖AFTER❖

The three of them had to fight through the sidewalk crowds just to reach the museum's side entrance. All they'd wanted was a quiet day when the museum was closed to the public, but when Nina and Fernandez had agreed on this Sunday in November, neither of them had thought to remember that it was the day of the New York Marathon.

But it was the most glorious autumn morning, Central Park simmering in fiery shades, and if it was bedlam out on Fifth Avenue, inside the Metropolitan it was wonderfully eerie in its silence. And that was the way Nina had wanted it for this one final, private visitation.

They had to troop up the grand staircase because the escalator was turned off. Nina lagged back with Fernandez, watching Bucky and Phyllis ahead of them, holding hands. Phyllis, it seemed to Nina, appeared the more nervous. After all, she'd never been to gallery twenty-seven before; for her, it was the fear of the unknown. It was different now, too, for Bucky, more than two months since the shot and the death. As they approached the Rubenses, he even called back, "Don't worry, Mr. Fernandez, I'm okay," and he put his arm, reassuringly, around his wife's shoulder.

That way, he steered Phyllis before *The Holy Family with St. Francis*. "Well," Bucky said to her, almost matter-of-factly, "that's me. When I was Margareta."

Phyllis stood closer, scrutinizing it, then she turned to look over to Bucky, her eyes beseeching. "What am I supposed to say?" she asked. "That you were kinda cute? I mean, Bucky, there's just no training for this in the wife's manual. Nobody's ever come to a museum with their husband before when he was...you know."

"Yeah," Bucky said.

Phyllis looked back at the painting. "Well, you had a sweet face," she decided.

"That's what everybody always told me," Bucky said, which sounded all the weirder to her.

"So, where's Adonis?" Phyllis asked then. By now, of course, she knew just about all of it; Bucky had told her everything about his romance with Constance.

He pointed down the wall, past the little Van Dyke, and Phyllis started to walk that way. But now, suddenly, Bucky held back. With a nod of his head, he gestured to Nina, and she stepped over to stand with Phyllis before the huge painting. Her eyes examined Adonis, up and down. "That was his love?" Phyllis asked Nina.

"Well, it was Margareta's, yes."

"Okay, I guess I got it," Phyllis said, and she went over, took Bucky's hand again, and without another word, they walked briskly out of the gallery. Of course, although Phyllis didn't notice, as they passed by Margareta, Bucky gave her a thumbs up for one last time.

Downstairs, they all thanked Fernandez, and he advised them to hurry if they wanted to get across Fifth Avenue before the marathon reached here. The three of them hustled down the sidewalk behind the crowds, and just managed to duck across before the cops closed off the street. The leaders in the marathon—two Kenyans and a Mexican—were in The Bronx and bearing down on Manhattan.

At her office, Nina took out her key, but just before she could put it in the lock, the door flew open. Hugh stood there. "I made the coffee already," he said.

Nina said, "Phyllis, Bucky—I don't think you've met my husband, Hugh Venable."

Bucky looked curiously at Hugh, then blurted out, "Hey, I know you."

"Jocelyn's service."

"Yeah, yeah." Bucky turned to Nina. "I told you how much I liked this guy. You never told me that you—"

Nina held up her left hand, showing off her rings. "We were just waiting for your blessing."

Impulsively, Bucky kissed Nina on the cheek. "Hey, a bride! Congratulations."

"Come on," she laughed, pushing him toward her office. Then, she turned back to Phyllis. "Enjoy the coffee. Bucky and I will only be a few minutes, I'm sure." And the two of them went into her inner sanctum, closing the door.

Bucky threw himself on the couch, giving out a big stage sigh. "You all right, Mr. Buckingham?" Nina asked.

"Yeah, I needed that. I had to say good-bye to Margareta."

"And Ollie?"

"Oh, I think I did that already, back when—"

"Yeah," Nina said, blowing on the coffee, waiting him out. And finally, he said, "All right, doctor, what did you decide about all this?"

Nina sipped her coffee. "Well, first I *know*—I know how sorry I am for Jocelyn and Constance." With her free hand, she crossed herself.

Bucky said, "Amen," and suddenly, he was struggling to hold back tears. Nina reached down and patted his shoulder.

"And then," she went on, "then I think...no—I'm certain—that there was a woman named Margareta who lived with her husband, Jan De Gruyter, in Antwerp around 1635, and..." Nina stopped and looked squarely at Bucky before she said this: "And as sure as I believe in God, I believe that you were that woman."

"Amen."

"I believe that you—Margareta—fell in love with a scoundrel...well, worse, a murderer. Charming and handsome, but a murderer. And he called himself Ollie then, and he became Constance Rawlings in this time and place. And I believe that Ollie and Margareta met at the house of Peter Paul Rubens, and then they were caught *in flagro delecto* by her husband—by your husband—and he murdered Ollie. But I believe that Ollie—and you—came back to life in this century, and by chance, you met each other in Philadelphia twenty years ago, and then, again, this past February 11th, you met again, reincarnated as Double Ones. That is what I believe."

"Yeah," was all Bucky said. "Exactly." Nina crossed over to her desk. Bucky asked, "What about your husband?"

"Hugh?"

"Yeah. I mean, he's a preacher. What's he think?"

"He doesn't want to talk about it, but the evidence is just too overwhelming—even for my Doubting Thomas. And you know, Bucky, I can't explain it, but Hugh did have some kind of change of heart...of mind. That very day Constance died. And then, after I showed him this..."

Nina picked up a large manila envelope. Bucky knew immediately it was from Europe. Even in the homogenized global economy, manila envelopes are the one thing made differently outside the United States. "This arrived a couple weeks ago," Nina explained, holding it up then coming over and sitting down next to him on the couch. "It's from Inspector Stoclet," she said, opening it up.

"Really?"

"In the beginning, I'd told him that Jocelyn was doing some sort of genealogical research in Antwerp."

"Well, that's kinda true," Bucky said.

"Yeah. Afterwards, I kinda forgot all about that, but damn if the inspector hadn't already gotten someone to start checking out the stuff I'd mentioned to him."

Nina took out the papers and went on. "These are some old records—copied from the Antwerp city archives. A fire destroyed a lot of records, and after the war most of them were moved from the town hall to an old building on Venusstraat, wherever that is, and even after all this time, not everything has been cataloged yet. Still, the inspector's man hit some pay dirt."

Bucky leaned forward, looking at the paper Nina showed him. "There's something called the *Liggere*," she said, pointing to the word. "Inspector Stoclet describes it as a 'book of membership'—a census, I guess—of old Antwerp. And sure enough, in 1635, a Jan De Gruyter is listed as residing on...are you ready?" Bucky nodded. "On

Schuttershofstraat."

"Schuttersh—? What?"

"Schuttershofstraat."

"I can't even say it."

"Yeah, well, if you go back and listen to the tape when you're speaking as Margareta, you say it loud and clear. And why not? It was the street you lived on." Bucky only shook his head. "And, by the way, that street's in"—Nina looked down and read—"*de derde wijk*—the third quarter. The same as where Rubens lived."

Softly, Bucky just said, "Go on," and Nina turned to the next page.

"The policeman working for Inspector Stoclet had no luck in finding any listing for a Jan De Gruyter in a couple of other places. One is something called *Eed*, which is 'a book of oaths,' whatever that is. Or the *Costuymen*, which is some sort of a law record of Antwerp."

"Nothing, huh?"

"No, but remember: a lot of records were burned years ago, and a lot more weren't complete or haven't been filed. But—now get this—the inspector's man did find the city tax records for 1635. It's called the"—Nina read—"*Tiende Penning*, which means 'Tenth Coin.'"

"Why?"

"Don't know. Doesn't matter what it's called. But what does matter is that these tax records were kept by the Spanish who ruled Antwerp at that time. And the *Tiende Penning* was very, very complete."

"Tax guys always are."

"Exactly. Now take a look." She handed to the sheet to Bucky. "See: Jan De Gruyter owned a house on Schuttershofstraat, where..."—Nina traced a line of fine ink penmanship—"... where he resided with his wife, Margareta, his two children, Adrien and Magdalena, and a servant—"

"Wow. Jackpot."

"—Clarissa Martens. You—Margareta—even mentioned her name to me."

"The woman who took care of the kids when I was with Ollie."

"Yep—they're all there: Jan, Margareta, the kids, the servant. The Spanish IRS didn't miss a thing."

Bucky whistled. "But you know," he said, "this is really just icing on the cake. If you'd showed me this a few months ago, I would've been stunned. But now? All this does is prove what I already knew, anyhow. What *we* already knew."

Nina smiled in agreement. "And there's one other thing."

"More?"

"After the police finished searching the city archives, they checked the records at Saint James Church." She passed him the photocopies. "The marriage of Margareta Engelgraef to Jan De Gruyter—October 30th, 1629. The baptisms of their children—Adrien in 1630, Magdalena in '32, and there: a third child, born in March of 1636, then baptized that fall on All Saints Sunday, at the time of their seventh wedding anniversary."

"So I *was* pregnant when Ollie was killed?"

"You most certainly were."

"But wait a minute, Nina. How could that child possibly have been baptized at Saint James? I mean, my husband had caught me in bed with another man. He wouldn't have tolerated keeping me around after that, would he? And would he go along with baptizing a child that wasn't his?"

Nina stood up. "I've thought about that. First of all, assuming that you'd still been servicing your husband—and De Gruyter sounds like a sex-on-demand guy—well then, he couldn't be sure whose child it was, could he?"

"I guess not."

"Margareta was positive it was Ollie's baby. So was Constance—the instant she saw him in the painting—'my deare childe.' But still, you know how men are."

Bucky laughed. "You probably know that better."

"Well, the proof is in the pudding. De Gruyter accepted the child as his, and he accepted Margareta back into his good graces." She ticked the paper Bucky held. "Mr. and Mrs. De Gruyter are both listed on the baptismal register—and it's certainly symbolic that they had the child baptized at the time of their anniversary."

"But, wait a minute. Didn't De Gruyter get punished? I mean, the sonuvabitch killed a man in cold blood. With a witness, uh, very close by."

"Yes, but that's it—he killed a man screwing his wife," Nina said. "In the seventeenth century, wherever you were in this benighted world, the courts tended to go kindly on poor, wronged husbands—especially those who discovered rather graphically that they were being cuckolded.

"I'm just guessing, Bucky, but I think this is possible, too. Somebody must have seen Ollie with Elsa—you know, away from Rubenshuis. Rubens had posted a nice reward. Especially after Ollie was killed, when there was a great deal of notoriety about the scandal, I suspect somebody fingered Ollie as Elsa's murderer. The *scutters* probably said case closed. So, you see, Jan De Gruyter wasn't really a murderer. He was more of a convenient instrument of justice who saved the city from paying the executioner."

"Okay," Bucky said, "so De Gruyter gets off, I...Margareta has the baby, and to keep up appearances, they baptize it at Saint James. You think maybe then he chucked Margareta outta the house?" Nina shook her head. "Oh no. I'd bet my life that Margareta and Jan stayed together. Maybe not happily, but yes, ever after. Look at the last thing on the baptism certificate." Bucky glanced down, puzzling over the handwriting. "It's the names of the godparents. See there?"

"Oh yeah."

"One godfather is Joannis Gansacker. Remember? It's his family that rescued Margareta from the orphanage. Mr. Gansacker was obviously a very prominent citizen. But now look at the other two godparents."

Bucky smiled as he read: "Peter Paul and Helena Rubens."

"The big guns. Margareta De Gruyter might have slipped into adultery, but she retained some very solid allies." Nina held up her two thumbs and forefingers, suggesting a picture frame. "This is the way I see it: Rubens assembled a sort of family court at Rubenshuis. He reverted back to being the diplomat. Probably no women there. Certainly not Margareta. No Helena. No Mrs. Gansacker. But Mr. Gansacker is there, and maybe the chief *scutter*. And Jan De Gruyter, for sure."

Nina paced about, playing Rubens, even stroking an imaginary beard. "And he says: 'Mr. De Gruyter, this has all been most unfortunate. Your dear wife was led astray by this evil Englishman, but you took care of that, *as any devoted husband has a right to*, but now it's time for you to forgive Margareta this lapse and proceed with your lives...as before.'"

Nina leaned over toward Bucky as if she were Rubens addressing De Gruyter. "'After all, my dear De Gruyter, you had yourself been behaving quite badly toward Margareta, who, as Joannis here will attest, is a wonderful lady.' And here Gansacker nods vigorously, and Rubens goes on: 'Both Mrs. Rubens and I have grown most fond of Margareta, too. And I'm sure, sir, that you would want to continue to live and prosper here in Antwerp, to worship at Saint James, to raise your family in our midst, under the protection of Our Blessed Virgin. What a shame it would be if your cloth business was found not to have paid sufficient taxes to the *Tiende Penning* or etc., etc.'

"And probably at that point, Bucky, Gansacker harrumphed on cue and said something like, 'Oh my, that would be so dreadful,' and Jan De Gruyter got the picture. It's possible that Rubens even told him that he and Gansacker were thinking of putting him up for membership in the country club—whatever the equivalent to country clubs was then in Antwerp. Make sense?"

"Perfect." Bucky slipped the papers back into the envelope. "So, I had Ollie's baby and went back to posing as Madonna."

"Even better. Posing with your child." Nina pointed to the envelope. "But one more thing. Take another look at the baptism certificate." Bucky retrieved it. "You didn't notice the child's name."

Bucky smiled broadly as he located the information. "Peter Paul," he said. "I named him Peter Paul De Gruyter."

Nina went back over to her desk and picked up a business card. "Inspector Stoclet also sent this name." She handed it to Bucky. "She's supposed to be the finest genealogist in Belgium. There's probably a lot more stuff she could uncover. Who knows? Maybe you could even trace your line right up to today."

Dismissively, though, Bucky flipped the card back at Nina. "No thanks. I can't quite see myself walking into somebody's house in Brussels and saying, 'Hi, I'm your great-great-great-great-great-great-great-great grandmother.'" He stood up, handing her the envelope. "No, that's enough, Nina. I don't wanna know any more."

She held up the envelope. "You don't even want this?"

He shook his head. "God, no. I'm just gonna try and forget it all—well, as much as I can. You're the shrink. You think that's best for me?"

"Yes, Dr. Winston, your *psychiatrist*, thinks that's best for you." Nina reached out and touched his shoulder. "More important, a good friend of yours named Nina thinks that's best for you."

For emphasis, then, Nina took the manila envelope and the genealogist's card and pitched them into the bottom drawer of her desk—along with Mr. Grady's old pack of stale Salems and the other abandoned artifacts of patients past. Only just then, from across the room, she heard Bucky say, "There's something else I oughtta tell you, Nina."

"Oh?"

He'd ducked his head, then raised it, but tentatively. "Well, can you keep a secret?"

"I think I've got a pretty good track record in that department."

"Okay, I'll take a chance with you. Phyllis is pregnant."

Nina blew him a kiss. "Why, you rascal, you." He beamed. It wasn't a buckysmirk. No, Nina noticed: it was very definitely a buckybeam. She came toward him then, holding out both her hands. "Well, I guess that's a perfect note to end on." He took her hands. "But, you ever have any more problems, you *ever* need a psychiatrist again—"

"Don't worry."

"Don't worry what?"

"Don't worry, Nina, I won't call you."

"Good. We're on the same page." She let go his hands, then, and put her arm under his, escorting him to the door. Only when they got there, did Nina look up and say: "All right, I'll tell you a secret, too."

"Yeah?"

"Remember once I told you I was unfaithful?" Bucky nodded. Nina pointed through the closed door.

"Oh, Hugh?"

Nina nodded. "And remember once you were trying to tell me about the color?"

"Sure. You said: 'Silver.' And I said: 'How'dja know?' and you said something like you always just imagined that silver was the color of rapture."

Nina shook her head. "No, Bucky, I wasn't guessing. I knew." And she pointed again, through the closed door.

"Hey, you mean, you and Hugh...? Really?"

"Uh huh. I'm pretty sure we're Double Ones. The instant I met him, there was just *something*. And there was silver, Bucky. Oh boy, was there silver."

"Do you know...when?"

"You mean when Hugh and I were lovers before?"

"Yeah."

"Believe me, I'm not going to try and open that Pandora's Box. Nobody's hypnotizing me. But, uhh"—Nina pursed her lips. "Incas. I think we were a magnificent Inca king and queen."

"Why you think that?"

"Oh, just a hunch. Hey, Bucky, you were a woman once. Don't you believe in a woman's intuition?"

Bucky smiled at her. "That's great, Nina. Are you happy?"

"Oh, Bucky, I'm so happy. Are you? We're not supposed to ever ask patients flat out: are you happy? So, tell me: are you happy?"

He considered that. "Well, I'm getting there. I'm learning to be happy again."

"Good," she said, reaching for the door. "You see, I'm sure it was your happiness—anyway, your contentment—that saved you. Constance never had the same pull to keep her here. I think that's why, eventually, when she was in Antwerp surrounded by the past, she fell back completely into the past."

"Yeah," Bucky said, and then, before Nina could turn the doorknob, he put his hand on top of hers. "Of course, Nina, even though I'm delighted for you—with Hugh—that does ruin my plans."

"What's that?"

"Well, you know, I was hoping—expecting—that next time..." He stopped talking, but with the most devilish buckysmirk she had ever seen, he just waggled his forefinger between her chest and his.

Nina said, "You mean, you and me?"

"Yeah, don't you think?"

Nina put a finger on her chin. "Well, it's a thought. I'll have to check my calendar, but when did you have in mind?"

"Now, I don't know about Incas," Bucky said, "but based on Margareta and Ollie, it's about three and a half centuries between shifts. So let's say, uh, around 2350—give or take the odd decade."

"It's a date, then," Nina cooed, and she reached up on her tip-toes and kissed Bucky ever so lightly on the lips. "You be the girl, I'll be the boy," she said.

"I'd like that, Doctor," Bucky said, and then they went into the reception room where Hugh and Phyllis were chatting. They all said their good-byes. But it was funny. Just as the Buckinghams stepped outside, the women's leaders in the marathon—a Tanzanian and a Finn—happened to come down Fifth Avenue right before them, so from all over the sidewalk, all around, at that exact moment there arose a great crescendo of cheers. Nina couldn't help it. She started applauding, too. But, of course, she was clapping for Bucky as she watched him disappear with his wife into the crowd.

He had made it. All the way back.

Hugh and Nina strolled home, moving away from the marathon mobs. They had Bloody Marys, which was reasonably sybaritic for newlyweds, while Nina did *The Sunday Times* crossword puzzle and Hugh watched the Jets. Hugh liked the Jets better than the Giants. "Why?" Nina asked, not because she cared, but because she felt it was a wifely thing to feign an interest in.

"Because the Giants are a very Roman Catholic team," he replied, presumably with some degree of seriousness.

"So, are the Jets a Lutheran team?" Nina asked him.

"Relative to the Giants, yes. Lutherans have to be grateful for small favors in New York. Anyway"—he looked at his watch—"it's almost time to go now."

"Go where?"

"On our honeymoon."

"Oh? Where we goin'?"

"You'll see."

"How long?"

"A week. But don't worry. We'll be back in time for the Jets-Ravens game on *Monday Night Football* next week."

"A week? I have appointments."

"No you don't. Roseann and I took care of that."

Nina shook her head in delight, then threw her arms around Hugh's neck and kissed him. "You're much too devious for a man of the cloth," she said. "But come on, I have to know what to bring."

Hugh opened the closet and brought out a new ladies' matching suitcase and garment bag, both full up. "The greatest trust a woman can have for her husband is to allow him to pack for her."

She nodded, but ruefully. "Are you really sure, Hugh? Marriage is dicey enough without taking a risk like this."

"I have the utmost faith in my ability to select your wardrobe," he said. "Now, shut up and dress for an overnight plane ride."

Of course, as soon as they checked in at Kennedy, Nina learned they were going to Paris. But it wasn't until they'd landed the next morning and were in the limousine Hugh had hired and she saw the skyline of Paris receding to the south, and then saw the sign that said, "Bruxelles, 200 km," that Nina figured out where they were going. "You devil, you," she said, but sweetly.

"You had to go. *We* had to go," was all Hugh said. They held hands and nodded off, Nina asleep upon his shoulder almost all the way to Brussels. Antwerp was an hour beyond. Hugh had made their reservation for the Hilton, and after they checked in, they walked around old Antwerp. In fact, they started with a sort of courtesy call to Rubens, pausing at his great statue in the Groen Plaats, which they could see from outside their window.

They went into the Cathedral next, and they said prayers there for the memory of Jocelyn, for forgiveness for Constance, and for the happiness of themselves. Nina also prayed for Bucky. She would always pray for Bucky.

Then they made their way forward, where above the high altar soared Rubens's great baroque work, *The Assumption of The Virgin*. Looking up at it, Nina couldn't help but notice how much the older fellow standing next to her towered over her. He must have been in his seventies, but he still stood straight as a tree, six-feet-four or more. He had red hair and freckles. It was only when he walked away that Nina saw that he was with someone—an old Asian woman, shorter even than Nina. He had to reach way down just to hold hands with her. "Now that's what I call an odd couple," Nina told Hugh.

"'God works in a mysterious way,'" Hugh said. "T.S. Eliot wrote that about a hippopotamus."

"How in the world would you know that?"

"You'd be surprised the stuff you learn that's good at starting sermons."

Back in their room, Hugh went over Nina's wardrobe. He showed her exactly what he thought she could wear every day in Antwerp, and next when they went to Bruges, and then finally back to Paris. "Well?" he said.

"Perfect," Nina replied. "You're my reward and I deserve you, but what a waste for womanhood that you aren't gay and could dress us all." They ate well and drank well and made love better, all silver, notwithstanding jet lag, and then, in the morning, walked to the Royal Museum.

They headed directly to the Rubens section. Soon, Nina moved ahead of Hugh, who studied every painting as if he were a curator. When she stepped into the next room, she saw them right away: the tall redheaded man and the little Asian woman. They were holding hands again, staring up at *Le Coup de Lance*, Rubens's painting of a Roman soldier spearing Christ upon the cross. Nina moved closer, fascinated at how completely enthralled they were. Why, she had not seen anyone so spellbound since...well, since Bucky or Constance.

When the couple fell back, collapsing onto one of the banquettes, Nina casually sat down herself and tried to strike up a conversation. "We're Australian," the redhead replied, and his little wife—Nina could see her ring—nodded. "From Adelaide."

"Oh, I want so much to go to your country," Nina gushed. She gestured toward Hugh, who was coming into the room just now. "My husband. Perhaps Australia the next time we travel. This is our honeymoon."

"Congratulations," said the woman.

"Well now," the redhead said. "You should only be as happy as we've been. This is our fiftieth."

"Fifty! Hugh, come here. These people are celebrating their fiftieth wedding anniversary."

"Well not exactly our anniversary," the redhead said. "Not for another three years that. But it was exactly fifty years ago this week that we met."

"November the twelfth, 1950," the wife said, and Nina smiled to herself that even if she had kept her original Asian accent, she had embroidered that with true Aussie dialect. She said "nine-een," as Australians say all the 'teens without a *t*.

Hugh approached and put out his hand, introducing himself.

"Roy Hewitt," replied the redhead. "And the wife is Sue."

Nina introduced herself, too. "Where in the world did you two meet?"

Softly, Sue said, "In my village near Chungju. In Korea."

"In the war," Roy added. "I was serving under your General MacArthur. We were on patrol, came into her village, my eyes fell on her, and I told the other blokes right 'en that this was the Sheilah I'd marry."

Nina shot a glance up at Hugh. "And you, Sue?" she asked.

"Oh yes. Neither my family nor Roy's could understand it, but it was, as you say, love at first sight."

"How absolutely wonderfully romantic."

"What brings you to Antwerp?" Hugh asked.

"Oh, this is our third trip," Sue said, although after she said that, she and her husband looked over to one another.

"We've become great Rubens fans," Roy explained.

Nina covered a little gasp. It all had such a ring to it. "Have you ever been to New York?" she said. "We have some wonderful Rubens in the Metropolitan."

Roy and Sue looked at each other again. She nodded, and he proceeded. "As a matter of fact, it was in the Metropolitan where we first, ah, came to appreciate Rubens so. We're just a couple of regular mutton-punchers, neither of us much for fancy art, but we were on a tour and bused with our mates to the museum, and that's where we found—" He stopped abruptly.

"My favorite is *Venus and Adonis*," Nina said.

"Well yes, that's nice, but the one across from it—"

"It's the self-portrait with Helena and young Peter Paul," Sue said.

"Oh yes," Nina said, "I know it well. It's so revealing of the family."

Roy and Sue glanced at each other again, then he took her hand, and making apologies that they must be off, they rose and departed. Nina and Hugh watched them go. Hugh said, "Look, I'm no Australian expert, but I know they used to have an incredibly stiff immigration policy for Asians. The Yellow Peril and all that. He must've had to be a bulldog to get her in."

"A soldier in a foreign land, in the midst of a war, meets a local girl. They can't speak the same language, they—"

"Double Ones," said Hugh, with a sigh.

"Are you being facetious?"

"No, darling, not at all." He sat down next to Nina and took both her hands in his. "I've been waiting for the right moment to tell you something. I was scared. I thought maybe if we came here, it would be easier, and—"

"Yes?"

And then Hugh told Nina about how he was standing in gallery twenty-seven when Constance fell to her death, and how he heard the dogs barking and felt the chill wisp of a breeze and then Adonis's leg, warm and alive. "Oh my God," said Nina. She fell against Hugh's chest, and he held her there.

Later that day, when they were strolling through the garden at Rubenshuis, they saw Roy and Sue across the way. He was carrying a bouquet of tulips. "Where in the world would you find tulips in November?" Nina asked.

"I suppose the right hothouse florist—if it matters enough." Right at that very moment, as a matter of fact, Nina and Hugh were standing by a sign which identified the great tulip beds that bloomed there in season, behind the little hedges that had kept Mr. and Mrs. Rubens's favorite flowers safe from any marauding peacocks.

Neither Hugh nor Nina were really very surprised when next they visited Rubens's burial chapel in Saint James and saw there—beneath the painting where Margareta as the Madonna held her baby—tulips scattered about. Nina was the one who noticed, however, that curiously, the flowers were not evenly distributed. Some were upon Rubens's tomb. The others upon Helena's, to his right. There were no flowers upon the tomb to the left, where Isabelle, the first wife, lay.

Nina thought about that and wondered, but it was not until she awoke at dawn the next morning that she understood. "Of course," she said out loud. She tore out of bed and ran to the window. She seemed to know what she would see there. And: yes. Before the great statue of Rubens in the Groen Plaats, there stood Roy and Sue, holding hands, gazing up at Rubens, as behind him, the first rays of the morning's sun began to brighten the cathedral spire.

Nina shook Hugh, rousing him. "Quick, get dressed," she snapped, starting to throw on a sweater herself. Hugh didn't question a thing; her urgency was sufficient for him to obey. Splashing water, running hands through their hair, tossing on jackets, they rushed to the elevator and out the hotel, hurrying toward the statue.

Roy and Sue saw them coming, and a bit wary, turned to leave. "No, no, wait," Nina cried out. And they did. She and Hugh caught their breath before them, and then, as quickly as she could, Nina searched their faces. And she said one word: "Margareta." And again: "Margareta?"

And yes, after a moment, some measure of recognition came to Sue's face. Then a smile. She turned to Roy, "Yes, yes. Margareta. My last Madonna." She stopped, embarrassed.

But, in another moment, he nodded. "Why, there was that awful murder..."

And then both Roy and Sue looked at Nina. "But how did—" she began.

"It's okay. It's okay. I've met Margareta." Nina was glowing. She turned to Hugh. "Don't you see, darling? Sue was Rubens, and Roy was Helena."

He nodded—and really, rather casually. "You know," he said, "Jocelyn told me once that the classic Double Ones of all time were Rubens and Helena."

Sue and Roy shook their heads, in the wonder of it all. "We often thought we were crazy," she said.

"No, no. You were them," Nina said. "You *were*." And she embraced them both, tears forming in her eyes.

The sun had risen just enough now, to come over the gables of Rubens's Antwerp, to shine down upon his statue, to light, for another day, upon his face. Beneath it, shyly, Roy and Sue smiled up to him, and then began to drift away, waving a little. Roy stopped and winked, and then they strode off, hand in hand.

Hugh put his arm around Nina's shoulder. "Now, that's the end of it," he said. "No more. It's just the twenty-first century for us from now on."

Nina cuddled up and mumbled agreement. And she did keep that pledge to Hugh that she made in the shadow of Peter Paul Rubens. But if Nina her best not to puzzle anymore about reincarnation, she did always wonder anew about the mysteries of love, of how a man and a woman might ever find each other's hearts. Whenever. Wherever. And how hard it is for any two people even to find just a little, tiny bit of forever to share.

About the Author

Frank Deford's work can be found across a broad range of genres. He has written twelve books on many subjects. Two of them, *Everybody's All-American* and *Alex: The Life of a Child*, were made into movies. Mr. Deford has also won numerous high honors as a magazine writer and is a member of the National Sportscasters and Sportswriters Hall of Fame. On the radio, he has been a commentator on National Public Radio for twenty years. On television, where he is now a correspondent for *RealSports with Bryant Gumbel* on HBO, he has won both an Emmy and a Peabody Award. This is his seventh novel. Mr. Deford resides in Connecticut with his wife, Carol.